Stephen Gallagher is the author of *Valley of Lights*, *Oktober*, *Down River*, *Rain*, *Chimera*, *Boat House*, *Follower* and *Nightmare, with Angel*. He lives in Lancashire.

PART ONE

A Doll's House

1

'Take all the time you need,' the woman said from over by the window. 'There's no hurry.' She looked out at the mid-morning traffic that was starting to move down in Chestnut Street and added, 'We do close the office at six.'

Ruth turned the pages of the brochure. Again. For what felt like the hundredth time in the past half-hour. She hadn't supposed that this was going to be easy, but even so . . . Her thoughts raced in a circle, full of purpose and getting nowhere like a dog trying to bite out a tick on its own behind. She was embarrassed.

She said, 'I'm usually very decisive. This isn't like me at all.'

Another page, another face. Another passably handsome middle-aged man with a perfect haircut and a lively spark in his eyes. They did that with lighting, she knew. It was nothing to go on.

She turned to another.

The woman said, 'If I had to guess, I'd say you were in business.'

'I suppose I am,' Ruth said.

'So many of our clients are. What line?'

'Publishing. Magazine publishing.'

'Would that be nationwide, or just Philadelphia?'

'Probably nothing you'd have seen. I sell advertising space in trade journals. Are they all this old?'

It didn't sound quite so blunt until it came out, and then it sounded positively crude. The woman, Mrs Eloise Carroll, looked over toward her with one drawn-in eyebrow raised.

'We don't call our gentlemen old, Ms Lasseter,' she said. 'We call them mature.'

7

'Only,' Ruth persisted, 'I don't want to turn up at this dance looking as if I came with my father.'

'You want to create an impression.'

'Yes, and not a desperate one. That's not the reason why I'm here.'

Eloise Carroll moved from the window, returning to her desk. She said, 'Ladies have all kinds of reasons for needing an escort service, Ms Lasseter. Believe me. Desperation is the least of them.' She leaned across the desk and flipped over a couple of the pages in the album that Ruth was holding. Another face looked up. Another God-almighty *grandfather*. 'What about our Mr Chapman? He's from England, too.'

'I'm not in England now,' Ruth said. 'I want a native.'

Eloise Carroll, still leaning across, lowered her voice a little and said, 'May I suggest something?'

'What?'

'Being tense will only affect your judgement. There's no need for it. Anything that's said in this room is said in complete confidence. The more you can tell me, the more help I can be.'

'I need an escort for one social occasion. That's all.'

'But an escort's just an escort. You seem to be looking for someone who'll fit a part. Am I right?'

She was right. After a fashion, anyway, and part of Ruth's problem was that it irritated her to acknowledge it. None of it was this woman's fault. Ruth was aware that she was being less than civil. She made an effort.

She said, 'It's for a trade event, like a society ball or a prom. My company's sponsoring it and we all have to go. One of the department heads has been my lover for nearly two years. He'll be there with his wife. He thinks she suspects. If I don't turn up with someone, then she'll know.'

Eloise Carroll lowered herself into the big padded swivel chair on the other side of the desk. The desktop carried a phone and a blotter and nothing else. Eloise Carroll would probably once have been described as a handsome woman.

8

RED, RED ROBIN

Stephen Gallagher

CORGI BOOKS

RED, RED ROBIN
A CORGI BOOK : 0 552 14293 X

Originally published in Great Britain by Bantam Press,
a division of Transworld Publishers Ltd

PRINTING HISTORY
Bantam Press edition published 1995
Corgi edition published 1996

Copyright © Stephen Gallagher 1995

Typeset in 10/11pt Plantin by
Hewer Text Composition Services, Edinburgh

Corgi books are published by Transworld Publishers Ltd,
61–63 Uxbridge Road, London W5 5SA,
in Australia by Transworld Publishers (Australia) Pty Ltd,
15–25 Helles Avenue, Moorebank, NSW 2170
and in New Zealand by Transworld Publishers (NZ) Ltd,
3 William Pickering Drive, Albany, Auckland.

Reproduced, printed and bound in Great Britain by
Cox & Wyman Ltd, Reading, Berks.

Handsome rather than pretty, and a lukewarm compliment in its time. But pretty wouldn't have lasted the way that handsome had.

She said, 'Well, you're not the first one to tell me this story.'

Ruth was surprised. 'You've had the situation before?'

'It happens all the time. What about our Mr Cooper? He's a professional actor. He won't let you down.'

'He's too old.'

'He's forty-five.'

'Well, he thinks too old. Haven't you got *anyone* who didn't pose in a blue rinse and a yachting blazer?'

'We've gentlemen of all ages up to sixty-five. But it's the older men who get the work. That's just the way it is.'

Ruth turned another page, and then another. The pages were actually see-through plastic pockets, photographs to one side with their printed details opposite. She was almost at the end of the book once again, and once again she was no closer to making any decision.

The last two faces in the book were boy pictures. Boys in tuxedo jackets, but they seemed completely out of place.

'How old's he?' she said, tilting the book for Eloise Carroll to see.

'That's our Mr Hagan. He's twenty-three. Turn up with *him* and you'll make an impression, all right.'

Ruth gazed at the page, and sighed. There was no lust in it, just wistfulness, and it wasn't particularly directed at the unlined face before her. 'God,' she said, 'to be twenty-three again. I wouldn't have had this problem then. The world was wall-to-wall with single males.'

'Time passes,' Eloise Carroll said. 'Things change. That's just life.'

Ruth knew what kind of choice she ought to be making. A man four or five years older than herself, distinguished-looking, good at small-talk; someone pleasant who'd support her and stand by her through the evening but who'd stick in no-one's mind, her own included. It should have been straightforward enough, the album was full of them. But she couldn't make the leap. It had nothing to do with years, and everything to do with self-image.

She said, 'I really don't know. Whatever I say now's going to be wrong. Do you have something I could take away with me?'

'We can fax to your office, but I don't suppose that would be appropriate in a case like this.'

'God, no.'

'Then I can give you photocopies,' Eloise Carroll said, rising.

A secretary in the outer office organized the paperwork while the two of them waited. If the woman was annoyed by Ruth's lack of decisiveness, she didn't show it. Maybe she was used to this kind of uncertainty; one of the more common factors involved in the job.

She said to Ruth, 'How long have you lived here?'

'Ever since I was twenty-five,' Ruth said. 'I was working for one of the big insurance companies and they sent me over on a three-year rotation. At the end of it I left the job rather than go back.'

'Why?'

'I thought I was in love with somebody.'

Strange, how it didn't hurt to say it now.

Eloise Carroll said, 'Was that in Philadelphia?'

'That was in New York. I moved to Philadelphia in 'eighty-four.'

'Do you ever go home?'

Without really intending to, Ruth looked toward the window. A couple of miles to the west, the chiselled glass towers of the city's business district now stood clear of the morning's earlier haze.

'This is home,' she said.

2

She walked along two city squares to where she'd left her car. It was on a lot where a ballroom had once stood and which had been fenced for contract parking. The air in the street was cool, but the inside of the car was hot and stuffy from the sun on the glass. She threw the folder onto the passenger seat, opened all the windows, and set off across town to her place of work.

Ruth drove a Pontiac 6000, her second American car in ten years. As soon as the stale air had blown through, she closed up the windows and turned on the air-conditioning. Then she switched on the radio. The crosstown traffic was slow but steady. Ruth was supposed to be at a meeting by eleven-thirty. She was cutting it close, but she could see no reason why she wouldn't make it.

She kept glancing down at the cardboard folder. This was ridiculous. Pick one and let's go, Ruth, she told herself. Just pick one and let's go. Any one of them's as good as any other.

But it was as if, every time, her mind turned aside just before the moment of decision.

About twenty minutes later she was stuck in a long line of traffic on Race Street, for reasons that were too far ahead of her to make out. A few people leaned on their horns, but their hearts weren't in it. About a half-dozen cars further on, two beggars in white shirts were working the lanes. Ruth checked the door locks and then picked up the envelope. She pulled out the Xerox sheets and started to look through. They'd been reduced, two pages into one. The copies weren't good, but they'd be good enough.

One of the beggars tapped on her window. She could see his paper cup out of the corner of her eye. She shook her head fractionally, but she didn't look up. After a few moments, he went on to the car behind.

As always, she felt guilty. She knew that she shouldn't, but she always did. Tough, but not tough enough. That was Ruth Lasseter's lonely secret.

Then she had an idea.

She dug out a bill from the parking change that she kept hidden behind some cassettes, and dropped the window. The heat of the day washed right back in on her. Holding the money up where it could be seen, she leaned out of the car and whistled.

It was loud. Ruth whistled with two fingers of one hand, like a boy, and she could hit a note that would scare a flock of birds out of a field of corn. The young black man with the paper cup flinched and then, looking a little uncertain, he started back up the line toward her.

'Hi,' Ruth said pleasantly, and reached out to stuff the money in his cup.

'Thank you. God *bless* you,' the young man said, with an intent politeness that seemed completely sincere.

'Can I ask your opinion on something?'

'I guess so.'

'Which of these men do you think I should take on a date?'

She held up the sheets like a set of flash cards, and started to give him a two-second burst of each. He was around twenty-five years old, well-built and good-looking. His footwear was all shot and filthy but his white shirt was spotless. He looked utterly bewildered.

'Why you asking me?' he said.

'I can't choose,' she said. 'They're all the same to me.'

'Well, they're all the same to me, too. Pick the one with most money.'

'It's not that kind of a date. You pay these guys.'

'For why?'

'They're escorts.'

'You're kidding.'

'No, I'm not.' Ruth glanced in the rearview mirror and

saw that the man in the car behind was watching the exchange with his mouth wide open. He shook his head in disbelief and then appeared to start expressing himself loudly in the solitude of his coupe. Up ahead, some of the vehicles were beginning to move.

The young man said, 'No woman who looks like you do has to pay to get a guy,' he said. 'Not on any planet *I* ever lived on.'

'Thank you,' Ruth said. 'It's not that I've got no-one to ask. I've got plenty of old boyfriends I could call on, but my new boyfriend won't have that. This is just to make him happy. He's very jealous.'

'You're drownin' me, now,' the young man said. 'If you got a boyfriend, what for do you need a date anyway?'

'Are you going to help me choose or not?'

'Uh-uh,' he said, backing off. 'Spin a bottle or stick a pin. 'Cause when it all goes bad, what *you* want to do is look back and say how somebody steered you wrong.'

'OK,' Ruth said, shifting into Drive. 'Thanks anyway.'

'Hey,' he said. 'Take me. I'll do it for free.'

'I told you he's jealous,' Ruth said. 'That would just about kill him.'

Graybird Publishing had space in the Somerville Building just a few blocks from Logan Circle, in a narrowing north-west corner of the city centre between the Schuylkill River and Fairmount Park. It was all wide streets and no pedestrians in this area, unlike those parts of town that reminded her of home – her original home, not the one that she'd made for herself here. The streets that reminded her of home had brick sidewalks and trees and neat row houses set back from the trees. The English north-country suburb where she'd grown up had featured none of these, which only helped to convince Ruth that nothing ever made too much sense if you insisted on looking at it too closely.

She left the car in the parking basement and took the elevator up to the lobby. Graybird had two floors in the building, the fourth and most of the fifth. The place was deceptive. On the outside it looked like a big old bank or a treasury building, fronted by immense classical columns and the kind of steps where gangsters always get shot in movies. Inside, it had been gutted and revamped to provide office space around an atrium big enough to launch a balloon in. All the fine old marble had been restored and polished and extended all the way up to the daylight in the roof. There was greenery and an indoor fountain, and ever-watchful security to make sure that these public spaces didn't attract the wrong kind of public. Mostly, the public stayed out and the spaces stayed empty.

Ruth crossed the floor and passed before the security counter on her way to the main elevator bank. Someone in a uniform was sitting behind the desk.

'Good morning, Miz Lasseter,' the uniform said as she went by.

She read off his badge without even a glance at the face above it.

'Morning, Aidan,' she said.

She'd missed the meeting. It was hard to be sorry. When she stepped out on the fifth she went over and ran her ID card through the reader, which let her through the glass doors and into company territory. Visitors had to press the buzzer and wait.

Once at her desk she threw her coat onto the back of the chair, switched on her terminal, and scooped all the internal mail from her in-tray and slid it straight into a drawer. Rosemary looked over the partition from the adjoining carrel and said, 'Hello, Ruth. Jake's been looking for you.'

'Any idea what for?'

'Nothing important, he said. I didn't know what to tell him.'

'You could have said I had an appointment to get my tattoo finished.'

'A tattoo?' Rosemary said. 'You? Where?'

'I don't want to say. Just don't expect me to sit much today.'

'Is that true?'

Ruth hadn't the heart.

'No, Rosemary,' she said, 'it's only a joke. I had some car trouble again.'

Rosemary made a sign of understanding, and dropped down out of sight. She wasn't tall. She had to sit on a cushion to type. Most people had fallen into the habit of referring to her as 'Little Rosemary' until the one memorable day when she'd exploded and it had taken more than an hour of diplomatic to-ing and fro-ing to entice her out of the women's room.

The little red light on Ruth's phone was blinking to indicate a backup of switchboard messages for her. She jiggled the receiver to kill it, set out yesterday's soda can, and then checked the overall effect. Woman at Work, it said to her. And if it said that to her, it would say the same to anyone.

So then she picked up a piece of scrap paper and walked off down the row toward the elevators. She saw the head of her section, who spotted her across the dividers and called her by name, but she waved the paper and said, 'Got to deal with this urgently, Jake, I'll be right back,' and then carried on.

On through the beehive. That was exactly what Graybird looked like to her, with everybody in their little private spaces that had no privacy. The carpet was deep and the colours were cool and all the lighting had almost the exact feel and texture of daylight, but it was a beehive all the same. It was never a good idea to step back too far and see your own place in it all. The plants you tended, the cards you pinned up. Exactly the same as everyone else. At a distance, you were no-one.

Group Services had real offices. Ruth walked past Gordon Parry's open door, and made for the snack machine at the end of the passageway.

She needed to do no more. They were lovers, they had radar. He would feel her presence like the passage of a magnetic field, making his heart race and raising the hairs on the back of his neck. She knew, because it was what his proximity could do to her.

He was approaching.

He stood behind her while she sorted out change for the machine, as if politely waiting his turn.

She heard him say, 'How did it go?'

'I'm going to need help,' she said. 'I can't make a choice.'

'What's the problem?'

'There's no problem. I just can't make a choice.'

'This is the craziest thing I've ever done.'

'Me too.' They were conversing in low voices and avoiding looking at each other, like prisoners in a yard under the eyes of the guards. She said, 'Can you come to the apartment?'

'Maybe Thursday. I'll try.'

She dropped some of the money. They bent together to pick it up, and their hands touched for a moment. Her heart was hammering as she walked back toward her desk.

She hadn't even looked at him.

Oh, Ruth, she thought to herself. The games we all play.

The chances we take.

3

There were a number of shops and services down in the windowless passageways off the atrium. Along with the barber shop and the florist and the copy shop and the Fed Ex desk, they included two gourmet cafés and a deli. Business tended to ebb and flow between them, depending on who'd placed the most attractive offer in this week's copy of the Somerville Building's internal newsletter. Rossini's café was offering free espresso and a dollar off with coupon, Moriarty's was two-for-one on sandwiches. So the four women of the Graybird ad sales department went down to lunch together at Spinks', which was offering nothing at all but was the only place with a table free.

Four of them sat around the table. Ruth, Rosemary, Jennie and Alicia. Because all the lighting was artificial, it could have been any hour in some below-ground bunker. It was too bright, and everything gleamed. Tiles, tabletops, silverware, everything. It was like a dining-room designed by an orthodontist. They talked about the morning's meeting, and the proposed measures for scaling down some of the less profitable parts of the company, and who was likely to stay and who would most probably be invited to go. Ruth, who hadn't been there, didn't have much to say on the subject. And much as she tried to take an interest, her mind would stray to a certain other matter.

'Hey,' Jennie cut in, leaning forward and lowering her voice. 'Look who's here.'

Ruth glanced around, and saw nobody. One of the building security people was passing with a tray, that was all. Big and slow-moving and mostly invisible, a blue shirt and a bunch of keys; but then she realized, it was the guard whom Jennie was eyeing. But she couldn't turn and look again. Not right away.

Rosemary said, with a pained expression, '*Please* don't drool. I'm trying to eat.'

'Do you think anyone would notice if I hid him in the trunk of my car and took him home?'

'Bill might.'

'I wouldn't bet on it. If I lay face-down on the table with a banana up my ass, he'd ask me where I put the fruit bowl.'

'Jennie!' Rosemary said, with a gasp of shock that wasn't entirely feigned.

'I don't care,' Jennie said. 'Somebody call him over. I've worked hard all my life, I deserve it.'

Now Ruth let her gaze drift and half-turned in her seat, hoping that the move didn't look fake and knowing that it did. But it made no difference. He wasn't looking her way. He'd settled at a table on his own and he was reading a newspaper, leaning over the table and turned slightly away from the room, as if to create a little private space in the middle of his day. It was, she realized, the one who'd been manning the desk when she'd arrived that morning. He'd known her by name, but she'd had to check for his. Aidan. Aidan Kincannon.

Aidan Kincannon, unlikely object of desire.

'I'll call him for you,' she offered, and started to raise a hand.

'Don't you dare!' Jennie said quickly.

Ruth became aware then that Alicia wasn't joining in. Hadn't taken her eyes off her for more than a minute, it seemed.

She said to Ruth, 'What about you? What's going to happen to you if the job disappears?'

'Same as everybody else,' Ruth said. 'I'm out on the street.'

'Won't you lose your right of residence?'

'I haven't thought about that.' It was true, she hadn't.

18

'You *must* have,' Alicia insisted. And Ruth felt herself being forced into an edgy smile.

'It sounds like I'd better start,' she said.

And Alicia said, 'What do you know that we don't?'

'What are you talking about?' Ruth said.

'Come on, Ruth. Let us in on the secret. Who do you have to fuck around here to be certain of secure employment? Then we can all form a line.'

Ruth looked at her levelly. She didn't flinch.

'Where did this come from?' she said.

Alicia shrugged.

'I don't have to sit here and listen to this,' Ruth said.

'Wait a minute,' Jennie said. 'Don't fly off the handle.'

'No,' Rosemary said. 'It was just a bad joke, wasn't it, Alicia?'

Alicia took a beat before she answered.

'That's what it was,' she said.

Ruth stood up, and pushed her chair back. It dry-scraped on the floor. She hadn't finished, but she was no longer hungry. She felt like someone cold to the touch around a white-hot core. She looked down at Alicia, who in spite of her supposed backdown remained defiant.

'I don't know what your real problem is, Alicia,' Ruth said, 'but deal with that. Don't try to take it out on me.'

She walked out of the coffee shop and back toward the elevators. She felt light-headed and, although she didn't falter, she also felt unsteady. It was as if she floated, and couldn't fall. Did Alicia know about her and Gordon? Did anyone actually *know*? Ahead of her in the passageway were two day assistants from the childcare centre in the basement, pulling along a wagon with about eight pre-schoolers sitting on it and two more helping to push. For once she didn't smile as she passed them.

The office was mostly empty when she got back. She went into her enclosure and sat down before her terminal.

There she took in the view of her domain, such as it was. A faded picture of her parents, one of her sister, one of her sister's children that was probably way out of date by now. A few similarly out-of-date gallery invitations, an old champagne cork still in its wire. A palm in a pot, its leaves steadily shrivelling. Ruth didn't have much of a way with plants; somebody would buy one for her, it would die slowly, she'd throw it out and then someone would give her another.

'Ruth?' she heard. 'Are you busy?'

She looked up. It was Rosemary. Ruth made a gesture that could have meant anything, and Rosemary took it as permission to stay. She pulled her chair around from the other side of the partition and sat down.

She said, 'I don't know what got into Alicia. Nobody agrees with what she said. I don't think she believes it herself.'

'Rosemary,' Ruth said, 'I really couldn't give a damn *what* she believes.'

'Please forgive her, Ruth.'

Ruth sighed. What could you say to a plea like that?

She said, 'Ever the peacemaker, aren't you, Rosemary? If Alicia's got some kind of a complex, then it's not my problem.'

'You need to understand something,' Rosemary said. 'Some of the others envy you. I envy you myself, sometimes.'

'For what?'

'Oh, come on. You're a grown-up single woman. You're the choice we didn't make, and you're looking pretty good on it. Whenever life gets rocky, we're bound to wonder if we chose wrong. When I was nine, I had dreams about being a bride. When I was nineteen, I married Prince Charming. Now he makes the kids laugh by getting them to pull on his finger just as he lets go with a fart. I still love him. But it's not the dream I had.'

'I can't handle that, Rosemary,' Ruth said. 'You can't ask me to take responsibility for it.'

'I'm not. I'm just telling you how it is.'

Alicia called by her desk after lunch, and apologized. Ruth told her it was OK. Jennie brought coffee for everyone, including Jake, who was then suspicious of them all for the rest of the afternoon.

The phones rang, the work got done. Some men brought a printer cabinet that nobody had asked for and then took it away again.

Ruth hardly thought ahead to Thursday at all.

4

Ruth's apartment was in a rehabilitated dry-goods ware-house alongside the access ramp to the Ben Franklin Bridge. The ramp was a massive arch outside her window, the space beneath it a dark cathedral in blue steel. As the traffic rolled over, it seemed to set every bass pipe on the organ singing. This was an old part of town that had been hauled from near-dereliction to upward mobility until recession had put on the brakes and left most of the rehabs with only part-occupancy. Five years ago she couldn't have afforded the area, but now most of them were offering deals. Ruth's was a simple studio, a big sitting-room with an open sleeping area overlooking it and a crawlspace under. On her lease agreement they called it a loft, although by New York standards it wasn't.

She kicked off her shoes and switched on the lights, low so that they'd gradually take over as the sun went down. She made herself some herbal tea in the kitchen, and carried it across to the couch. She didn't feel like eating anything, even though she'd left her lunch half-finished. Disinclined though she was to admit it, Alicia's attack was still churning her up inside. It was like a slap out of nowhere, something to make her head ring. They'd never been friends, exactly, but . . . my God, she thought, I never realized that the woman actively despised me.

It could only be envy. Envy or insecurity over a single woman, loose in a world of wives and mothers. Rosemary was probably right; Ruth's continuing existence must have seemed like a challenge to all of them. They'd see the way that some of their husbands twitched into life like dead meat when introduced into her company. God forbid that she should actually be happy as well.

She looked through the escort agency samples again, and tried to cut the numbers down to a few possibles. The one with the hint of a squint, *out*. One who looked like an actor she didn't like, *out*. Another that she didn't like the look of for no reason at all, *out*.

She slumped back on the couch, threw her head back, and groaned.

It hadn't been easy, even to pick up the phone. Gordon had passed her the number. He'd said that he'd checked it out and it was one of the legitimate places and not just a hotel handjob outfit, but how could she be sure? The very concept of a genuine agency seemed so archaic, a hangover of more innocent days. But there it was, the understanding social resource for the mature woman. Ouch. Companions for formal occasions, concerts, gallery visits, even shopping and city tours. The men on the books were mostly retired and doing it for pin money and their own enjoyment. And according to Eloise Carroll the clientele were mostly widows, middle-class and up, who called for a man because there was a man-sized space alongside them that they felt a need to have occupied. Nothing closer than that.

Well, if there was so much envy out there, this would be a way to defuse it as well as settling any suspicions that Mimi Parry might be having about her husband's late nights and New York stopovers. But that, Ruth was now beginning to realize, was the sticking point. The practical usefulness was undeniable. The hard part was that it made her feel just a little bit like a beaten dog, rolling over onto its back and showing its belly to end a fight. Life might be quieter afterwards, but at what price? It could be described as a form of appeasement.

But it could equally feel like a form of abasement.

Don't think, she told herself. Just choose.

But then, not thinking had never been as easy for Ruth as it seemed to be for some.

Midway through the evening, she picked up the phone and called the agency's answering machine. She said, 'Hello, Mrs Carroll. This is Ruth Lasseter, I came to your office this morning and took away a copy of your brochure. I've got it down to a couple of names; I'll call you in a day or so to check on their availability.'

She'd make a firm decision before the evening was out. Or tomorrow. Tomorrow would be just as good.

Her name was Frances Everline. She was forty-eight years old, twice-divorced, no children, and she was dying.

She hauled herself up off the bed, which was soiled with her vomit, and took a step toward the bedroom door. But she didn't get far. Her legs went from underneath her, and her face hit the carpet. It happened so fast that she wasn't even aware of falling.

For a while, she didn't move. She felt strangely comfortable here. It hurt, but it was like an arm's-length hurt. That this was dangerous, she knew. Slip far enough out of herself like this, and before she could stop she'd have slid too far ever to return.

The phone was in the next room. She knew that she'd have to get to that and dial 911 if she was going to have any hope at all. Lying here, she'd just get weaker. So she summoned what little strength she had left, and she started to crawl across the floor.

Her vision was distorted, like in a cartoon. The distance from here to the door seemed as vast as the view down a football field. From beyond the door to the phone would be like a desert still to cross.

But she'd try.

As she crawled, there was a clear part of her mind that berated itself and disparaged the person that she'd become in the past few weeks. She'd turned into someone that she could hardly recognize any more. From confident and self-possessed she'd gone to whining and dependent, and she could see the reasons for it only now. It was all because she'd felt that she was heading along a path down which she didn't actually want to go. But like a second-rate craftsman who couldn't bear to undo bad work, she'd done nothing but add to the situation and carry it further and ultimately make it worse. Where did she think she was heading? To happiness?

She stopped and half-lifted herself on her hands and dry-heaved, and brought up nothing but a couple of spoonfuls of green bile.

If this is happiness, the clear part of her mind was thinking, then you can keep it.

Her arms gave way then, and she dropped back to the floor. She lay there, shivering. Her vision was going, now. It was as if her nervous system was closing down on her, one department after another, with the last one out getting ready to turn off the lights.

Damn. And after she'd made it as far as the doorway, as well.

She'd never felt this weakened, not even by the worst fever. It was as if her joints had been disengaged and there were only a few cottony strands of muscle left to pull and make them work. But still she started to drag herself almost by her fingertips alone, feeling the nails tear as she dug them deep into the sitting-room carpet and into the backing beneath, and this way she began to cover the last few yards to the low table with the phone on it.

Frances would never have believed of herself that the hunger to live could be so strong. She'd always believed if ever she were to reach a state where only doctors were keeping her alive, then she'd much rather they'd pull the plugs and let her go. There were even letters to that effect in her lawyer's office, locked securely in his strongroom against the day that they might be needed. But she'd been clear-headed when she'd drafted them. Dragging herself across the carpet like this, she could see there was no way that she could have taken into account the determination with which she now clung grimly to that one remaining thread of gleaming silver that was her life.

She reached the table, and managed with a superhuman effort to get her hand up onto it. Her hand just lay there as the entire length of her arm trembled. Nothing in the muscles, all energy spent. She couldn't raise it any higher, she couldn't lift it to the phone. She could maybe push the buttons; but she wasn't sure if she could speak. She didn't want to try, and find out that she'd shot her only round. One word would do it. She hoped.

Her arm fell, and landed beside her face like a dead thing.

The table had a glass top. Looking up through it, she could see the underside of the phone. It might as well have been on a high shelf on some other floor of the building. The telephone cord went across the table and down by the leg, to where it ran under the furniture to the wall socket.

Could she manage this? This, at the very least? Frances reached across for the cord, and wrapped her fingers around it. She could feel the strength fading even as her fingers tightened. Then she pulled.

The phone slid across the table, caught on the edge and stayed there, resisting. It was maddening, like a sleeve caught on a door handle that wouldn't come away.

Then all of a sudden it flipped into the air and over, and it landed with a rattling crash on the floor in front of her. The receiver bounced free and landed on its side only inches before her face. She didn't even flinch.

Frances barely had to move her hand to stab out 911 on the touch pad, and then she didn't even wait for the operator to reply. 'Help,' she croaked, and no sound came out. Then 'Help,' again, and this time, just a rattling noise that could have been anything.

Oh, no.

No.

She'd come so far. She wasn't about to lose it now, not now that she'd run the full course and the only step left was to pick up the award. All she needed to do, she was thinking, was to hang on. Hang on while they registered her distress and locked the line open and traced it with the speed of which she knew them to be capable.

So then she swallowed, ready to try again, and it was like choking a marble down a dry pipe. It was then that she realized there was no operator's voice coming out of the phone. She'd misdialled. Or it had misconnected, and because of that she was wasting what little energy she had left.

She fumbled her hand onto the cradle. Pressed it down with rubber fingers in order to try again. But then she forced herself to hesitate, and she listened, and that was when her heart dropped like an elevator through fourteen storeys. The phone was making no dial tone, no buzz, no sound of any kind. There was nothing visibly wrong with the handset, but the line was completely dead.

Frances Everline beat her head weakly against her living-room carpet.

She wept.

And then, as if through miles of space, she heard a key being turned in the door.

Gratitude and shame rushed through her like unmixed torrents of hot and cold water. Apart from spraying vomit all around the bedroom, she'd fouled herself somewhere along the line as well. But help was here. That was all that mattered.

She saw him in the doorway. He was frozen there as in a flash photograph, his key still in the lock, an expression of utter surprise on his face as he looked down at her. Held against his chest with one hand was a paper bag from a Wawa all-night convenience store, and as he started forward the bag fell and hit the floor behind him with a sound like breaking eggs.

She spoke his name, making hardly a sound. He dropped to one knee beside her as the rich smell of chocolate filled the room. He had a weakness for hot chocolate and fresh doughnuts at ungodly hours after midnight. Her joke with him had been that, since she'd finally given in to temptation and invited him to move into her apartment only a few weeks before, he'd all but worn out the sidewalk between there and the store.

He lifted up her head, and all that she could keep on

trying to say was that she was sorry. 'Come on,' he said, and got his arm underneath her and rolled her over and hoisted her up, and from there he carried her across to the big armchair.

'What happened?' he said when he'd set her down in it. 'What did you do?' And as he said it, he took her face in both his hands. She could feel his fingers probing, behind her ears and on down the sides of her throat. He was checking her out, just like someone with first aid or medical training.

'I took all my tablets,' she confessed miserably. 'I took them all.'

'Why?' he said. 'Was it an accident? What were you doing?'

'I don't *know* what I was doing.'

She'd known. Whatever she'd believed at the time, she knew that she'd really had it in mind for him to get back and to find her much sooner than this. She'd never done anything like it before. If she'd any idea that this was how it was going to feel, she wouldn't even have flirted with the idea.

He was looking at her, and he was shaking his head, and his eyes were full of a kind of distant compassion.

Still holding her face in his hands, he said, 'How long have you been feeling this way? Why didn't you tell me?'

Frances said, 'I didn't know what to say to you.' Then she said, 'Please. I don't want to die. I need to get to a hospital.' And then she hesitated for a moment, because she felt a rising nausea and she was afraid that she was going to shame herself even further. But it abated, and she was able to go on. 'I tried to call an ambulance. The phone's not working.'

He said, 'I know about the phone. We'll get you to hospital. Don't worry.' He brushed the damp hair back from her forehead and said, 'Listen to me. You're not going to die, all right? Not today, anyway. I've checked your pulse. You've got a heart like a horse.

Whatever you took, you probably threw most of it up again.'

'I want an ambulance,' she moaned.

'We're not going to wait for an ambulance,' he said. 'I'm going to take you in the car.'

'Wipe my face first,' she said.

He smiled and he said, 'That's more like it. You're going to be fine.'

So he laid her head back against the chair and made her comfortable, and then he disappeared. Frances took a deep breath, and sighed. It would be so easy to sleep, now. So easy, and so dangerous.

When he came back, it was with a damp washcloth. It was warm, and he used it to clean her down.

'You're shivering,' he said, 'I'll bring something to cover you.'

This time, he seemed to take a while. But she drifted in and out of focus as she was waiting, so it would have been impossible for her to say exactly how long he was away. She was wishing that she could simply have stood up and told him what she needed to tell him. At least, that way, she might have kept some of her dignity.

When he came back with a tartan rug to put around her shoulders, she noticed that he'd changed his clothes.

'Come on,' he said, 'it's time to move.' And he lifted her forward to get the rug behind her shoulders. 'Can you walk?'

'No.'

'All right,' he said, and then he slid one arm under her and the other around her, and lifted her off the seat.

'Put your arm around my neck,' he said. 'Hold on to me.'

She clung to him as well as she could, and he navigated his way across the room and sideways through the door. They had to pass her bedroom on the way. She could see that he'd cleaned the room up and stripped the bed, and he'd re-made it with fresh sheets and a cover.

He's a good boy, she thought. She felt guilty at the way she'd been treating him. It was only somewhere deep underneath that a trace of doubt, a thought not quite fully formed, stirred concerning the questionable wisdom of housekeeping in the face of a medical emergency.

'Just pull your feet in as we get around the corner,' he told her, 'and then we're going down the stairs.'

They descended. Hers was the second-floor apartment in a subdivided house. They didn't head for the street, but for the back exit which would lead out to a set of parking garages across the alleyway behind the row. When they got there, the door was already unlocked and open and he was able to hook it with his heel to get them through. He must have come down and made everything ready as she'd been sliding in and out of consciousness in the chair. This was what had taken him so much time.

But why had he bothered to change the bed linen as well?

In the faint gleam thrown down from the windows of the buildings overlooking the alley, she could see that the door to her garage was already open. She was feeling sick and disoriented, the lurching of her progress down the stairs having disturbed her far more than the most nightmarish of fairground rides.

'I'm going to go back and get the rest of the stuff,' he said, as he raised her up higher and squeezed down the gap alongside the car. Frances experienced a hallucinogenic effect as the reflected lights of the night outside seemed to slide across the car's highly polished paintwork, and it was with a sense of bliss, the greatest feeling of relief that she'd ever known in her life, that she welcomed the sensation of being laid down into stillness and shadows. She was lying awkwardly, but that didn't seem to matter.

She became aware of him towering over her, a dark shape against darkness, framed as if in a window. 'I won't be very long,' he said. 'I've just got to go back for the doughnuts. Everything's going to be fine.'

And only belatedly did it begin to dawn on her that maybe it wasn't, as he reached up and brought down the trunk lid and put her into darkness.

5

'Did you choose somebody yet?'

It was Thursday morning. Gordon almost never called her on an office line and she, because he had an assistant who intercepted all his calls, could never phone him back. He had a cellular phone, and sometimes they'd talk on that. But only when she had a good idea of where he'd be.

'For what?' Ruth said, drawing him on.

'Don't make me say it out loud.' He lowered his voice, and she could almost imagine him casting a glance toward the door. No-one ever closed their office doors unless someone was being reprimanded or fired. It was like an unwritten company policy. He said, 'You know what I'm talking about.'

'Yes,' she lied, 'I think I chose somebody.'

'What's he like?'

'He's just one of the people they offered.'

'Good-looking?'

'Definitely.'

Gordon groaned. 'Oh, God.'

'I'll tell you what,' she said. 'You can look through the brochure tonight. See if you can guess which one I went for. You get it right, I'll give you a prize.'

'Ah.' There was an embarrassed silence and she knew, in an instant and in detail, exactly what was going to follow. 'Slight problem,' he said.

'Meaning what?'

'Meaning it doesn't look as if I'll make it. Nothing I can help. Sorry.'

'Don't apologize,' Ruth said.

'I'm not. But I'll miss seeing you.'

'Me too. Got to go.'

She hung up.

They'd agreed, in the beginning, that when something like this fell through one would never blame the other. And they didn't, as a rule. But it had inevitably become something of a one-sided arrangement. She couldn't complain, because she'd known how it would be. Ruth was no fool in this relationship. She hadn't wanted a husband. At least, not one of her own.

But it was a disappointment.

For some reason, the pagemaker program wasn't accepting input of her final copy. The deadline for *Art and Investment* magazine was only twenty minutes away. She tried to call Martin in Production on the floor below, but he wasn't picking up his phone. None of the other numbers for the department brought her a response, either.

It was quicker to walk down the one floor than to wait for an elevator. As soon as she emerged from the stairwell she could see that something was wrong.

There was a shirtsleeve crowd at the corridor's end and the crowd was, for want of a better term, rubbernecking at the glass wall which ran down one entire side of the Production Department. Most of Production was one big open floor where they ran traditional paste-up alongside the pagemaker terminals. It was an area of light and space and fairly continuous industry; more than two dozen titles were processed through here to varying deadlines, and the department had to be run like a switching yard. Holdups were costly, and the repercussions endless.

Ruth joined the crowd. She couldn't see much of anything other than the backs of people's heads and the ceiling beyond the glass, but it seemed that everyone who was supposed to be in there was out here.

'What's going on?' she asked Rozalia Bryce. Rozalia was part Native American and taller than most of the men.

'There's a lunatic with a knife walked in off the street,' Rozalia said. 'Security's got him cornered in there.'

'What does he want?'

'Someone to publish his autobiography.'

'Only in America,' Ruth said wearily, and started to ease her way through the gathering in search of Martin.

She didn't find him, but she did find herself up against the glass with a few of the people craning to see over her. The scene on the other side was about as undramatic as it was possible to get. Two distant figures were visible across a static sea of graphic artists' lightboards. They looked as if they were conversing, without tension or pressure. All of the tension seemed to be out here in the corridor.

Ruth looked around. Right alongside her was Herb Faux, production supervisor, amateur jazz player, two-hundred-pound short person. She said, 'Has anyone called the police?'

'They're on their way,' Herb said. 'Don't try to go in there, Ruth.'

'I wasn't even thinking of it. Did he hurt anyone?'

'He had a hold of Isabel Cardenas and cut off a piece of her hair, but that's all.'

Ruth glanced around behind them. 'Awful lot of guys out here,' she observed.

'The guard sent everyone out,' Herb said uncomfortably. 'This is how he wants it.'

She looked in through the glass again. Nothing much had changed in there, but as she watched she found that her sense of distance suddenly contracted as she realized that she knew somebody in the scene. Well, didn't *know* him, but recognized him at least. The building guard talking to the intruder, she could see now, was Aidan Kincannon. She could also see that there were a couple of the other security men behind a pillar and a bank of filing cabinets, and one of them was turning away and appeared to be speaking into a radio.

The intruder said something, jerking his head to indicate in the men's direction. Aidan Kincannon half-turned, and called to them. His voice didn't carry through the windows to the crowd. But the two men exchanged a glance and then backed off further, right out of everyone's sight.

She saw Aidan take off his uniform cap and place it on

34

a layout table beside him. He ran a hand over his hair. He seemed to be chatting, amiably; asking a question, showing an interest in the answer. The one facing him was weaving slightly back and forth as he stood. Ruth couldn't see the intruder's hands from here. Even at a distance he looked rheumy-eyed and unshaven. His stance was that of an old man but Ruth realized, with a sense of shock, that he was actually quite young.

Nothing was now as relaxed as it had at first seemed. The man was talking to Aidan with a dogged, unsteady earnestness as if he'd finally found somebody who'd listen after a long time searching. If he still had the knife, and it was almost certain that he did, then he was holding it out of sight.

The noise of an approaching siren came to them from the street outside. The man looked toward the windows. Aidan straightened slightly, alerted. He didn't move on him. But the man panicked all the same.

His hand came up and he made a lunging slash at Aidan. The corridor people gasped like a circus crowd. There was something in the hand. Ruth guessed it was his knife but it was moving too fast for her to be sure. Aidan caught the hand in movement and went with it, bearing it on down toward the floor and pulling the man along after. The intruder's balance hadn't been good, and now he lost it completely. The two men fell gracefully together, like a pile of toppling books, and disappeared from sight.

Someone threw open a door. All the eager guys dived through and into the big working area, flooding across the floor with all the not-so-eager-guys moving in their wake. Without even thinking about it, Ruth was with them.

Aidan had the man down and pinned. Expertly pinned.

'Stay back, please,' he told everyone. 'Nobody closer than this.'

One of the men said, 'Do you want us to do anything?'

'No,' Aidan said. 'No, thank you.'

'I can get the knife,' someone offered.

'Please don't try.'

Now the other security men came pushing their way through. The intruder was down on the carpeted floor, face squashed into the pile under Aidan's pinning hand. His arm was stretched out and held in a lock behind him, the blade still in his grasp. Aidan was leaning over him and speaking low. His tone seemed to be the same as before, although Ruth couldn't hear what was being said. It was like something private between them, unrelated to the absurdity of their positions. The man was nodding, awkwardly, so far as he could move at all.

One of the other guards dropped to one knee, and carefully disengaged the knife from the intruder's fingers.

'OK?' she heard Aidan say. And the man on the floor said, 'I think so. Thank you.'

The police arrived then, charging straight through. One of them collected the weapon as two more relieved Aidan, searching the man as he lay and then cuffing his hands behind him before raising him to his feet. Within a minute they were walking him out, two officers moving ahead to clear the way and others gripping his arms and holding him up so that he was almost weightless. He bobbed along in the middle of the blue-shirted pack like a fishing float.

Less than a minute after that, everybody realized that it was all over and in an instant the place was noisier than the kasbah.

Some officers stayed to do follow-up, but the other police dispersed toward the elevators. All the employees here had now bunched into excited clusters, talking at the tops of their voices; section supervisors moved through and made an attempt to get people motivated and back to their jobs, but their efforts all went for nothing as someone called out, 'They're taking him out of the building!' and everyone made for the windows. Ruth could hardly criticize; she was right there among them.

Looking down to the sidewalk below she could see three squad cars and a van, a traffic snarl-up, a crowd of onlookers, and all the office workers on every floor of the building opposite looking down as if into a bearpit. The last act of the drama was over in seconds. He was hustled across the sidewalk and into the van, the van and the cars all pulled out, and then there was nothing more to see.

As the audience finally broke up and everyone started to drift back toward their work stations, Ruth spied Martin and made her way over.

'Some show, huh?' he said. 'Guy pulls a knife on me, I'd sock him before I sat on him.'

'Yes,' Ruth said. 'I could see them holding you back.'

Somebody started to applaud then, and heads turned around. The cause of it was Aidan Kincannon, emerging from the department head's office after a brief statement-taking. Nearly everybody in the place joined in the ovation. Those who were seated moved to stand.

The security man blushed deeply, and didn't know how to respond. He nodded around sheepishly. Then he quickly put his hat on, pulled the peak down over his eyes, and headed for the doors.

Martin said, 'Now he's probably going to get dry-roasted for letting the guy slip past him in the first place.'

6

She'd an invitation to an opening at the Pentimenti Gallery in the Old City that evening. It was just around the corner from where she lived, so it was no big strain for her to drop by for half an hour. It would be quiet. Most of the galleries timed their openings for the first Friday of the month, and all the area's shops and restaurants stayed open late to make an occasion out of it. But this was an extra in the calendar. And now that her evening with Gordon seemed to have fallen through, any distraction from her disappointment would be welcome.

The Pentimenti was a long, deep, white-painted room with track lighting and a stripped wooden floor with its original old square nails still in place. She chatted to the owners and avoided the artist, who'd somehow formed an impression that she could enhance his career. He was young and slender, dressed all in black and with razor-thin pointy little sideburns and a stupid hat. The centrepiece of his show was a life-sized bronze of a kneeling woman with a real bicycle parked with its front wheel wedged in the crack of her behind. The piece was out in the middle of the floor, and people took turns at walking around it and studying it with their heads tilted to one side or the other.

'It's a statement about sexual politics,' she overheard him saying to someone who'd seemed interested.

Ruth was not big on art. Ruth sold ad space on financial magazines, one of which happened to be about art prices. She had an amateur's appreciation and she'd bought a few lithographs for her apartment, but that was as far as it went. She enjoyed the avant-garde most on gallery walls and at openings like this, where it cost her nothing. The artists that she'd met and liked all cared more about what they did than the figure they cut doing it, and were as likely to resemble barn-painters as anything. This boy was unlikely to join their company. Which was not to say that he wouldn't do well.

Walking home afterwards, she picked up some fresh bread and deli cheese for her supper. She'd planned something more elaborate, but now that Gordon wasn't coming she could save that for another day. She'd eat on the couch and watch some junk TV.

The Old City was a weird place. Comfortably weird now, but it had the air of somewhere that had been tamed and which had a more serious weirdness somewhere in its past. Galleries and seafood restaurants shared street space with air-compressor suppliers and wholesale shoe companies. All the rehab apartment blocks had names like the Wireworks or the Chocolate Works, except for the Chairworks where they still made chairs.

Ruth's building looked almost derelict on the outside, but that wasn't so much a design statement as a sign of the failure of those who owned their apartments to pay their condo fees. Ruth's rent was just under eight hundred a month exclusive of utilities, for which she reckoned she was entitled to see some paint. Her complaint was ongoing.

Once inside her apartment she put the locks on the door, changed into old clothes, and did a few stretching exercises on the carpet while channel-hopping with the TV remote. Everything that she found was either dross or advertising, but there was always the promise of something better further on. It never happened, but the chance was always there. She found an *Avengers* rerun, but it was ending.

She felt low. She was denying it, but she did.

Ruth got herself a glass of water and sat down, flushed and breathing hard. She closed her eyes and tried to concentrate. The counsellor who'd taught her this technique had recommended that she exercise first. She didn't understand why, but it seemed to work.

Her eyes stayed closed. But in her mind, they opened

after a few moments and she looked across the breakfast bar.

The kitchen was always whiter in here than it was in life. Cleaner. Newer. Brighter. Sharper. Like a transparency, lit from behind.

The teenager across the counter said, 'It's this escort agency thing, isn't it?'

'I suppose it must be,' Ruth said.

His name was Anthony. He'd been Anthony for about as long as she could remember. He appeared to have been raiding her refrigerator to make up a monster sandwich that now sat on the counter in front of him. There was stuff hanging out of it that she knew she didn't have. He didn't pick it up.

He said, 'Why?'

'I don't know why,' Ruth said. 'I thought it was a cool kind of answer to the problem. But it doesn't make me feel like a smart operator. It makes me feel . . . '

'Stupid?'

'No. It's like when you walk past a mirror that you didn't know was there. You see somebody and it's you, but you don't realize that for a second. You thought things were going great, but there was this sad-looking stranger.'

'You mean it's like disappointment.'

'I suppose I do.'

She was expecting him to say something but he didn't, not right away; he was looking at her and he was half-smiling and she knew that he wasn't thinking about anything other than her, and that unnerved her a little. Which was ridiculous because any thoughts that he expressed, they had to be her own. This scared her sometimes. It scared her because, on occasions, the voice that she heard most definitely wasn't hers. Or anything even like it.

He said, 'Well, it gives me the opportunity to tell you this. This great life you're so in control of. It's like four well-chosen objects in an empty room. It's boring, Ruth.'

He'd surprised her.

'Is it?' she said.

He looked down, and flicked at something nonexistent on the countertop. He said, 'What's the loveliest thing you ever saw?'

'You already know,' she said.

'Tell me anyway.'

'It was a horse chestnut. I found it when I was nine. I must have stared at the colour of it for an hour.'

'Who painted it?'

'No-one did.'

'Did you go looking for it?'

'I just saw it when I was walking.'

He persisted. 'What happened to it?'

'It got dried-out and the colours all faded and then somebody stole it out of my drawer.'

'And where were you?'

Ruth remembered.

Her mind went back to that big, almost-empty children's home in the Cheshire countryside. She'd been taken by an aunt to spend a couple of weeks there, late in one year. It was the first occasion that she'd been away from her parents for any length of time, apart from a hospital stay which she'd been almost too young to remember.

It was an institutional place, county-owned, built to give deprived kids and their carers a break from the inner city. She hadn't realized it at the time but she was the aunt's passport to a cheap holiday; it wasn't that her aunt didn't have any money, just that she couldn't pass up a bargain. Ruth remembered its huge empty rooms and its musty sanatorium furniture. She remembered sitting on the waxed wooden floor in the lounge, looking through the twenty-year-old books on the shelves while it rained outside and the other children played loud and rough somewhere down miles and miles of corridor.

It had felt like exile. It certainly wasn't an experience she'd have chosen. But somewhere in it was that one perfect moment that she'd never forgotten.

She realized what it was that the boy was telling her. That sometimes you had to be thrown into things because that was the only way you'd ever find your way through to something you didn't even know you wanted. That real life was a falling into darkness, out of control; and that whatever she'd been creating for herself, here, real wasn't quite the word for it.

Anthony said, 'Do you honestly think Gordon's the one?'

'I don't know,' Ruth admitted.

'You never will, unless you push him and find out.'

But Ruth wasn't certain. She'd made her choices and one of those choices as far as Gordon was concerned was, so far into my life and no further. But suppose that were to change. Suppose they were to move their affair into the open and take all of the consequences that came along with that. She ached for him sometimes, thought of him often. But what if the heat and the ache and the mystery were all bound up together with that sense of the forbidden? Would any of the awe and the passion remain? Indeed, would anything remain at all?

'What if he isn't?' she said.

'Then, what do you actually lose?'

The door buzzer rang.

'It's him,' the boy said with confidence.

'It can't be.'

'Let me tell you. If it's him, then it's fate.'

Ruth opened her eyes. She was alone.

And the door buzzer rang again.

For a moment she was disoriented. She'd been sitting *there*, now she was sitting *here*. But stirring herself as if yanked out of a dream, she got to her feet and went over to the entryphone and touched the reply button. 'Yes?'

It was Gordon's voice that came up the wire. *'It's me, Ruth,'* he said. *'I have less than an hour.'*

She felt dazed. 'Come on up,' she said, and pressed the bar that would let him in. Then she unlocked and took the chains off the apartment door, crossed the room and folded her arms to wait.

Gordon arrived within a couple of minutes. She could hear him approaching down the hallway.

'Lizzie's got a birthday party at a friend's house in Francisville,' he said as he swept in and closed the door behind him. 'I could either stay around and watch two dozen five-year-olds destroy a magician or I could slip away.' He turned to face her, looking expectant. 'Where are they?'

'Where's who?'

'The guys in the brochure. The rent-a-wreck boys I was supposed to come and see.'

Ruth indicated for him to go over and sit down, and she went to get the copied pages.

'They're not wrecks, Gordon,' she said as she handed him the papers and settled beside him. 'They're mature gentlemen.'

He made a face, and started to look through them. She sat and watched him. He wasn't brilliantly good-looking and his hair was starting to thin. But his eyes were kind and his grin could stop her heart in its tracks, sometimes, and he'd an eagerness about everything that could be infectious.

After a while she said, 'Aren't you taking off your coat?'

'No time,' he said without looking up.

'Do you want a drink?'

'You have one if you like. I don't want to risk Mimi smelling it on me. You know, while we're going through all this, she's talking like she can hardly be bothered to come along? She says she socializes enough for her own job, and it bores her.' He shook his head. 'God, look at this bunch. There are more rugs here than an Afghan market. Which one did you pick on?'

'I've not made the final decision,' Ruth said.

He looked at her. 'I thought you had.'

'It's not as easy as I thought it would be.'

He held out a page, comparing one with another, and said, 'I know what you mean. It's going to be weird. I'll have to keep reminding myself it's not for real.'

Ruth was thinking to herself, I'm not going to do this. But then she opened her mouth to say something else altogether, and out it came.

She said, 'Why don't we save ourselves all of this? You be my date.'

Gordon looked at her blankly. 'What are you talking about?'

'You take me to the ball.'

'Jesus, Ruth,' he said. 'You pick your moments!'

'If anyone asks, just say it's a professional thing. Like when movie stars take each other to the Oscars.'

'Nobody would believe it, Ruth. They wouldn't believe it even if it was the truth.'

'All right then, so it's not a professional thing. Look at all the trouble we're going to. If we're worth all that, maybe we ought to consider if what we have is worth more.'

Gordon stared at her. She could see that she'd actually frightened him.

He said, 'I can't talk about it now. This is something you really have to think through.' He took her hand. 'I'll tell you what. Let's get this event out of the way and then . . . then we can discuss it properly.'

She knew.

'Sure,' she said.

'Impulse is *not* the way to go with something like this,' Gordon went on, warming to it now that he saw he had an escape route. 'You've got to agree with that.'

'Whatever you say.'

And then something else seemed to cross his mind. Light dawned in his eyes.

'Wait a minute,' he said. 'Was this a test?'

She gave a tight smile that neither confirmed nor denied it. Gordon was clearly relieved. He let her hand fall.

'It was, wasn't it?' he said, breaking into a grin, and Ruth shrugged and said nothing.

He checked his watch, made a show of surprise at the passing of what had to be the shortest hour on record, and jumped up onto his feet. 'Don't play with me like that, Ruth,' he said, placing a hand on his chest. 'My old heart won't stand it. I love you and I want to be with you. What else do you need to know?' Then he held up one of the brochure pages. 'Him?'

Ruth gave a pained look.

'Gotta go,' Gordon said, and went.

The Barclay Hotel stood on the corner of Rittenhouse Square. In most people's minds Rittenhouse Square stood for Old Money, although as a rule the old money was a memory and the buildings around it were now high-rise commercial property just like everywhere else. At the heart of the square was a public park, and at the heart of the park stood a large and classy-looking canvas marquee. It had been raised there only hours before and it was encircled by a ring of private security to hold out the curious. It was a warm evening, and there was music drifting over from it already.

Ruth took a deep breath as she entered the Barclay from the sidewalk. Her heart was beating like a bride's. Ridiculous, but it was. The lobby was long and white, and lit by chandeliers that mellowed it all down to cream and gilt. Faced by it, she hesitated.

'Are you Ms Lasseter?' a voice behind her asked.

She turned, and saw that it came from a uniformed concierge at his desk by the door. 'Yes,' she said.

'Your guest is waiting for you in the cocktail lounge.'

'And where would that be?'

He indicated for her, and she followed a baronial passageway which led off the lobby and around into the bar. She was a few minutes later than she'd planned, but she didn't rush. Not in these heels, buster. She checked herself over in a big mirror as she passed it.

The cocktail lounge was deep in darkness, the main illumination being from a nightlight candle in a glass at the centre of each table. Twenty beads of light, one overall dim golden glow. The walls were panelled with Chinese scenes, painted in gilt on dark canvas and stretched on wooden frames. The only bright splashes were the red jacket of the bartender, and the baseball game that he was watching on the TV behind the bar. The colours of the field were vivid and wonderful. Ruth wondered why sports fields on TV sets in bars always looked vivid and wonderful.

There was only one other person in here. He rose to his feet as soon as he saw her.

'Mr Hagan?' she said, as she made her way through the tables toward him.

'I'm Tim,' he said. 'You're Miss Lasseter.'

'Ruth.'

'Thank you for choosing me.' He moved out to meet her and took her proffered hand in a gentle clasp, holding it for a moment before letting it go.

My God, she was thinking. What have I done? He's so *young*.

In this light, and probably in any other light as well, Tim Hagan looked even younger than his twenty-three years. A well-groomed, fit-looking boy in a tuxedo. But no schoolkid. He wore it too well for that. He was broad-shouldered and clear-skinned, and he had a razor-sharp haircut and the wide, clean-lined jawbone of a male model.

He was even better than his picture. He was utterly, utterly unbelievable.

And Ruth thought again, What *have* I done?

She said, 'I've got a few things I want to run through with you before we go over.'

He stepped back, so that she could go ahead of him to the table where he'd been waiting. There was a tall glass with what looked like mineral water in it, apparently untouched.

He said, 'Can I get you anything to drink?'

'This won't take that long,' Ruth said.

He glanced at the bartender and shook his head briefly as they sat. The bartender returned his attention to the game. Tim Hagan looked at Ruth attentively, hands folded on the table before him.

'Don't do that,' Ruth said, half-amused and making a brief waving-away gesture.

He looked anxious, as if he'd been tripped in a detail. 'Do what?' he said.

'You're making me feel like a schoolteacher.'

He moved his hands from the table.

'Sorry,' he said.

'I don't know how much the agency has told you.'

'I had a briefing from Mrs Carroll.'

'Did she seem to disapprove of anything?'

He seemed politely puzzled. 'I don't understand.'

Ruth said, 'She couldn't exactly contain her dismay when I phoned to make the final arrangements. She all but pleaded with me to reconsider.'

'Mrs Carroll said nothing about that to me.'

'She didn't say anything about . . . an age difference?'

'What age difference would that be?'

She watched him. Nothing changed. She gave him the chance to falter or smirk, but it didn't happen. His gaze was steady and it held her own.

Ruth let through a slow smile.

'I think this is going to work out fine, Tim,' she said.

'I hope so,' he said.

There was a perceptible sense of relaxation then, as if they'd swapped passwords and agreed their ground and no longer needed to be quite so much on their guard. Over at the bar, the head waiter from the adjoining restaurant came through and started to ring up a drinks order for his diners. Ruth was beginning to think that she could happily have spent the evening right here. The candles across the tables were like a field of stars reflected in a still pool.

But how realistic would that be? How long before they ran out of small-talk and the true size of the gulf between them was uncovered?

Don't even dream about it, she told herself.

She said, 'I don't know how much Mrs Carroll already told you. But I'm going to save both of us a lot of embarrassment and say that you don't have to fake anything tonight. I'm not saying you should tell everyone that I hired you. But trying to pretend we're something we're not is just ridiculous. We should act like friends who've hooked up for the evening because it's expected. You know,' she added, a little lamely, 'like when movie stars take each other to the Oscars.'

'I understand,' Hagan said. 'You don't have to tell me anything more.'

'Well, what do you say? Shall we go over?'

They rose, leaving his drink still untouched.

They walked out of the hotel and across the park toward the open-air ballroom which, like some magic garden in a story, had appeared out of nowhere and would vanish again in the morning. The main canvas had been raised over the fountain at the heart of the park, and side-awnings covered the approach walks in each direction. Across each path stood a wooden barrier with the words POLICE LINE on it, and behind each barrier stood a grey-jacketed security person. Outside the barriers, early-evening park life went on more or less as normal. People strolled, their dogs met and tumbled, the homeless staked a claim on their benches for the night. The last rays of the sun were gilding the upper floors of the high-rise blocks above them.

The entranceway at the south-east corner was lit up like a fairground booth and overstocked with flowers. Ruth and her guest were checked off the list, and then they made their way up a red carpet to the receiving line to be greeted by members of the board and the owning family. The latter, an elderly couple and their even older brother, looked as well-bred and frail as rare violins. The Chairman of the Board was impressive. He remembered her, or at least he was completely convincing in appearing to. As she moved on down the line, she could hear him being equally convincing with someone else.

After the logjam of the receiving line, everyone emerged into a courtyard area around two sides of the fountain that was like a holding pen. It was the cocktail hour, and drinks were being served. Four men in dinner suits, one with a ponytail, were running the free bar at a long and well-stocked table.

All the male guests were in black tie. The women were in more brilliant plumage. Ruth didn't, as yet, see too many that she knew.

Glancing around, Hagan said, 'I didn't get much time to prepare. I looked through some books on modern art last night and learned a few names.'

'You shouldn't have worried,' Ruth told him. 'These are finance publishing and society people, not an art crowd.'

'I already forgot most of the names anyway,' he admitted. 'Except for Mark Rothko. Is he likely to be here?'

'Not *too* likely, Tim,' Ruth said. 'He may be modern, but he's dead.'

He was relatively unfazed.

'Someone's waving to you,' he said.

She turned to look. A woman was squeezing by in a dress that was sequinned like fish scales, but then as her line of sight cleared Ruth could see Jennie and her husband, Bill. She'd met Bill a number of times and she knew, beyond a doubt, that this was not his kind of an occasion. It had probably taken a big bribe or some serious blackmail, first to get him into a rental suit and then to come along.

Jennie was in something ankle-length with frills down the front and a ruff at the neck. It gave her a look like a waitress in some chain of Southern-style restaurants, or a plantation house guide. She gave the once-over to Ruth's tight black little designer number and said, 'Well, look at you! I'd die to be able to fill up a dress like that.'

'You could fill it right now, kid,' her husband said from beside her, hands in his pockets as he scanned the crowd. 'The problem is what we'd do with the overflow.'

Ruth reached for Hagan and drew him forward slightly. 'Jennie, Bill,' she said. 'This is Tim. He's a friend of mine, and he's my date for tonight.'

Jennie turned to look at him, holding out her hand.

Ruth waited for the shockwave. It came, with a built-in delay for disbelief.

'You are?' she said, and then it hit so hard that she all but took a step backwards. 'You *are*.'

'I'm very pleased to meet you, Jennie,' Hagan said with just the right note of formality. 'And you, Bill.'

Jennie was still a little dazed, but she was recovering fast. She said to Hagan, 'Have you . . . known each other long?'

'You know,' Hagan said, 'I really couldn't put a time on it. Sometimes you just click with someone and right away it's like you've known them your entire life.'

'Well,' Bill said, not looking at anybody in particular, 'that's not unfeasible.'

Ruth couldn't be certain, but she was fairly sure that Jennie kicked or somehow distracted him at this point. Under the adjoining marquee, the band started to play and a singer started to sing.

Hagan turned to Ruth and said, 'Perhaps you'd like to dance?'

Jennie looked as if she needed the recovery time. Ruth said, 'See you both later,' and then she allowed Hagan to guide her off through the crowd.

'I said you didn't have to lie,' she told him as they eased their way through. Ahead of them there was a youngish man in a flamboyant white dinner suit, billowy as a sheik's pyjamas, who breezed onto the dance floor tugging his girlfriend by the hand like so much cargo.

Hagan said, 'Why do you assume I was lying?'

'Oh, Tim,' Ruth said with a smile as they stepped out onto the boarded deck. 'You'll go far. Can you dance to this kind of stuff?'

'Please,' he said with a pained look. 'I'm a professional.'

They danced.

The band was a six-piece outfit, old-time musicians with a lot of mileage under their belts. They did nothing showy and they didn't lay a note out of place. Right now, they were playing Cole Porter.

'You're good,' Ruth said after a while.

'I know,' Tim said simply.

That cracked her up, and she started to enjoy herself.

She started to recognize more co-workers and a few clients. The event started to take on an atmosphere. Coloured lights were being played over the underside of the marquee, and as flying insects darted through the beams they seemed to be momentarily afire. She thought that she saw Alicia and then, next time around, she confirmed it. Alicia was dancing with her husband Frank. Ruth didn't exactly catch her eye, but she knew that she'd been seen and recognized. Alicia had a stunned look, as if she'd just been struck by something and was waiting for a puff of wind to blow her over; her husband said something to her that she didn't seem to hear.

Ruth looked around for Gordon and Mimi, but she didn't see either of them. They'd be around somewhere by now, perhaps back in the courtyard where the canapés were being served. Maybe Gordon had seen *her*.

She moved closer to her escort. They fit together almost in interlock.

When the band stopped playing, taped disco music took over. Everyone applauded and the numbers out on the floor dropped by about half. Ruth looked around again. Damn it, Gordon, she was thinking, you should see this. He was paying for it, after all. And wouldn't *that* just get under his skin?

But instead of Gordon she spotted another figure, one that she hadn't expected to see. There was an instant in which she recognized him but couldn't make that recognition absolute, a kind of finger-snapping moment in which obvious connections refused to be made; and then it came together, and she realized that it was Aidan Kincannon again. He was in an ill-fitting dinner suit with a drink in his hand, glancing around after watching the dancing; there was a kind of pleasant, open look on his face as if he was trying to broadcast a general signal to anyone who might have been interested that he didn't feel at all uncomfortable, not really. If ever Ruth had seen a fish out of water, Aidan Kincannon was it. He worked for the building's people and not for the company, so there had to be some special reason for his being here.

'I think they're serving champagne,' Hagan said as they ducked away from the disco.

'How do you know?'

'I heard the corks being pulled. Would you like some?'

'Yes,' Ruth said, 'I rather think I would.'

'Will you be all right if I leave you for a minute?'

'Of course I will.'

Hagan moved off, and Ruth took aim through the crowd for Aidan Kincannon. She took the opportunity to exchange greetings with one or two people along the way, but she didn't stop for anyone.

Aidan seemed to become aware of her belatedly. He smiled, and didn't quite seem to know what to do with his hands as she covered the last few yards.

'Hello, Aidan,' she said. 'I almost didn't know you out of uniform.'

'That's what everyone's been telling me,' he said.

'I hadn't realized you were going to be here.'

'Somebody stuck an envelope with an invitation in my locker yesterday.' He made a wry face. 'I've been given to understand that it's some kind of a reward.'

'I saw what you did to earn it. I think you deserve more than this.'

'Don't tell me,' he said, 'tell the boss. Who's your friend?'

'Just a friend,' she said, playing it down for the first time all evening.

'Well,' Aidan said, pointing with his glass, 'he's looking for you.'

She looked over to the other side of the room and there was Tim Hagan, a champagne flute in each hand and scanning for her. She waved, and saw that she'd caught his eye.

'See you later,' she said to Aidan. And Aidan nodded,

pleasantly. She felt awkward about abandoning him again, but she wasn't sure what else she could do. Except maybe to feed a poisoned hors d'oeuvre to Bill, and to give Jennie a hard push in Aidan's direction.

Hagan handed her a glass and said, 'I've heard your name being whispered three times in the last five minutes.'

'Let them talk all they want,' Ruth said happily. 'Let's circulate.'

They circulated.

There was an art to keeping a conversation going in circumstances like these. No tale was ever completed, no story reached its point. New people were always drifting up, and new introductions were always being made. Jake brought over some clients with whom she'd dealt by phone for two years but whom she'd never met. Others, she sought out. Hagan stayed by her side throughout, there when she needed him to be, taking a step back when she didn't.

'You're doing well,' she told him after a while. A buffet had been unveiled in a side tent and there had been something of a stampede, leaving them alone with some empty tables where they could sit for a minute and recharge. The tables were draped with bronze-coloured cloth, the seats upholstered in red and gold to fit in with the general décor of open-air opulence. Floral displays were like hanging gardens, suspended above each. The effect, upscale though it undoubtedly was, seemed to Ruth like the world's most expensive carousel art.

Hagan inclined his head with a smile and said, 'Thank you. I'm enjoying it all.'

'But it's not the kind of evening you'd choose for yourself.'

'How do you know?'

'Well, what is there here for you?'

He made a show of thinking it over, of running through the options. 'There's you,' he said.

'Thank you,' Ruth said, knowing that she'd done no more than ask for this. 'Enough.'

'You don't think I'm serious,' he said.

'I'm going to change the subject. Where are you from?'

'Try to guess.'

She had no chance. Ruth had come to the conclusion long ago that she had no ear for nuance in speech. 'You're a Southern boy,' she said. 'I can hear that much, but that's about all.'

'And I thought I'd lost the accent.'

'How long have you lived in Philadelphia?'

'Not very long.'

She shook her head. He had a half-mischievous look that suggested that he could lead her on like this all night, if she wanted him to.

She said, 'You don't give much away, do you?'

'No,' he said.

Ruth knew a going-nowhere streak when she saw one.

'Let's go and eat,' she said.

The society columnist from the *Inquirer* was there. Ruth had seen him earlier; he'd arrived on a bicycle, wearing a bowler hat. He was leaving the buffet table just as she and Hagan arrived and joined the line. The food had been presented with an artistry that even the thorough wolverine-rout of the last ten minutes couldn't obscure. There was crabmeat on the shell, chicken on a skewer, teriyaki on a bed of lettuce; there was a chef out of sight somewhere in the back, but all of those handling the service looked as if they were in their teens. The girl on the salad bar wore a brace on her teeth.

As they passed down the table, the woman in front of Ruth suddenly turned to her.

'It's Ruth, isn't it?' she said. 'We haven't met before. I'm Mimi Parry.'

Ruth felt as if she'd been caught out. For a moment, she didn't know what to say. Gordon's wife was a character who'd lived in her imagination for some time now, someone with a changing image and an almost

55

cartoon-like personality. Mimi the dragon. Mimi the fire-breather. Mimi of the five-times-a-year sexual appetite.

This woman didn't look like *that* Mimi Parry at all.

Ruth said, 'How are you, Mrs Parry?'

'Nice to know you,' she said, and they managed to shake hands while still holding their plates. Ruth saw Gordon look back and see them doing it and then look again, startled. She'd been within a couple of yards of him and she hadn't even known it. Seen from the back in the line, he was barely distinguishable from all the other slightly balding middle-managers. So much for the bond they were always going to share.

'Gordon?' Mimi said. 'Get us some paper napkins, will you?' And she drew Ruth away from the table as if there was something pressing that they had to discuss.

'Yes, Mimi,' Gordon said hollowly as they left him behind.

With a glance toward Hagan, who was still back in line getting his plate loaded, Mimi said, 'Don't tell my husband, but I'm seriously thinking of trading him in for a model like yours. The problem's going to be finding someone who'll have him.'

Ruth smiled weakly.

'Good luck,' she said.

'Where'd you get him?'

'From Boys'R'Us. His name's Tim.'

Mimi laughed out loud. A couple of people looked. 'Pardon me,' she said as if she'd belched. What Ruth knew of Mimi was that she was a working woman herself, a lawyer in a midtown office. She'd risen in her profession, and it showed in her manner. She seemed to be practised at putting people at immediate ease and making them feel interesting.

'We're going to have to meet and chat properly, some day,' she told Ruth; and then Hagan came over to join them, his plate laden as if he was stoking up before a siege, and Mimi said, 'Hello, Tim. We've been talking about you.'

'Really?' Hagan said pleasantly.

'We've been talking about you, too, Gordon,' Mimi added drily as her husband arrived with the napkins.

Gordon had a hunted look. 'Saying what?'

'Nothing you'd want us to repeat.'

Mercifully, some old friends came over and howled with delight and fell upon Mimi and Gordon, and that was effectively the end of the exchange. Ruth backed off with a relief that she hoped wouldn't be obvious. She felt as if she'd just crossed a narrow plank above an alligator pool.

Hagan seemed to get a sense of her feelings, and asked if anything was wrong. She said that there wasn't. But she gave him a mental mark for his show of concern.

After the food they switched on the address system and there were some speeches, a couple of presentations, and then a prize draw based on coatroom numbers. Ruth could only marvel at the spectacle of people in thousand-dollar outfits digging their tickets out and squinting at them like bingo players, all for the sake of a big stuffed teddy bear that was going to take up so much house room and pick up so much dust that it would inevitably come to be detested over the years. It was won by Becky from the subscriptions department, whom Ruth reckoned probably deserved it. After that the company president, looking older than God and much better-groomed, took the mike and thanked them all for coming and sent them forth to enjoy themselves. He handed the mike to the singer, and the band struck up again.

'Back in a couple of minutes,' Ruth told Hagan.

'Are you sure there's nothing wrong?' he asked her, but she reassured him again.

The ladies' powder room was in one of two white tents at the quiet end of the area. Just about everybody was either on or close by the dance floor now. Staff down at this end were picking up trash and bagging it.

Inside the powder room, facilities were basic. One transportable chemical toilet in a booth, one table with

57

mirror and chair, and a basketwork bowl of complimentary sachet wipes.

Rosemary was there before the mirror, making a few repairs to her hair and makeup. She seemed slightly flustered.

'Are you all right, Rosemary?' Ruth said.

'I got a little overheated out there,' Rosemary said. 'Did you hear about Alicia?'

'No. What?'

'She left early. She wasn't feeling well.'

'What a shame,' Ruth said.

She hadn't meant it to carry any weight or to sound at all sarcastic, but somehow a note of that must have crept in. Or perhaps Rosemary thought she picked up a shading that simply wasn't there.

Turning from the mirror, she said, 'Do you know what you're *doing*, Ruth?'

Ruth looked her straight in the eye. 'For the first time in a long time, Rosemary,' she said, 'the answer is, not entirely.'

'It may not be my place to say it, but . . . you could have been his mother.'

'That's something I *think* I would have noticed. If a forty-year-old guy turns up with a young woman on his arm, you can't hear yourself talk for the sound of his friends slapping him on the back. I spend the evening with a younger man and suddenly I'm Elvira, Mistress of the Dark. He's just a nice boy, Rosemary, and he happens to be my escort for the evening. He also has a life of his own.'

'Well,' Rosemary said lamely, 'I'm only saying.'

'Thank you, Rosemary. I promise you I'll bear it in mind.'

'You may not realize how vulnerable you could be.'

'He's my escort, Rosemary. That doesn't mean he's got his hand in my pants.'

'There's no need to be coarse about it, Ruth,' Rosemary said; and the hurt in her eyes was so great and so genuine

58

that Ruth was beset with an almost overpowering sorrow. But what had been said could not be unsaid.

'Excuse me,' Rosemary said. She went on out of the tent, leaving Ruth alone.

Back in the midst of the party a few minutes later, Ruth scanned the crowd for Hagan. For the moment, she didn't seem to be able to see him. Then somebody bumped into her from behind and she turned and saw that it was Laura, Jake's wife. Where Jake tended to be perpetually harassed and depressive, Laura was the complete opposite. Ruth liked her a lot. She had a sheepish-looking Aidan Kincannon in tow and she was hauling him toward the dance floor. She was lightly tanked-up and totally unconcerned.

'He went thataway,' she said to Ruth, and pointed out toward the gardens. 'Come on, cowboy,' she then said to Aidan, pulling on his arm.

'Thanks,' Ruth said.

'Excuse me,' said Aidan Kincannon as he was yanked on past her.

The party was moving into its later phase now. The champagne had done its work and the music had moved uptempo. The dinner suits and gowns were unwinding and starting to frolic. There was even some sedate and comparatively tasteful jiving going on.

'Look at them all,' she heard some man say as she eased herself around the periphery of the crowd. 'That's how it was, back when Dinosaurs ruled the Earth.'

Aidan Kincannon was happily dancing with Laura, his necktie undone. There was no sign of Jake anywhere, which wasn't too much of a surprise. He was probably clearing up what was left of the food. When it came to fast living, Jake was a slow trailer hitched up to Laura's Ferrari.

She found Hagan outside of it all, out in the shadowy no-man's-land between the light and the movable barrier across the path. Behind Ruth, the canvas glowed like mother-of-pearl from the bright lights within. There was a photographer now working somewhere inside, and every now and again the marquee was further illuminated as if by the flash of a bumper car's pole.

Hagan was seated on a low wall, looking out across the darkened square with a half-empty glass in his hand. He appeared to be deep in thought, and didn't seem to be aware of her approaching.

'I apologize if it seemed I'd abandoned you,' Ruth said.

He looked around and started to rise abruptly, but she put her hand on his shoulder and pushed him back down as she sat beside him.

'Were you looking for me?' he said. 'I'm sorry.'

She took his drink from him, sipped from it, and handed it back.

'What are you thinking?' she said.

'How unlikely it all is,' he told her, looking down into his glass. Straight orange juice, so far as Ruth could tell. 'How you can plan the things you do but you can never plan the way you'll feel.'

'Have you been reading my mind?' she said.

Out beyond the barrier, about fifty yards away, a mounted Park Policeman went by in the night. His horse was huge and dark, and his helmet caught a glint of the perimeter lights as his mount carried him by with loose and free-flowing ease. A hint of the beast in the stillness of a city night. Horse and rider made no sound.

Hagan said, 'That man back in the food tent. The one who's married to the lawyer. He's the one, isn't he?'

'How could you tell?'

'I was reading your mind.'

'I'm serious,' she said, and she nudged him playfully with her shoulder. They were close enough for that. 'What gave it away?'

'I saw you look at him,' he said. 'And your eyes went kind of sad. As if you'd already decided to let him go. Have you?'

Ruth breathed deeply.

'I don't know,' she said. 'But I didn't realize I was

hiding it so badly. That's something I'll have to watch.' She smiled faintly in the shadows, and looked down at the ground. 'I'm glad I picked you, Tim,' she said. 'I'm glad it wasn't anyone else.'

'So am I,' he said.

She'd a sense that there were a thousand things that could have happened, right then. More than a thousand.

But they stood, to go back to the party. She linked her arm through his as they moved.

8

Somebody had come up with the bright idea of building a champagne fountain without actually taking into account the fact that they were using the wrong kind of champagne glasses, and the crash that followed almost drowned out the band. The bread-roll fight was another low spot. Some of the senior management people were out there after that, hard-eyed and cruising and making their presence known; not overtly taking names, but there to give the signal that they'd be damned well ready for it if things went any further. Couples with babysitters to relieve started to make a line for their coats. The free bar closed and the dance numbers turned slushy. A few people talked about going on to a club. All too soon, for Ruth. She felt tight and light, as if she'd been breathing in some thinner, purer kind of air. She didn't want to go to any nightclub. But she didn't want to end this yet, either. She felt like a runner, only just beginning to find her stride and her rhythm as those around her faded and fell away.

There were a couple of people that she still had to seek out and talk to, but when she checked around she learned that they'd already gone. Hagan stayed politely at her shoulder as she enquired. He seemed aware of the room but whenever she turned to him, his attention would return to her and was complete. It wasn't like having a boyfriend along. More like an eye-on-the-ball and attentive bodyguard. She wouldn't have imagined that she'd have liked the sensation. But she found that she did, rather.

Maybe it depended on who it was. Ruth didn't give of herself easily. She didn't like to let anyone under the ropes. Mostly, she'd allow them in and only then find out what they were really like, which was never quite as she'd expected. Or else, she reasoned, you let them in and then that changed how they thought of you, so by the very act you made them different.

In which case you couldn't hope to win, ever.

'What do you want to do from here?' he said.

There were guidelines to be followed, at this point as at the beginning of the evening; nothing special, just a version of the simple precautions of a first date with a stranger in the here-and-now. Meet in a public place. Avoid misunderstandings. Part like a couple of fencers, guard still up and protective layers intact. Take separate cabs or, if sharing, be dropped off last and don't risk being overheard when giving the address.

'You'd better get this for me,' she said, passing him her coatroom ticket. 'Then I'll drive you home.'

'I could get a cab. It's all included.'

'We don't need a cab.'

As well as the line for coats, there was another for taxis that was moving just as slowly. Waiting close to the exit for Hagan to return, Ruth found herself side-by-side with Gordon as he was reaching the head of it.

'Congratulations,' he said in a low voice and with a peevish streak in his tone that he wasn't quite managing to conceal. 'There isn't a woman in the place that you haven't managed to shock, scandalize or make green with envy.'

Ruth knew that he was exaggerating. But she also knew that, in a more limited way, he wasn't wrong. Her actions tonight had been the neutron bomb of bad behaviour, blasting the targets that she'd wanted to hit while leaving the major structures undamaged. Half the women here wouldn't even have known her name. The other half would probably have to struggle to forget it.

She said, 'Which category includes Mimi?'

'For some reason, Mimi seems to think you're wonderful. It's a shame I couldn't have brought the two of you together in some other life. You'd probably have a lot in common.'

'You mean, besides you?'

'Ruth!' he said under his breath, not daring to turn and look around.

'Here's your cab,' she said. 'Where's your wife?'

Mimi Parry was right behind her.

'Good night, Ruth,' she called out pleasantly as she passed.

Tim Hagan brought her wrap, and put it around her shoulders. They walked out into the square. There were still a few late strollers at the barriers. They were chatting easily to the security people, pointing things out, asking questions. But nobody paid the two of them much attention as they passed. She took Hagan's arm again, and leaned against him. She could do that, couldn't she? What the hell, she'd hired him. It was a fine summer's night and it felt good to share the sensation of being alive. No more than that. And it was clear he didn't mind, because he put his hand over hers and pulled her in close.

They'd no more than a hundred yards to walk to reach the all-night attendant parking which stood, along with three or four other neon-lit facilities, in an alleyway between two modern buildings on the square. They waited at the yellow line for her car to be driven up.

'Thank you for tonight,' Ruth said. 'I hope the evening wasn't too much of a strain.'

'No strain at all,' Hagan said. 'I think I learned a few things about myself.'

'Like what?' she said. But the attendant brought her car then, so she never got to find out.

He wasn't even going to get in until she insisted, and then he gave in with grace. It only occurred to her as they were emerging from the end of the alleyway that he might feel awkward. She looked at him, but she couldn't read him. He was looking out into the night and was stroking his jaw with his hand, as if absently checking the closeness of his shave.

And what, she wondered to herself, did *you* learn about yourself tonight?

'So where to, Tim?' she said.

He gave an address out in Society Hill. Which was a surprise. She'd been expecting University City, maybe, or somewhere across the river. Society Hill had been something in its day, and wasn't exactly the barrio now. It stood some way south of the Old City where she lived; but whereas much of the Old City had been reclaimed from a run-down waterfront zone, Society Hill had always been a prestige residential area. She'd checked out its prices when she'd been looking to move, and she'd backed off fast. It was a district mostly of colonial town houses, the very same streets that often made her think of home. A postcard of home, an idealized dream of home; the home they reckoned you could never go back to, because in truth it had never been there.

Now she was curious. Whatever impression she'd formed of Hagan, projecting her guesses into the gaps left by his good-humoured evasions, money had never been a part of it. Poverty, yes. She could see him as a poor boy with one good suit and his wits and a drive to rise. Making contacts, working his way; she couldn't imagine any other scenario that would put him onto the agency's books.

But that was just a kind of groundless romanticism, she realized now. The kind of impulse that made sad women on ocean cruises dream about the lifeguards at the pool. She was no virgin, and he was no gypsy. Life, it seemed, had an endless capacity to frustrate one's expectations.

She drove around Independence Square and down through the main tourist quarter, where the city had bulldozed the ground around a handful of key historic buildings to leave them standing in parkland like rock plugs on a volcanic plain. A few late visitors were peering through the glass of the Liberty Bell pavilion, but otherwise the sector was floodlit and quiet.

It didn't take her long to find the address. It was a low-rise building amid the row houses, designed to blend in. Three storeys with attic space above, cellar windows at street level, bars on the cellar windows. The street was short, and tree-lined, and quiet. They'd offset the east–west streets when they were laying out this part of the city, deliberately misaligning the ends so that young men wouldn't be able to race their carriages along them. There was a big van close behind her, and it was too narrow here for Ruth to stop. She had to circle around the adjoining streets a couple of times before she could find a space to pull in.

'Is this where you live?' she said.

'It's where I've been staying,' Hagan said. And then, abruptly, almost blurting it out as if he'd been trying and had finally failed to hold it back, he said, 'Come home with me.'

'What?'

'Don't do anything you don't want to do,' he said. 'But I don't want it to be over yet. I'm asking you to stay with me a while longer. Just to talk.'

She was lost.

'Tim,' she began, 'I . . .'

He held up a hand and shook his head. He was avoiding meeting her eyes. There was a hint of a stammer when he spoke now, in complete contrast to his easy manner throughout the evening.

He said, 'Don't answer. Take a minute to think. I'm going to run ahead and check on a few things. I'll leave you in the car. If you're gone when I come back, then that's entirely your choice. You won't see me again, you won't even have to explain.'

He got out of the car, then, and crossed the street to the house without looking back. She watched as he let himself in, first through an iron security gate and then through the main door beyond. The Pontiac's engine was running.

There was no question of her going with him. It couldn't happen. But even though she knew how it had to be, her inner reaction was a strange mixture of ecstasy and dismay. Dropping like a weight, soaring like a bird. To know that she dare not. But know that she could. This was the high point of the evening and there was nothing that could happen from here, *nothing*, that could be anything other

66

than the start of a downhill roll. So best to cut it clean, and go out high.

She'd be gone when he returned. That much was certain.

Lights came on in the second-floor apartment. She could see up to plaster mouldings and stripped woodwork, and a turning fan that cast a giant and ominous shadow across the ceiling of the room. She couldn't see Hagan from here, but she knew that she couldn't stick around any longer because he'd come down and find her waiting there and get entirely the wrong idea.

Ruth wondered what he'd run ahead to do. Tidy the place? Make sure that someone hadn't come home without warning, a girlfriend maybe?

Or his parents?

Oh, *God*. His parents. Wouldn't that be terrible? So terrible a thought that it was almost exquisite. It occupied that strange, strange ground between torment and bliss.

Now she'd better go.

But he was standing in the doorway with the hall light behind him. A backlit silhouette, watching, waiting. Ruth switched off the engine and got out of the car.

As she reached him, her eyes met his. He stepped back, by way of invitation, and she went on into the hall. As she started to climb the thickly carpeted stairs, her legs trembled so much that for a moment she was afraid that they might give way under her.

The apartment door stood open. No bare little garret, this. And not his, either, even though he closed the door behind them and moved across to the kitchen with a clear air of familiarity. She could tell at a glance, the style wasn't him. Not the glass coffee table, not the expensive rug it stood on, not the green porcelain dragons nor the dried-flower arrangement in the fireplace.

Whose, she couldn't say. It all looked immaculate, unlived-in. From over in the kitchen area he said, 'I can offer you an espresso or a cappuccino. There's a machine that does both.'

Ruth said, 'What am I doing here, Tim? If you can give me an answer to that I'll be happy because, God's own truth, I really don't know.'

Hagan moved out to stand before her. He took both of her hands in his own.

He said, 'Your hands are shaking.'

'So are yours. Look at the two of us.'

He leaned forward and down, and she raised herself to the kiss. It wasn't perfect, but it was powerful. He dropped her hands and their arms slid around each other, and when they broke off they continued to hug, fiercely, her face turned into his neck. Ruth didn't know if the sensation running through her was the hammering of Hagan's heart or the echo of her own.

'I think I'm going to explode,' she whispered.

'Good,' he said.

Out of all the details betraying the place as not his own, those in the bedroom spoke louder than any. Lights came on to reveal lush fabrics and deep gold, more like a luxury stateroom than a young man's place.

He was only passing through. Gypsy after all.

Now he was standing behind her. She could see herself and him in the ornately framed mirror across the room. Its glass had an amber tint, so that anyone looking in it would be flattered as if with a tan. It was head-to-toe, a full-length dress mirror. He placed his hands on her back and slid them outward, slipping the thin straps of her black dress over her shoulders. The dress glided down and hit the floor in one rapid cascade. Ruth saw it go, reflected in the glass. No catches, no snags, not even a wriggle.

Let's see Alicia do *that*, she was thinking with a fierce and almost demonic sense of pride . . . it would probably catch on her hips and hang there, like she'd stripped to the waist for a wash.

There she was. Hair up, no bra, the most expensive silk underwear that Gordon could afford. Black stockings and pumps, all the power of her sexuality tuned and aimed like a loaded gun.

She turned to Tim Hagan and placed her hands on his shoulders. He was as tight as a wire. He could hardly bring himself to look down.

'Don't be afraid,' she said.

Hagan swallowed, hard.

'I want to be,' he said.

9

Ruth picked up her clothes and dressed in the living-room while he slept. The lights were off and the drapes were still open. Above her, the ceiling fan was still. The only sound was the rustle of silk on skin and the occasional passing of a car in the street outside. She could see the room around her in shades of grey. Full of grain, like film pushed to its limit.

She was breathless, even now. She was high. There was an elation within her that just wouldn't let her come down.

Carrying her shoes in one hand, she tiptoed back in and crouched by the bed. She could see him by the faint red light of the display on the bedside alarm. He was face-down, sprawled, his head turned aside and half-buried in the pillow. The pillow was satin, and carried a shine. His face was completely open as he slept, like a child's.

'Tim?' she said. 'Are you awake?'

She'd barely breathed it. He stirred a little and she thought that his eyes opened a fraction, but he wasn't really there.

It was enough. 'That was better than wonderful,' she whispered, talking as one might to a patient in deep coma; not expecting to be heard, and yet believing that the words would somehow bypass all the barriers of consciousness and reach down to settle in some important place. 'But we've each got a life, Tim, and I'm not part of yours. I won't forget this. But never again.'

He stirred a little more and then turned over and she froze, waiting to see if he was going to haul himself all the way up into wakefulness. She was hoping that he wouldn't. Anything more that might be said out loud right now could only serve to bring down the moment.

He breathed in. Held it. Then let it out slowly, as if he'd turned from wakefulness in the last instant.

She straightened up and backed off, through the door and across the darkened sitting-room. Halfway over she tripped on the phone cord, and the clatter of the handset as it leaped into the air was like the sudden startling-up of a bird. She grabbed at it, fumbled it, dropped it with even more racket onto the hard surface of the coffee table.

Holding it still, she waited.

Then, moving carefully, she righted the handset and replaced the receiver. As an afterthought, she picked it up and checked it. No sound came from the earpiece. No tone, no static, nothing. She wondered if she'd broken it but then, it hadn't landed all that hard. Maybe it wasn't connected. She laid the receiver on the table alongside it, as kind of an indication.

Did she have everything? She did. She let herself out of the apartment and eased the door shut behind her with a faint click. Her shoes were still in her hand. She didn't put them on until she reached the place downstairs where the carpet ran up to the front door.

Ruth found that she couldn't get out into the street. She got the door open, but it was the barred security gate on the other side that was the problem. It needed some kind of an electronic release from the inside, and she couldn't see where it was.

She sighed. She was going to have to wake him after all. But what a lousy arrangement. What if they had a fire?

She went back down the hallway and, instead of climbing the stairs, continued toward the rear of the building. A swing door let her through into a much plainer service corridor with dim but constant emergency lighting. At the end of it was a solid-looking door with a vinyl sticker on it, red on white and reading FIRE EXIT. It had a crash bar that was secured with a pin on a chain, like a grenade.

When Ruth pulled out the pin and leaned against the

bar, the door popped open easily. As it swung out into the night she belatedly wondered if she was going to set off an alarm and bring every resident in the place downstairs in their skivvies, but nothing happened. She stepped out into an alleyway behind the row, with some parking garages opposite and beyond them the high walls and razor wire of another row's yards. There was a faint moon over the rooftops, marbled behind cloud, and yellow sodium security lighting over the garages. The door closed behind her, and she heard its bolts drop.

This wasn't a good time to be out in the open, even in an area like this. But her car was only around the corner.

And being honest with herself, she felt untouchable. Not stupid enough to believe it, but it was the way that she felt. She stepped out through the shadows. The alleyway was paved with herringbone-patterned brick, and was a little uneven.

Hell on the kind of heels she was wearing, but Ruth didn't mind. She was fireproof.

She hadn't put a foot wrong all night, and she wasn't about to start now.

10

Monday morning was something to remember. Ruth was able to enjoy the faint but invigorating whiff of scandal that hung in the air like fallout.

She'd spent a quiet Sunday; newspaper sections and a late breakfast in the morning, a drive out to buy a few things she didn't really need in the afternoon, an evening spent catching up on various TV stuff that she'd taped and never yet bothered to see. A day of low engagement, and long reflection.

She realized that the voice she'd raised in her mind had been right. She'd got her life under control, but she'd effectively limited it within the lines of her own imagination. How had she described it? Like four well-chosen objects in an empty room. Which would have been fine, if she'd been prepared to keep on investing it with the imaginative energy to keep everything fresh. But people didn't work that way, she realized now. Everyone yearned for bright lights and fireworks. Everyone grew up wanting to live in a dusty tent and travel the world. But almost everyone grabbed some kind of safer-looking option and felt more at ease with routine. Which they then blamed, because of the way that it kept them tied down.

You had to surprise yourself every now and again, she'd concluded. She'd let off the brakes for one night, and she'd found magic.

And that was where she'd leave it, because magic never survived a close inspection the second time around.

Shortly after eleven, Aidan Kincannon called by Ruth's work station. She knew him immediately now, without having to check on his badge. He seemed far happier in uniform than he'd been in formal wear; he'd seemed almost defenceless, then. But along with the uniform there was a sense of distance that she hadn't been aware of a couple of nights before.

He'd taken off his hat, and was holding it as he looked down at her. He said, 'Miz Lasseter? If you get a minute in the course of the morning, could I ask you to call by the security office?'

'Concerning what?' Ruth said.

'Some flowers came for you. I'll need to know what you'll want us to do with them.'

'Couldn't you bring them up with you?'

'That's why I need you to call by,' he said and, without explaining further, he moved off.

Rosemary was further down the office. 'I wonder what's the matter with *him* today?' Ruth heard her say.

She'd made peace with Rosemary in the course of the morning. Sometimes she made Ruth want to bang her head against the wall – her own, if not Rosemary's – but the woman's motives could hardly be faulted, even if her methods were guaranteed to irritate. They'd had a heart-to-heart in the staff social area along by the vending machines and the water fountain. Ruth doubted that she'd convinced Rosemary that she was going to do anything other than burn in hell for the life she was leading, but at least she felt less guilty about going on with it.

Flowers, now? She'd collect them later, on her way down to the car. That would be easier than having them in the office. People would ask, and she'd have to make up answers. Gordon wouldn't have put his name on the card, but there was bound to be a message of some kind.

Well, the benefits of her walk on the wild side seemed endless. The most electric sex in years, a boost to her ego of NASA-like proportions, and Gordon scared of losing her. Life could be a lot worse than this.

He called her just before eleven-thirty.

'Congratulations, Ruth,' he said. He'd told her last week that he was going to be up in New York for the day, and

74

the extra distance was probably intensifying any insecurity he might be feeling.

'I couldn't help it, Gordon,' Ruth said happily. 'The devil made me do it.'

'Did he go home with you?'

'Of course he didn't,' she said, which was God's honest truth. 'Why, are you jealous?'

'It's not a joke, Ruth. We were supposed to achieve something serious and what did you do? Some fucking camouflage. Now there probably isn't a company wife in town who hasn't got your picture on a dartboard.'

'What does Mimi think?'

Gordon gave an ironic-sounding snort. Coming down the line, it nearly deafened her. 'She says she took to you,' he said. 'She says she thinks you're an original. She says she wants to fill the house with a few interesting people on our anniversary, and you and your marvellous boy are top of the list.'

'Is that the real reason?'

'Don't take her at face value, Ruth. She was suspicious already, I think you just made things worse.'

'Suspicious? Why, Gordon? The woman never even met me before.'

'I don't know. One day she just looked up and said, "So, who's Ruth?"'

Ruth felt something inside her turn stony and cold.

She said, 'You never told me this.'

'I don't know where she got it from.'

Ruth said, 'Don't send me any invitations. I can't come to your house. I'll make an excuse.'

'Ruth,' Gordon said miserably, 'I'll tell you straight. I'm in hell. I don't know there's anything you can do that'll make a difference.'

'Are you going to leave her?'

'She's a lawyer, Ruth. I'll be walking the streets in my second-best underwear.'

'Do you want to see me?'

'I don't dare. I'll have to call you.'

He sounded despondent. Really despondent, and not just the way that people might try to sound to get sympathy out of others. She said, 'Well . . . thanks for the flowers, anyway.'

And Gordon said, 'What flowers?'

The door to the building's security office was on an empty-looking corridor behind the elevators on the ground floor. Ruth knocked, and went in. Aidan Kincannon wasn't there; it was an older man who swung around in a padded chair to face her. Behind him was a bank of monochrome screens showing rock-steady views of the atrium, the parking garage, the loading bays behind the building. The lighting was stark and the air-conditioning was loud.

She said, 'I'm Ruth Lasseter from the fifth floor. Apparently there's some big mystery about a bunch of flowers.'

'Miz Lasseter?' the guard said, and pulled a clipboard over to check for her name. Then he nodded and, standing, called to the back of the room, 'Take over for me will you, Joe?'

Another man was already on his way around from where the grey lockers were, carrying coffee in a styrofoam cup and holding it by the rim like a rare isotope.

'Hot?' she said.

'Nah,' he said, turning the now-empty chair around to sit in it. 'I got thin skin on my fingers.'

The older man gathered up some keys from the end of the desk, and led the way out. As they walked on down into the service part of the building where Ruth had never been before, Ruth said, 'I don't know why there has to be such a performance. Most times you just let the delivery boy drop them by somebody's desk.'

He stopped to unlock what looked like an unmarked storeroom.

'Most times,' he said, 'that's exactly what we do.'

He stepped in, and switched on the light. There were no windows in here, and the walls were bare. Apart from some computer shipping boxes that were stacked over in one corner, the room was full of flowers.

Thousands of them. Wall to wall. A literal truckload.

Ruth looked around in disbelief. The sheer scale of it all was disturbing, and the range of bright colours was hard on the eye. A real paint factory explosion, and a jungle of fern along with it. The scent alone would have been overpowering. It was as if someone had walked into a store and ordered everything on display; she was almost sure that she could see a funeral wreath in there, peeking out from under.

The guard pulled out a handkerchief, and sneezed.

'Excuse me,' he said.

Ruth said, 'Who sent them?'

'I was assuming you'd be able to make a guess.'

'Wasn't there a card or a message?'

'Not unless it's buried in there somewhere. What do you want to do with them?'

She looked around the room. Flowers were just flowers. But on this kind of a scale . . .

'I don't want them,' she said.

'Well,' the guard said, 'they can't stay here.'

'I don't care!' Ruth said, hearing the rising note in her voice but unable to check it. 'Get rid of them!'

She turned. Suddenly she had to get away. She left the guard looking helpless and calling after her, and she headed away from the storeroom almost at a run.

She nearly ran into Aidan Kincannon, walking down the corridor from the office they'd left. Looking down and with her hand to her head, she didn't see him until the last moment. She gave a start and swerved, and he caught her elbow as she almost stumbled.

'What is it?' he said.

'Nothing.'

'Are you all right?'

'Yes,' Ruth said, and with an effort she recovered a little of her poise. He let his hand fall. 'Yes. Thank you.'

'Quite a sight, isn't it? Looks like someone bought the store.'

'I really don't want them,' she said.

'Would you rather take them home? Give me your keys and I can put some in your car.'

'I don't want them at all. I don't even want to see them. Please. Can you get rid of them for me?'

He studied her for a moment. Ruth felt uncomfortable, but what more could she say?

He seemed to understand.

'I'll take care of it,' he said.

Back at her desk, for the moment not even thinking about whether she'd be overheard, Ruth called the escort agency. Mrs Carroll was unavailable, but would return her call as soon as she was able. She was probably sitting with some other client, patiently smiling through yet another process of hesitation and delay. When Ruth had hung up the phone, she sat back in her chair and stared at it, disconsolately.

What exactly was she going to say?

The phone rang, startling her. She picked it up.

'You left without saying goodbye,' said the voice of Tim Hagan, reproachfully.

For a moment, Ruth couldn't put it all together. But then when she did speak, she didn't try to conceal her anger. 'It was said. And it was final, as well.'

'Did you get the flowers?'

'Tim, that was ridiculous. You've embarrassed me. You've made me regret what we did, and that's the last thing I wanted to do.'

'I don't see the problem. I thought you liked me.'

'I like you, Tim, but I'm not going to see you again.'

'I'll tell you what,' he said. 'Take a few days to think it over and then I'll call you at home.'

'I'm not giving you my home number. And no-one else in this building is going to give it to you, either.'

'A phone call! That's all we're talking about!'

'No!'

78

Rosemary, passing, had slowed and was watching her. This was exactly the aspect that Ruth hadn't ever wanted to present to the world. She swung around to face away from the room.

Hagan was saying in a bewildered voice, 'Ruth, what *is* this? I tell you I like you, and you're treating me like I did something terrible!'

'I know,' she said, 'I'm sorry. It isn't your fault. But don't send me flowers, don't call me again. I'm starting to realize that I made a mistake.'

And then she hung up on him.

11

Ruth had no idea how she got through the afternoon. She made an excuse to dodge going outside for lunch with Jennie and ate alone, at her desk, attempting to read a magazine but doing little more than to stare right through it. She kept turning back the pages and realizing that she'd gone over them without a single word having registered. She could read them a second time and it was like all-new material. For the rest of the day she put on a headset and typed audio copy, continuously, keeping the words running through her mind in a calming stream.

When the chance came to leave early, she took it. On her way through the concourse she looked for Aidan Kincannon at the main desk, meaning to apologize for her earlier testiness and to ask if he'd been able to handle the problem she'd thrown at him. He was there, but he was busy; he was handing over to someone else, and rather than disturb him further she went on by.

After only a few strides, however, she heard him calling after her.

'Miz Lasseter?' he said. 'Can you hold on for a moment?'

She waited as he hurriedly completed the handover and then crossed the foyer to join her.

'I hope you didn't have second thoughts about the flowers,' he said as he walked with her toward the parking elevator. 'I got rid of them for you.'

'What did you do?'

'I called a couple of hospitals. Some volunteers came over in a van and took them away.'

'Thank you for thinking of that.'

They reached the doors, and he hit the call button for

her. He said, 'It seemed like a waste, just to dump them. I hope I did right.'

Ruth glanced at the indicator board; the elevator car was coming up already. She said, 'I'm sorry if I seemed abrupt.'

'I don't know about abrupt. I wondered if you were upset.'

'Just a little,' she admitted. 'It passed.'

He said, 'If ever you have a problem I can help with, you should call me.'

'I will.'

'I don't just mean getting rid of unwelcome gifts for you. I mean anything.'

The elevator arrived and the doors opened. It was empty. As she stepped inside, she turned and faced the security man. She could see that he was in earnest.

'OK,' she said. 'Forgive me if I was rude. Thanks again.'

And as the elevator doors closed to leave him standing in the concourse, Ruth couldn't help remembering the way that he'd handled the intruder of a couple of weeks before. It was the kind of thing that tended to stick in one's mind, rather. The man, they'd all heard later, was a long-term mental patient who'd been skipping his medication. His sister usually kept a check on him, but for once she'd been ill herself. A couple of road accidents and running muggers apart, this had been the closest to real-life violence that Ruth had ever seen. But what had stayed with her was the gentleness with which it had all been managed. Even with his face mashed into the carpet, it was as if Kincannon had allowed the man to hang on to some vital scrap of his dignity.

The doors opened onto the parking basement, and out she went.

Eloise Carroll hadn't called her back. Ruth had decided what she was going to tell her when they finally got to speak. Give your boy a tug on the leash and tell him to get professional. Tell him not to call.

Make him stay away.

Only a few moments after she'd started her car, she could sense that something was wrong. The engine didn't sound right. She got out and crouched down and looked underneath, half-expecting to see some piece of the muffler hanging, but nothing obvious showed. She was sure it was less than a year since she'd had the system replaced, anyway.

Ruth dusted herself off and got back in. It sounded fine now. Perhaps she'd imagined it.

But as she ascended to street level, it was ten times worse. It sounded like she was dragging a train wreck along in her wake. She looked at all the indicators on the dash, and none showed anything wrong. The oil pressure was normal. Nothing was flashing. But as she picked up speed toward the Parkway, the screech became excruciating.

Everything had been fine when she'd driven in this morning. And the alarms set automatically whenever she locked it, so between that and the camera surveillance in the garage it seemed unlikely that anyone could have been interfering. But could something so terrible-sounding happen while the car was standing still? Ruth could claim no mechanical knowledge at all. She could change a tyre, in theory, but she'd never actually had to do it.

She could pull over. But that wasn't exactly advisable.

It wasn't that the traffic didn't get policed in the rush hour. Quite the opposite. The police cruised the streets in vans with mounted loudspeaker systems, watching for motorists making illegal stops and blasting out a warning like the Voice of God whenever they did. This would either get them on the move again or, if they'd stopped to make a visit to a bank or a store, it would send them sprinting back across the sidewalk to their vehicles. But the police weren't the only ones with their eyes open, and there were opportunists whose vehicles carried no markings. What if one of them got to her first? Other cars around her would be no protection. People would watch whatever happened, and never even think to act.

Hard to believe, but it was there on the news almost every night.

She slowed for a red light. The note dropped to a whine. Heads still turned. Ruth sank lower into her seat, and wished for it all to be over.

Movement in the side-mirror caught her eye. Someone was coming up behind the car, threading and dodging his way through toward her. A young black man in a clean white T-shirt.

But no paper cup, this time. The T-shirt came with a cop's uniform and motorcycle helmet.

He eased the big patrol bike level with her window, and stopped. She wound down the glass.

'Do you need me to call you some assistance?' he said, raising his voice to be heard over his own engine and hers.

'The engine's been running fine,' Ruth said. 'I don't know why it's making such a racket.'

'You want to get that investigated as soon as possible. Don't run it any further than you have to.'

'I'm almost home.'

The light turned to green and everyone around them began to move. There was maybe a nanosecond's grace and then people a few cars back started to hit their horns.

'Drive on,' the motorcycle cop said. 'I'll follow you.'

And he did, staying close behind her until she made the turn into the secure parking garage of her co-op. At which he swept past, and accelerated off with a roar.

12

Whatever was wrong with her car, it sounded expensive. Nothing that went wrong with a car was ever cheap. Ruth had a savings plan to cover such contingencies, but as a general rule she lived close to the limit of her means. She'd few assets and, whenever she planned badly or hit an unforeseen expense, she could find herself getting awfully close to the wall. So she could live in a dump and take no winter vacations and keep money in the bank. But who, exactly, would that serve?

People sometimes asked her if she minded living alone. She told them that she didn't, it was fine, she put a value on her solitude. Which was true, except that on evenings like this she was apt to find solitude shading over into loneliness.

One source of pressure too many, that was all. First Hagan overstepping the mark, now this. First thing tomorrow she'd leave the car at the repair shop, and mid-morning she'd be sure to speak to Eloise Carroll. End of the day, her life would be back in balance.

Sitting on the couch with the TV switched on and its sound muted, she closed her eyes and laid back her head and waited for an image to come. But nothing did. No presence formed, no young voice spoke.

Damn.

She opened her eyes, and looked at the phone.

Gordon would almost certainly be on his way home by now. This was a monthly thing, and it always went the same; the afternoon meeting would end by five and at six he'd be on the Metroliner out of Penn Station and heading for home. It was nearly seven now, so he'd still be travelling.

Ruth picked up the phone and pressed the autodial for his cellular number.

He didn't like her to use it, but what the hell. She was low. The fact that this was at least partly of her own doing was neither here nor there.

It rang out for a while, and then the line opened to static and silence. Dialling cellular always struck her as a leap in the dark, like making a call into the Twilight Zone. Sometimes it seemed to Ruth that it wasn't unfeasible that one should dial a digit wrong and get a dead person picking up at the other end.

She said, uncertainly, 'Gordon? Are you there?'

And Mimi Parry said, 'Hello, Ruth.'

Ruth was totally wrong-footed. But only for a moment.

She said, 'I'm calling from the office. I've got some stuff I need to get to Gordon. Do you know if he's got a fax number in New York?'

There was a silence. Then Mimi said wearily, 'Don't insult me, Ruth. And don't embarrass yourself any more than you already have.'

Even though she was feeling the ground slip away from under her, Ruth ploughed on. She said, 'I don't know what you're talking about, Mimi.'

'I know, Ruth. Not for how long it's been going on, but I *do* know.'

Ruth sat there, feeling cold and small.

Her mind raced in search of some further manoeuvre. But all that she could manage to say was, 'How did you find out?'

'For certain? Only with this call. But I've suspected ever since the day I pressed the redial on this thing and got your answering machine. Then it was just a matter of waiting until I met a Ruth who matched the message.'

'I'm sorry, Mimi,' Ruth said miserably.

And before hanging up, with an edge in her voice that was as sharp as any blade, Mimi said coldly, 'I don't think you know what sorry means.'

13

Gordon appeared at her desk the next morning. In person. This was unprecedented. But then, all the rules had now changed.

He glanced to the side and said, 'Could you go to another part of the office for a minute, please, Rosemary?'

Ruth couldn't see around the partition from where she was sitting, but on the other side of the cubicle wall she heard a reaction from Rosemary like that of a startled rabbit. Ruth heard her grab up a few things and retreat in a hurry. Something had been getting around the building, Ruth didn't know how. Or maybe it was just the look on Gordon, that dangerous aura of a man who had scores to settle but who suddenly had nothing to lose.

Ruth said, 'A minute. Is that all I'm going to get?'

'The worst part's over,' Gordon said. 'The bomb went off and we're all still standing. I'm not going to leave her, Ruth.'

It was what she'd been expecting; but like any anticipated blow, it still knocked the wind out of her when it came. Ruth had been working this moment over, again and again and again. Pacing her apartment, lying awake, riding the subway in. Wondering what he'd say to finish it. Wondering what *she'd* say if he wanted it somehow to go on.

Not even knowing what she wanted, for sure.

She said, 'Oh.'

'It's not a surprise, then.'

'Should it be?'

There was regret in his eyes. But it was like a regret for something whose loss now allowed him to breathe again.

He said, 'The truth of it is, I'd still rather be with you.'

Ruth stared up at him. 'Don't you dare tell me that now,' she said, stung.

'It's true,' Gordon said. 'You think I never *would* have left her? You're wrong.'

'So what were you waiting for? Someone to give you an order?'

'I had you figured early,' Gordon said. 'That was more than you ever wanted of me, Ruth, and don't try to deny it.'

'Jesus, Gordon, you're unbelievable.'

'What you and I had was as close to happy as we were going to get. I'd lie alongside Mimi late at night and my chest would ache for thinking of you. But whatever you've told yourself, Ruth, you had me just at the distance you were ready to handle.'

'I've heard enough,' Ruth said. If they'd been anywhere else, she could have walked out on him and slammed the door in his face as he tried to follow.

But he persisted. 'Why'd you choose me, then?' he said. 'Why'd you choose a man you couldn't have? You're so damned careful over everything else. Look at the facts of it, Ruth. The only relationships you'll tolerate are the ones that don't leave a mark.'

Ruth picked up her half-empty mug of cold coffee and threw it over his suit.

Gordon took a quick step back, and it mostly hit his shirt. It wasn't hot, but by the look on his face for a moment he was expecting it to be. He stood there with his hands outspread, dripping onto the floor.

'Nice, Ruth,' he said. 'Very mature.'

'Go away,' Ruth said.

'I'm going. And while I'm trying not to think about you at three in the morning, I've no doubt you'll have found some setup where you can keep some other guy nicely at arm's length.'

He moved to go, but she couldn't leave it at that. She followed him. Down the line of carrels and right out across the office's open area. There were people out here and their heads were turning, but Ruth no longer paid them any attention.

She said, 'Damn you, Gordon, don't say that to me.'

'Calm down, Ruth,' he told her. 'People are watching.'

'I don't care.'

He turned his back on her and walked on, out past the department's reception desk and toward the elevators. She went after him raising her voice.

She said, 'Did I piss you off because I picked out a boy? Is that what this is all about?'

'I don't know if you picked him out or picked him up,' Gordon said over his shoulder. 'I knew I should have done this over the phone.'

'Fuck you, Gordon,' Ruth said with all the venom she could muster.

Gordon wheeled around and turned on her, but he lowered his voice to an intense near-whisper.

'I don't believe it,' he said. 'You're the one who sank us, and I have to listen to this. Grow up, Ruth. Nothing's going to change. You'll find plenty more dogs waiting at the gate.'

She looked around the nearby surfaces for something to throw.

Gordon stabbed a finger at her.

'Don't,' he warned. 'I'm serious.'

There was a hole-puncher in her hand, a good weight and a few sharp edges. Gordon was still staring at her, hard.

She couldn't do it. She let her hand drop, and Gordon turned and walked out through the glass doors toward the elevators.

Ruth slammed the hole-puncher back onto the desk and returned, blindly, to her own little part of the office. She was aware of people appearing from all over like small animals emerging from cover after a thunderstorm, but she acknowledged no-one.

She threw herself into her chair and tried to look at her screen. But she couldn't see it for tears. She was vaguely aware of Rosemary appearing, very tentatively, at her shoulder.

'Fuck off, Rosemary,' she said.

'I'm going to pray for you, Ruth,' Rosemary said.

'Do that, Rosemary,' Ruth said, 'but keep it quiet. I have a headache.'

She was murder to deal with that day, and she knew it. Others avoided her although there were a few who, quite plainly, had made up some excuse to stop by the department just so that they could get a look at her from a distance. She didn't oblige them any more than she had to. They wanted to see exhibits, they could go to the zoo.

Somebody bade her good night as she was leaving the building, but it didn't register with her until it was too late for her to reply. She was out, she was halfway down the front steps. There had been worse days than this in her life. Not for a very long time, but there had. She'd get through.

She walked down to City Hall, where she could pick up the Market–Frankford line for the short subway ride home. She had to fight her way through serious numbers of men in dark suits with black briefcases. The city's underground transportation system was fast and noisy and utterly functional. It wasted neither space nor time, and it was not for the inattentive. It was all brushed steel and blue, darkness and din, and it moved at a speed that kept everyone just slightly off-balance.

There was no seat for her, but that didn't matter. She wasn't going to be on board for long. The carriage was like the most basic of buses, with all its windows open for the most basic of air-conditioning. Ruth checked her watch as they slammed on through darkness and other trains on parallel tracks whipped by, sucking wind through the carriage. She was hoping that her car was going to be ready and that she was going to be able to get to it before the workshop closed.

At Thirteenth Street, a man stepped on through the

door closest to her. He was bearded and neatly dressed in a zippered jacket with a vinyl shoulder bag. Ruth's heart sank at the sight of a paper cup in his hand with a few dollars and coins in it.

And as the train moved off, he announced loudly, 'Good evening ladies and gentlemen, I *am* the Reverend Dyer and I *am* a minister of the church. My institution has *no* financial support other than through the generosity of others. I ask you to please give whatever you can, and God bless you.'

He swept through the carriage with his paper cup, God-blessing those who gave and bypassing those who didn't. Ruth stuffed in her last one-dollar bill, which left her with a couple of twenties until she could get to a MAC machine. At the next stop, the man was out and gone.

The train moved on. People came and went, and Ruth got a seat. She was thinking about what Gordon had said. She'd been thinking about it, on and off, for most of the afternoon. It tormented her. It tormented her because he was right. Arm's length and no more; that was the affair she'd wanted, and that was the natural limit of the affection that she'd found.

At Eighth Street, she belatedly realized that another figure, similarly equipped to the last if not half so presentable, had stepped on board and was standing just inside the open door.

'I am a United States veteran,' this one announced. 'I lost five fingers in an accident. I cannot get employment. I am homeless and I have no money for food.'

This person was identifiably a down-and-out. Now people were quickly getting up and disembarking, moving to other parts of the train; Ruth belatedly caught on, but already the doors were closing as she started to rise.

She was on her feet now, so she moved to the end of the carriage. There was a connecting door here that led to the next coach and resembled the door to a meat safe, but there was a notice stuck on its window that read DO NOT PASS WHILE THE TRAIN IS IN MOTION. She stopped there.

Through the double layer of glass, no more than ten

or fifteen feet away on the other side, she could see Tim Hagan.

He was sitting and reading a magazine. The other carriage weaved in relation to hers, a slight and continuing mismatch of two worlds. He didn't look the way he had on the night of the ball, but it was unmistakably him. His hair was uncombed and he was in jeans and a pair of Converse basketball boots that were all frayed and coming apart at the seams. His jacket was nondescript and all punched out of shape. He looked almost shabby, one in a crowd.

But it was still unmistakably him.

When the train pulled into Fifth Street, she saw him lean back and crane to watch the platform outside through the open door. He'd positioned himself so that he could be up and off at a moment's notice, if he had to. As the doors closed, he settled back and returned his attention to his magazine.

She could see the cover now. It was one of her titles, the company's, one of those on which she sold copy space. Not exactly the usual thing that a commuter might be seen to read. And not easy to get hold of casually, either.

There was little doubt in Ruth's mind. He was following her. He was following her home, so that he could find out where she lived.

He started to look up.

Ruth turned around quickly, and was hit in the face with an almost overpowering odour.

It was the down-and-out, his two-fingered hand grasping the cup only inches in front of her face. The rest of the hand was knuckled and perfectly smooth, healed-over as if no fingers had ever been there. His filmy eyes stared as he swayed, patiently, with the motion of the train.

She gave him one of the twenties, just to make him go.

At Second Street, she moved to the door. But she didn't get off, at least not right away. Some of the crowd inside switched places with all of the crowd outside. She waited until the door was starting to close, counted a beat, and then threw herself at the gap. The door all but bit her in the behind as she hit the platform, smacking its rubber lips after her.

The platform had almost cleared already. The train was starting to roll and if he'd followed her, she'd have seen him for sure.

But she was alone here.

The station was light and airy, white-tiled walls and blue-tiled floors. But there was nobody manning the turnstiles, coming in or going out, and it was no place to linger alone. He might have seen her, at least. He might even now be switching trains only one station down the line, heading back in with only a couple of minutes lost.

She pushed through the barrier and almost ran up the stairway.

Now Ruth had to walk some way to pick up her car. North of here was an area of four-lane streets and big factory units of all ages, some of them a hundred years old with crumbling water towers on their roofs. Others were modern brick units, barely more than a couple of decades old. Some of them stood unused, surrounded by acres of empty parking asphalt with weeds breaking through. The repair shop was a fortified-looking yard and building alongside a shopping plaza. It was all but closed-up when Ruth got there, and the owner was just about to let the dogs loose for the night before going home.

'You caught me just in time,' he told her, and he walked her to the bay where her car was to have been locked away for the night. He wore a stained leather jacket and a trucking cap and he had a chipped front tooth. She asked if he'd been able to track down the problem.

'Something like this,' he said, 'it can take five minutes or five hours to find it.'

'So which am I going to be paying for?' Ruth said.

Instead of replying directly, the man held up a small piece of metal that looked like a bracket out of something cheap.

'You were lucky,' he said. 'Here's the cause of your trouble.'

Ruth peered. 'What is it?'

'It's called an exhaust whistle. They're about a dollar apiece in a novelty store. You slide one into the tailpipe and it sticks there and makes a sound like the engine's falling out.'

'Does it do any damage?'

'Just makes a noise.'

He handed it to her. She looked at it, uncomprehending.

'Thanks,' she said.

'No problem,' the man said. 'Kids, eh? But better this than they should slash your tyres or scratch your paint.'

14

The police had a system, and as Ruth was telling her story for the third time over she realized that she was in it. Jennie had been through the same routine with her burglary the year before. They prioritized the calls as they came in, and those that didn't appear to need immediate action were routed downstairs to the Deferential Police Response unit in the administration building's basement where half a dozen officers listened and clarified details and assigned report numbers. It wasn't a popular job, by all accounts. The DPR room was windowless and dull and right next to the jail cells, and for many of the officers it was a halfway stage on the return to duty after injury or illness. Ruth's harassment, because she was phoning it in from the safety of her apartment, was considered to be significant but scored low on the urgency scale.

'When he phoned you at the office,' the officer said after taking her details and hearing the story through, 'did he say anything that might have implied a threat?'

'Not directly,' Ruth said. 'No.'

'Indirectly, then.'

'He fixed my car and followed me. I'd have thought that was enough.'

'But can you say for certain that the two are connected?'

Ruth wasn't sure she liked the direction in which the conversation seemed to be heading. 'You're not going to take me seriously,' she said.

'Of course we are,' the officer on the line told her. 'Look, he's what, twenty-three? Compared to you he's no more than a kid.'

'Well, thanks. You don't know how good that makes me feel.'

'I'm talking in terms of experience. You probably gave him a shot of something that's more than he can handle and he hasn't been able to peel himself off the ceiling yet. It's probably just a crush, is what I'm saying.'

'I don't care what it is,' Ruth said. 'I don't want to be followed around.'

'It's not like he's some breather on the phone. He's traceable.'

'I can't tell you his address. I could take you to it, but I didn't keep a note of the street name or the number.'

'I'll tell you what we're going to do, Ms Lasseter. This report will be routed to one of our detectives and you'll be contacted over the next couple of days. He or she will probably talk to your Mr Hagan and get him calmed down. He'll understand that if he persists, he's in trouble. In the meantime, is there anything that you want to ask?'

'What protection will I have if he doesn't choose to listen?'

'Did he strike you as unstable?'

'I'd never have let it go so far if he did.'

'Then what we're almost certainly looking at here is a guy who needs some kind of a jolt to see the consequence of his behaviour. A lot of the time, that's all it requires. Otherwise, check your car before you use it and try to stay generally aware.'

A lot of the time.

Ruth sat in her darkening apartment for a while, wondering who else she could call. Not to ask for help, but just to feel connected. Part of a network, not so alone. But being in a network meant giving support as well as receiving it, and that hadn't exactly been one of her strengths of late. Not that it had always been so. Back in New York she'd been surrounded by a few close friends, a lot of familiar faces, and a wider group of people that she was always seeing around and might one day get to know better; there it was as if she'd overwritten her old life in England with the new, only then to scrap it all and start again when things started to go wrong. She'd moved to

Philadelphia with a whole series of burning bridges behind her. And Gordon had been right, since then it had been arm's-length relationships only.

She tried one of the old numbers. She didn't know what she was going to say, but she tried it anyway. A stranger answered, and she hung up.

She went to the window and watched the cars on the bridge for a while.

Ruth's number was unlisted, so at least no-one could find her through the book. If it hadn't been for that, Hagan might have been out there right now. Out there and watching for her, without her even knowing.

She pulled down the blind before she turned on the light.

Then she went around and up to the open sleeping area. Her bed was still unmade from the morning; she'd had to rush out at the last minute as usual. She opened the closet and took down a box of photographs from one of the upper shelves. The photographs were all in their lab envelopes, unsorted and unlooked-at in years. She wasn't even sure where her camera was, these days. She moved the envelopes aside and uncovered a small Italian nine-ounce pistol, wrapped in a big piece of kitchen paper. It had never been fired, at least not by her. She kept it handy and loaded with blanks, in case of intruders.

She returned the box to its place and took the gun downstairs, where she put it in her handbag and checked the weight. She could tell that it was there, all right, but it didn't pull the bag out of shape. She took it out again and made sure that the safety catch was still on, and then double-checked to see that it was loaded before she put it back.

Blanks. But nobody had to know they were blanks. With real ammunition she'd be too terrified even to think of using it, but blanks were OK. Taking a life was something she couldn't contemplate. But pretending to be ready to . . . if it came to it, that was something she could probably just about manage.

Ruth paused for a moment. And what did you learn about yourself today?

That some roads are better not taken, she thought. Regardless of how they appear.

15

As a follow-up to her outburst there was an obligatory supervisor's session with Jake the next morning, and it went exactly as she might have anticipated: disastrously. For Jake. Ten minutes into it he was admitting that he'd never been able to fathom what women actually wanted out of life, five minutes later he was telling her all about his problems with Laura, and at the end of the half-hour he was drying his eyes with a Kleenex out of her bag and thanking Ruth and telling her that he now felt considerably better.

When she got back to her work station, she called up the E-mail and the switchboard messages and found three requests for her to get back to the same Philadelphia number. It wasn't a number that she recognized. Normally she'd assume that it meant new business and would be onto it right away, but this morning she hesitated.

But what could she do? This could get out of hand, if she let it.

So she dialled, ready to hang up in a second if she were to sense anything wrong.

But a woman answered, who on hearing Ruth's name said to her, 'Thank you for calling me back, Miz Lasseter, my name is Rafaella Suarez. I am an investigator in the employment of a major credit card company. Can I ask you to confirm whether on the tenth of this month you took delivery of an order of flowers and other related gift materials to the approximate value of fifteen hundred dollars?'

All right, so it wasn't Hagan. But Ruth's defences were still up and she said, guardedly, 'I never ordered any flowers.'

'Did you take delivery of any order?' Rafaella Suarez

asked then. She was polite but her manner was perfunctory, as if she was ticking off boxes as she worked her way down a list of questions.

'I had them all sent away,' Ruth said. 'They were an unwelcome gift.'

'May I ask if you can tell me the identity of the person who ordered the delivery? I am requesting this information in connection with an investigation which may result in a criminal prosecution.'

'Are you saying he used a stolen card?'

'I'm afraid I'm not able to supply you with that information. Can you give me a name?'

Ruth hesitated. She didn't want to be drawn into this any further than she had been already. But then, to suppose that she wasn't right in the middle of it would be to underestimate the situation.

She said, 'I made a report to the police in connection with all of this. I think if you want to discuss it any further, you're going to have to talk to them. I'll give you the report number they assigned to me, but I think that's really all I ought to be saying to you right now.'

It took her a moment to find the number, which she'd scribbled on a blank page at the back of her diary. After Ruth had read it over, Rafaella Suarez said, 'I have one more question if I may, Miz Lasseter. Are you acquainted or in any way familiar with the name of a Mrs Frances Everline?'

She let the name run through her mind, but she didn't have to let it run for long.

'No,' Ruth said.

When she hung up the phone it rang again in the same instant, startling her. It was somebody at the desk downstairs to say that there was a man, a detective named Diaz, who wanted to see her.

Ruth glanced around. She'd have no privacy here. It was true that she'd already blown it regarding Gordon, but Gordon was only half of the story and the rest of it was something that she was even less inclined to have broadcast.

She said, 'Please don't send him up here. Ask him to wait. I'll come down.'

She quickly finished a couple of things, did what was necessary to put off a couple more, and then headed downstairs. A man in a suit was waiting for her in the atrium, watching the fountain and killing time. He wasn't at all ill-at-ease, as if he often had to wait around for people. He showed her his ID. The picture on it looked like a post-mortem photograph and his first name, as typed alongside his shield number, was Tom. Not Thomas, but Tom. Tom Gabriel Diaz. He was around forty, slightly pockmarked and with the darkest eyes she'd ever seen.

They went over into Rossini's and sat at a corner table. The place was almost empty at this hour, and the staff were busy in the back. From the way that her initial report had been handled, Ruth had been expecting little more than a return call and no real action. But after the initial pleasantries – minimal – Diaz's face had turned serious.

He said, 'The escort service had a break-in yesterday. Someone tried to get into the filing cabinets while everyone was out at lunch.'

Ruth's fingertips began to tingle. The immediacy of everything around her seemed to recede, just a little. She was glad to be sitting down.

She said, 'Was it him?'

'It would be one way for him to get hold of your home address. Don't worry, he didn't get it.'

'How can you be sure of that?'

'The filing cabinets stayed locked. Someone from one of the other businesses on the same floor heard him banging and swearing. They called building security, but we're talking about one old guy who's slow on the stairs. The intruder had gone.'

The intruder. Jesus. What had she *started*?

She said, 'Have you spoken to him?'

'We haven't found him yet. The address that he gave

to the agency when he registered himself was a false one. There's no such place. We *did* find where he's been living, though. We traced it through his box number.'

'I already know where he's been living,' Ruth said.

'This was a one-room apartment in a house in Brewerytown. It isn't like the place you described.'

Brewerytown? Brewerytown was a part of North Philadelphia and whatever it might have been, it was not Society Hill. Ruth said as much, and the detective said to her, 'You still don't recall an address?'

'No,' Ruth said. 'But I told your man last night, I can take you right to it.'

Diaz started to get to his feet. 'I've got a fellow-officer waiting in the car just outside,' he said. 'I'd like you to show us where it is. Will you do that?'

As they were walking out, Ruth said, 'You don't go along with the idea that he's just some boy with a crush, then.'

'Boy with a crush can be a dangerous thing,' Tom Diaz said.

Ruth belatedly thought about calling upstairs and letting somebody know she'd be out for a while, but by then they were already out in the street and crossing the sidewalk. The car was a big sedan like the ones that always parked across from the DA's office on Arch Street, mostly unmarked Plymouths with lightbars in their back windows and spotlights mounted on their door pillars.

Another detective waited behind the wheel. Pale and freckled and with thinning ginger hair, he was reading the back pages of a *Daily News* which he folded and slung aside as they were getting in.

Diaz sat with her in the back of the car.

'I assume there was nobody home at this other place,' Ruth said.

'All we found were the sheets on the bed and a dinner suit hanging on the back of the door. Some workout weights, and nothing much of anything else. If that's where he's been living, he's been living like a monk.'

They overtook a bus that had stopped for some reason

of its own. They went east along Race Street and as they cut through the southern fringe of Chinatown, Ruth said, 'You should be getting a call about the stolen credit card he's been using.'

Diaz looked at her blankly. 'Oh?' he said.

'A woman from some private investigation bureau called me already,' Ruth explained. 'You'll know who she is when you hear her. She talks through her nose and she sounds just like a machine.'

'What did she say?'

'She wasn't giving anything away, but she asked if I knew the name of a Frances Everline.'

She saw Diaz look forward and catch his partner's eye in the rearview mirror. The other man's shoulders lifted slightly in a shrug.

A whiff of the farmyard came into the car a few minutes later, sucked in and delayed through the air-conditioning from the line of horse-drawn carriages that had been lined up for business outside Independence Hall. Ruth settled back in her seat. The car wasn't very old, but the springs in its upholstery had obviously taken a pounding. She'd never ridden in the back of a police vehicle before. She felt safe, but she felt slightly distant as well. There was something dreamlike about this entire experience, and Ruth knew that it wasn't the kind of dream she'd be over-eager to recall upon waking.

'Take a right here,' Ruth said, and they turned onto Delancey Street.

This wasn't the exact thoroughfare, but she did remember it as being in the general area and she was sure that a short cruise-around would throw up some detail that she'd be able to recognize. Sunlight through the trees dappled the car and filled its interior with a roving filigree pattern of light and shade. She frowned, and had to screw up her eyes a little. She'd left her sunglasses back at her desk.

Many of the buildings had upper-storey flagpoles with the Stars and Stripes hung out. From what she could see through the windows, their rooms were small and pleasant and crammed with art and bric-à-brac, with plaster mouldings and carefully restored timberwork. Suddenly, she wasn't so sure. She'd a mental image of the place they were looking for and a vague sense of how she'd driven there, but it all looked different by day. Cars were nose-to-tail down one side or another, the same features came up again and again. Wooden shutters, iron balustrades, marble columns, stone porticoes.

'Not here,' she said. 'Try around the other way.'

They'd passed it once before she spotted it for sure, but on that second look she was certain. That cast-iron outer security gate was the giveaway. Their driver pulled into a gap a little way further down, and as he was getting out and crossing the sidewalk Ruth turned to Detective Diaz and said, with great firmness, 'I don't want to see him.'

'You won't have to,' Diaz said. 'We'll check the place out and then come back. I want you to stay right here in the car for as long as we're gone.'

And then he looked out to his partner, who'd returned and had crouched slightly to look in through the side-window.

'Name by the buzzer says Everline,' the other man said.

The two men went over to the building. She could see them trying all the doorbells until somebody answered, and then she saw them go in. That was it, for about fifteen minutes that felt more like an hour in their passing.

When the two returned, they brought nobody with them. Diaz got in alongside her and, in answer to her expectant silence, said, 'We talked to one of the neighbours. Frances Everline's a widow, lives in the second-floor apartment but it's been more than a week since anyone saw her last. One of them said there had been a young guy coming and going for a while, but it was like she was trying to keep him out of sight.'

'Is that it?' Ruth said.

'Just about. The assumption seems to be that they've gone off somewhere together.'

Diaz rubbed at the side of his face, looking out and thinking.

Ruth said, 'So what are you going to do?'

'We'll take you back to your place of work,' the other man said, starting up the engine. Ruth looked from one to the other.

'You're not going to discuss it while I'm around, are you?' she said.

'I don't know what I can tell you,' Diaz said. 'This could be something or nothing.'

'He spent fifteen hundred dollars on the flowers,' Ruth said, 'and he used the woman's credit card to do it. He must have run up some kind of a bill already for them to start an investigation. Does that sound to you like they ran away together?'

Diaz said, 'We're going to bear all that in mind.'

'Aren't you going to look inside the apartment?'

'It's a possibility.'

And there it was. It was clear to Ruth that the traffic in confidences was going to be strictly one-way, and so she gave up trying. The look in both men's eyes was unmistakable, though. Hard and beady, like a couple of lizards.

'You can let me out anywhere here,' she said as they came back on a route through the middle of town.

The driver said, 'We're not even close yet.'

'There's some stuff I want to pick up. I'll get a cab after that. Don't worry, I won't take any chances. Will you be wanting to talk to me again?'

'I should imagine that's extremely possible.'

They set her down by the Gallery shopping centre near the old Reading Terminal Market, which was about as close to the heart of things as she could ask. There were plenty of people here, but still she was nervous. She did her best not to let the policemen see. Diaz promised her that he'd keep her informed.

Ruth went into the modern mall and looked around close inside the entranceway for a directory. No big fan of mall shopping, for once she was grateful for the relative safety of a monitored environment. She found the board with its backlit map alongside, and checked through the numbers.

Pet store. Bookstores. Toys and games.

Sporting goods. Where were the sporting goods?

She knew there had to be a place, because she was fairly sure that this was where she'd picked out some Lycra exercise gear about eighteen months before. Someone had opened up a dance studio in between the Chocolate Works and Bridge View where they'd offered aerobics to classical music, and she'd signed up around the time of the gap that had separated the end of Ronan and the beginning of Gordon.

It wasn't Lycra that she was looking for now. Aerobics were tame stuff compared to the turn her life seemed suddenly to have taken.

Going home with Tim Hagan had felt pretty daring.

But nothing like so daring as the purchase of live ammunition.

16

Tom Diaz got back to her late in the afternoon, as others were starting to leave. She'd been out of the office almost until three, but no-one had commented on her absence. She seemed to have created an exclusion zone around herself into which even Rosemary wouldn't venture; God alone knew what anyone would have thought had they looked into Ruth's carrel and found her loading rounds from a box into the nine-ounce Bernardelli by the light of her terminal. If being a single woman with a known attitude was enough to clear the corridors ahead of her, then the prospect of Ruth Lasseter with an attitude and a gun would probably empty the building.

None of her convictions had altered. She still believed that to take a life would be unthinkable. But she'd formed a mental image that wouldn't now desert her, of being in the dark space between two public places and turning around to see Tim Hagan coming toward her with his face and his eyes all deep pits of shadow; and she called and he wouldn't stop, and she threatened and he wouldn't stop, and she fired and he wouldn't stop.

Her beliefs hadn't changed. But she'd begun to suspect that, in just such a moment, they might.

She'd half-loaded the magazine when Tom Diaz called her, and she quickly pulled open a drawer and swept everything inside as she held the phone tucked between her ear and her shoulder. Somebody might come by, and she wouldn't hear them approaching. Also she felt slightly guilty, as if Diaz might somehow be able to see what she was doing.

He said, 'We've been back to the apartment building in Society Hill. Talking to the credit card company gave us enough to go for a search warrant. Wherever Frances Everline went to, she left all of her clothes and a full set of luggage behind.'

'Oh, my God,' Ruth said. She sat back, level with the screen where she'd been checking her electronic mailbox as she'd worked with the handgun. A symbol changed and pulsed; something was coming in.

Tom Diaz said, 'Hey. Don't go reading too much into this yet.'

Which was fine for him to say. Ruth was the one who'd been followed. She was the one who'd made the big gesture that she'd now come to regret. She was the one who'd opened up Pandora's boxers.

She said, 'Was Frances Everline one of the escort service's clients as well?'

'Hagan – or whatever his real name is – only ever got one job as an escort, and you were it. He'd been on the books for more than three months before that, but no-one had bitten. We don't know how else he might have been earning a living. Judging by the stuff in his rented room, he's broke.'

Ruth was staring at the four lines of text that had just appeared on her terminal screen.

Numbly, she said, 'Listen . . . can I call you back?'

'I'll be out of the office until morning,' Tom Diaz said, and he seemed to detect the change in her voice. 'Is there something wrong?'

'As if I didn't have enough things to worry about,' Ruth said, still staring at the screen. 'It looks like I'm about to get fired.'

The message didn't say it in so many words. All it said was that Mrs Poliakoff of Personnel requested Ruth's attendance at her office before leaving. But anyone in the company would have known in an instant what this actually meant; Poliakoff was aka Harriet the Hatchet, and the hatchet always fell without much notice at the end of a day.

Ruth's head buzzed. She was going to be dismissed. Shed. Let go. Ruth had never been fired from a job before, and she hadn't seen this coming. The shock and the hurt were almost physical.

What was she going to do?

Gordon. My God, she thought, this is Gordon. His answer, with the justification she'd given him. The session with Jake yesterday had simply been a matter of form; she could have stripped to the waist and scourged herself in his office, and her contrition wouldn't have made any difference.

She stormed down the corridor and straight to Gordon's department.

His office was empty.

Ruth's immediate assumption was that he'd planned it this way; he was gone, his assistant wasn't at her desk, at least two phones somewhere around here were ringing. It was already after five, but Gordon wasn't one for dashing out early; he usually worked on alone until six or even later. She'd often done the same, and this was how it had started between them. Both of them supposedly staying late to work, both finding some excuse to flirt.

Ruth hesitated, some of her momentum lost. There was a sense of something odd going on, but she didn't know what it was.

Gordon's assistant came back less than a minute later, flying along with the air of someone thrust deep into the management of a crisis. She bypassed Ruth and grabbed up the phone, slammed it down again when she realized that the caller had given up, and dumped the armload of papers she'd been carrying onto the desk.

'Couldn't you get that for me?' she said as she went around to the other side. Her name was Debbie and she was hard and lean like a tennis player.

'It seems I don't work here any more,' Ruth said. 'Where's Gordon?'

'Mr Parry went out to buy a present for his wife.'

'I'll wait for him.'

'You can't. I mean, there's no point waiting, he's not coming back in. We just heard he got mugged on the street.'

'In broad daylight? In the middle of town?'

'They had to take him to the hospital. Nobody knows exactly what happened.'

Head spinning, Ruth walked back through the now-emptying building toward her own office. Gordon always reckoned that he carried a couple of spare bills in a pocket and his wallet somewhere else; mugger money, he called it, ready to hand so that thieves would cut and run. Lots of people did the same. The whole point of it was to avoid the quick escalation into violence that could occur even if there was no resistance offered but the response wasn't fast enough. She wondered what could have gone wrong. And she felt concern for him still, in spite of everything else.

Always assuming that it was as she'd heard, and nothing with a deeper significance. Tim Hagan knew who Gordon was, and he'd be no more difficult to follow than she had been. Having considered that, she couldn't imagine what advantage there might be in an attack on him. She wondered how badly he'd been hurt. She'd an urge to go to the hospital. But Mimi might be there already.

Back at her desk, she sat heavily in her chair and reached for the drawer. The memo preparing the way for her dismissal was still on her screen. Any doubts that she'd had about going out armed had now been dispelled. It was a scary prospect. But not half so scary as the alternative.

The drawer that she pulled out was empty.

'Hello, Ruth,' said a voice that she recognized from behind her chair.

17

She stared up at him.

'What are you doing here?' she said.

'Waiting for you.'

She'd spun the chair around. There was minimal space in the carrel, and he was mere inches away. Only the high back of the chair had screened him from her. He was looking down on her and he seemed relaxed.

He said, 'I don't know what I did to offend you. Whatever it was, I'm sorry. Please give me a second chance.'

'You're pointing a gun at me,' Ruth said.

'I know,' Hagan said. 'It's yours.' He leaned over her, and she shrank back; but her chair was jammed into the narrow space, and the castors scooted back no more than three or four inches before she was stopped. Hagan was more or less as he'd been when she'd seen him on the subway. He was still a good-looking boy, but he wouldn't turn women's heads the way he had when he'd been dressed to k . . .

Ruth pushed that thought away. 'Funny little toy you've got here,' Hagan said, as he raised his hand and Ruth started to flinch. But he only used it to point to his eyes, one after the other.

'Read these,' he said. 'Will I use it, do you think?'

She stared. Swallowed drily. She'd never seen anything quite like those eyes before.

'Don't find out the hard way,' Tim Hagan suggested. 'I'm certifiable. That's official. Don't argue with the experts. Stand up.'

Ruth didn't know how she did it, but she stood. She seemed to float up without conscious control.

'I'm not going anywhere,' she said. She wondered if there

was anyone left in this part of the building, anyone at all. But she knew that there probably wasn't. He'd have checked before he made his appearance.

'I think you'll find that you will,' he suggested. 'It's never the way you imagine. One thing I'll promise you, after this you'll know yourself better. There are lots of ways this could go. You could even be the one who saves me from hell. Wouldn't that be something?'

Ruth had no idea what he was talking about.

She said, 'Now what happens?'

'Now we leave.'

She couldn't leave with him. That was the worst thing imaginable. Or at least, it would be the first step on the inevitable descent to the worst thing imaginable.

But she seemed to have no choice.

They saw few people as they headed toward the elevators. Most watched the countdown to the hour and then took off like sprinters. Hagan put a hand around her waist and drew her close. No-one who saw them would notice the gun in her side. It was a lady's gun, a popgun. Useless over distance. But jammed into her ribs like knuckles, she didn't even dare to think of what damage it might achieve.

'What did you do to Gordon?' she said.

'No more than I had to,' Hagan said. 'All I wanted was his card for getting in. He screamed like a pig when I smacked him.' He shook his head. 'Some guys.'

Someone crossed ahead of them. A plea rose inside her. And then faded, unborn.

'Where are we going?' she said.

'First to your car,' Hagan said. 'Then we drive.'

'*Why?*' Ruth pleaded weakly.

But to that, he gave no answer.

He was very cool. When they reached the elevators and stopped, he continued to hold her close. To anyone who didn't know what was actually happening, it would look like a public display of intimacy. But its real purpose was to keep her feeling threatened and under control.

Intimacy, threat . . . from Hagan, she felt terror at the prospect of either.

The elevator doors opened. Aidan Kincannon was riding inside, and Ruth saw his eyes light up in recognition as he moved to step out and saw her there.

'Hello, Ruth,' he said. And then he took in Hagan beside her, and his manner seemed to change. It was as if all of the warmth, if none of the politeness, suddenly went out of it.

He held the door for them as they boarded.

'Thank you,' Hagan said.

But the security man didn't back off yet. He stood with his hand on the sensor bar, holding the door as it made repeated and ineffectual attempts to close. He was looking at Ruth and he said, 'Is everything all right?'

'Ruth's had a shock,' Hagan explained. 'I came in to take her home.'

Aidan Kincannon didn't acknowledge him. He was still looking at Ruth. She was trying to find some way to signal that she was in trouble, but she didn't know how to do it without Hagan becoming aware.

Aidan said, 'What exactly's happened?'

He was speaking to Ruth again, but again it was Tim Hagan who spoke. 'They found Gordon Parry in a back alley with his thumbs wired together behind him and a plastic bag over his head,' he said. And then he squeezed Ruth tighter, as if for necessary support. 'Look at her,' he said, 'she's shaking.'

'Ruth?' the security man said. 'Do you need anything?'

Look in my eyes. Read my mind.

'We'll be all right,' Hagan assured him.

'There's a doctor for the building who's always on call. I can phone him or I can give you his number.'

'Thanks,' Hagan said, with a clear note of irritation in his voice, 'but I know what she needs. I'm going to get her a long way from here.'

'OK,' said Aidan Kincannon then, and he backed off and let the elevator doors close. Her spirits sank even lower than before. The sound made by the doors as they engaged was like that of the gate to a cell.

'Fucking rentacop,' she heard a dismissive Hagan say as they descended.

They went on down into the parking basement and straight to her car. He knew exactly where it was; which bay, which side. A faulty lighting tube stuttered overhead.

'Now,' he said. 'You're going to drive, and I'm going to watch you. Let me tell you now, you'll prefer that arrangement to any other.'

He made her get out her keys. And then he covered her as she opened up and they both got inside. In the faltering light, she noticed that there were cats' pawprints in the dust across her hood. She didn't know from where.

He told her to start the engine. She said, 'Where are we going?'

'Out of town,' he said. 'Just like we told your friend.'

Ruth said, 'What did I do to you, Tim? I mean, that deserves this?'

But he didn't even acknowledge the question.

'Once we're out of here,' he said, 'head for Market Street and the expressway.'

She couldn't resist. It wasn't an option. Her mind looked for chances but her body, moving to some other command, let them slip by. She felt as meek as a mouse. As if she'd crawl and eat dirt if he told her to. She felt utter, utter despair.

She'd never known a terror like it. She'd no sense of self any more. It had been swamped, destroyed.

They were out in the evening traffic. Most of these cars would be homeward bound, but not Ruth's. The boy that she'd chosen was taking her away from her home, out toward the river and the west of the city.

They crossed the bridge. On the right-hand side was the General Electric Aerospace plant, a huge black-windowed warehouse of a place. Lined along the road were snack wagons with shiny aluminium sides, old beat-up buses with gas cylinders rolled underneath them to supply the ovens within.

Hagan seemed at ease. He had Ruth where he wanted her. He leaned back in his seat, and started to get expansive.

'Now, in situations like this,' he said, 'the police can't exactly say so in public but it's rumoured that their best advice for you would be to ram another car in traffic. That's on the principle that a call for help will often be ignored but vehicular damage will always get you a reaction. Let me explain to you what's going to happen if you try it. I'll shoot you once in the heart and once in the head. The first shot may miss the actual organ, but it'll disable you enough to allow me to place the second. Then I'll step out of the car and walk away. If there's a crowd, no-one will stop me.' He looked out into the evening. They were heading into the sunset. 'If anyone questions them afterwards, no two people are going to agree on what they saw.'

'Oh, my God,' Ruth said miserably.

Hagan looked up into the reddening sky.

'None of it has to happen, Ruth,' he said. 'It's entirely in your hands.'

18

An hour out, and her hopes had all but gone. It was as if she'd retreated into a room in some tiny corner of her mind and locked herself in. She'd read reports of women who'd been kidnapped or abused, who'd gone along with instructions even to their inevitable degradation, and she'd read them with disbelief. With the certainty that if it ever happened to her, she'd fight it out whatever the immediate threat. What could you lose, after all, when your very life was at stake? Not me, she'd thought, looking at those sad victims. Never me. She'd heard trial judges weighing up the cases after the event, trying to get a measure of the blame and saying, well, this one didn't fight much, this one went along . . . this one was no angel to start with . . .

And all that she could think now was, God forgive us all.

It was much simpler than she'd ever supposed. First you froze, and then you obeyed. And while you obeyed, the essential core of your volition stayed frozen. You lived from one second to the next. And you clung to that second like a drowning sailor to a raft.

'Keep it at fifty-five,' Hagan said. 'I know what you're trying to do.'

She let her speed drop back. She'd been allowing it to creep upward on the slim chance that they might get picked up on State Police radar, but Hagan was paying more attention than he'd been showing.

'You've done this before,' she said.

'Often enough to know all the angles.'

They were out on the I-76, still heading west. The city was behind them and they were deep into Pennsylvania countryside now; stretches of dense woodland, cattle farms, roadside ads for campgrounds with RV hookups. The Interstate was a two-lane conduit overhung by trees, with patched-up cracks in the concrete running before them in the headlights like fleeing snakes. Sixteen-wheelers and high-sided panel trucks powered by them in the next lane. She'd no idea where they were going. Hagan seemed to have some firm destination in mind, but he was giving nothing away.

'What are you going to do to me?' she said. It had taken her the last ten, fifteen miles of driving simply to get up the nerve to ask the question.

Hagan said, 'What's happening here is, I'm expressing my disappointment in you. I think I'm entitled to do that.'

Ruth fell silent for a while. A note in the mail would have been sufficient, she thought.

Then she said, 'What did you do with Frances Everline?'

He looked at her across the car. She didn't take her eyes off the road, but she could sense his gaze on her like some kind of radiation. Some crudely bottled source from which the shields had partly fallen, releasing its destructive heat in her direction.

'What do you know about her?' he said.

'I know it was her apartment that you took me to.'

'Who else knows?'

'The police.'

He was quiet for a while, taking this in. Ruth wondered if she'd helped or harmed herself by telling him.

Then he said, 'Frances was fine when I saw her last. She was in better shape than she was when I found her. The fact of it is, I looked after her.'

'But where is she now?'

'You'll know that soon enough.'

Her hands were numb on the wheel. She'd been gripping it so tightly that they'd lost all sensation. A car drew level in the outside lane, but it didn't pass. Ruth willed her fingers to open, to ease off, and after a few moments they responded. With the response came the pain of cramp, and the pins-and-needles feeling of returning circulation.

You can get used to anything, she realized. Even terror. Nothing stays raw, nothing stays hot; it starts to break down, it cools. It makes itself a place and settles in.

She remembered to check her mirror. Ruth couldn't recall when driving had last been a conscious act. Often, when she was preoccupied, she'd realize at a journey's end that she had no memory of her route or the travelling of it. But this, she reckoned, was a journey she'd never forget. If she dared anticipate having the chance to remember.

The car alongside her was still level, and hadn't passed. Hagan wouldn't allow her to speed, so she slowed to let it by.

The car in the next lane kept pace.

Ruth looked across and there, at the wheel on the far side of the banged-about Nissan that was matching her speed, sat Aidan Kincannon.

He took his eyes from the road ahead and looked at her. A big truck was coming up behind him, and any minute now he was going to have to speed up or fall back. His face was blank in the semi-darkness of the car, no expression on it at all, and his gaze was steady. He was still in his uniform, but he appeared to have thrown a dark jacket over.

She made no sound. But her lips made the shape of a single word.

Help.

His face didn't change. But his head inclined slightly, and then he returned his attention to the road ahead and the Nissan began to fall back. The big truck behind came storming on through the gap and passed by just as Kincannon got out of the way, its airhorn blowing off in a self-assertive blast. There had been no actual holdup. So the blast was just in case.

The Nissan's lights slid into place in her rearview mirror. Two yellow discs, no details behind. She risked a glance at Hagan. He was looking the other way. They were passing a sign for a service plaza about a mile ahead and Ruth said, 'We're going to have to stop the car.'

'Nice try,' Hagan said.

'You don't even know why yet.'

'I don't need to.'

The plaza would be a public place. She could see it coming up now, a group of grey-and-white colonial-looking buildings under bright lights. A Yogurt House and a Roy Rogers restaurant, gas pumps probably somewhere around the back.

She had to pass the exit without even slowing.

'I still have to stop,' she said. 'I'm going to throw up.'

'I'll make a deal with you,' he said. 'You don't throw up, and I won't put you in the trunk for the rest of the drive.'

They went on, the plaza dropping behind them.

'You've got me so scared,' she said, tossing it in as a late aside even though the plaza was now a lost cause.

'Try to live with it.'

Ruth's mind raced. Aidan Kincannon's lights were still there in her mirror. She hoped. The fact of it was, they could be anybody's lights now; a couple of cars had joined the highway from the plaza and there had been some jockeying-around as they'd merged. But she felt they were his. She knew they were his.

They'd damned well better be his.

Quietly, she swallowed some air.

Construction gangs had been working on the road along this stretch, and the rumble strip and the shoulder had been blocked off from the highway with a low, hefty-looking barrier of concrete sections. Over on the other side of the wall, big wagons and earth-moving equipment hulked unattended in the darkness. She couldn't have stopped anywhere around here even if she'd managed to persuade him. There was nowhere to pull in.

This was not good. She'd paused in her strategy, but the air that she'd started to swallow now lay like a pound weight in her stomach. She'd been planning to convince

Hagan that there was, indeed, a real risk of her puking in the car, but she'd timed it badly. Now she was losing control. She couldn't belch to command, it wasn't a girl thing. Couldn't play the *Lone Ranger* theme in her armpit, come to that, but then she'd never expected either skill to figure as a survival trait.

Ruth clamped her lips shut, but the air wouldn't stay down.

It came bubbling up in her chest, and it sounded just like the plumbing in an old house after midnight. Keeping her mouth shut only made it worse.

It came out like a wet horse fart.

'Oh, Jesus,' Hagan said, and reached across her to grab the wheel. He twisted it hard and it spun out of her hands.

She didn't know what was happening. They swung right into the concrete wall and she screamed and expected an impact, but there was none. She'd stamped on the brake already and she thought that's it, he's killed us both, but her Pontiac was sliding to a halt on the earthworks side of the barrier while the Interstate traffic roared by on the other.

Of course, they'd left gaps. Spaces for the construction workers' vehicles to come and go, and Hagan had swung them through one of those. Aidan Kincannon would have been taken completely by surprise and would have been unable to follow. He'd be gone already, with no way of getting back.

Her one hope. Her only hope. Now nothing more than a set of red tail-lights, lost among the rest and disappearing fast.

The moment that her car stopped rolling, Ruth flung open the door and scrambled out. Shaken as she was, she wasn't about to let this hard-won advantage go. Hagan obviously thought she was going to crouch there and puke, but she didn't. She hit the ground and ran.

She heard him shout. The hell with him. The more distance she could put between them, the more useless to him her little handbag gun would be. She'd been warned of that when she'd bought it. But then, all that she'd bought it for was the noise it could make.

She heard a crack. It was like a snap of elastic.

Is that it? she thought, and her spirits began to rise.

She hit the banking, and scrambled up into the woodland beyond. He was behind her, she didn't have to look back to know that.

The branches tore at her, slowed her. The undergrowth was like so much barbed wire. She realized then that she wasn't going to get away from him and lie low until he lost interest or the police came. If she carried on trying to fight her way through this, she wasn't going to get away from him at all.

She changed direction, back down toward the road. She could hear him tearing after.

All that remained of the dusk was a dull azure glow in the sky, with the first stars beginning to show. The only light was the spill from passing headlights, which gave a low background blaze like that on an airport runway. Traffic noise was a constant roar. Down by the shoulder stood a big dirt-moving truck with chrome bolts on its wheels, its cab dark and locked-down for the night. Ruth made for it. The banking had been dug out here and the soft, sandy-coloured earth piled in a mound; she went over it, sliding down the other side like a dune-runner, and then dived to the ground and went under the truck.

When she came out on the other side, she knew that she had a matter of seconds before he came skidding around and she'd be within his sight again. She crossed the shoulder and went over the concrete barrier and threw herself flat to the road.

The barrier sections were about hip-height, and curved outward to form a lip above her. The cars were running frighteningly close, and she'd no protection; she was down there in the road dirt and squirming along with their tyres passing inches from her face. She had to turn it away. She was screened from Hagan and he wouldn't know where she'd gone, that was what mattered. She started to crawl back along the road, into the oncoming headlights.

One or two sounded their horns, some tried to swerve. She was buffeted and sprayed with grit as they went by. The barrier sections were linked by pieces of rusty chain, and there were gaps. Through one of these she saw Hagan's feet, pacing on the other side. He was looking for her, but he hadn't yet fathomed the trick. She scrambled on past, before he could glance down.

Ruth knew that she wasn't going to be able to go on like this for long. But if she could buy some time to get up and flag somebody down, that would surely be enough. Someone would stop. Someone had to stop.

Didn't they?

Maybe she could get to her feet and make a dash across the road. She had a mental image of Hagan angling over to intercept her and then *blam*, he was just a big smear on the hardtop in the wake of a truck. She might make it. It wasn't inconceivable. But looking at the steady onslaught of vehicles as they poured out of the night and by, it seemed unlikely. She'd have to rise and then wait to pick her moment, and in that beat of time he'd be upon her again.

Gravel ripped at her elbows as she dragged herself along. Hurricane winds battered her as the biggest vehicles thundered past. There was grit in her eyes, and they streamed. Somebody blasted on a horn, terribly close, and she heard a screech of tyres and thought, Oh shit, this is it. Misjudgement. Oblivion. Ruth stopped and hunched down, making herself as small against the concrete as she possibly could.

A red pickup truck sailed by, brakes kangaroo-pumping as they locked and spun, locked and spun. The driver had slammed on his hazard lights and was weaving to a halt. There was nowhere to pull over, so he was stopping right there in the road. Other cars were having to switch lanes, fast.

He was getting out.

Ruth started to rise. He was moving toward her. She got the briefest impression; a blond barn-door of a guy, tough and square and someone not to mess with.

She opened her mouth to call out. But halfway up onto her feet, Ruth stumbled.

A hand caught her under the arm, and helped her the rest of the way.

'It's all right!' Hagan called to the pickup's driver, his voice at top note barely able to compete with the noise of the traffic. 'I've got her!'

And, as if it had been run through the slowing-down filter of a nightmare, every moment stretched and every detail pointed up and made more exquisite, she saw the pickup driver take in the message and then signal a thumbs-up and hop back into his vehicle. Ruth gathered herself for one single, banshee scream of '*No!* . . .'

Only to hear it disappear in the overwhelming howl from all the air-horns on a huge beer truck as it thundered by them, bearing down on the pickup like a big herd of buffalo. The pickup burned rubber and took off just in time, yellow hazards still flashing, diving out from under the monster with nothing to spare.

While Ruth was once more in the hands of Tim Hagan.

He helped her back over the barrier. All of the fight had gone out of her now.

He said, 'Can you still drive?'

'I don't want to,' she said. 'I want to go home.'

'If you're not going to drive, then I have to tie you up or put you in the trunk. I don't mind, it's all the same to me. If I tie you up I'll use wire, and it'll hurt. What's it to be? Can you drive?'

She nodded.

'Good,' he said.

'Don't hurt me,' she said. 'Please.'

'You're scared,' he said. 'That's good. It doesn't give me any pleasure, believe me, but it's your best guarantee of us getting through this.'

Getting through it. Getting through it to what? They were walking back toward her car. Her legs felt like rubber, and he was half-holding her up. At any distance, his actions would have looked like an expression of concern for a person in distress.

When they reached the vehicle he said, 'I don't think this is going to work, Ruth. Look at you, you can barely stand. You won't be safe behind a wheel. You're going to have to bend over the car.'

Not safe? she thought as he turned her and pushed her to sprawl off-balance against the passenger door of her Pontiac. Clearly his notion of safety was arbitrary or, at the very least, relative. He pulled her arms behind her back, and she felt a sudden biting pain as he ran something around her hands and twisted it tight. She cried out, but he didn't respond other than to say, 'Don't try to move,' as he went around to the driver's door, opened it, and reached inside.

She heard the hollow clunk of a catch releasing, and the hood sprang up a couple of inches.

'Damn,' she heard Hagan say. 'Where's the one for the back?'

He leaned farther in and he fumbled around some more. He was going to carry out the other part of his threat, and put her into the trunk for the rest of the ride.

Ruth could hear him muttering inside the car. She knew what he was looking for but she didn't help him out. She was watching the red lights that were heading her way.

Strange. They were like approaching eyes. They resolved themselves into tail-lights, flaring bright as the car beyond them braked. The car was backing down the shoulder toward them on this side of the concrete divider.

She could see now what Aidan Kincannon must have done. He'd overshot the gap as they'd pulled in without warning, but then he'd carried on either to the next opening or to the end of the works. There wasn't the space to swing a car around, and so he'd had to turn in his seat and steer backwards into darkness as fast as he dared. It was a perilous-looking ride. She realized, as he dodged about and over-corrected, that he could barely see where he was going.

In fact, he was concentrating so hard on the immediate ground under his wheels that he didn't even see her car until it was almost too late.

The Nissan braked. Ruth and everything else lit up red. She was trying to get out of the way but she couldn't get her balance. The slowing Nissan hit her car at about five or ten miles an hour and shunted it back just as Tim Hagan, realizing that something was wrong, was moving to climb out.

Ruth slid and hit the hood as the car was knocked out from under her. She'd been trying to get her hands apart. The wire bit deep, but it had been carelessly done. She saw Aidan Kincannon getting out of his car and running. There was a gun of some kind in his hand, a revolver.

He reached the driver's door of her car and flung it all the way open. But there was an instant sound of a shot from inside the Pontiac, and Aidan went backwards and down without even bringing his own weapon to bear. Ruth looked in through the windshield and saw Hagan scrambling across to get away from Aidan and out of the passenger door. Her hands still weren't free but as he got it open and started to clamber out, she kicked it shut. His forehead rose to meet the moving glass and he rebounded off it, hard, falling back and out of sight. Ruth managed to roll over and get her footing, and as she went around the car to Aidan she finally managed to prise her thumbs out of the wire loop that had been twisted around them.

Aidan was lying back against the concrete barrier, one hand clutching his throat, blood all around it. She crouched before him, not knowing what to do, not knowing where to start; but with his gun hand he reached up and shoved her aside, and then with his way clear he started to pump shots into the car.

Ruth had to cover her ears. Her cut hands were bleeding down her wrists.

'Stop!' she shouted. 'Stop!'

But he only stopped when his gun was empty and the hammer fell onto dead chambers. Once, twice, and then he let his hand drop.

Now it was comparatively quiet.

Gingerly, Ruth reached up and opened her car's perforated door. The car was empty, the opposite door open to the night. She looked back at Aidan, and he grimaced.

Her own little handbag gun was sticking out of the seat, jammed in between the seatback and the cushion. She worked it free and as it came out, she glanced through the rear windshield and saw Hagan.

He was on his hands and knees about fifty yards off, crawling away down the shoulder. She saw him try to rise a couple of times, but mostly he was just worming his way along. From here she couldn't tell for certain whether he was shot, or stunned, or what.

She slid back out of the car.

'He's going to get away,' she said.

Aidan was shaking his head hard, swinging it from side to side and unable to speak.

'He's unarmed now,' Ruth said. 'I can stop him.'

She started to run. Her side hurt, her hands hurt. She overtook Hagan easily, dropped to a crouch before him, and levelled her gun at his face as he became aware of her and halted his crawl.

'Enough,' she said. 'We're going back.'

He looked up at her, dully. Then his eyes focused into the barrel of the Bernardelli right in front of him.

'Is this the end of it?' he said.

'Yes, it is.'

'I mean, the end of it all.'

Ruth's hand was steady.

'Only if you want it to be,' she said.

It started to go wrong, then. Hagan gave a brief nod, and closed his eyes. He waited.

Traffic pounded on by on the other side of the barrier.

Ruth felt as if she'd been wrong-footed. This wasn't what was supposed to happen. He was supposed to submit, to give up the game and do as he was told. As she had. The positions were reversed.

But the roles, it seemed, were not.

Her hand started to shake.

He opened his eyes.

'Apparently not,' he said.

He struggled to his knees, and then he got to his feet. Ruth could only back off, helpless. She was still holding the gun on him, but it was useless to her. She couldn't bring herself to pull the trigger, and he knew it. That was the difference between them.

He swayed, and wiped down his cheeks with both hands as if clearing away the waters of the baptized. Then he took a deep breath. He didn't appear to be holed or otherwise damaged.

'If you're not going to stop me,' he said, 'then I'll have to go on.'

He sucked at something as if at a loose tooth, and then spat blood.

'Pity,' he added. And he began to walk stiff-leggedly back toward the cars, squeezing his head in both hands for a moment as if to press out the pain that she'd caused him.

Ruth stood there, powerless. And then belatedly she realized that not only was he walking toward the cars, he was walking toward Aidan Kincannon. She moved to catch up. If Hagan tried to do him further harm, surely she'd stop him then. It wasn't weakness that stayed her hand. Weakness wasn't the word for it.

But Hagan went to her car, not to Kincannon. She reached the fallen security guard just as Hagan was starting the engine. Aidan had pulled out a handkerchief and jammed it between his neck and shoulder like a violinist, except that the handkerchief was red to overflowing. In this awkward and pained-looking position, he was attempting to reload his revolver with trembling hands.

The Pontiac started to pull back, disengaging from the

Nissan with a sound of tearing metal. At this, Aidan aborted the attempted reload and slammed shut the cylinder.

The damaged Pontiac swept past them, reversing toward the gap through which it had originally left the road. Aidan swung his arm around to follow. He dry-fired on four empty chambers and then, finally, got off a couple of too-late shots as the Pontiac swung out and re-entered the traffic.

Back on the highway now, Hagan accelerated past them and away.

Ruth turned her full attention to Aidan. He'd been hit, all right. There was so much blood around the wound site that it was impossible to tell where, but at least it didn't seem to be through his throat as she'd feared. At her best guess it seemed to be a few inches to the side, through the muscle between the neck and shoulder. Dangerously close to the main artery, but so far as she could see there was nothing that was actually spurting.

She looked around. As part of the construction work they seemed to have dug up the emergency phones along this stretch. She'd have to try to get him into his own car, and onward to medical help. 'Can you speak?' she said.

His face twisted in pain and anger. She was heartened. He seemed too furious to die.

'Shit,' he gurgled.

'I couldn't do it,' she said. 'He dared me to.'

'You should've,' Aidan said.

Ruth couldn't look him in the eyes. 'I know,' she said. She knew.

PART TWO

An Enemy of the People

19

Late one Saturday afternoon, Aidan Kincannon took a phone call at home. Home was his house in north-east Philadelphia, where he'd lived ever since inheriting the place when his mother died. After the breakdown of his marriage to Angela he'd spent a month on a friend's couch and then most of a year in a pit of a one-roomed apartment, counting the stains on the ceiling and trying not to wonder how they got there. Then this place had come along. Talk about a mixed blessing. But at least he had somewhere he could bring his two children at weekends, and space besides.

The voice on the line said, 'Who's that?'

'I'm the guy who pays the phone bill,' Aidan said. 'Who's that?'

'Detective Tom Diaz of the city police. Can I talk to Ruth?'

Aidan had met Tom Diaz twice in the course of the investigation that had followed Ruth's abduction. But that had been almost a year ago now, and everything seemed to have cooled off. They knew what they knew, and it led to nothing more. They hadn't had a call from the police in almost four months.

He said, 'She's working today. What's it concerning?'

'You can tell her that we think that we know where he is.'

'Should she worry?'

'If what I just heard is right,' Diaz said, 'she can *stop* worrying.'

They talked some more, and Tom Diaz enquired about his health, and then Aidan hung up and went back to the kitchen to get the coffee that he'd left brewing when the

phone had rung. He was trying to decide whether he ought
to call Ruth at her place of work and tell her the news. He
knew that the boss didn't like his staff to take personal
calls in working hours, but this surely had to be a justified
exception.

Ruth held down two jobs now, and the two combined
didn't bring in half the salary she'd been drawing before
getting fired from her last one. Her day job was in what
could only be described as a keyboard sweatshop, a suite
of rooms upstairs from a peepshow on Arch Street where
women sat shoulder-to-shoulder transferring written data
onto disk. Electronic scanners could do the same work
faster and more cheaply these days, but the sweatshop
gave more accuracy. Ruth had once explained to him
how they did it, but he still didn't understand. They
paid her per thousand key depressions, and they didn't
pay her much.

Then two evenings a week and all of Saturday – like
today – she worked in a discount bookstore south of
South Street, where she spent her time in the basement
slashing open boxes and then sorting and stacking their
contents onto the shelves. The books were set out as
review copies but they were obviously warehouse stock,
the same they supplied to the regular bookstores. You
could pick up just about any hardcover from their
so-called 'Eight Miles o' Books' at half-price within a
few days of it coming out. Even Ruth couldn't work
out how they managed that one. For this she got paid
by the hour, and she stayed on as late as they'd let her.
Unless business turned out to be slow, tonight she'd be
there until ten.

He tried to call the bookstore. But nobody picked up
the phone.

Ruth had one of the rooms upstairs in the house, and she
gave Aidan rent. She paid her rent in cheques that he never
cashed or took to the bank. Like him she was supposed to
be healed, and like him she carried her pain well-hidden.
But Aidan's discomfort was physical, and he knew it would

132

eventually fade. Hers ran deeper, and seemed to flourish unseen.

She was so private. She told him almost nothing. She'd been getting letters from the Department of Justice that he knew she hadn't been answering, but he didn't feel able to ask her why. He had something that he'd wanted for a long time and never thought that he could possibly have, and that was Ruth Lasseter in his home. Long-admired from a distance, and now his to hold. But something was missing. It was as if there was a place inside her that she retreated to alone, and that he could never go to with her.

He tried the bookstore a few more times over the next couple of hours. Only once did he get through, and he spoke to someone whose voice he didn't recognize. He was put on hold for so long that he didn't realize that the call had been lost until a message from the phone company cut in.

Dinner reached the table from the freezer via the microwave. He watched half of a movie on cable, and then half of another on some other channel.

And then a little after nine-thirty, he locked up the house and went out to his car.

He'd traded the Nissan for a three-year-old Chevrolet. Ruth's car had been fit for nothing other than the scrapheap when they'd finally found it, and then for some reason she'd done badly out of the insurance. She used mainly public transportation now, and rode the bus home on Saturday nights. Aidan didn't like her doing it, Ruth didn't like him saying so. She didn't like it if he turned up to collect her, either, but tonight it was something they'd both have to live with for the sake of the news that he'd bring.

Standing alone on the street, riding alone on the bus. How could she face that, after what she'd been through? But somehow she did; for some reason, she chose to.

He drove into town, taking the Delaware Expressway almost to Front Street and then down through Queen Village. South Street, which cut across the middle of the village, was a centre of late activity filled with restaurants, fast-food places and that general sense of the bizarre found in counterculture areas that had turned respectable. It was skateboards on the sidewalks, loud music in the cars, T-shirts in the shops. Below South Street was residential, black residential mainly, with young women and girls out on the sidewalk watching their small children play while the men sat apart on benches or front stoops. It was Aidan's belief that you could always guess the neighbourhood by the music you could hear as you were driving through, from rap to Hispanic to a kind of constipated white rock. In an area like this one, it could change character completely over a distance of a couple of streets.

There was a lot of clearance going on in the neighbourhood around Eight Miles o' Books. It had hit business, although business went on. He parked the car across the street, by a seven-storey building which presented a still-perfect façade on one side but whose brick walls had been torn out on the other, floor after floor, exposing its iron framework like a skeleton. The bookstore was in an old row of shops. It was now after ten, and one of the managers was pulling the security shutters down as Aidan walked over.

'Did Ruth Lasseter leave yet?' he asked the lockup man.

'If she didn't,' the man said, 'she's in there till Monday.'

'Do you know where she goes to get the bus home?'

The man didn't know, so Aidan got back into the car and circled around to see if he could find her SEPTA stop. It was a warm night. So warm that mothers had come out of their homes on quieter streets to lean against the cars with tiny babies on their shoulders, soothing them there because the heat wouldn't let them settle in the house.

After a few minutes he caught sight of Ruth, standing alone under a light on one of the emptier throughways. She held a brown paper grocery bag against her chest and she seemed to be scanning the night. He stopped the car across from her, and then signalled to her and waved. She started to walk toward him, and he could tell at first that she hadn't recognized him or the car. But then as she approached and realized who it was, the tensions of her body seemed to alter.

She bent over to look into the car. She didn't look pleased.

'What are you doing?' he asked her.

'Waiting for my bus,' she said. 'Why did you come for me?'

'Don't start an argument, Ruth. Please. Just get in.'

She got into the car and stared ahead, coldly. As if the gesture wasn't only unwelcome, but he'd wrecked something for her as well. He sometimes wondered if she met someone else. She could be secretive enough.

Aidan said, 'Detective Diaz rang. They think they may have found him.'

She looked at him then. There was no need to ask about whom he was talking. 'Where?'

'Out past Mechanicsburg, not two miles from where he dumped your car. There's a creek that's culverted under the highway. It gets overgrown and they clear it out every year. The road gang found him in that.'

'What was he doing there?'

'Nature was stripping him down. He was dead, Ruth. Dead for the entire year. Chances are that he got hit that same night while he was walking on the shoulder in the dark. A few cars knocked him around before he ended up in the ditch. The drivers probably didn't even know.'

It was a lot to take in, he knew it. It would drag back to the surface a lot of feelings that she'd almost certainly been trying to suppress, and she'd need time to come to terms with it all.

He started the car, and they set off.

After a while, Ruth said, 'I'd want to see proof.'

'They've got him in a little county morgue,' Aidan told her. 'I don't see there's much doubt in the matter.'

'I mean before I'll believe that it's him.'

'Someone's going out there on Monday. I don't know if they'll do an autopsy there or bring him back into the city. He can't be much more than teeth and bones by now, it'll be more like archaeology than anything. But they've got our statements. They know what he was wearing.'

'He's not stupid.'

'He's not anything, he's dead. They're going to prove it so even you'll have to accept it. What's in the bag?'

'Nothing,' Ruth said.

'Heavy-looking nothing.'

He drove along in silence for a while and then Ruth said, belatedly, 'It's something to read for the weekend.'

'That's interesting,' he said. 'Let me see it.'

She sat without speaking or looking at him. She was almost sullen.

'Let me see it, Ruth,' he repeated patiently.

They were back on the expressway now, and the light wasn't bad. Reluctantly but obediently, she reached into the bag and drew out the contents. He took his eyes off the road for long enough to glance over.

'Pearl handles,' he said, as if he couldn't help being impressed. 'Where'd you get it?'

'A pawnshop,' she said.

'Is the safety on?'

She put the safety on.

'Jesus,' Aidan said, appalled. 'Put it away.'

Nothing much more was said until they got home. Aidan was angry, because it wasn't the first time that something like this had happened. Aidan's house was in the older part of its neighbourhood, on a narrow street that was barely more than one car's width across. The street had trees, and iron posts to keep vehicles from its sidewalks. The trees leaned inward in a cypress-grove effect, and the posts were topped with cast-iron rocking-horse heads. Aidan's house was tall and narrow and dark, its upper storey lost among the leaves. Some of the other houses had window boxes and flowers in the tiny garden space out front. Aidan had built a wooden parking deck on his.

Ruth went inside first as he locked up the car. She waited for him in the sitting-room, knowing that something was coming.

He stood before her.

'Why, Ruth?' he said.

She looked up at him, upset and defiant. 'How can you ask me that?' she said.

'To protect yourself? No. People trying to protect themselves don't stand out there in the open like they're hoping to draw some enemy fire.'

'I wasn't doing that.'

'You've been daring him.'

'I haven't.'

'You never want my help. You're scared as a kitten but you never want protection. Why'd you move in with me, Ruth? Was I just the cheapest option, or did you really think I'd be too dumb to notice what you were doing?'

'I haven't been doing anything.'

'I took a call for you last week. It was another one of those escort places, they were ringing to apologize because their brochure hadn't been printed yet. This was South Carolina. Why?'

'He's a Southern boy,' she said reluctantly.

'*Was*, Ruth.' Aidan insisted. 'The word now is was.'

'So if he's been dead all this time,' she countered, 'what does it matter anyway?'

'He may not be out there, Ruth, but plenty of others still are. Look at me and listen to me. Not bringing yourself to blow his brains out when you got the chance doesn't make you responsible for him ever after. It doesn't make you responsible for anything. He's gone. Can we please start to live now?'

She did it again. The dumb treatment. The routine where she stared at him wide-eyed and simply took it in, until he'd blown off all his energy and had nothing left to say. She didn't argue further, she didn't try to justify herself.

Just waited it out, and then went on as before.

When she'd gone upstairs, Aidan sat in a chair and held his head. He didn't know how to get through to her. He'd thought that the news about Hagan might make some difference, but seemingly it hadn't. He could understand her to a certain extent. A world with Hagan still out there, always just out of sight, always with the chance of finding him around the next corner . . . it was bound to seem as if every moment held a little taint of poison. Victims of violence were never quite the same people again. They could recover, they could get strong. But never the same as before.

It was called survival. Now that Hagan was known to be dead, the process ought to begin.

But, seemingly, no. Because it appeared that for Ruth, dead simply wasn't enough.

20

Sometime around two in the morning, as he lay awake in darkness, he heard a movement from the direction of her room. Aidan had always left his door a few inches ajar so that he could pick up the night sounds of the house. He'd done it even before the children had been born. He heard the creak of a loose board on the upper landing, and then the whisper of moving air that was the door to his room being pushed all the way open. He knew what would happen next.

There was the sound of a single footstep as she crossed the floor, and then the bed bounced as she slid under the covers and curled up meekly against him. As always when she did this, she'd shed the washed-out and oversized T-shirt that was her regular nightwear. Her presence might have been a sign of genuine contrition, or it might have been an act of manipulation; the likelihood was that it was both, inextricably mixed.

She fitted against him, pressing her behind into his lap and moving gently for the reaction that she knew she'd inevitably get. But when it came, he didn't act on it. He held her more tightly.

'I think I'd die for you,' he said. It was easier to say such a thing into the darkness; somehow it became stripped-down and simple and sincere. 'When I first used to see you around the building, I don't think I even noticed you much. But over time it just stole up on me. Isn't it strange, how that happens.'

She was still, and said nothing.

And Aidan said, 'This is the dream I used to have.'

'I'm sorry, Aidan,' Ruth said, and started to draw away from him; but he put his arm across her and held her as she was. She settled back. The spark had gone now, but so had any hint of pretence.

He said, 'I wish I could do whatever it took to make you happy.'

'Maybe from now it'll change,' she said. 'I don't know.'

There was silence for a while.

Then Aidan said, 'We should find out for sure by the end of the week.'

'I don't think I can wait that long,' Ruth said.

21

So that was how they came to be driving out on the Sunday morning down the same road where it had all happened, heading for the small Pennsylvania town where the mortal remains of Tim Hagan supposedly lay. There wasn't much doubt in Aidan's mind. It was exactly the kind of fate to which the Tim Hagans of this world inevitably came. Detached souls, drifting unloved, doing their damage, dying alone. Whether Ruth could accept it or not had nothing to do with the facts, and depended entirely on her state of mind.

Construction work out on the road had been completed some time ago now, and there was no clue to where the events of that night had taken place. Aidan watched for it, and he knew when they'd passed it; but of the spot itself he had no sense at all. He glanced at Ruth every now and again, but as usual she was giving nothing away.

It was a problem. No matter how much the human spirit yearned for order and understanding, what it mostly had to deal with was a mess. Pick out of it what you could, and hope that you'd get enough to go on with. The local newspapers and a couple of the national tabloids had taken an interest in the story, but they ran into the same kind of problem. It was an interesting hook but it was unfinished business, without quite the critical mass to make a satisfying tale.

'Take the next exit,' Ruth said, the map open across her knees.

Beneath the Interstate was the usual immediate sprawl of motels, gas stations and restaurants. Power lines running from pole to pole overhead, and access roads crumbling around the edges. A hand-painted sign offered 800 feet of frontage for sale, and then there was a phone number, but most of the phone number had peeled away. There was an antiques co-op, an open-air hardware store. The place had the feeling of being pitched rather than built, but then they drove a few hundred yards on and took another turnoff and found that there was a place behind the place, a township suburb of pleasant homes and painted fire hydrants and small children who ran between the houses without any sense of danger.

Aidan cruised slowly, looking for the police department. Cars outside were usually the best indicator because in a place like this, the building itself wouldn't be much. They were probably looking at no more than two or three officers and a chief, with backup from the State Police.

It was redbrick and modern, set back from the road. It had space for a dozen cars but only two were now parked outside. There was nobody behind the counter, but their presence brought a patrolman out of the office at the back. He was young and blond and square-headed, and very tanned apart from a couple of pale flashes like racing stripes at his temples where his sunglasses usually covered.

Aidan said, 'We're the witnesses you got the call about.'

The man looked alert, but blank. 'What call's this?'

'The body you found in the culvert? We're supposed to help with the identification.'

Now the patrolman's look became one of dismay. 'You want to take a look at *that*?' he said.

'Not out of choice,' Aidan assured him. Ruth stood behind his shoulder and said nothing, as they'd agreed.

The patrolman said, 'Nobody's called us.'

'Can you check?' Aidan said. 'We came a long way for this and we'd really like to get it over with.'

He looked from one to the other. 'Which of you's the witness?'

'We both are,' Aidan said.

Ruth couldn't stay out of it any longer.

'Where are you keeping him?' she said.

The young man thought it over.

'Please wait here for just one moment,' he said.

He left them and went into the back office, where he could be seen through a partition of obscured glass. It gave him the look of someone whose identity had been concealed for TV news. They saw him check over something on a desk, then move away and become a set of even less distinct blurs of colour. He was talking to someone.

Ruth said, in a low voice, 'Did we make him suspicious?'

Aidan was watching to see if the man should pick up a phone. 'He's going through the motions,' he told Ruth. 'It's not that big a deal.'

'I suppose we could get into trouble.'

'We've a legitimate interest. All we don't have is a formal invitation.'

The young man returned without, so far as Aidan could tell, having talked to anyone outside of the office.

He said to them, 'What exactly is your relationship to the deceased?'

'Miss Lasseter's the one he abducted,' Aidan said. 'I'm the one he shot.'

The patrolman nodded, unable quite to conceal that he was impressed.

'OK,' he said. 'You know what condition he's in.'

'We've been warned about what to expect.'

But the young man couldn't help glancing toward Ruth. 'He's been partly in water,' he said. 'They don't come any worse than that. I think they sprayed him with something, but I don't know that it's helped.'

'Excuse me, Officer,' Ruth said, 'but the deader he looks, the happier I'll be.'

He picked up some keys from behind the counter.

'You want to follow me in your car?' he said. 'I'll show you where to go.'

'If you can tell us where,' Aidan offered, 'we can find it for ourselves.'

'And if I don't come with you,' the young patrolman said, 'you won't get in.'

They followed his cruiser through what passed for a downtown district. With the exception of the Fruit Bowl, which was a produce supermarket the size of a football field, most of the commercial buildings resembled small churches with steeply pitched roofs and white steeples. The actual churches looked like abandoned sheds. The two cars drove out under a massive iron trestle railway bridge to reach the county hospital on the outskirts of town.

It wasn't a new-looking building, but Aidan couldn't have put a date on it. They parked on a service road around the back, and the patrolman walked over to a windowless door and rang a bell. The door was opened about a minute later by an elderly black man in a green apron.

'Heyyy, George,' the patrolman said.

'Uh-huh,' the man said, dourly.

'Can you look after these people for me?'

The man stared at Aidan and Ruth. The whites of his eyes were the colour of bone. 'What do they want?' he said.

'They're here to make an identification on the body from the culvert; 'parently the city called ahead.'

The man in the green apron shrugged, and stepped back to let them enter. The patrolman was already backing away.

'I'll leave you in George's capable hands,' he said. 'Stop by on your way out and let me know how it went.' He looked at Ruth once again. 'If I was you,' he said, 'I wouldn't do this.'

'I can handle it,' Ruth said.

'I watched when they were getting him out. That was as much as *I'd* care to handle.'

Once they were inside, George led them down a badly lit corridor and into a room that had no windows at all. It had been painted mostly in a yellow that was the colour of bile.

'Wait here,' he said, and he moved over to the corner and reached up to switch on a black-and-white TV monitor. The monitor was on a bracket that had been bolted to the ceiling. The tube warmed up slowly, the picture rolling.

George banged it a couple of times on the side with the flat of his hand to make it go steady. Then he shuffled off, leaving them alone.

'Now what?' Ruth said.

'Watch the screen,' Aidan told her. 'See what comes up.'

Nothing came up for a while, apart from what seemed to be a downward view of the floor with the leg of some piece of steel furniture visible in one corner. It had a bright reflection on it that burned out a part of the picture. But then, after a few minutes, a gurney was manoeuvred under.

'Is that it?' Ruth said.

'That's the boy.'

Ruth approached the monitor, eyes raised to the screen, until she was as close as it was possible to get. The detail was mercifully poor, and the lack of any colour lent the process a kind of academic detachment. Aidan recognized the upper half of a heavily decomposed body lying on its side. It had been wrapped in sheet plastic, the plastic turned back to expose what was left of the face in profile. The hair was still in place but the nose and jaw were gone. The facial flesh had seemingly been caught in the act of boiling off in a froth.

The screen spasmed and rolled a few times, giving the face a momentary and horrible semblance of animation.

Footsteps approached down the corridor. The elderly black man came back in and stood waiting behind them. He was wearing see-through disposable gloves that covered all the way to his elbows and above. Ruth turned from the screen to look at Aidan.

'I can't tell anything from this,' she said. She didn't seem at all disturbed. 'Can't I get a proper look at his face?'

Aidan looked at George. The man said, 'I can move him around, but that's all I can do. I can't turn him over on my own. And there's only me here of a Sunday.'

'I can help you turn him,' Aidan said.

'You can't go back there.'

'It's all right. I used to be a cop.' He looked at Ruth. 'Are you OK?' he asked her.

She nodded. She was perhaps a little paler. The fact of it was, she'd been pretty drained-looking for a while.

Aidan followed the man down to the mortuary cold room, about fifty yards further on down the corridor. There the body lay on its gurney under the camera, which was the simple kind used for security work. It was usual to strip and wash the cadavers as they came into a place like this, but here clothes and tissue had become impossible to separate. The body lay more or less as it must have been found.

Aidan said, 'Can I get some of those gloves?'

He put them on, and looked at the arrangement. Apart from the camera there was no monitor, no intercom, no way of checking how the image would look. There was a deep scent of decay under some sweet chemical overlay.

'Don't keep on holding your breath,' George suggested. 'The quicker you suck it in, the sooner you get over it.'

Yeah, right. Holding his breath anyway, Aidan took hold of a part of the plastic sheet and helped the man to reposition the remains. They were heavier than they looked, considering that so much of them was gone. The smell reminded Aidan of the time he'd had to dig up a dog toilet, only it was a hundred times worse. Like having the world's worst halitosis sufferer belch right in your face after a rich garbage dinner. Because of the lack of feedback, they could only point the worm-eaten face at the camera and hope it was coming through.

The teeth showed through the cheeks. The eyes had dropped right back in.

'They look like his clothes,' Ruth said from immediately behind Aidan.

He almost dropped the sheet, which would have been a serious mistake. Still holding it, he looked over his shoulder. She'd followed them in.

She seemed emotionless. Anyone who didn't know her would probably have said that she was still unaffected. But Aidan, who knew every slight contour of her face, could

146

see the tiny pulse by her eye that was hammering at the speed of a mosquito's wing.

Trying to keep it matter-of-fact, he said, 'The hair looks about right, too.'

'I don't know, though,' Ruth said. 'That could be anyone.'

Personally, Aidan wouldn't have pursued it so far. But as he and George carefully lowered the remains back onto the gurney, he said to the other man, 'Were there any personal effects?'

George went over to a filing cabinet. Aidan looked at Ruth again. 'Still OK?' he said.

She shrugged and swallowed, hard. No, not OK. But not about to back off, either.

They moved over to a side table, where George laid a sealed bag before them. They couldn't open the bag, so they had to look at everything through the clear plastic. Aidan smoothed it flat on the table for a better view. He saw some keys and coins, a wristwatch, a wallet half-eaten by something, shredded fragments of the wallet's contents.

'Those are the keys to my car,' Ruth said.

Aidan looked more closely at the keys. They were on a metal key fob with enamel colours laid onto it, a souvenir from Walt Disney World. Not unique.

But under the circumstances, he thought, pretty damned conclusive.

Ruth waited out in the corridor while Aidan stripped off the throwaway gloves and scrubbed his hands. He could still smell the place as they walked out to his car but then he realized that the smell was on him, and in his clothes. Ruth seemed not to notice. He wondered how long it would take to disperse. He could shower and he could wash his clothes as soon as they got back to the house, but by then it would probably have invaded the car.

His thoughts about Hagan were dark, and lacked pity. In death, as in life, the boy fouled wherever he touched.

Aidan wondered if Ruth wanted to stop somewhere, to sit for a while; maybe get something to drink, perhaps even talk over what they'd done and seen. Undam some of the feeling that she'd been holding back for so long. But it seemed that she didn't.

She only wanted to go home.

Well, at least she was calling it home. Aidan got them back onto the highway, and didn't try to draw her out any further. He fiddled with the radio until he found the NPR station that he knew she liked to listen to. It was playing something classical.

Nearly an hour had passed when she suddenly said, 'He'd already dumped the car. Why'd he bother keeping the keys?'

'Stop it, Ruth,' Aidan said.

She was quiet for a while.

'Only wondering,' she said.

22

They got back early in the evening. Aidan showered, Ruth
went into her room. When Aidan came out, he could
hear her moving around above him. At one point she
was dragging stuff across the floor. When he'd dressed,
he made some coffee and carried it upstairs. With a mug
in each fist, he tapped on her slightly open door with
his foot.

'Come in,' she said.

She'd pulled out a big suitcase from under the bed, and
it was open on the rug. For a moment he almost panicked
and thought that she was packing, but then he could see
that she'd been emptying it, not filling it with clothes, and
most of what she had in there was paper. Some of the papers
she'd sorted into stacks, other items had been screwed up
and tossed into a pile across the room for later disposal.

He said, 'What are you doing?'

'I'm trying to get rid of all this stuff,' she said, gesturing
at what lay before her. Most of it, he'd never seen before.
Brochures. Letters. Newspaper clippings, all pertaining to
the kidnap. But not so many clippings, because it hadn't
been such big news.

'It *was* him, wasn't it?' Ruth said. She was looking up at
Aidan, and there was a note of appeal in her voice. Reassure
me. Even if it's wrong. Even if you have to lie. Tell me what
I most need to hear.

'It was him,' Aidan said.

She seemed helpless. 'I ought to feel better than this,'
she said. 'Why don't I?'

'It doesn't happen like that.'

He crouched down beside her and put an arm around
her. The papers in her hand slid to the floor and scattered

where they hit. She resisted for a moment, out of habit more than anything, and then she allowed herself to break training. She leaned against him. After a few moments, she was crying.

'Why, Aidan?' she said. 'Why'd he pick on me?'

'He didn't pick on you. You just happened to be the one who fell into his way. It was nothing personal.'

'But it *was* personal! That's the whole point! How personal can you get? Saying it could have been anyone doesn't help. It wasn't anyone. It was me.'

He rocked her a little. 'You can have your life again, Ruth. That's the best revenge you can take.'

She prised herself away from him, then. She'd dipped, she'd touched, she was back in the air. 'It's got nothing to do with revenge,' she said, leaning forward and scooping up some of the pages she'd let fall. 'I just wanted to understand. Look at these.'

They were envelopes, returned mail, with the official return-to-sender overstamp partly obscuring the address. But he could still read the name. Mrs J. Hagan on some, Jessica Hagan on at least one of them. An address in Brighton Beach, New York.

'I wrote these to his mother,' Ruth explained. 'One of those reporters helped me track her down.'

'In return for what?'

'Nothing.'

'That's something you don't hear every day. Didn't you get *any* replies?'

She shook her head, slowly. 'Not a one.'

'Walk away from it, Ruth,' Aidan urged her. 'And be grateful that you can.'

'I'll try,' she said. 'Can you give me a hand to get all this stuff downstairs?'

Aidan was thinking that it would all have been a lot easier to handle if it had been left unsorted in the suitcase, when the crest on one of the envelopes caught his eye.

'Wait a minute,' he said, reaching for it. 'What's this?'

'Oh,' she said, waving a dismissive hand, 'those are just

forms and things. The immigration people keep writing to me.'

'You haven't even opened most of them. This could be serious, Ruth.'

'It's their standard package, they send them to everyone. I already went through it all. I'm settled here now, they don't even apply.'

He pulled one out of a torn-open packet. It was an application for employment authorization. Fee, thirty-five dollars. There were six or seven other forms in there with it, in varying pale hues.

He said, 'There's stuff here you should have passed to your new employers.'

She took the packet from him.

'I said I'll deal with it,' she told him. There was a noticeable edge in her voice.

They made a fire out in the barbecue in Aidan's tiny back yard. He hadn't used it in at least two summers, and for two winters it had stood out there when he should have cleaned it up and taken it in. The grill was rusted and he had to drain water out of the main part. But when they finally got it going, the paper was consumed quickly and the ashes rose into the air, still glowing like scraps of burning night.

Ruth watched as they were carried upward on the breeze, flaring red and then winking out.

'All I have to do now is believe it's really over,' she said as they went back inside.

'Now I'm taking you out,' Aidan said. 'It's not a celebration, think of it like a ritual. We draw a line under it, we wake up in the morning, we go on.'

She went upstairs to get her coat, but she was gone for longer than he'd expected; not a lot longer, but when she reappeared she'd changed some of her clothes and added a quick dash of makeup. Aidan took this to be an encouraging sign.

As they walked out to his car, she said, 'Where are we going?'

'Just a place I know,' Aidan said.

'Oh, God, Aidan,' she said, 'not another cop bar.'

'It's not a cop bar,' Aidan said, annoyed and not trying too hard to hide it.

'OK,' she said. 'Sorry.'

About halfway into town he said, 'What's so bad about a cop bar, anyway?'

'Nothing,' Ruth said, and looked out of the window.

As they passed under a bridge and the light changed, he could see her reflection. Aidan could have sworn that she was making a throwing-up face.

23

He took her to Downey's, which was about as unlike the cop bar that he'd once taken her to as anything he could imagine. In the cop bar, the lights were so bright that you could hardly see the projection TV and the waitresses wore rubber-soled gym shoes with their uniforms. Downey's was an Irish pub on Front Street with dark wood, green marble, brass rails, and a thousand tiny golden lights picking out all the beams and the angles in the walls and the ceiling. The panelling had been brought over from a Dublin bank, and was deep and rich. The décor included photographs of the Pope and various baseball players, and a lot of old radios and other stuff that made it look as if the staterooms of the Hindenburg had collided with a junk shop. The staff were young, loud and cheerful, and managed the trick of flirting with each other without annoying the customers. It got crowded at nights. If this place didn't raise Ruth's spirits after the day that they'd had, it was unlikely that anywhere would.

They got a table in the dining area, which had padded seating and exposed brick walls.

'All right?' he demanded of Ruth as a waitress went off with their order.

'This is fine,' Ruth said, as if it was almost too obvious a question to merit an answer.

'Oh, good,' Aidan said with exaggerated sarcasm that he didn't really mean. Well, not as much as he was laying it on, anyway. Ruth's reaction had been a heartening sign. There had been a time when she hadn't seemed to care about her surroundings. She'd simply accepted wherever she was put, like furniture.

'I wasn't meaning to insult you,' Ruth said.

The beer arrived. Aidan was big on beer. He'd an empty bottle collection taking up space in his basement that Ruth had said, even in the absence of any other evidence, had been enough to prove to her that here was a man who lived on his own.

Aidan took a long drink, and let out a sigh that turned into a hiccup. He covered his mouth with his hand. Ruth was trying not to laugh into her own drink, and she was spraying it up into her face.

'I shouldn't go back to those cop places anyway,' he said after. 'I left, it's over.'

'Why'd you *really* give it up?'

'Exactly why I told you. Money. The Atlantic City casinos were expanding and they were hiring cops from all over for security. The prospects looked great but we were all like turtles on the beach. Only so many ever make it to the water. I had to face the fact that I'd chosen wrong and I was never going to be management material. I'm too likely to say what I actually think. But if you're in that line and you don't climb the ladder, all you get to do is watch the money. That fascination fades.'

'I thought it might be something more dramatic. You know, like you threw down your badge and walked out.'

He shook his head, and smiled faintly. 'Only in the movies,' he said.

Ruth said, 'Do you miss it?'

'What, the casino?'

'No. Before.'

'Yeah, I miss it. Back then I used to think a private security guard was the lowest form of life. But you never know.'

'No,' Ruth said. 'You never do.'

They shared a contemplative silence for a while. Through the half-open kitchen hatch, Aidan could see occasional sheets of flame rising on the range. It looked as if they were having a refinery explosion in there.

Aidan said, 'Why don't we do a deal? I won't drag you

154

to any more cop bars if you'll wipe the slate and say the hell with Timothy Hagan.'

Ruth raised her glass.

'And the horse he rode in on,' she said.

Their food arrived, Aidan's turkey sandwich and Ruth's seafood chowder. Aidan watched her, and his heart almost sang. It was as if a leech had been removed, and her bloom and colour were returning before his eyes. All in a matter of hours, and after confronting a sight that would have given most people a year of nightmares but which instead seemed set to end a year of hers.

He said, 'Did I tell you I get the kids again next weekend?'

'Well,' she said, with an air of neutrality that seemed diplomatic, 'that's good.'

'Are you sure about that?'

'Of course.'

'I was starting to wonder if there's anything in the way you seem to disappear when they arrive.'

'I don't disappear. I feel awkward with them, I'm not denying that. But you're the one they come to see, not me. That's why I stay out of the way.'

'I'd like them to know you better,' he insisted. 'I'd like us all to do something together next time. Can we do that?'

Aidan sensed that he'd gone about as far as he dared on this for the moment. If she just said no then fine, he'd back off. But he hoped that she wouldn't. She was a private person, he wanted to respect that. She couldn't have lived alone and independently for so long without being anything else. But the urge to bring her more fully into his life was a difficult one to resist. She'd been out there for so long, and life was so short, and when it ended then that was it, that was the person you were. The person that you always intended to be tomorrow counted for nothing.

She said, 'You shouldn't be asking me. You should be asking them.'

'I'm asking you first.'

'Then, yes,' Ruth said. 'Of course.'

Later on in the evening, when they were walking up toward where they'd left the car, she linked his arm.

Aidan said, 'You should have seen this whole area twenty years ago. It was a *lot* different then.'

He saw her glance around. They'd left Front Street and were passing a church and its well-tended graveyard. The gravestones were weathered like half-dissolved lozenges, but the grass was carefully barbered. Some of the tombs had small flags, Stars and Stripes of a size that a child might wave, planted in the ground before the old stones.

She said, 'Was this your area?'

'For a while. It was a serious dump until your hippie entrepreneurs moved in for the low rents and started to set up businesses. There was another old church about three blocks down that way, I don't even know if it's still standing. I remember this fourteen-year-old girl had got hold of a gun and spent the day on the streets trying to sell it for thirty dollars. It got to the end of the day and she hadn't found any takers, so she sat down on the church steps and shot herself with it.'

'That's a sad story.'

'Yeah, but that's not why they still tell it. The bullet didn't go straight through. It tumbled around inside her skull and came out sideways. This cop was running up the steps to her and it took his hat clean off. They all remember his name. But no-one remembers hers.'

'Do you?'

'How would I?' Aidan said. 'I wasn't even there.'

It started to rain as they reached the car. Lightly at first, no summer thunderstorm, but as they set out for home it rained harder. It had eased off by the time they arrived, but it was still enough to wet them as they ran from the car to the house. Hardly a soaking. Once inside, Ruth bent her head and shook the drops from her hair.

They went upstairs. At the door to Aidan's room, she put her hand on his arm.

'You don't have to,' Aidan said.

'I want to.'

The droplets in her hair were still wet and cold. The rest of her wasn't.

24

Next Saturday morning, Aidan drove out alone to collect
his children from their home out in the western suburbs.
They lived there with their mother and the man whom
Aidan still thought of as her new guy, even though it had
been more than five years since she'd remarried. They'd
spent longer with their stepfather than they'd ever spent
with him. The place where they lived was pleasant, better
than Aidan himself could ever have given them, although
he consoled himself by reckoning that some of the parts
of town that he had to pass through to reach it weren't
exactly the best.

Like the street he was driving along now. Big houses in a
long row set back from the street, most of them with canvas
awnings. Many of the houses looked solid, but one didn't
have to stare too hard to see that their timbers were rotting.
One or two of them had been shored-up or even boarded,
and their awnings hung like rags. People sat out front with
nothing better to do than watch the cars go by.

Aidan had long ago given up trying to work out what
had gone wrong. It just had, that was all. It had started
when Jeff was born, it had redoubled when Jeff was four
and Imogen had come along. Angela, his ex, seemed to
respond to motherhood by taking to martyrdom in a big
way. She suffered nothing in silence. Maybe if it hadn't
been for the children they could have carried on, like a
weld that never gets tested. He'd reached a certain point
and then he'd walked out on them. Sometimes when he
was telling the story he lied, said that she'd taken the kids
and gone. Walking out was nothing to be proud of. He'd
known that even then.

For a while he'd been convinced that the fault was all

hers. But looking at her now, and seeing how different was the life that she'd made for them, he wasn't quite so clear. She was happy now. There was a new baby, seven months old; he'd sent them a card and a gift. And if she was happy now, why couldn't she have been happy before? There was only one factor different in the equation, and that was Aidan himself.

Alchemy, was all that he could attribute it to. You changed, and you were changed by, the person you were with. You chose, you hoped. And that was all you could do.

He switched on the radio, and set it searching through the FM stations. It landed on Eagle 106, and he left it there. Lite rock. Everything now was either lite rock or golden oldies. When the lite rock tracks started to turn up on the golden oldies stations, Aidan was going to ask a close friend to shoot him in the head.

Jeff had passed thirteen this year. As far as he was concerned, Aidan was most definitely the King Across the Water. Imogen, having been no more than a baby at the time of the breakup, was more ambivalent and uncertain. There were no tears from *her* when they got ready to go home. At first he'd spent too much on them during his access time, bought them things and annoyed the hell out of Angela, but then he'd grown out of that. Money had been tight for a while anyway. As he'd told Ruth, Aidan had been part of the last police exodus that had been sparked by expansion out in Atlantic City, but it hadn't worked out. A lot of ex-officers had gone out there to work in casino security and some had done well, but the hours were long and the work could be tedious and gruelling. The sixty-five mile commute each way hadn't exactly been a picnic, either.

Something else that hadn't quite worked out.

He made the turn. Maple Street. It looked exactly the way you'd expect a place called Maple Street to be. Modest duplex housing on raised land above street level, all the houses with front porches, all of them two storeys high and surrounded by lawn sloping down to the sidewalk. All neat, all newly painted, always a couple of them for sale. They had gardens at the back, as well.

Aidan had never been inside the house. He'd been invited, but he'd never gone in. Even though there was an armistice of a kind, there was still an outstanding dispute over property that was grinding toward no particular resolution. His falling income had forced him to renegotiate the monthly payments that he made for the children's support, and now in recompense Angela's lawyers were trying to claim a part of the equity in his mother's old house. It didn't matter to them that he lived there; it was an asset, and they wanted a piece. The lawyers wrote each other letters, and he and Angela carefully avoided the subject whenever they met.

He stopped before the house, and checked his watch. Ten minutes ahead of time. He planned to wait in the car until they came out, but when he glanced up they were heading down the driveway already. Jeff leaping the steps two at a time, all awkward with his bat ears and goofy grin, a ringer for those pictures of Aidan at the same age. Imogen with her clean dress and a careful hairdo walking after, carrying the favoured doll of the moment and too dignified to run.

She held it up so that it could see the car. She was talking to it.

The long day stretched ahead.

And Aidan felt his heart lift, unbidden.

25

'This is the main escape route for these two floors,' the fire officer said. Her name was Candy and she was a demon on detail. 'You've got to have access through here at all times.'

'That's usually the case,' Aidan said. 'I'll find out who locked it.'

He made a note on his clipboard, and the fire department's safety officer made a note on hers, and they moved on to the next part of the check.

Another half-hour, Aidan was thinking, and he could go for his break. It wasn't that Candy was bad company. They'd known each other for years. But it was a big and complex building, and the permit checklist could seem endless. He'd tried to dodge and shift it onto Oliver, but Oliver had dodged and it had shifted right back.

He tried not to yawn.

As they were walking down the east stairwell, Candy said, 'If you had to be any female Hollywood star, which one would you choose?'

'Female?' Aidan said. 'You mean like, a woman?'

'It's got to be a woman,' Candy said. 'That's the whole point of the question.'

Aidan considered as they descended between the fourth and the third floors.

'I'd be any lesbian,' he said. 'Then I could keep all the same wardrobe.'

'You can't just say that,' Candy said, checking the free opening of the stairwell doors as they passed. 'You have to pick an actress by name.'

'Clint Eastwood,' Aidan said confidently.

'Come on.'

'No, Clint Eastwood. She's *definitely* a lesbian.'

They found a couple of dead bulbs in the exit signs and another impeded escape route. Candy told him a sick joke about a recent plane crash, and then they went back to the security office and cleared up the paperwork and then she left. Aidan put the necessary dockets into the system and then stuck a magazine in his back pocket and headed out for the coffee shop before anything else could come his way.

Saturday had passed without Ruth's presence. She'd told him on Friday night that she was going to have to work a full day in the bookstore. He and the children had spent most of it around the house, apart from a trip into town for lunch in the food court at Liberty Mall and a visit to the Green Onions comic store for Jeff to buy the latest copy of something called *Sandman*. The store had a minor claim to fame in that it had once been rammed by a United cab that had mounted the sidewalk and taken out the entire window. A passing lawyer had pulled out a camera and then passed around his card. Meanwhile an indigent on the sidewalk was offering to sell his eyewitness story for two dollars to anyone who was interested.

Only in America.

Mostly, the two of them seemed content just to mess around the house when they came to him for the day. They'd read, watch cartoons on TV, go through his record collection with him. Occasionally they'd squabble, and he'd have to break them up. But once he'd realized that they felt more at ease when he didn't make elaborate plans, a lot of the tension went out of their visits. Back in the early days, he'd almost exhausted the guidebook. He'd probably hit rock-bottom when he started taking them to see paintings in churches. He could still remember the time when they'd been confronted by a picture titled Jesus Breaking Bread. Jeff had called it Jesus Breaking Wind and he'd had to hustle them out of the cathedral.

'May I join you?' a voice said. 'It's only for a minute.'

Aidan looked up from his magazine. Gordon Parry was standing over the table.

'Please do,' Aidan said, puzzled.

He was sitting in Spinks' at what he'd thought was going to be a quiet corner table, with a cup of coffee and a corned beef sandwich. It was close to the lunch hour and, thanks to the latest coupon drive, the place was already three-quarters full. Gordon Parry pulled out the chair across from his own. He set down his espresso cup, laid alongside it the lime-green cardboard folder that he'd been carrying, and sat down.

'How's Ruth?' Gordon said.

'Doing fine,' Aidan said warily. 'Getting better.'

'Good. You don't have to tell her I asked. She's living with you now, right?'

'What if she is?'

Gordon Parry opened the folder with an uneasy glance around the restaurant. He drew out a copy of a magazine that had been folded open at an inside story, and he slid it across the table to Aidan. Aidan picked it up and studied it. It was one of those magazines that were always around in racks by checkout desks. Puzzles, diet tips, fashion hints, a few human interest items and a lot of beauty-care ads.

Gordon said, 'I don't know if you've got any influence over her or not. God knows, I never did. But tell her she's got to stop doing this.'

The headline read *Talk To Me, Victim Begs Would-be Killer's Mother*. The one-page article that followed referred to Ruth by her first name only, but gave Hagan's details in full. There was a photograph of a cowering model who clearly wasn't her, being loomed-over by an unseen figure who clearly wasn't anyone.

'I heard all about this,' Aidan said, briefly scanning through. As far as he knew, this was something that Ruth had reluctantly agreed to months ago and which had been in the pipeline for so long that she'd all but forgotten about it. 'She's been trying to find a way to come to terms with what happened, that's all.'

'Well, I wish she'd come to terms with it in some other way. This stuff gets in every supermarket.'

Aidan handed the magazine back. 'What's the problem?' he said. 'You don't even get a mention.'

Well, he thought . . . not by name, anyway.

'And you think that means that no-one's going to know? I found this on the Xerox machine in my department. Listen. My home life couldn't be more shitty if you squeezed it out of a dog, I'm in therapy for the bad dreams I still get, and the last thing I need is to lose any more face around here.'

'I'm sorry, Mr Parry,' Aidan said. 'You did what you did. It really isn't my problem.'

Gordon pointed down at the magazine. 'Are you saying that some part of what happened was *my* fault?'

'No,' Aidan said evenly. 'What I'm saying is that next to Ruth's happiness I couldn't give a flying fart for your standing in the office.'

Gordon's eyes widened slightly. This was clearly not the kind of talk he expected to hear from a building employee who wore a uniform with his name on the pocket. He leaned forward.

'I'll tell you something about that woman, Aidan,' he said, with a quick glance down at Aidan's tag for the information. 'Free advice from one who knows.'

'I don't want it,' Aidan said.

'She's nobody's victim.'

'Hey. Enough.'

'What happened to her, she as good as went looking for . . .'

He stopped then, because Aidan had reached over and dipped his finger in Gordon's coffee and was now flicking the drops at him to make him shut up.

Gordon Parry over-reacted, leaping up and scraping his chair back. Some heads turned.

'Oops,' Aidan said.

Gordon was frantically checking his suit jacket to see if any of the coffee had hit. He looked as if he was trying to shake a wasp out of it.

'Do you know how *long* it takes to get the stains out of this?' he demanded.

'Next time,' Aidan suggested, 'try listening.'

Gordon looked at him, incredulous.

'You're as mad as she is,' he said, as if this was something that was only just beginning to dawn on him.

'That's probably true.'

Gordon seemed to become aware of his surroundings again. The fact of it was that those who'd glanced over were no longer looking, and most of them were from other parts of the building anyway. But he dropped his voice to a lower tone and said, 'Tell her this, then. Tell her it's no problem for me if she just wants to get on with her life. But if she's going to insist on making more waves, then I'm going to have a hard time dissuading Mimi from making some calls.'

'You got her fired, Gordon,' Aidan said. 'What does that leave?'

'It leaves her a resident alien with no steady employment. Think about that one as hard as you like.'

Aidan said, 'Don't forget your magazine.'

Gordon picked it up and stalked off.

Aidan tried to find his place and carry on, but it was pointless. Gordon had messed up his mood, probably for the day. He took a few more bites of his sandwich and abandoned the rest. As he was leaving Spinks' he passed a woman that he recognized as one of Ruth's old co-workers, the only one who'd been in touch with her at all since she'd left.

'Ugly scene?' Jennie said as she went by with a tray.

'Ugly guy,' Aidan said, and went back to work.

26

He might have been too hard on Gordon, he couldn't really be sure. It wasn't in Aidan's nature to be mean, and even when he rose to it with justification he'd be taunted by doubts when the moment had receded. Gordon had been given quite a beating when Hagan had jumped him and taken his swipe card, and a couple more minutes with the bag over his head would have made it a kindness to leave it on. He was supposed to be fully recovered, but it had aged him a little. Part of his face around one eye now had the look of a really good car body repair, the kind that you'd run your hand along and admire when the real point was that you weren't supposed to be able to spot it at all.

But then he thought of Gordon with his hands on Ruth, the two of them on the rug in that big apartment that she'd had, and the man's suffering became a little easier for Aidan to bear.

He was standing in one of the side bays that same afternoon, watching a truck unload some leather furniture for the new East Coast office of an advertising company, when the radio on his hip broke into life and he got the message that there was a phone call, and it was the police, and they wanted him now. Somebody was on her way out to relieve him. The somebody was Janice, one of three women on the security team.

'They're holding on the line for you, Aidan,' she told him when she got there. 'What did you do? It sounds like they finally caught up with you.'

'I don't know,' he said as he handed over the loading bay keys.

'Hey,' she said, 'I hope it isn't bad news.'

Aidan said, 'I'm not expecting any. But I *am* hoping to hear something good about this dead person.'

All the same, he hurried. The first thought into his mind had been for the children. When he reached the office, Joe was on the phone at the desk but he pointed to one of the others that was lying off the hook.

Aidan picked it up and, feeling like a man about to step through a doorway where there might equally be a solid floor or a long fall on the other side, said, 'This is Aidan Kincannon.'

'It's Tom Diaz,' the voice at the other end of the line said. 'I've got Ruth here. Can you get away for a couple of hours?'

'What's wrong?'

'She's fine, but she needs someone to take her home. She also needs some serious talking-to and I don't think she'll take it from me.'

'What's she done?'

'Come see.'

The address that he was given was south of Market Street and not too far from the middle of town. A hotel, in an area of several city squares where the hotels didn't have the best of reputations. Walk on through, and you'd never even know it; you'd see tidy-looking streets with antique shops and picture framers and dry-cleaning services. Nothing too outrageous there. But ask anyone who knew the city for the location of a fleabag hotel or two with some notoriety, and they'd send you straight to it.

What could Ruth have been doing there? Perhaps she'd had an accident. But judging from the tone of Tom Diaz, Aidan didn't think so. He cleared it with his supervisor, threw a jacket on over his uniform, and headed out to see what might lie behind the call.

The hotel had been half-grand, once. Now it looked like a set from a Vincent Price movie. All the gilt was under dust, all the high ceilings seemed to gather and trap the gloom. Aidan was directed upstairs by a desk man in stubble and a ponytail who clearly didn't appreciate the impact on business of police cruisers on the sidewalk outside.

He travelled up in a cage elevator that made a noise like a train in a mine. The upper corridors were tall and narrow and even gloomier than the foyer. Windowless, they had chandeliers that cast a sick-looking light. The carpet didn't look too bad. Until one really looked.

All of the doors were firmly closed, except for a couple some way ahead. Outside one of these, two uniformed patrolmen were conversing and there was a steady clamour of more people beyond. Aidan couldn't tell how many from the sound alone. Eight, maybe a dozen. A young detective emerged with his ID out on his coat and headed down toward Aidan, sliding on past with a murmured excuse-me. When Aidan was close enough to see into the room he saw that Ruth was in there, seated on the bed. Somebody was sitting next to her, others were standing around and talking over her head. She glanced up, and her eyes met his.

'Ruth?' he said.

But Tom Diaz was pulling him along, past the open doorway and toward the next room down the corridor.

'In a minute,' Tom Diaz said.

They went inside. This room was pretty much like the last, only bigger; they had a connecting door between them, but it wasn't open. Two lab technicians were dismantling a volume of monitoring and recording equipment that wouldn't have disgraced a field intelligence unit in Vietnam. Silver-grey cases were stacked by the door, ready to go. Others lay open, with so many cables and wires that they were suggestive of unfinished transplant surgery.

Something lay on the table, bagged and tagged.

'Do you recognize this?' Diaz said.

Aidan recognized it. It was the pearl-handled revolver.

'I understand she bought it in a pawnshop,' he said.

'It isn't registered.'

'I think she's got a licence,' Aidan said, but without too much hope.

168

'Not for this, she hasn't. God Almighty, Aidan, what does she think she's doing?'

'I don't know. You're the one who made the call.'

'Do you recognize the setup here?'

Aidan looked around. The camera that was being lifted back into its case was the probe kind, a little fisheye lens on a stalk that could be pushed through a hole in a wall and still give a view of the entire room on the other side.

'Yeah,' he said. 'You've got some kind of entrapment going.'

'We had a complaint,' Tom Diaz explained. 'From a group of fucking *pimps*, no less. They all got together and made it formal.'

'A complaint over what?'

'The story was about some woman who was picking up boys on the streets. She'd take them to a hotel and pay cash for a room. Once they were inside she'd lock the door and the next thing the kid knows, he's got a gun in his ear and he's looking at a photograph. Guess of who.'

Aidan didn't have to guess. 'Hagan's dead,' he said. 'What's the matter with her?'

'Dead, but he won't lie down. She knows it in her head, but that's not enough. He's haunting her now.'

Aidan pulled out the dressing-table chair and sat, helplessly.

'She saw the body,' he said. 'What more can I do?'

'I know all about that little excursion, too,' Tom Diaz told him. 'I can't keep this one so quiet, Aidan. There's going to be follow-up.'

'I'll try to explain it to her.'

'Good luck.'

Aidan looked up at Diaz.

'Can I take her now?' he said.

He was half-expecting Diaz to shake his head and to find that, while they'd been talking, Ruth had already been walked out to the cars and was on her way across town. But the approach on this seemed to be one of taking a low profile and letting the paperwork lead. Diaz gestured toward the connecting door, and as Aidan started to move Diaz said to him, 'Start by explaining the concept of wasting one's time. Doesn't she even realize that male prostitutes do it for guys?'

Ruth was signing some forms. She was calm, and she showed no emotion. Only her eyes were scared, and only Aidan looked into those. Somebody inside one of the other rooms was shouting as he led her toward the elevator.

As he was driving her home, she said, 'I wouldn't blame you if you decided to throw me out.'

Aidan let it sit for a while.

'I'm not going to,' he said.

27

At home, that night, Aidan lay on his bed and watched TV on the portable in his room for a while after midnight. But he couldn't concentrate, even on that. So he aimed the clicker and switched it off and lay back. He stared at the patterns on his ceiling in the dark.

After a while, he heard the familiar creak of the upper-landing floorboard. He didn't move. There was the suspense of anticipation, and then the slightest of changes in the room as his door opened and another presence entered it.

A shadow moved.

She climbed into the bed again and snuggled up against him, contritely, like a small animal for warmth.

'You can't keep doing this, Ruth,' he said. 'It's not fair to me. You crawl in here and say sorry, then it's all supposed to be fine again.'

She froze up at the implied rejection, and then she moved to climb out again. But he caught hold of her.

'Don't go,' he said. 'Talk to me.'

'You don't want to hear sorry,' Ruth said in the darkness. 'That's all I've got that I can say.'

'Why did you lie?'

'I didn't lie. I know he's supposed to be dead. I want it to be over. But him being gone doesn't mean it's the end.'

'What does it matter?'

'It matters.'

'Why?' Aidan said, bewildered. 'Do you think he's going to come back? Or is it something else? I mean, do you think you ought to understand his motives, or something? Is that it? Don't bother. He was past forgiveness, Ruth. Don't waste your life.'

'I don't know what I want,' Ruth said.

There was silence for a while. Then he said, 'Why did you avoid the kids again at the weekend?'

'I didn't avoid them,' Ruth said. 'I had to work.'

'I phoned the bookstore on the day to find out what time you'd be home. They weren't even expecting you.'

'Oh,' Ruth said.

'Just oh? What happened to that entire conversation we had? Was *any* part of it genuine? I wouldn't ever want to push you into anything that you don't want to do. But don't tell me one thing when you're thinking something else.'

'I can't talk to children,' she said, her voice sounding remote in the darkness. 'I don't know how.'

'So here was your chance to get some practice. They're not some other species. And it's not entirely inconceivable that you could still have one of your own.'

She lifted herself slightly, and looked down on him. A hint of moonlight from the window reflected on the wet part of her eye in the darkness.

'I can't, Aidan,' she said.

'What do you mean?'

'I can't.'

'You're not that old.'

She drew away from him. Not completely, but enough to create a space between them.

'It has nothing to do with age,' she said. 'It's just not going to happen.'

'Tell me,' he said.

And then, after a moment in which nothing was said and nothing stirred, 'Tell me, Ruth.'

When she spoke again her voice was flat, expressing nothing. 'It's because of a termination I had when I lived in New York,' she said. 'For what seemed like all the best reasons. I was young, I wasn't ready, my career was taking off, I'd have plenty more chances. Five days after the procedure I woke up and I thought, my God I've wet the bed. But I hadn't wet the bed. I was bleeding. I had to go back into hospital for more than a week, and then that was it. The damage was fixed, and so was I. No-one ever came straight out and told me I'd just thrown away the only chance I was ever going to have, but that was what I'd done.'

'Was that why you moved out of New York?'

'The relationship broke up and I couldn't bear to stay. It hits you harder than you could ever believe. You wouldn't think it could hurt, being told you can't ever have something that you didn't even want yet. But it does.'

Aidan didn't know what to say. He tried to think of something helpful, something consoling. But he couldn't.

'I tried all kinds of counselling,' Ruth went on. 'There was a woman in Greenwich Village told me that as time went by I'd probably start to imagine the baby as a real grown-up person, and that I shouldn't turn away from that. Just let it happen, give him a name, talk to him. She was right, that's what I did. I used to be able to close my eyes and see him. Right up until not so long ago. I can't do it now.' She took a deep breath, and sighed. 'So that's another thing he's taken from me.'

'Come out with us next weekend,' Aidan said.

'No,' she said.

She stayed for a while longer.

Then she climbed out of his bed and, without another word, went back to her own.

28

The next morning, there was a near-silence over breakfast. Aidan tried to keep the tone light, but Ruth was just going through the motions. It was clear that nothing he could say was going to make any difference to the overall mood. She answered when he spoke to her. She was neutral and polite. But she brought nothing to the conversation. She stared at the wall for most of the time and then, when she was done, she got up from the table and went to get herself ready for work.

Aidan wondered what he was going to do with her. Every time he thought they'd sorted something out, she'd go off and do something that went against all that had been said. It was like having a junkie in the house, someone desperately full of good intentions but still stealing one's money and shooting up in some dark corner when no-one was looking.

But junkies had people who loved and feared for them, too. And at least an addict could have been made to bare her arms to show healing scars and her skin free of new tracks. With Ruth, there were no such signs. The destructiveness of Ruth's pain brought with it no visible stigmata.

When she'd gone out, he sat alone. The way that he was feeling at the moment, it was as if Ruth were some strange creature that he'd fallen for and managed to capture. But the chances of a happy ending seemed slim. It seemed more likely that, were he to persist, she'd blindly tear him apart as he tried to embrace her.

Was it wise to go on?

Was the choice even his?

He picked up the phone and called the security office and made an arrangement to take the morning off. He cited personal reasons. By then it was after nine, and after he'd rung off he was able to make another call to fix up the appointment that he'd need.

Ruth would get forty-five minutes for lunch. He didn't let her know that he was going to be there, but at twelve-thirty he was waiting outside the building.

It could only be a matter of time before this row had to come down. They'd built a new Convention Center north of the Terminal Market and now the entire area was being thoroughly, almost savagely redeveloped. About a score of the old businesses still hung on, surrounded by dust and grit and construction sand. There were big cranes overhead, blasted-out pits where buildings had once been across the street, demolition workers' trailers and temporary fencing, a hard-hat area for half a mile around. And there they still managed to stand, in the midst of it all: Anthony's Barber Shop. The Baltimore Shoe Service. The All-X Triple-Treat Adult Cinema.

And the peepshow where Ruth worked over the shop.

It had signs in the window framed by coloured bulbs like a carnival sideshow. One of them read WOMEN ARE WELCOME. Hung out over the sidewalk was a board for Visa and MasterCard, and below that a truck's side-mirror had been bolted to the doorframe to give a view of the street to anyone just inside. The windows of the data transcription agency on the second floor and above were, by contrast, utterly anonymous. They were rented to a separate company, and all that they shared was the address.

Aidan checked the time. He felt slightly nervous, slightly insecure. He reckoned that it wasn't a sensation that he'd care to get used to. He hadn't been so formlessly anxious since dressing up on the night of the ball. Three hours of agony, and a huge bill for suit hire, and barely a word with the one person that he'd gone along hoping to see.

Minutes passed, and nobody seemed to be coming out. A couple of dozen yards along, an olive-skinned boy of about nine years old stood at a public phone, repeatedly trying to make a call while his mother sat watching from a doorway with a smaller child in a pushchair.

Two women emerged, a young one and an older. A United Parcels truck brought a delivery.

Then Ruth.

She was blinking in the sunlight, and it was a moment before she registered her surprise at seeing him. His unexpected presence made her falter, almost defensively.

'I want to talk,' he said.

'What's so urgent?'

'Come on, I know you don't get much time.'

They walked across the street toward the Reading Terminal Market, where Ruth – and just about everybody else who worked within reach – went every day for lunch. Dust blew through, like in a desert. Big dumper trucks, as they passed, raised a blinding haze in the air.

Taken at first look, the Market was a huge mass of people in an old train shed. Closer inspection didn't alter the impression. The cast-iron structure covered an entire city square from Twelfth Street going east and, with the exception of a few modern-looking air ducts hacked into its sides, had changed little in the previous hundred years. Stalls inside sold spices, fresh fruit, cured meat, flowers, live crabs and lobsters with their claws taped for safety, fresh ground coffee and musty old paperbacks. One entire corner was given over to Amish merchants who brought in their goods from Pennsylvania Dutch Country and whose traditional dress intensified the feeling of being in some weird way station outside of normal time and space.

Aidan found them a couple of seats at Pearl's Oyster Bar on the Twelfth Street side. It consisted of a long, U-shaped counter and some window space with an open-sided kitchen. A wooden ship's figurehead towered above the cashier's stool. Ruth's pale skin was tinged green by the neon of the window sign above their table. The first time that Aidan had ever become aware of Ruth, really aware, her hair had been the colour of sun-lightened hay. He could remember the moment. He'd been standing behind her in the elevator. Her hair had been up then, and the soft down in the nape of her neck had caught his eye and he'd been beset with an overpowering feeling of certainty and longing. They'd talked about it since and she'd called it her deaf, dumb, and blond phase. Since then she'd let it go to its natural, much darker colour.

'I spent half an hour getting some advice from a lawyer this morning,' Aidan explained.

'I can get a lawyer of my own,' Ruth said.

'Have you spoken to one yet?' he said, being fairly sure that she hadn't.

She shook her head.

'I don't think you've grasped the situation, Ruth,' Aidan said. 'You know what the maximum penalty is for the illegal purchase of a firearm? It's five years in jail and a five-thousand-dollar fine. Just because it was easy doesn't mean it wasn't wrong.'

She looked disbelieving.

'Is that what I'm likely to get?' she said.

'They rarely enforce it. What you'll probably get is a lighter penalty and then be deported. Have you thought about that?'

She took this in slowly. She seemed to be stunned. If anything, this seemed to be worse news than the prospect of jail.

'Deported to where?' she said.

'Back to where you came from.'

'But I live *here*. It's home. I don't have anywhere else now.'

'But you're not a citizen,' Aidan said. 'I checked out your position, Ruth, and to put it mildly, it's a mess. You came in as an employee of an international organization, but then you switched jobs and cities without altering your status. You had more than the minimum seven years' residence. You could have made the change at any time.'

'I did all that. I was late, but I did it. Everything was going through the system. I thought I was OK.'

'You would have been. But now you've got a firearms

offence against you. As soon as they get a conviction, you get a hearing. After the hearing, then you're almost certainly out.'

She seemed dismayed.

'What am I going to do?' she said.

'Do you want to go back?'

'No. I mean . . . there's no place for me there now. I let everything go.' She started to panic, and her voice began to rise. 'God Almighty, Aidan,' she said. 'I may not have much here, but it's where my home is. I lost everything else. Am I going to lose this as well?'

He covered her hand with his and held it, firmly. 'There is a way around it,' he said. 'You're going to have to think about this very hard.'

She looked at him, ready to grab for any lifeline. 'What do I have to do?'

'You and I get married.'

The look became a stare. But at least it wasn't a suspicious stare. It was more of a smacked-in-the-face-with-something-awesome stare.

Aidan said, 'It doesn't have to be me. It could be any eligible male US citizen. But I'd be able to apply for waivers and then for resident status on your behalf. I know you don't love me, Ruth, and this isn't some angle I've come up with. I wouldn't do it for anyone else. But I'd do it for you.'

'Married?' Ruth said bleakly, as if that was the only word out of any of it that she'd taken in.

'Don't answer right now, because I know what you'll say. Think about it. You had the life that you chose, but you lost that. You're on the point of losing everything else as well. You could do worse than me, Ruth. If there's any way it can be done, I think I can make you happy.' He got to his feet. 'That's all I'm going to say.'

And then he left her there, alone, to think it over.

In a large house on the fringe of the area known as the Garden District of New Orleans, a woman named Theresa McCall sat by the kitchen table and turned the pages of a

178

magazine. It had been brought in by the three-days-a-week maid to read during her morning break, and then left in the newspaper stack to be tied up with string and put out for collection. Theresa always rescued the maid's magazines and read them when she was alone. She could easily have afforded her own. But that wasn't a McCall kind of a thing to do.

Theresa wasn't a snob. Not a conscious one, anyway. But the idea of laying down money in public for housewives' mind-candy would never have occurred to her. Undignified, perhaps. Not something she'd care to see herself doing. Whereas raiding this stuff out of the garbage caused her no problems at all.

The maid got the magazines second-hand from her sister, who filled in all the word-puzzles and usually filled them in wrong. Sometimes she cut out the recipes, as well. Theresa wasn't sure why, but sometimes when she saw the badly formed letters and the square holes in the pages she felt a twinge of something that was an odd mixture of disdain, pity and – hardest of all to explain – envy. The reason for the envy was something that she couldn't begin to pin down. She'd never actually met the maid's sister, but from what she could tell the woman was dirt-poor and hardworking. Theresa had never worked at a job in her life and, being widowed and buoyed up by insurance capital and a steady investment income, she wasn't about to start. Mostly, she felt that her own life was settled. What was to envy?

Only sometimes, at her lowest points, did she feel that there might be something at her life's heart that felt suspiciously like a void. To think so little, to tax one's mind even less . . . to be dumb and to be happy, just like something in a zoo.

But she went to church more than most, she did believe in God. There was no void. There was not.

She looked at her horoscope. Romance and surprises ahead. Then she looked back to the human interest story on the page that preceded it. She'd read that twice already, and it had hit home just a little too hard.

Today, she was starting to feel, might just turn out to be one of those low spots.

There was a rush of water through one of the kitchen's walls. All of the pipework from upstairs came down through here, and when the shower was running it sounded like a downpour. Unused to there being anyone in the house along with her, Theresa instinctively glanced out through the kitchen window. The sky was heavy, but there was no rain. It hadn't rained in weeks, and the humidity outside was getting hard to bear. The garden was in full flower but the grass was dried-out and burned, and it was as if just a little of the colour had been pulled out of everything. The light in Louisiana was like nowhere else that she knew. A strange, zinc-and-pastel kind of light. At its brightest, it was the brightness of a pearl.

Now she could hear him moving around.

He'd said that his name was Christopher, but she was no longer so sure. A couple of times when she'd said his name when speaking to him, he hadn't responded to the sound of it straightaway. He'd apologized, and said that his thoughts had been elsewhere. Theresa's first feelings of unease had begun around then.

Prior to that, of course, she'd been like a duck on helium; high as a kite, quacking happily, light in the head and probably making no sense. She'd met him at some social event out at Loyola University, something connected with the library. He'd been escorting someone else. Someone had told her that he was recently arrived back in town and that he seemed to be networking like crazy, sleeping on floors and being careful not to take advantage of anyone or to wear out his welcome. He was said to be a research student of some kind, but no-one quite knew what he was supposed to be researching.

She'd seen him again, in someone else's company at the Women's Club, and it was there that she'd made him an offer of accommodation should he ever need it.

He'd been on her doorstep the next day.

That had been five weeks ago and, after the first few

days, their relationship had become intense. But it was the kind of intensity, she was coming to realize, that developed between mothers and the sons that track them down after decades apart. He was, after all, barely half her age.

She went through to the laundry room which connected the house to the garage, and she replaced the magazine somewhere in the middle of the newspaper stack. Then she went upstairs. The house was big, but it wasn't quite a mansion. Four bedrooms, two bathrooms. He'd emerged from the shower into the master bedroom, and he was drying off.

'Did I hear the phone ring?' he said, half-looking back over his shoulder at her. His skin was reddened and smooth and his hair was in dark spikes. There was a light spray of freckling across his shoulders. The towel was one of her biggest, and he had it slung around him like a toga. He was standing in front of the dressing-table mirror and he was using one corner of the towel to dry out his ears.

She said, 'Were you expecting someone to call?'

'Who knows I'm here?' He looked back again and caught her eye and grinned, as if he'd trapped her into giving something away.

'Nobody knows,' he said reassuringly. And then he said, 'But it worries you, doesn't it?'

'The phone didn't ring,' Theresa said. It was true, she had tried at first to keep their liaison totally secret. But there was the maid, and then there were the neighbours . . . She said, 'I'm not ashamed of us. But I *do* have friends in this town who wouldn't know how to handle it.'

'Why give them the problem?' he agreed.

'Exactly,' she said, and she sat on the bed as he screwed up the towel and slung it in the general direction of the laundry basket. She found that she was trying to avoid looking at him directly as she said, 'What are you doing today?'

'I have to find one of those little photo booths and get some pictures,' he said. 'Everybody wants to see ID with

181

a picture on it these days.' He looked at her with a faintly hopeful expression. 'I don't suppose I could give this as a mailing address?'

'Well,' she began, 'I . . .'

'No,' he said, 'you're right. I'll find a way around it. No problem.'

Now that he had his shorts on, she felt less awkward. She watched him for a while as he continued to dress.

And then she said, 'What do you want out of life, Christopher? At the end of the day?'

'Any day in particular?'

'All of them.'

He thought for a while, and then shrugged.

'I don't know,' he said. 'What does anybody want?'

And Theresa couldn't answer because she didn't know, either. All that she suspected was that it was something different for everybody. And as to what it might be for her . . . she knew that least of all, she was starting to realize now.

Something else she suspected. She suspected that he was deeper than he made himself out to be.

'Can I use this hairbrush?' he said.

Something in her moved. She didn't want him to.

'Of course,' she said.

As he turned away from her and began to brush back his hair with quick, hard strokes, Theresa said, 'I'm going to have to go away for a while.'

'When?'

'Very soon.'

'You want me to house-sit? It's no problem.'

'No, Christopher,' she said, 'I don't want you to house-sit.'

There was a moment's pause.

'You want me to go,' he said.

Now that it was out, she felt suddenly guilty. She said quickly, 'I'll pay for you to go into a hotel. I don't want to see you sleeping on anyone's floor.'

He turned to face her. 'You don't have to pay for me

to do anything, Theresa,' he said, quite gently. 'I didn't come here because I wanted your money.'

'I'm sorry. That's not how I meant it to sound. But you knew it was going to have to end sometime, didn't you?'

'I knew it was going to end,' he said. 'It always ends. I just didn't think it was going to be today.'

'Are you upset?'

'Of course I'm upset.'

'Are you angry?'

'No.'

He laid down the brush. Theresa said, 'Look, I know you're not well off right now. It's nothing to be ashamed of. Would a thousand dollars be enough to keep you going?'

'I appreciate the thought,' he said, 'but it isn't necessary.'

'Now I think I've offended you,' she said. 'I'm making a terrible job of this.'

'Hey,' he said, and he walked over to her barefoot. She got to her feet, uncertain, and he put his arms around her and gave her a big, enfolding hug.

He said, 'I've been happier with you than I've been in a long, long time. Nothing can ever take that away.'

'Me, too,' she said.

'Do you want me to go today?'

She didn't reply. She tried to, but instead she found that she burst into tears.

'What's the matter?' he said.

'I don't *want* you to go at all.'

'Come on,' he said. 'Be brave. Finish what you've started.'

He broke off the embrace, and wiped the tears from her face with the edge of his hand. They smeared on her cheeks, and she tried to tidy herself up with her sleeve. She felt like a complete mess.

He said, 'You go downstairs and make us some coffee. I'll be right behind you.'

She walked out of the bedroom and toward the stairs, still dabbing at her eyes. She could hardly believe that he'd made it so easy for her, and yet he'd still managed to make her feel that their relationship mattered. So understanding. Along with her relief, there was a hint of disappointment that what they'd had was going to slip away so easily. It wasn't that she wanted it to leave scars. But some kind of change, some kind of mark to remember it by . . . was that so much to ask?

Which was the question in her mind as something hit her hard from behind and pitched her forward. For a long moment she was flying, arms outstretched in terror, and then she struck and rolled all the way down to the foot of the stairs. She could have counted every one of them. The hallway floor at the bottom was of waxed woodblock, and she landed flat on her back and hit that hardest of all and felt every ounce of breath suddenly explode out of her.

Theresa lay, gaping up at the ceiling like a landed fish.

She couldn't draw breath again. She could taste blood or something like blood, vile and sour, but she couldn't draw breath.

He came down after her. She saw him descending, saw him reach to roll her over onto her face and her shoulder screamed; but it was the kind of scream that only she could hear, and he rolled her over anyway and she almost fainted.

She saw him take a lamp from a hallway table and jerk the flex from it, and then he used the wire to lash her arms behind her from the thumbs all the way up to her elbows. Her arms were afire and felt weak, and she couldn't move her fingers.

'Don't call out,' he said. 'You'll be amazed at how distressed I'll get if you make a noise.'

And then he left her. She could hear him moving back up the stairs, quickly but in no desperate hurry. She gagged and rasped again a couple of times and then, with desperate gratitude, she beat the invisible barrier and managed to suck in one halting breath.

Another followed. The blood roared in her ears, but she was breathing again.

He was up there for a while. Theresa couldn't move.

Her arms were locked behind her, and it was as if she'd been trussed like a bird for the oven. After a while she could hear something so familiar but so odd in its context that it took her a while to place what it was. It seemed absurd.

He was vacuuming.

A few minutes later he came downstairs, carrying the sheets from the bed in a bundled armload. Stepping over her, he went on through the house and she heard the door to the laundry room open and close. He came back a few minutes later, and crouched beside her.

'How are we doing?' he said pleasantly.

'You pushed me down the stairs!' she said. It sounded childish and petulant, but there was nothing in her emotional armoury that could possibly match the occasion.

He said, 'I didn't start this process, Theresa, you did. Don't complain about it now.'

Somebody was coming to the door.

Theresa felt her heart leap in hope and she opened her mouth to shout, but the boy placed his hand over her nose and mouth and pinched her nostrils shut. She tried to shake her head, but his pinch-grip was firm.

She could see the vague shape of the person, through the opal-grey etched glass of the front door. She was close to blacking out.

She heard the flap of the mailbox outside on the porch, and saw the figure turn away and fade.

Too late in the day for the mailman. Advertising flyers, probably. Or coupons for the local stores.

He let go, leaving her gasping. Then he went back upstairs and when he reappeared, he was bringing down his luggage one-handed and wiping everything down with one of her washcloths as he went along. She realized then what he was doing.

He was removing all traces of himself from the house.

He stepped over her again. Theresa heard the opening of the door to the laundry room and then the further, fainter door through into the garage. One of the car doors opened, and then it slammed. Please, God, she thought. Let him just take the car and go. Please. Let him start it up and take it and leave me lying right here.

But he came back for her, and helped her to her feet.

'Come on, you old bag,' he said, and started to walk her down toward the garage.

'What did you just call me?'

'I'm sorry,' he said, 'that just slipped out. Will you be able to drive?'

'You've broken my arms!'

'That's too bad. Look on the bright side, I won't have to keep you tied up.'

He walked her through the laundry room, steadying her over the one downward step. Her knees almost went as her feet hit the floor. The big washing machine was churning away, sheets tumbling in the suds behind the little round window. She could feel the heat and the humidity rising as they went through into the garage, to where the air-conditioning didn't extend. It was a two-car garage, but she only ran the one. The door to her white Mercedes stood open and he helped her into the back where she lay, face-down and trembling, across the seat. A tear dripped onto the leather and ran cold under her cheek. The numbing shock of her fall was starting to wear off and an ache, a deep ache without hope of relief, was beginning to spread through her bones. He'd left her again now, and when he returned he threw her coat and her bag into the car with her and slammed the door.

She knew that he'd opened up the garage by the light that was falling onto her face. She felt the car start up, saw the shadows move. He stopped the car outside and went back to close the doors.

'You want to sit up?' he said as he got back in behind the wheel. 'I can sit you up if that's what you'd prefer.'

'I need a hospital,' she said. Her voice sounded scratchy and her breath came back into her face from against the leather, making her reddened eyes smart even more. She closed them, squeezing out another hot tear.

'You're probably right,' he said as he checked in both directions before making the turn out into the street.

'Well, why aren't you taking me to one?'

The car bounced, almost bottomed-out, and twin lances of pain shot from her wrists to her shoulders. The streets were a mess around here, all consisting of baked, cracked asphalt with concrete sidewalks that had buckled and shifted like tectonic plates. The light coming into the car was the brilliant filigree of sunlight through overhanging trees, and she guessed that they were pulling out onto St Charles Avenue. St Charles had real mansions. Mansions with porches, mansions with cupolas, mansions standing with only the tiniest strips of land to surround them and only yards back from the street. Some of the porches had swings where the owners could sit and watch the passing stream of cars heading into and out of the middle of town.

Was anyone watching her now?

'You know,' he said, 'there were all kinds of ways that this could have gone. You could have been the one who saved me from hell. Wouldn't that have been something?'

'You're demented,' she said miserably, not even making an attempt to humour him.

'I'm worse than demented,' he said. 'I know exactly what I'm doing.'

The pain in her wrists intensified as they began to swell. She tried to shut it out of her mind, but she only succeeded in putting herself at a slight distance so that it hurt no less but it simmered rather than boiled. Her skin felt stretched and numb. But at the core of her limbs were white-hot rivers.

She didn't know how much time passed. Probably no more than about ten minutes which, assuming that he was heading away from the middle of town, would put them somewhere around Carrolton and the I-10. She'd heard a streetcar bell, but that had been some way back. The air in the car had cooled and freshened now. Theresa thought that she wanted to die. But almost as soon as the thought had formed, she knew that she didn't. She didn't want to die at all, not today. And not ever, if it could possibly be arranged.

After that first ten minutes, they stopped somewhere.

Surely somebody's going to look in the car now, she thought. Somebody must. With all the stop-start of the traffic, some van or a bus or some similar vehicle must surely draw in alongside and, human nature being what it was, they'd take a peek. Even if it was only out of envy of the Mercedes; she didn't care about the reasons as long as they looked and saw her lying there. Once they saw her, they'd have to know that something was wrong.

Without saying anything, he turned off the engine and got out of the car and left her there. She heard the sound of the electric door locks, engaging all at once.

Theresa started to wriggle her way upright. Without the use of her hands it seemed almost impossible, but she pushed her face into the seat and worked her way up an inch at a time. They were in the parking lot of a shopping plaza, she saw as her face came up level with the window. It was built around a Winn Dixie supermarket with a few satellite businesses, including a Baskin Robbins and an Eckerd Drugs. There were very few cars, and these were all lined up close to the buildings and some distance away.

The interior of the Mercedes was starting to get warm again already. The summer air in New Orleans could strike like engine heat. Theresa had her shoulder against the door. She lifted and flopped, gaining an inch or so every time. One arm felt useless, the other was mere torture.

Turning, she hooked a finger in the door catch. She was sure that she felt bones grate as she pulled. Central locking with the key set the car's alarm, and opening the door from inside would trigger it. It was a safety feature. It sure as hell ought to get her some attention.

Even before the door was open, the howler set off. It was the sweetest, crudest music she'd ever heard.

It howled for one second. Then his key in the lock shut it down.

'I got you some painkillers,' he said, leaning in

through the doorway. 'Now tell me I don't show you any consideration.'

Theresa was in a daze. No-one came running.

When he'd opened up the car he sat her upright and she cried out as her weight rested back on her bound-up arms. He leaned her forward and looked at her hands, and seemed to decide that he could release her without much risk. This ought to be good news, she knew, but somehow she could only receive it with dread. Carefully, he moved her hands around and laid them in her lap. They stayed where they were put.

From the paper bag that he'd brought back with him, he took a white plastic container and shook four tablets out of it and into his hand.

'Why are you doing this?' Theresa said as she watched, but he took no notice of the question.

'I'm sorry,' he said. 'I forgot to get you anything to drink. You'll have to swallow them dry.'

'I can't.'

'Try.'

She did her best to choke them down. She didn't recognize where they were. There must have been scores of plazas like this throughout the outskirts of the city; hundreds, even. Doing small business, all the big traffic pouring by. Beyond the edge of the parking lot and across the boulevard, Theresa could see a roadside produce stall that had been set out under umbrellas in the shade of a big oak tree. They were selling creole tomatoes, fresh white corn, and peaches, all out of the back of a van. Too far away to call to, too remote for any appeal. They'd handwritten signs on the roof and set out all along the sidewalk, and the entire arrangement looked like a travelling show pitched by the roadside. In the middle of it all, a black child of about ten years old sat on a folding canvas chair and fanned herself.

And right in that moment, half-believing that it was one of the last sights that she might ever see, Theresa looked on the light and the shade, and the colours of the fruit, and the way the canvas hung, and the slow motion of the lazily moving fan, and thought that it was possibly the most heartbreakingly beautiful sight that she'd ever witnessed.

He told her, 'We'll be stopping again in a while. I'll try to get you coffee or something then.'

He held her by the shoulders and lowered her onto the back seat, and then he part-covered her with a rug even though the car was stifling again. One of the big tablets lay unswallowed on her tongue. She'd almost no saliva and so it continued to lie there, bitter and undissolved.

They drove on. They were out on the highway, maybe the causeway; jointed concrete sections were going under the wheels in a steady beat. The effect was almost hypnotic. She didn't exactly doze, but she lay there in a stupor. The day rolled by and her thoughts fizzled out and became one long, empty, static-like buzz. When she whimpered, he switched the radio on and turned it up loud.

It took her a long time to realize, at some point along the way, that the car had stopped moving and she was alone in it again.

She looked up. She could see the heavy, lowering sky through the window. She saw a Frisbee slice across it.

Slowly, she raised herself to see.

The car was on the forecourt of a general store, on what appeared to be a country road in the middle of nowhere. The frontage of the building was long and low and painted a kind of drab green, and there were a couple of Exxon pumps out in front. Over by the entrance doors there was a pregnant woman in rubber flip-flop sandals, wearing a red T-shirt and a ponytail. She was holding a small child by the hand and exchanging pleasantries with an older black man in a baseball cap who was climbing into a battered Toyota pickup.

Another child was standing only a few feet from the car, and he was looking at her.

He was holding his Frisbee, one of the moonlight, glow-in-the-dark models. Their eyes met. Theresa tried to call for help. Her lips moved but no sound came out.

The child was riveted and pale, eyes wide as he backed away. Then he turned and ran, and then Theresa knew that it was hopeless. From where he stood he must have looked like some terrible, pale, pain-racked witch, mouthing silently through the windshield.

She started to beat her head against the door glass.

When the young man came back from out of the store, she was sitting with her forehead against the window.

'Hot chocolate and doughnuts,' he said. 'I brought a selection. I'll let you have first pick.'

He gave her some more of the painkillers, and helped her to get them down with a few sips of the chocolate. It was scalding. Then she obediently tried to chomp down some of the food, but it tasted like cardboard and stuck in her mouth.

'Better?' he said brightly. He was holding her up with his arm around her shoulders.

She shook her head.

'Don't be ungrateful, now,' he warned, and she could tell that it wasn't a joke.

She said, 'You're the boy in the magazine, aren't you?'

His expression didn't change, but everything seemed to skip a beat.

'What magazine?' he said.

So, haltingly, she told him about the story that she'd read. The human interest story. One of those things that happened to other people.

She said, 'I read it and I thought, Well, I'm luckier than her.'

Theresa's body began to shake with sobs. He held her, almost tenderly.

'Hey,' he said soothingly. 'There, now.'

Gently, he laid her back down on the seat and then went around and got in behind the wheel. Theresa felt slow-witted and sick, the chocolate and doughnut lying uneasy in the pit of her stomach like a pint of oil and a stone. The car moved off and she closed her eyes, and again time started to slide. She was vaguely aware of him making several stops over the next hour or so, leaving her locked in the car; every time she formed the intention of raising herself and making another escape bid, and every time he returned before any of the thoughts had been translated into action.

She could guess what he was doing. He was stopping at places so that he could look for a copy of the magazine.

She did sleep. She must have. Because suddenly he was shaking her by the sleeve, reaching back from the driving seat without taking his eyes off the road and saying, 'You can sit up, now. We're nearly there.'

'I can't sit up,' she said.

They rolled to a halt and, after getting out of the car and being away from it for a few minutes, he came back and opened the door and reached to help her out.

It hit her again, that engine-heat atmosphere. So thick with humidity that one almost had to drink the oxygen out of it. Her head swam and she wanted to faint. But he caught her and he held her up.

'Come over here,' he said. 'Let's take care of you.'

He walked her toward a cypress stump. They were at the end of a dirt road, where it ran out somewhere in the swamplands. There was open water to one side, not-so-open water to the other, and dense undergrowth ahead. There was a path into it, of sorts. No road sounds, no sounds of cars or civilization of any kind; just the steady drone of insect life and the occasional call of a tree frog, a sound like a bass string being scratched with a nail. Hanging out over the water there was the sliding ruin of what appeared to be an old-time fisherman's cabin, part treehouse and part rotted deathtrap.

He sat her on the stump, and used some of the sachet wipes from her bag to clean up her face.

'You're looking better now,' he said encouragingly. 'You want some makeup? I'll have to put it on for you if you do.'

She shook her head at makeup.

'Come on, then,' he said.

He helped her up and started to walk her. Heart pounding in terror, she watched herself in disbelief as she complied. He seemed to be utterly sincere in his belief that he was treating her with kindness, here. Break and run, she told herself, even though she knew she would never get far. But her legs kept on walking with that half-controlled, jerky motion, like a frog's under the application of a galvanic wire.

Then Theresa saw the yawning square hole ahead and started to scream and struggle, at which he picked her up bodily and carried her forward and pitched her in. She cleared the sides and landed in a mess of mud and branches and darkness, the only light now being the square above her.

He threw her handbag in after and called in, 'I've brought a new friend for you. Be nice to her, now.'

And Theresa realized that whoever he might be talking to, he wasn't talking to her.

There was the sound of stone against concrete as the slab cover was replaced. Theresa screamed, finding a voice that she didn't realize she had, but it made no difference.

Darkness.

She waited, and listened. Nothing.

It stank down here, rank as old weeds, and the darkness was total. But she could feel her handbag, which had landed on her. It was open. If she could find her house key, there was a little flashlight on the key-ring that she could use. Nothing much and with only a watch battery to power it, but it was good enough for close-quarters lighting.

She used her good hand, as she was beginning to refer to it in her mind; the one that had no grip but wasn't quite completely useless. She couldn't get the thumb-and-forefinger pressure to make the tiny flashlight work, but she managed to fumble it up and into her teeth where she was able to clamp on it and bite down. The light flickered and came on, shining out into the darkness with an illumination the colour of pale tea.

What she saw.

Not weeds. Not branches.
But skulls and bones, long hair and jewels.

Outside, the young man finished up the job of pulling
vegetation across the concrete cover. Everything grew so
fast out here that the traces would have all but disappeared
in a matter of weeks. Even he had trouble finding it,
sometimes.

He turned and walked back toward the Mercedes. The
driver's door was still wide open. He got in, and picked
up the magazine that he'd bought about an hour before.
He slammed the door and turned on the engine to restart
the air-conditioning. His shirt was sticking to him after
his efforts out in the muggy air, making wet patches that
felt icy as the cooler air hit them.

The magazine was open at one of the stories. He read
the headline again.

Talk To Me, Victim Begs Would-be Killer's Mother.

'Damn,' he said.

29

It was about a week after Aidan's unconventional proposal when Ruth, instead of heading for home after the day's work changed some of her clothing in the data agency's toilets and went across town to meet him for the evening. She hadn't given him an answer yet, but she'd been stirred into making an effort to open up a little more. It was as if he'd brought a few things into sharper focus for her; as if, while she'd been thinking that she'd already lost everything, he'd shown her that what had gone so far had been only the top-dressing. There was more beneath, which she'd been taking so much for granted that she hadn't even seen it.

Or hadn't until now, when the threat came for even that to be taken away.

Now she was making a serious effort to get back in touch with the things that she valued. The commonplace things.

And whatever still stirred in her heart, she swore. To herself. That she'd try to hold it down.

She wore her big wool coat, a touch of lipstick. The days were still warm but it could be cool in the evenings. She rode the bus to the area where once she'd worked, and walked the last couple of hundred yards to where the Fitness Club stood opposite a big white brick church.

Aidan had signed up here after the shooting, mainly because of its closeness to his job and the employee discount available. Ruth knew that the injury, though healed, could still cause him considerable pain even after all this time. He'd been unable to work for twelve weeks and it had been another six months before he'd been able to raise his arm fully. He had a physio programme here that he followed twice a week.

'I'm supposed to meet Aidan Kincannon,' she said to the receptionist. 'Did he sign out yet?'

'I don't think so,' the receptionist said. 'Take a look in the book.'

He hadn't, so she moved to the rail to look for him. Club reception was at street level but the gym extended down into basement level beyond. The gym had white walls and a wooden floor, and hanging silks to take the glare off the overhead fluorescents. There was a big fan on the balcony beside Ruth that was blowing cooler air down into the space.

The floor was crowded with men and women who'd made time to work out before heading for home, but Aidan immediately saw her and came over. He was quite a sight. Where everyone else was wearing designer sportswear, Aidan wore a big and ancient football shirt that made him seem barrel-chested, outrageous Bermuda shorts that made him look bandy-legged, and canvas sneakers that had started life as white tennis shoes and now looked as if some down-and-out had found them on a dump. His regular workout gear. He resembled a kids' favourite incorrigible uncle at a barbecue.

'Hi,' he said, looking up and towelling sweat.

Ruth said, 'Is that how you plan on being dressed?'

Aidan spread his arms and looked down at himself. 'Yeah,' he said. 'I thought so. Won't I fit right in?'

'The depressing part is that you probably would.'

'What time do we have to be there?'

'It starts at seven-thirty.'

He slung the towel over his shoulder. 'I'll get in the shower,' he said.

'Don't rush,' she told him. 'We can make it.'

As he walked off toward the changing rooms, Ruth watched him go and felt something inside her move at the thought of what he'd done for her. He was decent and devoted, genuinely one of the nicest people she'd ever known. She wished that she could clear everything else out of her life, and deal specifically with that. But she couldn't, and it was a heartbreaker; he might slip away from her, simply because of her inability to hold on to him. She could fight it, but it was like fighting some impediment. The harder she tried it, the harder it became.

She moved back into the reception area. There were a few low seats around a coffee table with a basket of flowers on it. Down the wall was a line of brass plates listing all the corporate memberships of businesses and hotels in the surrounding area, her former employers among them. Ruth sat down to wait.

She thought about Tim Hagan. Working out in his room in Brewerytown, learning his dance steps, probably practising his smalltalk in the mirror as he went about the job of redesigning himself into a sleek and charming machine of his own invention. Dead or not, he was still there in her mind like a memory-resident program in a computer, ready to pop up out of the background any time that she happened to miskey.

Aidan came up the stairs, showered and dressed now. They walked out together.

'How's your shoulder?' she said as they headed down in the direction of his car.

'It's fine,' he said.

'I don't believe you.'

'Well,' he conceded, 'it hurts still. But it's what we action movie aficionados refer to as, "just a flesh wound".' He winced. 'Just a fucking flesh wound. What do they know?'

'I think of how close he got,' Ruth said. 'I still go cold. I wonder for how long that's going to keep on happening.'

'I don't know,' Aidan said. 'I don't think that ever goes away.' There was a few moments' silence. Aidan looked down as they walked along.

Then he said, 'Any more thoughts on what I suggested?'

'I've been thinking about it,' Ruth said. 'I'm still thinking about it. I'm sorry, Aidan. I'm doing the best that I can.'

He didn't press it. He said, 'Did you see the lawyer today?'

'They switched people on me.'

'What does that mean?'

'It was a different person to the first time. He couldn't even find the other one's notes. I had to tell the entire story from the beginning, all over again.'

'Jesus,' Aidan said blankly.

'He said I shouldn't worry too much,' Ruth said, wondering why she felt an urge to cover up and justify the fact that she was getting exactly what could be expected from the firm that she'd hired. Lawyers were like everything else, she'd found; there were Cadillacs and there were Fords, and there were bottom-of-the-range clunkers. 'He said the system's so overloaded that everything takes for ever. Even if it goes against me, I can appeal.'

'Yeah, and guess who benefits most if you have to go through that? I wish we could afford you someone better.'

'The law's still the law,' Ruth said.

'I know. And no guarantee is still no guarantee.'

There had been a time when people had said of immigration lawyers that they'd descended to their trade by dint of being unsuccessful in any other area. Corporate work and international employee mobility had changed all of that, but one simple fact remained. Ruth's was a rock-bottom case and she couldn't afford the best. Aidan had offered to help her out, but he had only one asset – his house – and that was still the subject of litigation.

It was a problem. Which was not to say that it was a problem without a solution.

It was simply that the answer scared her just as much as the question it aimed to address.

Aidan was taking her to a reading in a bookstore. Or she was taking him. The initiative was his, but the territory was hers; he'd pushed her into this, there was no other way of describing it. He knew that it had been one of her pleasures in the life before Hagan, and when the store's events guide had come redirected in the mail from her old address he'd almost bullied her into choosing a date. He hoped it was going to work out. He'd seen her beginning to make an effort over the past week or so, and he felt that it would. Aidan was no great reader himself, but he'd fake it if he had to. He'd look interested at gallery openings, sit still for some avant-garde performance at the Painted Bride.

Anything.

Anything, to be able to watch her bloom again.

It was a civilized-looking place, with wide aisles and light oak fittings and a deep green carpet. One of the assistants recognized Ruth.

'I thought you might have moved away and left us,' she said.

'I've been out of circulation for a while,' Ruth told her.

The reading area was on the second floor, adjacent to a coffee bar and set out with straight-backed black plastic chairs facing a blondwood lectern. At seven-twenty-five only a few of them were occupied, but an announcement downstairs doubled the audience size in the space of a minute. Just before the start time, a young man came out and fixed a live microphone to a bracket on the lectern to give the reader a fighting chance against the espresso machine and the electronic cash register across the way. The audience were an assorted bunch, one or two of whom looked as if they'd had to be let out in order to be there.

'Admit it, Aidan,' Ruth said to him. 'This isn't exactly your scene.'

'It is so,' said Aidan.

'You barely have a book in the house that isn't by John D. MacDonald.'

'I'm heavily into the classics,' Aidan insisted. 'Right now I'm reading James Joyce. *Ulysses*.'

'Since when?'

'Since nineteen seventy-two. So far, I'm eight pages in.'

'So you haven't picked it up in a while.'

'Not since nineteen seventy-three.'

The author was a young man in ordinary clothes. Too damned young, was the opinion of Aidan, who when he was reading liked to think that he was getting the thoughts of someone who'd knocked around a little. The young man stood back, trying not to look embarrassed, as one of the bookshop staff stood at the microphone and reeled off a few future events before busking his way through an introduction. Then the author stepped up, took off his jacket, fiddled with the microphone so that the speakers made noises like the wrong end of a bowling alley, confessed his nervousness at reading, and then started to read.

He'd picked out a passage that was written completely in dialogue, and proceeded to read it without the slightest change in rhythm or inflection. Aidan hadn't got a clue what it was about. Something about dogs and bathrooms. After a while his eyes started to wander; they started to wander longingly to the espresso bar, and then, fearful of being caught out, he switched his attention back to the lectern. Ruth was leaning forward. She seemed to be enjoying herself.

After the reading part the author asked if there were any questions, and there was a behind-shuffling silence until someone stuck up a hand and started the ball rolling. After that it seemed to loosen up a little, although Aidan was no less lost. His attention wandered and came back into focus again. Someone was saying, 'Who did you write this book for?' and the author was saying, 'Do you know, in a very real sense, I wrote it for myself.' Afterwards the author moved to a table where maybe a dozen copies were piled ready for signing, and nobody else moved at all except for those on the fringes who got to their feet and dipped out of sight behind the pillars, like mice darting for safety before the cat's attention was turned upon them.

Aidan looked at Ruth with what he hoped wasn't too hopeful an expression on his face, and to his relief Ruth smiled and raised her eyebrows and they moved to go.

It was a pleasant evening. As they walked down Walnut Street, Ruth said, 'Clear up one thing for me, Aidan.'

'Name it,' he said.

'Why did you ever start on *Ulysses* in the first place?'

'I heard it was a sexy book,' he admitted.

'It's a major work of twentieth-century literature.'

'So I quickly found.'

Ruth stopped.

'My God,' she said dully.

They'd entered Rittenhouse Square. A row of lights burned among the trees like pale moons. People were lounging on the benches, strolling through, cycling through, skating through. They'd been through here before and she'd had no big problems; Aidan looked around for the cause of her dismay.

A yellow Ryder truck had been parked there and behind it, just starting to rise on its tubular frame skeleton, was the shiny white fabric shape of a canvas marquee. More than a year had gone by since the ball, and it seemed that something like it was about to happen again.

'I'm sorry, Ruth,' he said. 'I didn't know.'

The work gang had sectioned off the area with tent poles across trash cans and were working under the late evening sky. The muted glow of park lighting made clear shadows of everything, painting darkness onto dark.

She took his arm and gripped it, and they walked on.

She said, 'Why won't he leave us alone, Aidan?'

'Dead people are like that,' Aidan said. 'They've got no consideration.'

'I can't quite get myself to believe that he's gone.'

For Aidan, this felt like a breakthrough. Never had he known her to speak so openly on the subject before. It was as if the tangle of her emotions had knotted up to choke her off. Her fear, and her shame at being afraid. The guilt of knowing that she'd had an opportunity to stop him for good and been unable to take it.

And more. Other, deeper feelings that she'd never expressed and that Aidan couldn't begin to imagine. At last, perhaps, the knot was beginning to relax.

He said, 'Do you think you'd feel any better now

if you'd pulled the trigger on him when you had the chance?'

'I don't know.'

'Well, I don't think you would. I know guys who've shot people. Women too. It takes less than a second to do it and then you carry it around for ever.'

'I still want to talk to his mother,' Ruth said. 'There are some things I want to ask her.'

'And then do you think you'll feel better?'

At least she gave him an honest-sounding answer.

'I don't know,' she said.

30

It emerged that there was a good reason for the unopened return of Ruth's letters to Jessica Hagan. Because when she and Aidan showed up in Brighton Beach in the hope of persuading the woman to a meeting, they found that the address passed along to Ruth by the magazine reporter had been wrong. Right apartment number, wrong apartment building. Aidan knocked on a few doors and made a few guesses, charmed a widow or two and got them onto the right track. And then when they located the apartment, Mrs Hagan wasn't home.

'You go down the boardwalk, you'll find her,' a neighbour told them. 'She's down there a lot. She sells second-hand clothes for a Mexican when the Mexican's woman can't work.'

Brighton Beach, out across Brooklyn from the centre of New York, had once been a middle-class Jewish area and was now home to a large number of immigrant Russians. The apartment block in which Jessica Hagan lived was huge and brown and castle-like, looking out over the sea with its name and a phone number painted vertically down its side.

Out on the seafront, Aidan asked around some more. Brighton Beach ran on into Coney Island, once the city's playground and now more like a war zone peopled by refugees. The shapes of the old parks were still there, but the parks themselves were all but gone. There were large patches of waste ground with half-heartedly fenced and vacant lots in between, rides that had been left and were slowly rusting, a complete rollercoaster that was no more than derelict towers and gantries and rails. The streets that had once led down to the beach stood utterly empty –

of cars, of buildings, of everything. Only the boardwalk was in good repair.

Parallel to the beach ran a two-tier elevated railway, and in the shadow of the elevated had been pitched a market, of sorts.

Beside a shutter-fronted store selling discount furniture there was a flea market of big metal freight containers with their end doors open. The containers looked like deep, dark caves. One was filled with second-hand mattresses, another with used tyres, most of the others with junk where the choicest items had been set out in front – an old toaster, a squash racquet, a home gym for a hundred dollars. And lots of hi-fi decks, of makers and makes unknown. Some way farther along were the less ambitious enterprises, goods unloaded and laid out from vans and automobiles. Jessica Hagan wasn't hard to find among the mostly Spanish-speakers.

'Mrs Hagan?' Aidan said to her. 'This is Ruth Lasseter. She's been writing you letters, but I don't think you'll have received them.'

The woman looked dazed. Then she looked at Ruth, without any sense of recognition.

'What do you want?' she said.

'Only to talk.'

'Are you from the newspapers again? I had it up to here with the newspapers. You've got no right to chase me around.'

'We're not here to harass you,' Aidan said. 'Ruth Lasseter. Doesn't the name mean anything?'

She looked at Ruth again. She was an older woman. Not too much older, but life had knocked her out of shape and slowed her down before her time. She wore a plaid coat and sat on a folding stool by her employer's wares, new and second-hand clothing. Some of the goods had been draped on a waist-high hurricane fence, the rest laid out on towels along the sidewalk before it. The stuff looked as if it had been spilled from a wreck. Although her hair was mostly grey, her skin was pink and tight like a baby's.

Still looking at Ruth, she said, 'Are you the one he's supposed to have hurt?'

Ruth nodded, and Aidan could see how nervous she was.

'I didn't see the boy in more than five years,' the woman said. 'And then only because he needed money. I don't know what he did or he didn't. If you want to take it out on someone, I don't want to listen.'

'That's not why I'm here,' Ruth said.

'Then, what?'

People around them were starting to take an interest. Not a partisan interest, nor even a sympathetic interest. Attention was gathering around them like sand around a stick in the desert, raising a dune out of nowhere simply by being there.

Ruth said, 'I'm just here to talk.'

'I got nothing to say on the subject. You catch me out on the street like this where I can't walk away, that just isn't fair.'

'Please, Mrs Hagan,' Ruth persisted. 'You must feel something too. Don't you think it'll help?'

'Help who?'

'I have dreams about him. Your son. And they're not good ones. I don't see any way they're ever going to stop. Five minutes is all I ask.'

'I don't have five minutes,' the woman said. 'This is my busiest part of the day.'

'What time do you finish, here?' Aidan said.

They got a grudging concession out of her. Another woman would be coming to take over at two o'clock, and maybe she'd talk to them then. She'd think about it. But don't expect much. 'Cause she'd nothing to say.

Aidan couldn't think of anything more that they could do. So they backed off, leaving the woman to handle her big rush of nobody except for a man with a Handicam, scanning along the goods on show like a tourist in a famine village. Aidan put his hand out to guide Ruth, and she came

205

away reluctantly. She looked at him, helpless and a little bit desperate.

And he said, 'One step at a time, Ruth.'

They walked along to the Stillwell Avenue station, the end of the line for the elevated and once the point of arrival for as many as a hundred thousand visitors in a single day. Now there were just a couple of identical old, stiff, lame-looking mongrels wandering around looking for somewhere to do their business. The dark concourse underneath was like somewhere that had been buried undersea for twenty years and then drained and put back into service without any attempt to tidy it up. In it stood a candy store selling salt-water taffy and, behind that, an old-style coffee shop where Ruth and Aidan seated themselves at the long counter and let half an hour go by with little to say.

'What exactly are you going to ask her?' Aidan said.

But Ruth could only shake her head, as if she'd had an almost mystic certainty that something would happen when they met and was dismayed to find it all falling apart even as she approached.

When they returned to the market with more than twenty minutes still to go, they found a stranger on the folding stool and Jessica Hagan nowhere in sight.

31

They caught up with her less than a quarter of a mile away. She was heading for home. Aidan hung back, and let the two of them walk together. He couldn't hear everything that was being said. But he could hear most of it.

'His daddy left the family when Tim was no more than eight,' the woman was telling Ruth. 'He was a metal worker, a strong man. But not strong in his character. I'd married him in Jersey City, but we lived in Indiana for a while. We'd moved there because he thought the work would be better. Once he'd left us he lived in some rooms on his own and then in a trailer, and then last of all he moved into the nursing home where he died. Tim was a teenager by then. He used to borrow money from his father and some nights he'd sleep on the couch at his place. He stole from him, once. He gave the money to some girls he knew who were setting up in their own apartment. When his father died, he said he was going west to look for work but then two months later, he showed up on my doorstep and told me he hadn't even left town yet. I gave him the fare for the bus and that's the last time I saw him.'

Ruth said, 'Do you know where he went?'

'I don't think he ever got any further than Pittsburgh. He didn't write me more than three letters in all that time. He just seemed to be drifting around from one place to another. He wasn't what you'd call a good worker. He didn't like to be told what to do. But you had to push him to get him to do anything at all.'

'Was he ever in trouble with the police?'

'One time when he was thirteen. He stole some tapes out of a car and they caught him running away. And then two years ago I got a police letter about a fire in some motel where he'd been living. He'd given my address when he was checking in. He'd never even been to see me here. I don't know what else I can tell you. I can answer your questions, but . . . I somehow raised a stranger, is all I know. He always wanted to *be* somebody. But he never stuck at anything.'

'What kind of a child was he?'

'He liked to be out of doors. Loved animals. He could play on his own for hours. And he did well enough in school. I kept all his report cards. I tied them up with a ribbon along with his letters. What's your name again?'

'Ruth Lasseter,' she said. And then, 'Ruth.'

'Don't ever have children, Ruth. You'll regret it if you do. All they bring you is pain. I didn't see him in years and he didn't give me a single good word to say about him in all that time, and still I cried when they told me he'd died.'

Her apartment was bigger than it looked from the hallway, and neater than Aidan had expected. While Jessica Hagan went to get the letters, he and Ruth sat on a couch whose springs bulged like a bag of snakes. She'd little other furniture, including a Zenith black-and-white TV that looked as if it had been picked up on the flea market and a kerosene heater in the blocked-off fireplace, probably from the same source. Aidan had an overpowering sense of a life running out toward its premature end, shedding just about everything as it went. Home and family, already gone. Hopes probably gone long before. Girlish dreams? Did they ever go? Or did they echo in these rooms even now?

She came back with the box.

'This is all there is,' she said. 'I'm sorry about your pain, Ruth. If reading these helps it in some way, then I reckon it's only your due. What else can I tell you? I'm sorry he turned out bad. I'd have loved to have a good son like other women get, but I didn't get one. I don't know what made him into what he was and if that's the answer you're looking for, I'm not the one who can give it to you.'

She placed the box in Ruth's hands. Her own shook, slightly.

'I'll bring these back,' Ruth said.

'I'm counting on you to,' Jessica Hagan said. 'They're all I have left. The only recent photograph I had, I loaned it to those newspaper people. They never gave it back to me and they didn't even use it.'

Aidan said, 'Do you want us to get you anything?'

'I want you to go, now,' she said.

They walked back to get their train. Ruth held the box to her like a baby's coffin. Aidan was thinking about his boy and his daughter, about how he'd feel if anything were ever to happen to them. Distanced from them though he was, he couldn't imagine going on with a life from which they'd been taken. He almost certainly would, because people did. And the thought that he'd do it only served to anger and upset him even more.

About two hundred gulls were wheeling above the army recruitment cabin across from the station. Leaving the birds' cries behind as they went in under the tracks, Ruth said, 'Nothing connects. It just gets worse.'

'You know what I think?' Aidan said. 'I think you fell for him.'

She looked at him, shocked.

'It hurts me to say it,' he went on. 'But I think he came along and filled a space that no-one else could fill for you. The fact that the boy was a twisted-up shit just makes the whole thing a tragedy instead of a fairy story.'

'It's not true,' she said.

'Don't I wish,' Aidan said. 'He's dead and you're still hungry, and that's why we're here.'

He sat with his head resting against the glass of the window, watching the Brooklyn landscape go by as the train headed back in toward Manhattan. They were passing a breaking yard for school buses with a river behind it, the back ends of the vehicles out over the water but with their flat tyres still on the asphalt. Then at roof-height past hundred-year-old buildings, their huge satellite dishes almost level with the train's windows. He was no longer sure that it was such a great idea for them to have made this journey. It looked good from a distance, a necessary pain. But close up, he wondered if it was worth it.

His daddy left the family when Tim was no more than eight. A strong man. But not strong in his character.

The words kept running through Aidan's mind, and squirm as he might he couldn't escape the discomfort that they brought.

'This isn't him,' Ruth said.

Aidan glanced toward her. She'd taken the lid from the box and she'd untied the ribbon, and for most of their journey so far she'd been taking out papers and unfolding them and laying them on her knee and on the seat beside her.

Aidan said, 'What do you mean?'

'He told me he was a Southern boy,' she said. 'It was there in his voice. Tim Hagan never went South in his life. Nothing else fits, either. Hagan never stuck at anything. He didn't even graduate. This boy taught himself to dance, he built himself into something, he even studied for the evening when I hired him.' She pulled out a snapshot of a young teenager, in bright sunlight with his face in the shade of his own shoulder-length hair. 'Look at this picture, Aidan,' she said. 'It was taken ten years ago, but still it's nothing like him.'

Aidan barely even glanced at it.

'So what?' he said.

Ruth was blank; obviously this wasn't the reaction she'd been expecting to hear.

She said, 'What do you mean?'

'So he lifted some drifter's ID,' Aidan said. 'When was it ever an issue?'

'This is *important*,' Ruth insisted.

'Only to you. I don't care what his name was. He did what he did, and he got what he got. Stop trying to conjure him back into life. I've got a limit, Ruth, and you're starting to push it.' He looked out of the window again. 'I'm sorry I said I'd come out here.'

Ruth backed off, and maintained a diplomatic silence thereafter.

She wouldn't have to make the journey again. Because Jessica Hagan was dead before morning.

32

Ruth tried to call her from the station between trains, and again several times that evening. She wanted to tell the woman that whatever the real Tim Hagan might have done in his life, the crimes against Ruth were not on his slate. And regardless of the fact that he'd disappeared from sight, there was no longer even any proof that Jessica Hagan's errant boy was dead. But she got no reply.

Not until after eleven, when the call appeared to be diverted and a man's voice started to ask her business. Ruth hung up, suddenly scared, although she couldn't have explained why.

Aidan reluctantly made a few calls of his own the next morning, from the security office when he'd arrived at his work. And that was how he was first to learn the truth.

'They're trying to decide whether to treat her death as suspicious,' his contact told him when phoning him back after half an hour. Aidan's contact was Joe McDade, with whom he'd once trained and who was now one of the senior people in the Public Affairs Office of the Philadelphia police. Joe seemed to know everyone, everywhere; Brooklyn or the Bahamas, there was always somebody with whom he'd been on a course or to a convention. He drove a school bus outside hours and had recently picked up his twenty-year service award. Aidan had felt a pang of envy at the time. It was clear to him, looking back, that his own decision to leave hadn't been the best that he could have made. But then there were some paths that, once taken, held no prospect of return.

Joe said, 'The fire department found the place full of smoke and her in a closet. It wasn't a sensible place to be, but you know how people don't think straight when they panic. What they can't rule out is that someone put her in there and then started the fire to cover their tracks. Kids see someone who lives alone and spends no money, they always have to think there's a big wad of cash hidden somewhere around the place. There's an autopsy scheduled for ten o'clock. If anyone handled her first, they might know it then.'

'How did the fire get started?'

'From the heater in the sitting-room. There's a difference between kerosene and gasoline, only she didn't seem to know it.'

Aidan didn't try to get hold of Ruth straightaway. He could imagine how she'd react to the information. It wasn't simply that the sudden death of a known person, even of a once-met stranger, was always a shock. Aidan wasn't immune to the feeling, and he'd seen it happen more than most. But in Ruth's case it would stir right in with the rest of her paranoid brew and she'd leap to all kinds of conclusions.

He got hold of Tom Diaz instead.

'What's happening with Tim Hagan's body?' he asked, after waiting more than a minute for Diaz to get to the phone.

'Don't ask me,' the detective said. 'I don't keep track of everything. I think they're going to release it for interment.'

'What about the forensic stuff?'

'I don't think we're doing any. No prints and the lower jawbone's gone . . . and it's not like we don't know who he is. We may just have to rely on what we've got.'

'You might be hearing from Ruth on that,' Aidan said, and went on to explain.

'Ohhh, God,' Tom Diaz groaned, dispiritedly.

'Don't worry,' Aidan said. 'Whatever his name was, at least he's still dead.'

Ruth was back in the suite upstairs from the peepshow, pounding the keyboard as usual. Her hands ached and her eyes hurt and her head buzzed, but all this was normal. There were eleven other women in the room at identical terminals, and the constant *yuk-yuk-yuk* of the keys was like a cocktail party in an ant farm. Listen to it long enough and it merged, became a quiet roar.

Most of the retyping that took place here was to produce digitized versions of existing text for CD-ROM and other retrieval systems. Scanning wasn't yet accurate enough; everything was retyped by two different people whose work was merged and compared to pick up any errors. Which meant that the typists didn't have to be the best, just fast. Ruth produced about eighty thousand characters a day. The fastest could reach almost double that, when pushed. Ruth had worked on textbooks, journals, reference works, legal documents . . . it was at the point where she was barely aware of content any more. Some listened to music on headsets while they worked. Ruth had no need.

Ruth had thoughts enough to occupy her, whatever else might be happening.

It was plain to her that Aidan didn't much care whether Tim Hagan and the boy who'd attacked her were one and the same person. As far as he was concerned, the perp had been found dead in a ditch and given them a convenient end to the story. Except that for Ruth, a story had to be more than a bunch of mysteries and a gabbled conclusion. To be a story, it had to make sense. And without sense, there was no hope of satisfaction.

She'd chosen him. Slept with him. Suffered at his hands. For him to remain as such an enigma . . . well, it just wasn't acceptable.

When the time for lunch arrived, she made a note on her worksheet and went for her coat. She socialized with the others sometimes, but not often. Usually she picked her time so that she walked out alone, and she went over to the market and found some corner of stillness while the life of the place seethed all around her. In her bag there was always an improving book and a piece of junk. Whichever she read depended on her mood. Often, she'd rest her eyes and wouldn't read at all.

Walking over, she wondered if Aidan had managed to speak to Jessica Hagan yet. He'd promised he'd try. Ruth felt odd about this entire aspect of the affair. She'd gone into the box of letters with a ferocious sense of certainty, only to see her certainties fall apart. The only one that she was left with was that the paths of Tim Hagan and her assailant must have crossed at some time. Probably around the time that Hagan had started to drift westward; the police questionnaire about a small-town fire was the last piece of dated evidence that fixed him in any location. It was the only interruption in two years of silence.

Maybe the real Hagan was spinning out his low-achiever life somewhere, unaware of how his name had been taken and used.

Or maybe he wasn't.

All of this made her feel like an archaeologist. An archaeologist of pain. She'd the urge to dig and to dig until she could find the source of the hurt and then she could clean it off and bring it into the light. It would still be what it was. But power over it would then be hers.

She got a seat on one of the garden-furniture tables at the Bassetts turkey sandwich stall, which had been relocated to a windowless spot at the back of the market while renovations were under way. Ruth was hoping that the renovations wouldn't amount to much. The Market had the kind of atmosphere that one could easily improve to death. Yellow board ceilings and open pipework and cold brick floors and bad lighting – these made the place, they didn't hold it back.

However it all turned out, she only hoped that she'd still be around and able to see it.

She bit into her sandwich and got out some stories by Joyce Carol Oates. The possibility of her deportation was a subject from which her mind always skated away. It was like an ominous symptom on which she didn't like to dwell. It seemed so unfair. No matter what had happened to her, this was home. You couldn't simply choose or change your home at will, you just knew it when you were there. It was her last fingerhold, and they were threatening to knock it away.

Damn it. She was thinking about it. Someone slid into a seat at the table alongside her, and without looking up she hitched along to make room. When the subject needed rational consideration, she couldn't bring herself to give it. But then when she wanted to blank it out of her mind, it wouldn't go away.

She became aware of being looked at. The short hairs on the back of her neck were rising.

Ruth turned to the person who'd sat down beside her.

'Hello, Ruth,' said the boy who had once planned to hurt her, and whose name was not Tim Hagan.

33

He said, 'Were you expecting to see me again?'

He'd a white linen jacket, well-worn but not cheap-looking, over a T-shirt. He'd a slight tan and he looked well-groomed. Yet again, someone different. She couldn't meet his eyes. She felt that if she looked into his eyes, they'd be like a couple of dense black marbles.

She glanced around, trying not to move her head so it wouldn't be obvious, and he noted it.

'Don't worry,' he told her, 'you're perfectly safe. Shall I tell you why? Say, Yes, Tim.'

'That isn't your name,' Ruth said. She felt frozen. Rooted. But she wasn't going to let him dominate her again.

'That's one of the reasons why I'm here,' he said. 'Think about it, Ruth. I'm talking about your own best interests now. For God's sake, Ruth, don't stare. Close your mouth.' He looked all around, as if a sudden thought had struck him. 'Do they have cameras here?'

Ruth felt almost too dazed to speak.

But then she managed to say, 'Why have you come back?'

He put his elbows on the table and leaned forward and lowered his voice, as if they were intimates. Ruth shrank back from him, but she managed not to lose it. 'What was I going to do,' he said, 'write you a letter? I came back to point something out that you clearly haven't realized yet. I've moved on. I've cut the links, as far as this town's concerned I'm a dead person now. As a dead person, I've got no worries. Nobody's looking for me and I've nothing to fear. There are two ways for me to stop being a dead person. One would be to draw attention to myself, which would be stupid.'

'Then why are you here?'

'I'm taking a risk to point out the fucking obvious, Ruth. The easiest way for me to blow my cover would be to do harm to you now. But as long as I stay dead, you're out of danger. If that one thing changes, then everything changes with it. Do you understand?'

'What's the second way?' Ruth said.

'You keep on doing exactly what you're doing. It's not wise, Ruth. I may not want to show myself, but accidents can still happen.'

'You're threatening me.'

'The opposite. I'm offering a truce. You go your way, I'll go mine. We draw a line and that's the end of it.'

'I've got just one question about that.'

'No questions.'

'Will you go on doing what you do?'

Silence. Then . . .

'What I do from here on will be no responsibility of yours,' he said evenly.

He pushed his chair back, and started to get to his feet.

'I know you're going to judge me,' he said. 'I can't help that. But there's something I wish you'd understand. Something with you that I never had from anyone else. I live in hell, Ruth. Wherever I look, it's all that I see. But there was just one moment when I really thought you were going to be the one who'd lead me out of it.'

'What happened?'

'It passed,' he said.

And then he turned and walked away.

34

That evening, when Aidan returned home, it was to find his house fully secured and bolted and with every light blazing, inside and out, including the one he'd installed over the car deck and which came on when anybody moved around within range. And it wasn't even dark yet.

'Ruth?' he called into the hallway. 'The chain's on the door. You've got to let me in.'

He could hear her coming down the hallway. She unhooked the anti-intruder chain and let him in, and then she replaced it after and put on the night security bolt as well. It engaged with a bang and was probably stronger than the door.

'What's the matter?' Aidan said, watching her and wondering what could have happened to bring on this sudden and intense burst of nervous activity. Had she heard about Jessica Hagan? He didn't see how, but that had to be it.

'I've seen him,' she said.

'Who?'

She didn't reply, and after a few moments for her meaning to sink in Aidan felt as if he was on the point of beginning a long trip down an elevator shaft without the use or aid of an elevator.

Ruth seemed to be anticipating his reaction, and she said, 'I really did see him, Aidan. Don't say you're not going to believe me. I couldn't handle that.'

'Where?'

So then she told him of the encounter, start to finish, and every now and again he looked around helplessly as if he'd been trapped here, right here in the hallway with his coat over his uniform and the bag he carried to and from work, nailed into being her audience and being given no chance even to step inside and settle. If she saw this, she didn't take it in. Or if she took it in, she didn't act on it.

When she'd finished, Aidan said, 'This is a hell of a lot to swallow.'

'I know that,' she said. 'I'd probably feel the same way if I hadn't actually seen him. But what's so unlikely about it? It's obvious that he picked someone up on the road and then left him to rot in his place. Don't tell me he's not capable of that.'

'Supposing it's so. What do you want to do about it?'

'I'll have to go back to the police. But you'll have to be with me, Aidan, they'll never believe me if I go on my own.'

Aidan was thinking that they'd never believe her if she went along with her own polygraph expert and Billy Graham for a witness. But what he said, feeling as if he was crashing through the undergrowth but knowing that there was no way of guiding the conversation around with any more subtlety, was, 'Would you consider talking to a doctor?'

'Damn you, Aidan,' she said, 'that's exactly the kind of reaction I'm so scared of. What's the big problem, here? Last time I told you he faked his name, you shrugged it off and you said so what. You made me feel stupid for even being surprised. Now I'm telling you he did it again. He did it again because that's what he does. There's probably another ditch somewhere with another heap of festering meat in it that no-one can put a name to, and that's how he became Tim Hagan in the first place.'

'Ruth,' Aidan said, getting to the point where he wanted nothing more than to get into his own house and take his shoes off and throw himself into a chair for a while. 'How can I put this? Shut up.'

'No,' Ruth said.

'Then I'm going out.'

'Don't leave me on my own.'

He was turning to the door already, but he stopped. He

didn't really want to go out. He didn't have anywhere to go.

Ruth said, 'I don't want to be alone here.'

Aidan sighed, a big one.

'What am I going to do with you?' he said wearily.

'I know what you're thinking,' Ruth said. 'You think he's dead and I'm just wishing him alive. Well, I'm not. If I could turn back the clock, I'd pull that trigger and I'd live with whatever came after. But I didn't, and he's here!'

He looked into her eyes, making sure that he left her in no doubt. He was taking her seriously. But he didn't believe her. That there was a big problem and that he was prepared to address it, of that there was no question. But he wanted her to understand that in his mind it didn't revolve around some ghost, it revolved around Ruth herself. He wouldn't be scared off. Although scared he certainly was.

He said, 'Can you prove it to me?'

Ruth returned his gaze without flinching. Her face was pale, her eyes wide and dark. Adult and child, and no firm line between.

'If you loved me like you said,' she told him, 'I shouldn't have to.'

She lay with him that night. She didn't move out of contact at all; when he slipped out of bed to go to the bathroom at around two in the morning, it was to return to find that her eyes were open and she was waiting for him. When he climbed back in, her eyes fell closed and she slept on as if without a break.

Aidan didn't know which prospect scared him more.

That she might be telling the truth, which seemed unlikely.

Or that she'd now started living out her nightmares, which filled him with a sense of unutterable despair.

35

The next morning, at breakfast, Ruth couldn't eat. She showed no sign of getting ready to go out.

She said, 'I feel sick every time I think of it. I suppose you think this is some kind of a performance.'

'No,' Aidan said. He was thinking that a performance would almost be preferable. Like a barking seal. You throw it the right kind of fish, and then it's happy. With this there could be no such simple remedy.

'But you think I'm ill,' Ruth persisted.

'I never said that.'

'He's even smarter than I thought,' she said. 'I'm not only warned off. I'm discredited with you as well.'

'Stop it, Ruth,' Aidan said quietly.

'Well I am, aren't I?'

The phone rang out then, and Aidan went over to pick it up. Ruth left the room, and he heard her on the stairs a moment later.

'Aidan?' said the voice at the other end of the line. 'Tom Diaz.'

'Hi.'

'Is Ruth with you?'

'She just went upstairs,' Aidan said. 'Do you want to speak to her?'

'No, that's not necessary. I'm just calling to ask how she's doing. Is she going to work today?'

Aidan wasn't sure how to answer. As far as he was aware, Ruth hadn't told anyone else of yesterday's supposed encounter. He said, 'I don't think so. She's up and down. You know.'

'What about you?'

'I'm fine. What can I help you with?'

'Not a thing. Just trying to keep up to speed.'

After they'd finished talking and he'd hung up, Aidan sat and thought for a moment. Something here felt wrong, but he didn't exactly know what. They weren't friends. Cops didn't ring for a chat, with nothing they wanted to ask and nothing they needed to know. He'd been one. He knew.

He cleared a few of the breakfast things away, deliberated a little longer, and then dialled the Race Street number and asked for the detectives' department. A woman whose voice he didn't know picked up at the other end.

He said, 'This is Mike in the Chem Lab. I brought the Winnebago in for Tom Diaz to look at. Do you know what his plans are for the day?'

'I couldn't tell you for sure,' she said. 'A couple of Immigration people came in early and they just went out of the office together. He didn't say when he'd be back.'

'Do you know where they were going?'

'They're arresting some woman. I'd leave it until after lunch hour, at least.'

'That probably answers it,' Aidan said. 'Thanks.'

He became aware of Ruth as he was dialling the next number. She'd reappeared silently and was standing in the doorway, watching him, alert to the fact that something was happening although she couldn't yet know what.

The law firm's operator took more than a minute to answer.

'I need to talk to whoever's supposed to be representing Ruth Lasseter,' he said when he finally got through.

'I'm sorry,' the operator said, 'there's no-one available right now.'

'Thanks a lot,' Aidan said, and hung up.

He sat with his elbows on the table and his hands in his hair, thinking so hard that he probably looked as if he was trying to hold his head together.

'Are they coming for me?' Ruth said.

'I don't know. I think so.'

'I thought you said I had time.'

'Six months to a year is average. How long you can hold

223

out beyond that depends on a good case and a less than lousy lawyer, neither of which you appear to have.' Aidan's mind raced.

He couldn't leave her, couldn't stand around and see her taken away. His own selfish reasons apart, how would she function? She was walking wounded and she needed his support. That wasn't vanity on his part, it was a fact. Everybody needed somebody, and he was all she had.

'I don't want to leave the house,' she said.

'We've got to deal with this, Ruth,' he said. 'We've got to start dealing with it now. I'll be with you. Nobody's going to hurt you again. But if we stay here and they come for you, there won't be anything I can do. Don't you understand that?'

'You're talking to me like I'm a child,' she said.

'For God's sake, Ruth,' he said. 'We've got fifteen minutes at the most. Get back upstairs and pack a bag.'

Aidan's Chevy drew up in front of the house on Maple Street, and he had to duck down slightly in his seat to look across Ruth and up the sloping lawn to the building. It looked neat and white and perfect from here. The grass had been cut since his last visit. With nail scissors, to judge by the neatness of its edges.

'This is where Angela lives now,' he explained. 'She did pretty well for herself, wouldn't you say?'

Ruth said, 'Why are we here?'

'Not my style, though,' Aidan went on. He'd never been much of a home-maker. There had been a garden behind the house where he'd lived with Angela, and the only times he'd felt moved to mow the lawn were those when he'd needed to find the golf balls that he'd lost.

'Aidan?' Ruth said.

'Kids'll be at school,' he told her. 'It's good timing. You want to stay in the car, or come inside? It's better if you come. Then we don't give the neighbours the wrong idea.'

She came along with him.

Mostly he didn't even need to walk up the driveway, because the children watched for his car and came out to meet him. That had been with the exception of one or two occasions on which there had been arguments, when they were clearly propelled out of the door toward him.

Angela opened the door herself. She couldn't disguise the fact that she was surprised to see him standing there.

'Aidan?' she said, uncertainly.

'Hello, Angela,' he said. 'Is it all right to come in?'

It was obvious that he'd caught her off-guard. 'The children aren't here,' she said.

'I know,' he said. 'I have to talk to you. This is Ruth. Don't worry, we're not going to embarrass anyone.'

There was a cry from the new baby, giving vent to its feelings from somewhere inside the house behind her. It was almost as if this forced her hand. She stepped back, and they entered.

She seemed to be alone with the child. Aidan felt awkward enough, and he could only imagine how Ruth must be feeling. Angela showed them through into the kitchen where the baby sat in a high chair, eating the usual kind of baby slop. Or rather, complaining at being abandoned in the midst of eating the usual kind of baby slop. The kitchen was bright and modern but it wasn't anything like as spotless as the way she'd tried to keep their old one, back in the days when ostentatious housekeeping had been one of her weapons of war.

Angela said to Ruth, 'I hear things about you.'

'I can imagine,' Ruth said.

'You're Australian,' Angela said in surprise on hearing her speak.

'Not even close,' Ruth said tightly.

And Aidan quickly said, 'I'm going to need a pen and some paper.'

He and Angela went into another room, leaving Ruth with the baby. Aidan wondered how good an idea this might be; as they left, he glanced back and saw that the kid was watching Ruth and looking stunned.

His expression hadn't changed when they returned a few minutes later. Angela picked up a spare bib, cleaned mashed banana off the baby, and lifted it out of its chair.

'What's the matter, Stinkbomb?' she said. 'You want to have a nice sleep in the car?'

'Stinkbomb?' Ruth said.

And by way of reply, there was a loud banana-fart as Stinkbomb kicked and bicycled his short legs in the air.

They went back out to the Chevrolet, and sat in it waiting for Angela's Civic to emerge from the garage. The automatic door was left to close as the two cars headed off down the street.

Ruth said, 'Do I get to find out what's happening, or not?'

'Angela and I just did a deal,' Aidan told her. 'We settled the argument over the house.'

'Meaning what?'

'Meaning, basically, she gets it. She buys me out of my share and she gets the title. I wrote her a letter of agreement. She's getting a serious bargain, and she knows it.'

'But for what?'

'So we can get you a more expensive lawyer. One who's got some clout and a decent grasp of the situation and who answers the phone when you call, and who can piss from a great height onto the friends of Mimi Parry. We get a cash deposit here and now and the balance on sale.'

'How much?'

'Don't ask,' Aidan said.

Ruth said, 'Aidan, what are you telling me? That you're practically giving your house away?'

'I said she was getting a bargain,' Aidan said. 'I didn't say I was stupid.'

'Does this mean you believe me about the other thing?'

By 'the other thing' she clearly meant her supposed encounter with a living, breathing, walking, talking Tim Hagan.

'The other thing has got nothing to do with this,' Aidan said.

They followed Angela's car to a bank which stood outside a west-of-city shopping mall and shared a corner of its parking lot. Aidan and Ruth waited in the Chevy as Angela went inside. The baby's car seat lifted out all in one piece, like a little ejector seat, and went in with her.

She came out a while later, reinstalled the child in the Civic, put on the radio to give him something to listen to, and came over to their car. She was carrying a large white bank envelope.

Ruth moved into the back so that the two of them could tie up the details of their deal. She stayed silent for a while, although Aidan could sense that she was busting to say something.

Finally, out it came.

'Exactly how legal is this?' she said.

Aidan turned to give her a pleading look. Angela was turning as well.

Ruth went on, 'That's just a letter. It's not a binding contract, or anything. What's to stop us taking your money and then saying you still have to fight for the house?'

'Drop it, Ruth,' Aidan suggested.

'It's only fair to say it, Aidan,' Ruth insisted. 'I've got enough on my conscience already.'

Angela said to her, 'You obviously don't know Aidan quite as well as I do.' And then she turned to look at Aidan in the front of the car, and said, 'Is she the one you got shot for?'

Aidan, uncomfortable, shrugged and looked out of the window.

And he heard Angela say to Ruth, 'I hope he thinks you're worth it.'

Aidan signed the letter, and handed it over in exchange for the envelope. He didn't count the money, but folded the envelope and slipped it inside his jacket. Ruth made no comment as she climbed into the front of the car again; Angela's Civic was already way over on the other side of the parking lot and rejoining the homeward traffic.

She looked down, not meeting Aidan's eyes.

Aidan said nothing.

They headed out of town. Ruth didn't ask where they were going and Aidan wasn't going to offer any more information until she did. After a while they made a stop in a rest area, which had a single building containing a King's Family Restaurant and a McDonald's with toilets and a shop. They walked to it across the oil-stained concrete of the parking lot, which was surrounded by open fields and woodland. In the field across the way, new saplings had been planted and stood in their white protective plastic tubes. There was an odd and unsettling effect, because these were ranked in orderly rows like gravestones.

The King's Family Restaurant was decorated in a vaguely Victorian domestic style, with print wallpaper and brass lights. Aidan sent Ruth ahead to get them a table, and fed some change into one of the public phones.

After a couple of minutes, he was talking to Tom Diaz.

'You've been causing me some serious embarrassment,' Diaz told him. 'Wherever you both are, get back in here.'

'Give me a week,' Aidan said.

He could almost hear Diaz leaning back in his chair, looking up at the ceiling and sighing.

'No chance,' he said.

'What's a week?'

'It's out of my hands. What do you think you're going to achieve, anyway? All you've done is make everything worse. Bring her in.'

'You know damn well that once they put her on a plane, that's it.'

'Get on it with her, then, if you're so firmly attached. They must have dress-up rentacops in England too.'

Ignoring the insult, Aidan said, 'Did you find what happened to Frances Everline yet?'

'No we didn't,' Diaz said. 'What of it?'

'If you get rid of Ruth and Hagan's still in action, you lose your one and only living witness.'

228

'You really believe all that?'

Silence.

'Yeah,' Diaz said, 'that's what I thought. Let her go, Aidan. She's too damaged. She's using you and she's taking you down with her. I know it sounds hard, but that's the way it is.'

36

The next morning, Aidan left Ruth taking a shower in their room at the Crown Point Motel and walked down toward the office. They'd arrived late, and grabbed the last unit. Most of those who'd been staying here were working drivers, and they'd packed up and shipped out already. The motel was an L-shaped motor court with a huge black-mesh satellite dish out front. By night it sat under a forest of big, bright roadside signs that promised more excitement than the buildings down below. By day the signs were just so much dead clutter on the skyline.

'Was everything all right for you?' the woman in the office asked him. She was well-built and in her fifties, and her voice had a husky crack in it. As if it was usually louder, but she'd been shouting from a mountaintop.

'Everything was fine,' Aidan said. 'Now can I ask you something?'

'You can try me.'

'Is there anyone around here with the legal power to marry people?'

'I hate to break the bad news,' the woman said, 'but I already got something that passes for a husband.'

'I'm actually serious.'

'In a pig's ass.'

Aidan leaned forward, with an earnest expression.

'Are these the eyes of a liar?' he said.

She studied him, still not quite sure whether or not he was joshing her. Light seemed to dawn on her face as she looked closely at his.

'No!' she said, with clear delight.

'I've been chasing her for ages, and I finally got her pinned down to a yes.'

'And you want to do it *here*? Right in this town?' Now she was looking doubtful.

'Today, if we can,' Aidan said.

'I saw the lady when you arrived last night,' the woman said. 'She's a nice-looking girl for a man with such a serious taste problem. Which is what you must have if out of the whole state you pick a place like this to get married in.'

Aidan said, 'My best friend got married in Las Vegas. The ceremony was conducted by a woman with big hair and fifteen facelifts, and they all posed on the wedding photographs with an Elvis impersonator. Don't tell me *I've* got a taste problem.'

'What's the rush?'

'I'm an old-fashioned romantic. And I want to get her nailed down before she changes her mind. Are you on my side, or not?'

'I'll tell you what,' the woman said, moving back into the office and reaching for a phone. 'I'm going to call cousin Jimmy. Jimmy can fix anything.'

As she was making the call, Aidan leaned on the counter and scanned the office. A big, baleful German Shepherd looked up at him from underneath a table. On the wall by the counter a little note read *Dogs Are Welcome* and beneath that was a newspaper clipping: *We never had a dog that smoked in bed, got drunk or messed the room up. If your dog can vouch for you, then you're welcome too.*

The woman hung up the phone.

'Jimmy's on his way,' she said.

Aidan thanked her, and she drew them both a cup of coffee from the percolator in the office's little kitchenette. Her name, she told him, was Lisette. Lisette was a name that associated itself in Aidan's mind with someone small and dark and wearing French underwear and although he couldn't, for certain, have said why, he found himself suddenly having to rearrange his preconceptions. As this Lisette set his coffee down before him, Aidan said, 'Were you here around the time of the fire?'

'Which fire's that?' she said.

'Why, you had more than one?'

'You're talking now about before we bought the place and did it up. This is a good location for a family motel, but the last people ran it like a flophouse. People used to cook in the rooms and there was two or three fires every year.'

'The one I'm thinking of,' Aidan said, 'someone died.'

The woman inclined her head in recognition.

'That was the one that closed them down,' she said, and then she reached up to a place on the wall on the other side of the counter window and brought down a store-bought picture frame.

'My husband had this hung out where you're standing,' she said, turning it around and laying it on the countertop before him, 'but I didn't think it was much of an advertisement so I had him put it out of sight.'

The frame held a yellowing newspaper clipping from the front page of what appeared to be a local journal. It had faded so badly that the image was hard to make out. Some of the adjoining text was visible, but cropped too closely to be read. The photograph showed the end of the motel building with a fire truck standing outside.

Aidan said, 'Did they give it any more coverage than this?'

'Oh, to be sure,' the woman said. 'This is a small town and it's the biggest thing that happened since the dinosaurs left footprints. Everyone came over the weekend and took pictures. How come you're so interested?'

'Someone I know may have been involved.'

'You mean, like the boy who died?'

'Could have been. I really don't know for certain.'

'Well, that was the big story when it all finally came out,' Lisette said. 'The boy who got all burned up here was the one whose daddy killed all those women back in Louisiana. Is that who you mean?'

Aidan felt like he'd suddenly been shot to a place that was a million miles away.

'In that case,' he said, not wanting to encourage her to any more questions, 'I think I made a mistake.'

Lisette shrugged, and moved to return the picture frame to its usual position.

'Here's someone for you,' she said as she reached up to rehang it on its nail.

Aidan turned to look. And froze.

There was a police cruiser parked across the doorway outside, and a uniformed police officer in sunglasses was pushing through the glass doors and into the office toward him.

37

'This is Cousin Jimmy,' the woman said. 'Tell him what it is you're wanting to do.'

Jimmy was the local Chief of Police. He was lean and good-looking, balding only slightly, and he'd a neatly trimmed moustache. The sleeves in his uniform shirt had creases like knives. He listened as Aidan explained and then he said, 'It's easily done. Undoing it can be the difficult part.'

'I've been through that as well,' Aidan told him.

'Well,' Jimmy said, 'then there's nothing I can tell you about it. Let's go and talk to some people.'

They got into the cruiser, and went out for a ride.

The town was a full day's drive out of Philadelphia and about ten miles over into Maryland. It stood in a long, low rambling green valley that led up to a blue haze of mountains in the distance. It was too far out ever to have been one of the 'marriage factories', as they'd once termed places like Elkton that stood just over the state line, but since he and Ruth were here anyway it would do them just as well.

'My whole life's tied up in this town,' Jimmy told him as they drove along. It was a long while since Aidan had sat in a police cruiser, and he'd never done it as a civilian. It was an odd feeling. Jimmy went on, 'It may not be postcard-pretty, but there's a lot who like it. I was born here, I'm related to half the people. I've got a piece of four different businesses and my wife runs the souvenir shop.' He pointed out of the car. They were passing a near-ruin of a frame house, set back from and overlooking the road they were on. 'That's my uncle's house,' he said.

Aidan turned to look back as they left it behind them. The place had no roof, just a gracefully fallen-in roofline that made it look as if it had been punched from above.

'Where's your uncle?' Aidan said.

'Oh, he's gone. The place is falling down, but no-one wants the land. I don't suppose you've thought of settling around here?'

'Well, we're going to have to plan for something,' Aidan said.

'Don't mind me banging the drum for the area,' Jimmy said. 'I look on it as part of the job. You want wedding flowers, I can get you a good discount.'

Aidan had imagined that they'd be heading for a courthouse or some similar official building, but they drew up alongside a huge permanent furniture tent sale pitched on a rise by the road. The furniture had been set out on the grass in front of the big canvas awning. All of the chairs and tables and couches were factory-new and had been taped up in thick polythene to keep them pristine. They stood like the sheeted dead, hundreds of pieces in regular rows.

Aidan followed the Police Chief up an aisle of grass toward the sales office at the back, and there they met the local Justice. His name was Bill Wheaton and he was thickset and ginger. Jimmy explained the situation while Aidan hung back and felt a little stupid.

'Where are they staying?' the Justice asked when he'd heard the story.

'Over at Crown Point with Lisette and Bob.'

The Justice looked at Aidan. 'You'll need blood tests and witnesses,' he said.

'I'll fix all that,' Jimmy said. 'I already called Dr Sheffield. Any other reason for holding it up?'

'Only caution and plain good sense. And when did a man getting married ever show any of that?'

They all walked out together through the open-air sales floor, back toward where the Chief's car waited. Maybe the weekdays were always slow, but nobody had turned out to browse. The stuff looked like a careful inventory for a departed civilization. The Dralon people.

Jimmy said, 'There's a nice room up at the Northgate Inn. I could call ahead and we could do it there.'

'My house is nicer than that shithole,' the Justice said. 'I just had the hall painted. We'll do it right there and save these people the money.'

They went around the outskirts of town on the snow road and then back in along Technology Drive. Technology Drive appeared to have been named in hope and marked out in lots, but the only building that Aidan could see was a big old warehouse with an empty parking area around it and a hurricane fence and a padlocked gate. The edge of town was marked by a bargain barn. The bargain barn was a ramshackle old building, surrounded by dead refrigerators and cookers and freezers.

Jimmy said, 'I wasn't trying to cost you money back there.'

'I never thought you were,' Aidan said.

'I don't have any more than a quarter-interest in the Northgate anyway. You see this road we're on? I closed this entire road for a movie company once. They wanted to land a jet on it. I said no problem. I'll do *anything* to get a movie company into this town. Later on I can show you a barn they moved.'

The business district seemed to consist of half a dozen antique shops and a diner, the Jesus is Lord Hall, and a big US Mail Office serving the area. The diner, near the big junction opposite the Dollar General Stores, was called Glory B's. Jimmy pointed out the Gracious Giving Gift Shop, sounding his horn and waving to his wife as they went by. The shop had a big sign hung outside reading *Truck Load Sale*.

Aidan was looking at a white building just ahead.

'Is that the library?' he said.

'It is.'

'I'd like to look in there. Could I do that?'

The librarian, inevitably, was some second cousin or

236

other of Jimmy's and the two of them chatted about family while Aidan checked through the back files of the local newssheet. Issues for the previous twelve months were all in a big book, and everything earlier was on microfilm. The library was small, but the facilities were as good as he'd seen anywhere.

Aidan threaded up the reader with the spool for the first half of the previous year and then, after checking that he wasn't being watched, he took out the letter that had been in the bundle with Tim Hagan's papers. It was short and formal, asking the recipient to get in touch with the Police Department to endorse the statement he'd neglected to sign when interviewed. Hagan had, according to this, been one of those resident at the Crown Point Motel on the night of the fire that had closed it down.

He spooled to the date of the incident. The big headline for that week concerned the theft of a photo and frame from a gravestone in the local cemetery. But the next issue had the fire story, and Aidan recognized the picture of the burned-out end of the building from the one he'd seen back at the motel. He fed some quarters into the machine, fiddled with the framing and the focus for a while, and then started to take some copies.

After that, Jimmy took him back to the Crown Point. They made one more stop on the way, at a store where Jimmy grabbed a bottle of champagne from behind the counter and presented it to Aidan. The store was one of those where he was part-owner. He volunteered himself as a witness and said he looked forward to meeting Ruth. A radio call came in as he was setting Aidan down by the office, and he zoomed off to answer it with his arm resting out of the cruiser's open window.

The forecourt had almost cleared now. Alongside the motel office there was a gold-coloured pickup truck, unlicensed and unfit for the road and more battered than any toy, with the words 'Farm Use' daubed on its side.

Tiny greenfly-sized bugs covered the white door of their unit. Aidan knocked, and called out Ruth's name. He

237

heard her taking off the lock and chain, and then she let him in.

The air-conditioning had been running ever since they'd checked in, but it hadn't quite dispersed the musty odour that had hit them when they'd first walked into the room. Aidan closed the door behind him. The carpet was so thick underfoot that it felt as if the floor was giving way.

'It's mostly fixed,' he said. 'How've you been?'

'I've just been lying on the bed and watching TV,' Ruth said. 'Someone knocked about an hour ago. But I didn't hear you call, so I didn't answer.'

'It was probably the housekeeper.' A little self-consciously, and not wanting to refer to it directly, he set the champagne bottle down. It was the kind made in California. He said, 'How are you feeling now?'

'Strange,' Ruth admitted.

'I've got stuff to tell you,' Aidan said. 'Sit down.'

She sat on one of the twin beds, and Aidan aimed the remote control at the TV to lower the sound to background level before sitting opposite her. The drapes were unopened, and most of the illumination in the room was from the reading lights above the beds.

Aidan said, 'We already know somebody died in a fire here. They got statements from everyone who was staying that night. Tim Hagan was here but his statement didn't get signed. The fire happened because one of the residents was using a camping stove in his room. The stove ran on kerosene but it was a gasoline fire. Does that sound at all familiar?'

Ruth nodded, slowly.

'Hagan was gone the next morning,' Aidan went on. 'The body left behind in the room was very badly burned, but there was enough in his pockets to identify him. He was an itinerant worker, Louisiana-born. His name was Pete Michaud. The police were looking for him after a series of assaults on women in Cameron County. He'd worked there for more than a year. He drove a dumper truck at an

238

incinerator plant, which is kind of ironic. After the fire, they closed the file.'

'He switched, didn't he?' Ruth said.

'Pete Michaud became a dead person. But it was the real Tim Hagan who did the actual dying. This guy Michaud took his name, his ID, everything. And went on to bigger things. There's his picture.'

The photograph of Michaud had appeared in the next week's issue of the local journal. As Lisette had suggested, the fire had been the biggest hard news story to hit the area in ages and the team of the *News Examiner* had kept on scratching up new angles for more than a month.

Aidan had taken several copies of this page at various light levels, and he showed her the best of them. Even this hadn't come through too well. It was a functional, non-flattering, head-on portrait, probably taken in a booth or by someone with an instant-picture camera. The subject had the stare of an arrestee. He was plumper than when Aidan had last seen him, and he had hippyish hair and a beard. But it was definitely Ruth's dancing companion and would-be abductor, seen here at around the age of eighteen or nineteen years.

Peter Michaud, supposedly burned to death and conveniently unrecognizable. The Southern boy whose daddy, as the *Examiner* had never tired of pointing out, had killed all those women in Louisiana.

Aidan said, 'They lifted that from his ID card at the cremator.'

Ruth studied it, and seemed to shiver.

She said, 'He did it here, and then two years later he did it again. Can I take it that now you believe me?'

'I believe you saw him again,' Aidan said. 'I apologize.'

She looked up at him.

'I never *dis*believed you, Ruth. I wouldn't have brought us here if I did. Read the rest of it.'

Ruth looked through the various copies, and then continued to read. With nothing new to report they'd started to dig around to fill out the picture, and Peter

Michaud's family history had provided a more useful mine than most. It had been a clippings job, mostly. But some of the clippings were kind of remarkable.

As she was reading, Aidan said, 'Now, there's something you have to decide.'

For a moment, she couldn't quite tear herself away. But then she was listening.

'They're not likely to deport a material witness. So what we've got fixed here this afternoon doesn't necessarily have to go ahead. Unless you choose for it to.'

There was a long pause. It had taken Aidan a while to get up his nerve to point out her options, and now he was beginning to feel sorry that he had.

But then she said, 'Ice the champagne.'

'Is that a yes?'

'I suppose it must be.'

Aidan had wondered how he'd feel about it, were the moment ever to come. Right now he felt like a man standing on the rail of a high-span bridge over a mile-deep gorge, contemplating the beauty of the light on the water as he made ready to leap.

He picked up the plastic bucket from alongside the TV, and went out to look for the ice machine.

Ruth didn't expect him to be gone for more than a couple of minutes, but she hooked the chain onto the door anyway. If she'd been nervous before, now she felt as if she'd taken a step even closer to the heat.

Pete Michaud.

Peter Michaud.

The match of the name to the person would take some time for her to get used to.

She took a deep breath. Was she doing right, here? Aidan had stuck by her and done so much for her. If she felt able to stand unaided again now, that was mainly thanks to him. She owed him, if only for that.

Didn't she owe him? And although it might be enough of a reason, was it the right one?

She sat on the bed again, and read on. Aidan didn't come back. She supposed that he must have bumped into someone, the motel people again, and got held up in conversation.

Still he didn't come back.

Ruth went to the window, twitched apart the drapes, and looked out. The glass was dusty and the day beyond it appeared washed-out and bright. Their car was still in the same place, but now there was no other in the forecourt. She couldn't see Aidan. But she could see the ice machine, in plain sight under the overhang at the far end of the 'L'.

He'd been gone almost half an hour. She wondered if she could get up the nerve to go out alone and look for him.

She looked at the door, and the chain on the door. She wondered how secure those chains really were. The screws that held it were pretty small. They looked as if one determined kick would spring them out of the wood.

The photocopies lay on the bed, forgotten for the moment. She would read them all. She'd carry on reading when Aidan got back.

She waited. And waited.

And when the police chief's cruiser and the doctor's station wagon drew up outside more than an hour later, Aidan still hadn't returned.

PART THREE

When We Dead Awaken

38

Right away, we could see that there was going to be trouble.

We could see it the minute that he brought her into the house, the two of them stumbling and giggling and Daddy saying Hush, and how they'd wake up the kids and everything. But he never came up to see if we were asleep. She missed the peg and dropped her coat in the hallway, and then the two of them just went on through into the other room where the booze and the big couch are. He didn't even close the door all the way behind them.

I looked at Kathy and Elaine, and they looked at me. We knew what was coming, and nobody even had to put it into words.

There was something about her. Big. Loud. Like a lady wrestler, gone to fat. She had blue eyelids and red lips and she laughed like a man. The last one had been the same and Kathy had reckoned that she probably *was* a man, underneath, but I wouldn't let her sneak downstairs to look. I'm the oldest, I have to show a sense of responsibility.

'What are we going to do?' Elaine said.

'We'll wait,' I told her. 'It may not be so bad, this time.'

They wanted to believe it, I could see as much in their eyes. But they didn't, and neither did I.

As quietly as we could, we got to our feet and went into my room.

We'd emerged at the sound of the car, wondering if

he'd be coming home alone tonight or with company. My room was on one side of the hall, Kathy and Elaine were just across from me. We knew that if we kept our lights off and laid ourselves flat with just our faces up against the banister rails, it would be almost impossible to see us from down below. Not that it had mattered, because neither of them had even glanced upward. Just lurched in, goosed each other like they were both squeezing cushions, and lurched on.

If that's what passes for fun when you're a grownup, I'm of the opinion that it isn't much to look forward to.

Elaine wanted to play Atari but I put on the TV instead, and we all sat together in a nest made out of the pillows and bedding and watched the late movie. It was one of the *Omen* movies, the one where Damien's grown-up and rides a horse. We were just at the part where the lady TV reporter finds Damien lying curled up and naked under a back-to-front cross and starts to wonder if there's perhaps something he hasn't been telling her about himself, when the noise started up again from downstairs.

This was after about half an hour. It was a pattern, of a kind. First slam the car doors, then into the house giggling and tiptoeing, some clumsy sounds of glass against glass, and then about twenty or thirty minutes of silence before the argument started. And she could shout, could this one. Kathy looked at me and I could see the apprehension in her eyes, so I just turned up the sound on the TV. It wouldn't matter if they could hear us downstairs, not by now. It was like a journey. You reached a certain point, and beyond it you knew there was no turning back.

Downstairs there was some banging and crashing, and we heard a couple of screams. Then there was some sobbing and then everything went quiet again. We all kept our eyes on the TV screen, and we all pretended we heard nothing.

And only when the movie was over did we get to our feet and go downstairs.

It was now after one in the morning. We switched on

the stairway light because we didn't want to trip and fall. There wasn't much danger of being seen or heard by the neighbours; the house is in woodland with its own creek and about three acres all around it, and there's no direct line of sight with anybody. When it's dark you can just about make out a single streetlamp at the end of the driveway on the ridge road, but that's all.

Kathy pushed open the door. We all stood in the doorway and looked into the room.

Daddy was on one end of the couch, his head thrown back and his arms flung wide like he'd been caught in the act of belting out a song. Except that he was snoring, and his head was bobbing slightly with the vibration. Every time he reached the end of a breath, his fingers twitched as if his hands were trying to make little claws.

The woman was at the other end. Or rather she had been, and now she'd slid down onto the floor and was lying there like a whale on a beach. Her face was all mottled and her tongue was sticking out farther than it had any right to.

'Uh-oh,' said Elaine.

We saw to Daddy first. We tipped his head forward and sat him there for a few minutes until the two girls were able to take an arm each and get him to stand. He could just about help himself when he was like this, but he moved like a sleepwalker and didn't really know what he was doing. They aimed him toward the doorway and he went along with them, a kind of unguided missile.

'Get him upstairs to the bedroom,' I told them. 'I'll make a start down here.'

I put the Scotch away. One of the glasses had got broken on the floor, so I first had to get together all the pieces and then mop up the spill. Then I straightened the cover on the couch and took a cloth and wiped around everywhere that she might have touched. I had to step over her a few times while I was doing this. I was never certain where Daddy picked up his women, because it was hardly something that I could ask; but I had a suspicion that he found them crying in dark corners in bars. She was even bigger than she'd looked from upstairs. Stretching to step over, I almost fell on her. I know for a fact that big women weren't Daddy's type, and yet he always brought the same kind home. Mother wasn't big at all, so doesn't that prove it?

I crouched down by her head and looked into her face. Her eyes were slightly open and there were clusters of blood spots under the makeup, as if tiny fireworks had burst inside her skin.

I said, 'Lady, I can see you're going to give us a problem,' and just then I heard Daddy start to shout.

So I ran out to help. Kathy and Elaine had managed to get Daddy about halfway up the stairs, but now he was shouting and fighting them off. It wasn't serious fighting because he was moving like a man in a dream or under water, but it was making life hard for them. I came up behind and said 'Easy, Daddy, easy,' and he turned and looked at me. The turn was like old clockwork, and the look was a heartbreaker. One eye was wide open and the other was half-closed, and the half-closed eye was a red ball. He stared at me with no recognition at all, but at least he'd calmed down and I was able to take one of his arms and guide him onward.

We put him on his bed and stripped off his trousers and his tie, and then we left him in his shirt and his underwear and covered him over. He just lay there, eyes closed and snoring again. There wasn't anything else that we could do for him, so then we went back downstairs for another look at his lady friend.

Nothing had changed since I'd left her. I don't know what we'd have done if she'd moved or shown some sign of life; after all we could hardly let her go off and tell anyone of what had happened, not now. I didn't like to picture myself putting a cushion over her face and sitting on it until she went still again. The notion seemed kind of cruel.

We stood around her and we stared for a while.

'Jesus, she's fat,' Elaine said.

'I know,' I said. 'I know.'

I'm the oldest, but I can't say I'm the strongest. There were two years when I was small that I spent going in and out of hospital for one thing after another, and I don't think I ever fully caught up. Kathy, now . . . Kathy was a tank. She didn't look much, but she could hit harder than any boy I knew. Nobody ever picked on me because they couldn't stand the thought of having to run in fear when a girl came after them, which she most certainly would. We stuck together. Even without Mother we were a family, after all.

Kathy took one of the woman's arms and Elaine and I took the other, and we heaved. She shifted about an inch.

'This is going to take a while,' I said. 'Let me think about it.'

I went back to the hallway and got her coat. It was red, and like her it was heavy. I took it through and spread it on the floor beside her, and then the three of us all got together and rolled her onto it. That wasn't easy, either. She kept getting halfway and then flopping back, and for a while I was thinking that we'd never be able to do it. But then we gave one last big heave-ho, and she rolled over like a ship.

I was gasping. But Kathy patted me on the shoulder.

'She might be easier to handle when she's stiffened up a bit,' she said.

'I know,' I said. 'But that won't be for hours.'

We at least had to get her out of the house before morning. Once outside we could drag her into the shed or even just cover her with an old tarpaulin until Daddy was out of the way and we could finish the job, but the simple fact is that there's no easy way to hide a dead fat lady indoors. Put her in a chest or a closet, and she'll go rigid on you and you won't be able to get her out again until she loosens up after a good twelve hours or more.

And who knew *what* could happen in that twelve hours?

We all lined up and got a grip on the coat, and we started

to drag. The coat collar began to tear at first, so we had to stop and rearrange everything before we tried again. It was slow progress but we got her across the floor where a doorway led through to the kitchen, and there we had a problem because the three of us all got bunched together and we couldn't squeeze through.

Something moved upstairs, and we all froze.

'Only Daddy turning over,' I said.

The woman had lost a shoe, and Kathy went to retrieve it while I sat on the kitchen floor and got my breath back. Details like that can really mess you up if you don't keep on top of them. She tossed the shoe onto the coat and stepped over the woman to rejoin us.

'Better move the table,' she said.

We moved the kitchen table to give us a clear run to the back door. Once through the door we'd be outside, but then there would be two steps to manage. But at least we'd be going down them, and not up.

Getting her across the kitchen floor was a lot easier. The floor was tile instead of carpet, and it made a difference. Even so it was a considerable strain, and when we got there Elaine sat down heavily and said, 'That's it, I've had enough.'

It isn't only that Elaine's the baby in the family. She's also something of a complainer. You have to know that, and you have to manage her or else she'll just throw up her hands on everything and say, 'Well, *you* do it.' You always know when she's come into a room because she announces her presence with a heavy, exasperated sigh. Then you're supposed to ask what's wrong so that she can tell you.

I said, 'Now, everybody listen. We're going to do this and we're going to do it *tonight*. Just us and nobody else. Because Daddy's going to wake up and come down for breakfast in the morning, and if he sees her lying here by the door he's going to get a pretty good idea there's something wrong.'

What we're talking about here is impeccable logic and there was nobody there in that kitchen who could give me an argument, mainly because the one who'd probably be most inclined to was elsewhere bending the ear of Jesus. I looked at Kathy and Kathy nodded, and I looked at Elaine and Elaine stuck out her bottom lip and looked dark. But for once she didn't argue.

'Here's how we'll do it,' I said. 'Kathy, you and me are going to go to the shed and get the boards. Elaine's going to stay here and listen out in case Daddy starts wandering around again.'

'With *her*?' Elaine said, eyeing the body distastefully.

'Yeah, with her,' I said. 'Don't worry, she isn't going to bite.'

'She's really ugly,' said Elaine.

'Try not to let it depress you,' I said.

Kathy and I went out to the shed. It was a cool night and there was a starry sky, and most of the leaves had fallen from the trees by then so there was a clear view of the stars through the woodland all around the house. We could hear the running of water in the creek and the cry of some far-off animal and, just for a moment, the passing of a car on the main road about a quarter of a mile away. We stopped and waited, but nothing turned down the ridge road toward us.

The boards were two shelves on the shed wall. They weren't fixed on their brackets but before we could get them down we had to take off a number of half-empty paint cans and gluepots and bottles and a lot of other dusty stuff that seemed to have been there for ever. We didn't worry too much about where anything belonged, and we could put it all back afterwards in any order and Daddy wouldn't know. He kept his stock in here and he moved it all around so that he could work with his tools sometimes; otherwise it was mostly a dump for kid stuff like my old bike or Elaine's playhouse.

Daddy's stock was of wooden toyboxes that he made out in the shed and advertised in the newspaper for forty dollars apiece. He made other things too, porch swings and garden chairs which he kept stacked up on the back of his truck with a little framed FOR SALE notice and his phone number. Before he started up in business for himself he'd worked at a place out on the I-90 which supplied electric motors, but he'd been laid off from there. No-one ever seemed to phone, but occasionally he'd make a sale straight off the back of the Mitsubishi.

That was on the good days. He had maybe a couple of those every month.

Otherwise, he never had much call to come in here.

We got the boards and we took them back to the kitchen doorway, and we laid them outside over the steps like a ramp and that's how we got her out. It was nearly three in the morning by then, and Elaine was yawning and this time it wasn't just for effect. Even Kathy looked dead on her feet, although nobody looked quite as much so as the fat lady.

I'd planned to get her across the yard area behind the house and in among the trees where we could cover her over, but I could see that it wasn't going to happen . . . at least, it wasn't going to happen tonight. The troops were exhausted. So instead we kept up with the coat trick and dragged her past the sandpit and into the shed, where we then hauled out a few of the toyboxes and built them into a wall to screen her from the door. I checked, and you couldn't see her at all. It wasn't ideal, but it would do for now.

It was after four. We went inside, cleaned ourselves up, and all went to bed. I don't remember what I was thinking about as I went off to sleep.

I only know that it didn't take long.

I woke late in the morning. I knew that I'd overslept but all the same I just lay there, vaguely remembering the night before. Then suddenly it all came together with a bang, like a jet-propelled jigsaw, and I jumped out of bed. I could hear movement from downstairs as I got into yesterday's clothes, and I hoped that I wasn't going to be too late.

I checked on Daddy's bedroom on the way past. His bed was empty.

Everyone was in the kitchen. Daddy was at the table and Kathy was right behind him, and as I froze in the doorway she was making frantic signals to me that he couldn't see. *It's OK*, she was signing. *Everything's OK*.

Daddy looked up from his cereal, and he smiled.

'Morning, Peter,' he said.

The bad eye was closer to normal. It was just ordinary bloodshot, now. He looked pale and the lines on his face had a look as if they'd been dusted in with grey powder, but otherwise he was the same old Daddy again. Elaine was bringing him an Alka-Seltzer from over by the sink.

As she set it down beside him, he rumpled her hair as a kind of thanks and said, 'Did anybody notice what time it was when I got in last night?'

We all shrugged and shook our heads.

He sighed. 'These late business meetings,' he said. 'Sometimes I wish I could avoid them altogether.'

We all sat around the table and we talked about the things that we'd been doing and the things that we still had to do, when the fact of it was that the only thing on three of our minds was the problem of the corpse out there in the shed. Daddy seemed to have no memory of the previous night at all.

But that was usual.

After a while he slammed both hands flat onto the table and, rising, said in a bright voice, 'You know, I don't know what it is, but I'm feeling lucky today. I think I'll just get myself made presentable and then I'll make a couple of calls and then I'm going to hit the road. There's a place in Hammond showed an interest in putting some stuff on display when I last went by.'

Something went cold inside me.

I said, 'Do you want us to bring any of it out of the shed?'

'Well, thanks for the offer, but I've told you before about you kids not handling the stock. I'll see to it myself.'

He went upstairs, whistling lightly. And I can tell you, the moment he was out of earshot we nearly panicked.

'What are we going to do? What are we going to do?' Kathy kept saying, until I had to tell her to shush because Daddy was going to hear her voice through the floor.

'You and me are going to go out and move her,' I said, 'while Elaine keeps a watch right here.' I turned to Elaine. 'You hear him coming, you get him over to the other side of the house and keep him busy there until we're done.'

'How?' she said.

'You can be thinking of that while you're waiting for him,' I told her.

Kathy and I went out to the shed. When Daddy went for a wash and a shave he could usually be counted on to be missing for half an hour, at least. He liked to play the bathroom radio and take his time and make a real production out of it. Surely we could get her out and into the trees in that time; we could pile sacks or leaves over her, or even truck out all of the sand from the sandpit and bury her in *that* . . . anything to keep her out of Daddy's sight until he was out of the way, when by the sound of it we'd have the entire day in which to finish the job properly.

'We'd better put the boxes back too, or he'll know,' Kathy said.

So first we rearranged the stock as we'd found it, uncovering the fat lady as we did. She didn't look any better or worse than she had the night before, but now she looked it in daylight. I checked my watch. We'd lost ten minutes so far, we had another twenty. There'd be no more than fifty yards to cover, but it would be over rough ground and there were only two of us now.

'Let's do it,' I said.

We got her by the arms again except that by now, of course, she was a statue. She seemed to weigh like marble, too. Imagine trying to haul a dead cow around your living-room and then push it out of the doorway; that was the kind of problem we faced. We tried dragging her, we tried dragging the coat she still lay on.

I checked my watch again. Fifteen minutes gone. And the half-hour was an optimistic estimate anyway.

Kathy let go.

'I've got an idea,' she said.

She dived behind Elaine's upended playhouse at the back of the shed, and after about a minute's rummaging she came out with a skipping rope.

'A skipping rope?' I said.

'We loop this under her arms,' Kathy explained, 'and then we take an end each and pull. Like horses.'

'Let's try it,' I said.

We ran it under her shoulders then around her armpits. One side was easy, but on the other we had to work it through and touching her flesh was like handling a chicken fresh out of the refrigerator. I had to wipe my hands on my shorts and then the two of us each took a handle of the skipping rope and leaned back like we were in a tug-o'-war and pulled.

She moved, just a little. We braced our legs, we put our backs into it . . .

And she moved again.

Slowly but surely, we were getting her toward the door. That was only a matter of a few feet and I'm not pretending that it was easy, but we were doing it and that was encouraging. We got out of the doorway, she slid up to it and stopped. Stopped dead, if I can say as much.

'She's stuck,' I said.

'She can't be stuck,' Kathy said. 'We got her through there last night, didn't we?'

'Her arm's in the way,' I said.

And it was, too. It must have been the way that she'd been lying; whatever the cause, her arm was sticking out like a toppled mannequin's and was refusing to give.

'I'll fix it,' Kathy said, and she pushed me aside and took a hold on the doorframe for balance and then raised herself and put one foot against the arm and pushed. Nothing seemed to happen.

'If this doesn't work, I'm taking the shovel to it,' Kathy

said, and she started to use her entire weight to rock the arm back and forth like a car on its springs.

She never needed the shovel. I knew that the moment that I heard the arm crack.

We got back into position and then we turned our backs to the fat lady and leaned into the skipping rope like a couple of oxen, and with a lot of huffing and straining we got her over the threshold and began the long, slow journey across open ground toward the trees. I couldn't check my watch now. I didn't dare break off from what I was doing. Did you ever see those pictures of Egyptian slaves dragging the big stones that went to make the pyramids? Well, I know exactly what they felt like.

We'd gone less than halfway when Elaine came running out of the house.

'Get back in,' I gasped, losing my footing at the same time. 'Get back in before he comes out and sees us!'

But Elaine only said, 'There's a police car coming up the ridge road.'

I dropped the rope.

'Oh, shit,' I said.

There's a useful expression I've learned since, and it's *hoist with one's own petard*. Essentially as I understand it, it means all fucked up and all your own fault. We'd dragged her right out into the middle of the yard and put her on open display, where only a blind person with no dog could miss her. There wasn't the time to go forward, there wasn't the time to go back. We couldn't even stick a few feathers on her and pretend that she'd fallen out of a tree.

'Do what you can here,' I said. 'I'll try to keep them away from the windows.'

I ran for the house. My mind was racing, but I can't honestly say that it was achieving much. As I entered the kitchen, I could hear Daddy coming down the stairs to open the front door and any hopes that I'd had of the police car heading on for somewhere else just went. I could hear muffled voices now, and I turned and looked out of the kitchen window. The woman lay there like an anthill with legs. Kathy and Elaine were nowhere to be seen, and I honestly couldn't say that I blamed them.

The muffled voices were coming my way, and getting less muffled with every stride.

I did the only thing I could think of. I grabbed the rod and turned the slats on the venetian blind so that the light was still coming in, but you couldn't take a straight look out.

Daddy came into the kitchen first. He was saying, 'If the kids didn't turn the coffee machine off, there ought to be . . . ' and then he stopped, and said, 'Oh,' because the coffeemaker wasn't on and hadn't even been working for weeks.

'Doesn't matter, Mr Michaud,' the man behind him said, and the room seemed to fill from wall to wall with the terrifying aura of authority that came in through the door with that police uniform. His hat was in his hand, but that made no difference. And his voice was like an elderly uncle's, almost kind, but that made no difference either. I was awestruck, dwarfed in his shadow.

The policeman saw me, and winked.

He was older than Daddy, and bigger. I can imagine that under any other circumstances I might even have liked him on sight, but today most definitely wasn't the day for it.

He said, 'Don't take this wrong, but we've got to eliminate. Women out on their own go missing, it's something you've got to check up on. You don't remember talking to her at all?'

Daddy shook his head. 'I don't remember talking to *anyone*. I pretty much keep to myself when I go . . .' He looked at me then, and there was a barely perceptible hesitation. 'When I go into town.'

'Do you remember what time you left?'

Daddy frowned, and looked at me. 'Peter?' he said. 'Did I already ask you this?'

'You got home around ten-thirty,' I said, hazarding a guess and hoping.

It would seem that I got it just about right, because it appeared to be what the policeman most wanted to hear.

'Well, that takes care of that,' he said, brightening. But as quickly as the light touched his features, it gave way to something more serious.

He said, 'I'm sorry to be bothering you with this at all. I know what a rough year you've had, what with . . . '

And the two of them kind of nodded, acknowledging their way around the unsayable.

'A terrible way to go,' the policeman said. 'For her, and for everybody. Especially when you have to watch them heading downhill for so long.'

Daddy said, 'I've been luckier than some. At least I've had the kids to look after me and keep me going. I don't know how I'd ever have handled it without them.'

'Yeah,' the policeman said. 'A family's a blessing, all right. Of course, mine are all grown-up and gone now.' And my heart soared as he put his hat on, obviously making ready to leave.

'We can get out this way,' Daddy said, moving to the back door.

I gagged.

I was trying to speak.

The problem was, I couldn't think of a single thing that I could possibly say.

'Everything all right, Peter?' Daddy said with a puzzled, half-smiling look of enquiry as he opened the door to the yard and stood back for the policeman to precede him outside. 'Anything wrong?'

I smiled what had to be the most stupid smile in the history of goofiness, and shook my head.

They went out.

I stayed there, waiting for the bomb to burst.

I heard Daddy say, 'Those are my other two.' And the policeman say, 'Nice kids.'

Nice kids?

I waited for the next part, something along the lines of Hey, I see you have a dead fat lady in your garden, mind if I just go over and see if it's the same one we're looking for? And then maybe Daddy would say No, help yourself, we get a lot of that around here.

But all I heard was Daddy calling, 'If you're going to play with that thing, don't go leaving it outside all night.' And then a chorus from Kathy and Elaine of, 'Yes, Daddy.'

I couldn't believe what I was hearing. I snapped open a gap in the blind and peered through.

Daddy and the policeman were just disappearing around the side of the shed, heading around to the driveway at the front of the building. Out across the yard, Kathy and Elaine had spread out a dolls' picnic before Elaine's playhouse. I stared stupidly at the scene for several moments before I realized what they'd done.

The playhouse was a printed cloth tent over a frame of lightweight plastic tubes. For all its size, Elaine could just about carry it on her own as long as there wasn't a strong wind. Two of them together could have lifted it into place in a matter of seconds. You were supposed to break it down and pack it all away when it wasn't in use, but it was much easier simply to stick it on its side in the shed until the next time that it was wanted. At least that way, pieces didn't get lost.

It hadn't covered the woman perfectly, but you couldn't see that from the house. It only became apparent as I walked across the yard toward them and saw her top end sticking out at the back. She looked as if she was trying to crawl out from under. Only she wasn't, of course, she hadn't even moved. The skipping rope was still in place around her shoulders, the wooden handles lying on the ground to either side of her head.

Kathy and Elaine were looking up at me.

I said, 'I stalled them for you as long as I could. You should have heard me in there. I was brilliant.'

I don't know what it was; perhaps it was the policeman talking about Mother. But when Daddy came back inside he went down to his office in the basement and picked up the phone, and that's how I found him when I went down about twenty minutes later – sitting there with the receiver in his hand gazing blankly at all the unpaid bills in their clip on the wall, and with that faint howling noise coming out of the earpiece. You know the sound, it's the one they put on after a minute or so when you've forgotten to dial. I took the receiver out of his hand and set it down, and he looked at me. I was scared then.

But he knew me.

He didn't go out after all. His bright mood was gone, and he seemed to have forgotten any plans that he'd made for the day. He just hung around the kitchen, which in turn meant that the three of us had to hang around that stupid playhouse in order to keep a guard on what we had hidden inside. Sometimes he'd watch us from the window, which meant that we couldn't even take a shot at moving her again.

Only when it had started to go dark were we able to leave it and come inside. Elaine was happy. She'd spent all day in her element, organizing tea parties and handing out the plastic food.

Daddy said to me suddenly, 'Did somebody come to the house this morning?'

'I don't think so, Daddy,' I said.

And then he walked away again with a puzzled, uncertain look on his face as if he was trying to remember a dream.

At around seven he reappeared in his good clothes and said, 'I have to go into town tonight. It's one of those late business meetings, something I can't avoid. I want you to lock up and look after your sisters.'

And I said, 'I will.'

As soon as his car was gone, we put on the yard lights and went out to finish the job. With three of us on the skipping rope, we had her there in less than half an hour.

I took the lid off the tank, and we used one of the boards to lever her up and tip her in. What a strain. For a moment it looked as if she wasn't going to fit through, but we all stamped on her together and she went through with a pop. It wouldn't have been so easy if the tank hadn't been buried in the ground. All of the waste from the house was supposed to go in at one end and clean water was supposed to flow out into the creek at the other, but don't ask me how it worked. Kathy dropped the loose shoe in after.

We'd a flashlight with us, of course. I shone it through the hatch just to be sure that she hadn't got jammed halfway down. But she hadn't. In the beam I could see the faded prints of old dresses and odd bits of mildewed jewellery and some hair and some bones. Whatever this tank process was, it seemed to be taking its time.

The light caught on something that grinned.

'We've brought a new friend for you,' I whispered. 'Now, you've all got to be nice to her.'

And then I put the lid back onto the tank, and we all went into the house to watch some television.

39

It was night in New Orleans.

Ten twenty-five in the evening, and Ruth was following the lights of a streetcar as it headed out toward Carrolton Avenue. The avenue was broad and the streetcar lines ran up the middle of it, divided off in a central reservation by grass strips and bushes and power line poles. Either side of the tracks, traffic pumped by; whatever the hour, the blood still flowed.

Ruth was in a sedan that she'd rented that afternoon. As she went through the motions of driving, she tried to keep her mind clear of all reflection. This was not easy. It was as if she was shutting out a beast whose very name she dared not mention. Living in this moment and no other; trying not to look too far forward, determined not to look behind her at all.

To look back would be, in a most literal sense, too much for her to bear.

She was passing a church with a hoarding outside. Her eyes took it in, but in her mind it didn't register. Details slid by her, hard and bright, and nothing stuck. As night had drawn on the sky had failed fully to darken, staying almost opalescent with the reflected haze of the bright city. New Orleans, the low-lying crescent-shaped city within one huge bend of the Mississippi River, spread around her for miles.

She stopped for a red light. A flapping handbill caught her attention for a moment. The wooden power poles at every junction were each peppered with a thousand old staples, black and rusted like a crust of dead insects. The streetcar had already crossed and was picking up speed ahead, but Ruth looked away and let it go. It was the last remaining line in town, it was on rails, it could make no choices. It went where it went. Which was pretty much the way that she felt.

Ruth checked her written directions. She'd a map on the seat, but she'd given up on that. The address that she needed was somewhere close to the end of the line. It was late to be doing this. She wondered for a moment if she was being wise. But she didn't dwell on it for long.

Two cars stood at the end of the line where one broad avenue crossed another. They looked like old-time railway carriages with no train to pull them. One driver sat out behind while the other moved down his empty car, listlessly knocking the seatbacks over as he switched the vehicle around for its return journey downtown. Ruth could hear the seatbacks going, one clattering crash after another, fading into the distance behind her as she made the turn off the avenue and into the side streets.

She had to park and walk a little way. People had switched on their lights, but many hadn't yet drawn their blinds so that each home was like an illuminated doll's house with a many-layered domestic scene behind each window. The houses along here were an odd mix. There were Swiss chalets from a picture book, near-mansions going to rot, shotgun cabins maintained to near-perfection, and all of them side-by-side on the same residential street. As Ruth walked along, she was treated to the combined chorus of the back ends of a sequence of air-conditioning units. The street was of baked, cracked asphalt. Cars were nose-to-tail all along, leaving only one car's width down the middle.

Here was the house that she'd come to find. Well-kept, but overdue a fresh coat of paint. A porch at the front, and a light over the porch.

She stepped up to the door and rang the bell.

The door didn't open, but after a few moments she heard a voice calling out from the other side of it.

'What is it?' the voice said. A woman's voice.

Ruth said, 'I'm looking for Mrs Elizabeth Vermot. Is that you?'

'What's your business?' the woman said. There was an outer frame door with an insect mesh across it. The extra layer didn't look much, but it didn't help the sound.

Ruth said, 'I went to your old house, and your neighbours said you'd moved here.'

'It's very late.'

'I know, I'm sorry about that. I only got into town this afternoon.'

'Well, what's it about?'

'You were foster mother to the Michaud children after their father went away? Do I have the right person?'

There was a silence. After a few moments, Ruth began to think that maybe the woman had decided to clam up and retreat into her home, leaving Ruth to stand there unheard. But how else could she have handled it? She had to say it somehow.

But then the woman said, 'That's private to them and me. I don't talk about it. I'm sorry. Good night.'

'I'm not a reporter,' Ruth said.

'Not to anyone. Good night.'

Ruth started to feel desperate. And a little ridiculous, shouting through the door like this, but then she knew that she'd stand here and conduct the entire conversation at one remove if she had to. Anything, as long as she could get the woman to talk to her.

She said, 'I know Peter Michaud.'

'Peter died,' the woman said.

'That's not true, and I've got the scars to prove it.'

There was another silence. And then Ruth heard the woman say, 'Step back to where the light is.'

Ruth complied and, after a few moments, she heard locks being released and the door being opened. Elizabeth Vermot stood in the doorway, looking out at her through the dark mesh of the screen. Ruth felt like an exhibit. But she didn't move from under the light.

'What's your name?' Elizabeth Vermot said. She was wearing a loose-sleeved robe and obviously hadn't been expecting company. She was a tall woman, good-looking

264

still. Her features were strong and she rinsed her hair blond.

'Ruth Lasseter,' Ruth said.

'What did he do to you?'

'I'd rather not stand here and tell it.'

'You'd better,' Elizabeth Vermot warned her, "cause you ain't coming inside at this hour.'

Ruth took a breath. 'I . . . went with him,' she said. She couldn't quite bring herself to put it any other way. 'It was only the one time and it happened because I gave in to something I shouldn't have. But then when I stopped it, he turned on me.'

Elizabeth Vermot was watching her narrow-eyed, but it was plain to Ruth that none of this was a surprise to her. She wasn't necessarily swallowing it. But she wasn't discounting it either.

She said, 'What'd he do?'

'Tried to hurt me first. Then he found out he could hurt me more through someone I cared about.'

'Ruth, you say?'

Ruth nodded.

The woman hesitated for a moment, as if she was about to do something that went against all custom and habit. And then, in a tone of considerably lessened hostility, she said, 'I'll talk to you, Ruth, but it'll have to be in the morning. Where are you staying?'

'I don't know that yet.'

'There's a whole string of motels out on Airline Highway,' the woman said. 'None of 'em's pretty, but they won't break the bank. Come back in daylight and I'll talk to you then.'

Neither of them moved. Ruth wanted to say something more. But she couldn't think of anything.

'Thanks,' she said.

It was clear that both of them felt awkward now.

'Nothing personal, Miz Lasseter,' the woman explained. 'But my husband's in the hospital and I'm here on my own in the house.'

Pleading wouldn't help, and it might do her case harm. She'd gained some ground. Ruth knew that she ought to back off and be patient now. But what she felt was despair, sinking in her like a weight that she didn't have the strength to re-elevate.

'I understand,' she said. 'I hope it's not serious.'

'Well,' Elizabeth Vermot said, 'he had a stroke. We're waiting to see how serious it's going to be.'

'I can see you've got troubles enough of your own, without me adding mine.'

Ruth turned to leave the porch, and to go back to her car.

She'd reached the darkness at the end of the short driveway when she heard her first name being called.

Ruth looked back. Elizabeth Vermot had opened the screen door. She beckoned with a movement of her head for Ruth to return and join her inside.

She went.

The sitting-room had a polished wooden floor and a low leather couch. It was illuminated by a single reading lamp. Elizabeth Vermot led Ruth through to the kitchen at the back of the house, where the lights were brighter and where she'd apparently been interrupted in the act of making tea with a dipper.

'What's that accent?' she said.

'I'm English.'

'So how does an English woman come to get hurt by a boy like Peter Michaud?'

'It's on my own head,' Ruth admitted. 'I picked him for the job.'

Elizabeth Vermot was fishing out the dipper, holding it out over the kitchen sink like a dripping censer. 'You want some of this?' she said, looking back over her shoulder.

But Ruth had seen something that interested her, and she moved to the wall of the kitchen where hung a picture frame with somewhere between thirty and fifty different overlapping snapshots crowded into it. A scrapbook on

266

the wall. 'No, thank you,' she said. 'Were these all your children?'

'Every one of 'em,' Elizabeth Vermot said, with a tone that affected to imply a mountain of trouble but actually did more than hint at a mountain of pride. 'I've had them from babies to big lugs, for anything from two weeks to ten years. I'd get a lot of the problem cases. Straightened a lot of them out, too. There are some of them stayed in touch. Not all of them.' She'd moved over to stand by Ruth, and now she pointed at certain of the pictures. 'Him, him, her . . . they don't write often. But they do remember.'

'Have you given it up?'

'Well, with Curtis and his health, I'd've had to anyway. We sold up the big house and moved into this one.'

Ruth scanned the faces on the photo board.

'If you're looking for Peter on there,' Elizabeth said, 'you'll be wasting your time. Curtis wouldn't have it. His sisters are there, but not him. Peter was the reason for Curtis saying, enough. I said a prayer when I heard he'd died because I never knew a boy that needed one more. Now you seem to be telling me that I spoke out for him too soon.'

'You don't seem that surprised,' Ruth said.

'You knew him like I did,' Elizabeth Vermot said, 'you wouldn't be either. Let's hear it, Ruth. There's nothing in this house a person can't say.'

Ruth stumbled her way through her story. It wasn't as hard as she'd feared. She'd the sense that there had been many scenes like this one in Elizabeth Vermot's life and long career as a carer, late-night heart-to-hearts in kitchens where the day's end brought an outpouring of troubles. If one knew where to prod and when to listen, the rest would surely follow.

She left out one thing.

She left out the ending: the incident at the Crown Point Motel, and the nature of the phone call she'd received on her return.

Instead, she brought it to a conclusion by saying, 'I have

to find him somehow. If you know of any way I can do that, I'll be grateful to hear it.'

'You find him,' Elizabeth Vermot said. 'Then what?'

'That'll be mostly up to him.'

They moved through into the other room, and Elizabeth Vermot switched on a few more lights. She'd wanted to check that the VCR was running, as she was taping a show for her husband so that he wouldn't miss it while in hospital. Her undertone of anxiety would have been hard to miss. Ruth guessed that the prognosis for Curtis Vermot had been less than encouraging.

Elizabeth said, 'The three of them were sent to me about five weeks after their daddy was first put away. They'd been split up in different institutions since the time of the arrest, and they'd taken that badly. Getting them together under one roof again was the first priority. Me getting their trust was going to be the second. Elaine was the easiest, she was a little doll. She was a complainer, but she wasn't hard to handle. Kathy was the big handful. You know that she was killed?'

Ruth hadn't even known the names of the girls until now. All she'd seen were the second-hand reports in the newspaper coverage. 'I didn't know that,' she said.

'It happened when she was seventeen. She was out with some boys that she used to hang around with. I was always grounding her, and it never made a scrap of difference. Lock her in her room, and she'd go out through the window. These boys used to steal cars and race them around and then set fire to them. They were driving too fast along the top of the levee one night, and they lost it and the car rolled over. Two died and two walked away. Kathy broke her neck. I miss that girl still. She acted tough, but she'd a really thin skin. And a great sense of humour. When she was around, she'd make the place light up.'

Ruth said, 'Was her brother any part of that crowd?'

'Peter had moved out by then.' A twitch of a grim smile. 'Moved out . . . hell, I'd thrown him out. He was living back in their old house on his own, in spite of it being ruined by then and everyone telling him not to. He took a bedroll and he fixed up one room, and that was his home. I was supposed to drive out there and tell him about Kathy, but I let the police do it. I had looking after Elaine for my excuse if I needed one, but the fact of it is that Peter Michaud is the only child who lived in my house that I ever gave up on. I don't say that lightly. It ain't a job for people who think you can walk away.'

'What did he do?'

'Well, he was the oldest and I suppose he'd been hit the worst. He came to me all full of guilt, and all the kindness in the world couldn't get it out of him.' Ruth's expression must have been giving something away, because Elizabeth Vermot said, 'What's the matter?'

Ruth said, 'He's got to be the least guilty-feeling person I ever saw.'

'Well,' Elizabeth said, 'guilt's a complicated thing. You can get it when you didn't control something you think you should've. Pete thought he should have kept the family together, and he didn't. He couldn't cure his momma's cancer and he couldn't keep his daddy sane. You could tell that to his head, but his heart wouldn't let him listen. If he'd been a little bit more stupid and a lot more selfish, he'd probably have come through it OK. It sounds like a strange thing to wish for a person, but that's how it was.'

'So how did he react when he heard about his sister?'

Elizabeth sighed, and shook her head. 'I don't know. I never saw him then. But I'd guess that whatever he felt, he chose what he let show. He was good at that. I'd seen him learning how.'

'What do you mean?'

'Well, twice a week they all used to go for assessment and therapy. For Kathy it was like water off a duck. Elaine sucked it up and did real well. It was just what she needed, and I could see it did her a lot of good. With Pete they reckoned they were getting a steady improvement but if you ask me, he was just getting the hang of how to fool the professionals. Once he finally got his act perfect, they said he was fine.'

'Fine in the sense of what?'

'Being over his trauma. By every other indication, his life was a mess. He was kicked out of school. It got to the point where he just lay about the house all the time and I'd have to pick him up and throw him out just to be sure that he saw daylight once in a while. He wasn't over it. He wasn't over anything. He'd just dug a hole and buried it deep.'

'Does Elaine still live around here?'

Elizabeth Vermot looked at her hands, and then clasped them before her. 'I'm not sure I want to answer that,' she said.

'Maybe he's in touch with her,' Ruth suggested, and that earned her a look that told her she'd sailed right up to the line and over it.

'And maybe he isn't,' Elizabeth said. 'Do you want to talk about the Michaud boy or do you want to call it a night?'

Ruth took the hint. She said, 'What did he do after they kicked him out of school?'

'There were jobs,' Elizabeth said. 'He had a whole string of jobs but it was like he got a weird kind of satisfaction out of ruining his own chances. Like there was someone else watching, and it would hurt them more than it did him. The time he finally moved out of here, he was working in a slaughterhouse.'

Ruth felt something turn over inside her. She said, 'Did he kill things?'

'No, he just worked on the line. I think he cut up the chilled meat with a bandsaw for the next person to trim and pack. He'd bring home these coveralls all stiff with blood down the front. Talk about a mess, you couldn't put anything else in the wash along with them. There was this one night he told me this story about how a sow had escaped from the pens and had everybody chasing it around outside for more than an hour. So then the slaughtermen penned it up and let every male pig in the stockyard take a poke at her. This went on the whole day until the sow was all torn up and screaming, and then they killed her. I didn't say anything to him, but I phoned his supervisor the next morning. I couldn't believe that anyone would have given approval for such a job and, sure enough, nobody had. They thought he was still binding books for the library. They had him fired the same morning, and that was the day he came home and attacked me.'

'You mean physically?'

'He broke the one house rule I wouldn't ever bend. He wasn't the first. But he was damn near a grown man. We'd never had an easy relationship, but that was the absolute limit. I made him wait outside while I packed his bags.'

'I'm surprised that he went along with that,' Ruth said. 'He's not a person who handles frustration too well.'

'He needed a mother figure,' Elizabeth said. 'But I wasn't his mother. He just couldn't sort out the resentment from the need.'

Ruth said, 'Do you know where he might have gone to?'

'I have really no idea. I'm sorry.'

'And his sister? Can't I talk to her?'

Elizabeth didn't answer straightaway. She studied Ruth for a while. Long enough to make her uncomfortable, at least.

She said, 'I have to draw a line between helping you and hurting someone else. Elaine's been through a lot and she's still hardly more than a kid. She's got a job and a home and a boyfriend, and they're talking about getting married. What's behind her's behind her. I don't see any good reason for upsetting all that. Unless there's something else you haven't told me that's going to persuade me, I think it's best I say no.'

Ruth looked down. 'I don't want to say any more than I've said.'

'And yet you still think I'm going to send you to Elaine.'

'Please.'

'Why?'

'I think Peter's a lost soul. That's what makes him so dangerous. You can't scare him or knock him down or make him see reason; he just goes on. I had the chance to stop him once, and I didn't take it. So now everyone that he's hurt since then is on my conscience. One way or another I'm going to find him and try to bring him home. He stripped everything out of my life. I've nothing else left. And if I let go of this, I'll be gone just like he is. I have to find him. For his own sake, as much as mine.'

There was a sudden sound. A whirr of servos, the beat of a machine. The VCR had run to the end of its timer and was powering down. The lights on its fascia cut out. They'd been talking for over an hour.

Elizabeth Vermot got to her feet and went over to the window. The window ran from floor to ceiling and was screened by a thin-slatted venetian blind. She could look out. But nobody down at street level could look in.

She said, 'Elaine lives in Gramercy with her boyfriend now. I won't tell you her home address, but most days you'll find her on the checkout at the TG&Y. You can't miss it. It's right on the main street in the middle of town. Ask her, but don't press her. Don't spoil what she has. If you do, I won't forgive you.'

Ruth thanked her. There didn't seem to be anything else that she could say, apart from wishing her husband well.

As Ruth was leaving, Elizabeth said, 'You talk about scars. This is what he gave me to remember him by.'

Standing by the open doorway, she drew back the sleeve of her robe. On the inside of her forearm, white on white where the flesh was at its most vulnerable, was the perfect double-crescent of a human bite mark.

'He feels no-one else's pain,' Elizabeth said. 'But you can be sure he feels his own. Don't think I don't pity him, Ruth.'

She walked back to her car. And along the way, she became aware of something that she hadn't noticed before. Some people were sitting out on their unlit porches, dark in the darkness, watching unmoving and in silence as she passed by.

She drove out, past the big Canal Villere all-hours supermarket at the end of the street. A car overtook her, rap music rattling its windows. Teenagers gathered on the corner were watching the traffic go by and hailing their friends.

Ruth wanted to go on. She wanted to go on without stopping. But she knew that it was late, and she knew that there was little she'd be able to do before morning. She had to find a place to stay. And if she could manage it, she had to try to sleep.

She drove up and down for a while. The sense of motion was soothing. Aimless but temporarily satisfying, like food with no nourishment.

She passed the church again. Again, she saw the hoarding. It carried a message, hand-lettered and old-fashioned and simple in its wisdom.

It is better to build children, it said, *than to repair adults*.

It stuck for a moment.

And then it slipped away.

40

Ruth lay on her bed in semi-darkness.

Her car was in a numbered bay outside. Her room was a dingy twenty-eight-dollar cell with brown carpet around the bed and yellow patterned linoleum everywhere else. The linoleum was scratched, and around the door it was grimy. The walls in the bathroom were of plain cinderblock painted pink and the toilet roll was on some kind of a ratchet that jammed every half-turn, tearing the paper and saving the management money.

Her neighbour in the next unit was playing music, loud, on a portable stereo. It came through the walls like somebody shouting at a deaf person.

A cheap place. She'd chosen it at random out of a row of cheap places. There was a security chain hanging on the doorframe, but no bracket to fix it to. The door itself looked as if someone had been kicking at it to get out.

But then, it was Aidan's house money that she was throwing around now; to waste it on anything more than this would feel like a betrayal. She wondered if he'd approve of what she was doing. She could almost imagine his voice telling her, Drop it, Ruth. Let it go.

But she stopped that line of thought. Stopped it dead in its tracks.

She thought instead about Peter Michaud. Michaud in his slaughterhouse whites, their front starched with blood and as red as any robin. Then, after he'd drifted north, Michaud on a dumper truck, bulldozing the carcasses of condemned animals into the maw of a furnace. In her mind they were piled up into an almighty wall, stiff-legged and gaseous and tumbling into the flames. It was night, and he wore goggles and a grubby canvas mask, and he was bathed in reflected fire. Flesh burst as it burned, sparks flew.

And then Michaud on his hands and knees by the side of the highway, eyes closed, gun at his forehead, traffic thundering by as he waited patiently for that terminal light. This was no act of the imagination – Ruth could see it all and her own place in it in perfect detail, still.

There were gaps in the overall picture. But it was as if Ruth could begin to chart Michaud's descent into his own personal hell, one circle at a time and dragging down with him just whomever he could grab.

She thought of Elizabeth Vermot's parting words to her. About how Michaud recognized nobody else's pain, but felt his own so deeply. She envied him, she realized. Because what he'd done to her had worked the opposite effect. It was as if, instead of turning inward, she'd been laid wide open to the suffering of others.

The bass coming through the wall was almost terrifying. She could feel it inside her, coiled and vibrating. She didn't know whose music it was. Another bunch of self-conscious Bad Boys with leather trousers and corporate responsibilities, at a guess.

One more power chord, and then it ended.

Now there was peace.

'Turn it back on,' Ruth said softly into the night air.

And after a few moments, no more than the time that it would have taken to turn over an audio cassette, the music resumed.

Only then was she able to close her eyes.

And for a while, Ruth slept.

41

She drove out to Gramercy the next morning, heading out of the city on a causeway that shot like an endless bridge out across low, green swamplands. Gramercy was less than two hours' drive upriver, close to the Mississippi but not itself a river town. This was sugar cane plantation country. Many of the plantation houses were gone and those museum pieces remaining had lost most of their land, but some industry remained. Colonial Sugars held the riverside spot with a vast refinery of white towers and storage hoppers, and the settlement where its workforce lived stood a couple of miles to the north.

Gramercy had a big main street and a lot of back roads. A working town, nobody's idea of pretty but comfortable in its way. It had a general store called Bill's and a gun shop called Nick's. The dress shop was called Roussel's, and that was about as fancy as anything got.

Ruth found the TG&Y on West Main Street across from the Ace Lumber and Hardware Store. Something had knocked out the big red 'T' on the front of the building so that the lightbox behind it showed. It was a large, no-frills barn of a place selling household necessities at rock-bottom prices. Ruth went in through glass doors by which had been stacked blue plastic paddling pools and black plastic trash bins.

There was plain flat lighting inside, from fluorescent tubes high overhead. Ruth looked around. She'd seen the picture of Elaine on Elizabeth Vermot's collage board, but in the photograph she'd been thirteen years old. There were only a few morning shoppers in the aisles. The men wore sports shirts and baseball caps, and the women wore big pressed shorts and carried babies. The staff wore blue uniform tabards with red piping over their regular clothes, but the two women that Ruth could see putting stock onto the shelves were both too old. Somebody was waiting to pay for a garden rake, but there was nobody on the checkouts.

She could ask, she supposed.

But then there was the sound of flat heels hurrying on vinyl, and a young woman emerged from one of the aisles and hopped in behind one of the cashier's positions. Apologizing, she pulled out a key on a chain and unlocked the cash drawer.

Ruth picked up a magazine from a rack and went over to get into line.

She had more than a minute to study the girl as she waited. She was wearing a square button carrying her name on the front of the tabard, but Ruth was certain of her even before she'd moved close enough to read it. For one thing, Elaine hadn't changed much since the photograph. For another, she had the look of Michaud. Same colouring. Same eyes. Not quite the same smile.

'There's a real easy write-in competition in this one,' Elaine said as she ran the price of Ruth's magazine. The surname on the badge was different, but her first name was unchanged. Her accent was pure Louisiana.

'Aren't they always?' Ruth said. But then she noted a flicker of uncertainty in Elaine, and realized that she hadn't been making a joke. She remembered how Elizabeth Vermot had described her one-time charge. Open and uncomplicated, well-meaning, not necessarily among the brightest.

Elaine said, 'You want anything else? Shampoo's on a special this week.'

'This'll be fine,' Ruth said and then, without at all changing her tone, 'Aren't you the Elaine with a brother named Pete?'

The girl's friendly expression stiffened up a little.

'You must be thinking of somebody else,' she said.

'I don't think so,' Ruth said. 'You're Elaine Michaud. Or you used to be. Yes?'

Elaine looked around. Not for help, but in apprehension. So nobody here knew.

She said, 'What do you want?'

'Will you talk to me?'

'No.'

'Will you talk to me in some other place?'

'No. What is this?'

'I need your help in something,' Ruth said, 'it's nothing more than that.'

Over in the raised-up open office overlooking the sales floor, a man in a red shirt with a logo on the pocket had got to his feet and was looking their way. For nothing, perhaps, because there was nothing to see, but with a note of suppressed panic Elaine said, 'Don't do this to me. You're going to lose me my job!'

'All right,' Ruth said, and she paid for her magazine and left the store.

She moved her car over into the parking lot of the supermarket next door, from where she could get a view of Elaine through a window display of sunglasses, cheap watches, cake mix and kitchen towels. Ruth couldn't see her all of the time because she kept going off to another job somewhere else, but whenever she had to return to deal with a customer she came back into sight. Ruth could see that she was nervous, because when she was at the checkout she kept glancing out. But she never once looked Ruth's way.

As she was waiting, Ruth flicked idly through the magazine that she'd bought. She gave a shiver. Even on its lowest setting, the air-conditioning seemed to make the car too cold. But then whenever she turned it off, an immediate warm dampness began to seep into the car with an odour like old neglected clothes that had been packed away for too many changes of season.

The magazine wasn't unlike the one that had run her story. Talk about a strange feeling. They'd changed her words and they'd taken all the edges out of her life,

278

as well; they'd made her sound like a bad pitch for a character in a TV show. The model who'd posed was nice-looking, though. She wondered if others were reading about themselves in this issue with the same sense of alienation and dismay.

After a while, Elaine came out.

She went around to the front of the store and got into her car. She was still in uniform. The car was an old Dodge Diplomat with no shine left on it and rust breaking through all over like a rash. Ruth started her own car, and set off to follow.

They went down by the side of the store on Magnolia Street, past Bob's Photo Shop and on out into a newish residential development. It was a narrow strip of road, newly laid, and recently subdivided into lots. Houses stood on about two-thirds of them, some as yet unfinished. Where no houses stood, recent rainfall had collected in the hollows and turned the ground into a sponge.

Elaine followed the road around and then made a left onto Airline Avenue, where the houses were older but the pattern was the same. Wide lots, plenty of space, a variety of designs. There were mobile homes where the daylight shone under, on land alongside brick houses that looked like doctors' offices. Before the point where the avenue swung around and crossed the railway track, Elaine's car made a turn onto the driveway of one of the older houses.

Ruth drove by. She could see Elaine getting out of the Dodge and going inside. It was a plain one-storey house, well-kept and looking as if it had been extended a couple of times. It was painted green and had a tiled roof, apart from the porch overhang which was roofed in clean corrugated iron.

Ruth found somewhere to turn around, and went back. She left the car on what little shoulder there was and walked up to the house. The reason for Elaine's return home was soon apparent to Ruth as a young dog came bounding out through the open door and down the porch steps, stopping immediately to squat and pee copiously on the front lawn. Then it ran to her.

Ruth stopped, and stroked the dog's head. It was a big puppy, no more than a few months old. She looked toward the house. There were a couple of painted chairs on the porch, and towels drying over the porch rail.

Elaine emerged.

'Just what do you think you're doing?' she said, and she looked angry.

'I want to talk about your brother,' Ruth said.

'My brother's passed on, and it's no damn business of yours.'

'So,' Ruth said, 'you *are* Elaine Michaud.'

Elaine hesitated, caught out but still defiant.

'I'm gettin' married next spring,' she said, as if that made any difference.

'I understand that Pete's the only family you have left, now,' Ruth said. 'Is he going to come to the wedding?'

'He's *dead*!' Elaine almost roared, while her dog sniffed around the base of one of the big mature trees in the garden and started to hunker down for a dump.

'He's no more dead than I am,' Ruth said, 'and I think you know it.'

Elaine looked as if she was getting ready to burst. 'Get off of here!' she said.

'What are you going to do, set your dog on me?' The puppy, still fully occupied, looked back at them apologetically. 'You don't even know who I am,' Ruth went on. 'I'm not your enemy, Elaine. You could say I'm here on family business. I can tell you why inside, or I can tell the whole world right here.'

Elaine was incredulous. 'You think you're gonna come in my *house*?' she said.

'Please,' Ruth said.

This nonplussed Elaine. She didn't know what to do. She bunched up her fists and gave a *Grrrr*, and then turned around and stalked back inside. She slammed the

280

door after her and it bounced right open again. The door swung there uncommittedly; not an invitation, not entirely a denial.

Ruth went inside. There was nothing in the hallway except for an unmistakable smell. She moved down to the kitchen and said, 'Elaine? Can I come in?'

'You can stay right there until you explain yourself,' Elaine said, 'then you can turn around and go.'

Sheets of newspaper had been spread out all over the kitchen floor, and some of it had been soiled. Elaine had pulled on elbow-length rubber gloves and was gathering it up to change it for fresh. Ruth saw that there were some scratches on the door beside her, and the edge of the carpet had been chewed.

'I knew Peter in Philadelphia,' Ruth said. 'He was calling himself Tim Hagan then. This is after he was supposed to have died.'

Elaine, crouching, with a heap of newspaper bundled up in her arms, was watching her warily.

Ruth went on, 'He's got to be somewhere. There's a chance he may even have come home. Is there anything, anything at all that you can tell me?'

'Who are you?' Elaine said.

'My name's Ruth.'

'And what's my brother to you?'

'For one minute we were lovers. The next . . . I don't know what happened. But he hurt me. He tried to hurt me a lot.'

Elaine was shaking her head as she rose to her feet. 'You've got entirely the wrong person,' she said.

'OK,' Ruth said. 'Elizabeth told me you don't lie. Your word's enough for me.'

'When'd you see her?' Elaine said, reaching for her plastic sack and then missing it and having to look.

'I saw her last night,' Ruth said. 'She's fine. Curtis is in the hospital, though.'

'Why?'

Ruth started to tell her what she knew. And halfway

through it, Elaine suddenly said, 'I fell right into that one, didn't I?'

'It wasn't a trap,' Ruth said.

'I meant what I said,' Elaine insisted. 'Whoever it was you met in Philadelphia, my brother really is dead.'

'Does that mean you have no family at all, now?'

'My daddy's still alive, but he doesn't know me. He doesn't know anyone. It's kind of a blessing because it don't matter to him now that he's always gonna be locked away. He doesn't even recognize me when I go there. He sits with his face toward the wall and they feed him like a baby. Momma 'Lizabeth's the only people I got now. Her and my man Louis. Lou's got lots of family. Christmas at their place is like The Beverly Hillbillies. They all like me, too. You hear what I'm saying?'

'I think so,' Ruth said.

'I'm saying, I've got a life. Behind me I got nothing worth having. That's sad but in a way it's OK, because that's not the way I'm going. I got out. I'm not gonna go back in.'

'I'm sorry if I've bothered you,' Ruth said.

'I'm sorry if I was rude. I got no excuse for it.'

She shoved in the last of the newspaper and put a wire tie around the neck of the bag, and then Ruth followed her out and down the side steps of the house as she took it to put with the garbage. To the front of the house was the street, to the back was just open land that went out all the way to the sandy leveed edge of a lake or waterway.

Elaine said, kind of delicately, 'This guy you thought might be my brother. He didn't – you know, he didn't put you in the family way or anything, did he?'

'No,' Ruth said. 'It's worse than that. He makes love to older women and then he tries to kill them when they attempt to drop him.'

Elaine looked at her, not quite sure how to take this. She said, 'That's pretty sick, if it's meant to be a joke.'

Ruth said, 'Do I look as if I'm laughing?'

Elaine was frowning. She was looking beyond Ruth.

Ruth turned and looked back toward the street,

wondering what was wrong. She was just in time to catch sight of a uniformed cop running between two of the houses. He was overweight and holding his hat on, trying to be quick and surreptitious and light on his feet. The effect was like one of the dancing hippos in *Fantasia*.

Elaine gave Ruth a withering look, slammed down the lid on the trash can, and stormed inside. Ruth followed her.

'This has got nothing to do with me,' she said. 'I swear it to you, Elaine.'

'Get out of here.'

'I didn't even know.'

Elaine went straight through the house and out onto the front porch; Ruth emerged behind her just as an unmarked car was coming around from the direction of the tracks.

'Hey, Lucius,' Elaine called to the puppy. 'Come on, Lucius, get inside.'

The car had pulled up now, and four men were getting out. Ruth had no idea of what was happening, and the fact that Philadelphia detective Tom Diaz was the third man out of the car did nothing to help her understanding. The others looked like agency heavyweights, FBI or worse. The big puppy was frolicking around their legs as the first man showed Elaine some ID while, from behind him, Tom Diaz said, 'Thank you, Ruth. Nicely screwed.'

The suit in charge said, 'Can we all step inside, please?'

'I want to call Lou,' Elaine said, and she looked scared.

'You don't have to be afraid,' the suit told her, in a tone that conveyed no reassurance at all. One of the other men took Elaine's arm and they all went inside, except for Ruth and Tom Diaz who were left out on the porch.

Tom Diaz seemed ill at ease in the climate. There were tiny beads of sweat shining in the roots of his hair.

He said, 'What did you get out of her?'

'Nothing,' Ruth said.

'Ruth. . .' Tom Diaz said with a note of warning in his voice.

'That's exactly what I got,' Ruth snapped angrily. 'Don't you dare point your finger at me. You are *way* overdrawn at the fucking Ruth Lasseter Bank of Goodwill.'

She led the way into the house.

The furniture in the sitting-room was mostly basketwork with cushions, hardly built to last but inexpensive and cheerful. Elaine was seated, surrounded by the suits and a couple of the uniformed policemen who'd come in through the back of the house. She looked pale and dismayed. Ruth felt for her deeply in that instant.

'She knows nothing,' Ruth said sharply. 'Don't stand over her like that.'

The man in charge looked at her. He was rugged-looking despite the business suit and hair that appeared to have been cut by laser.

He said, 'We're just about to explain to Miss Michaud why we felt it necessary to put her house under surveillance.'

But Ruth's eyes were now on the man just behind him, because the man just behind him was bringing out a pocket-sized cassette player; for Ruth it was almost as if the room underwent a hallucinatory swing in its proportions and she could see little but the machine, and that more clearly than anything, as the man reached forward and set it on the smoked-glass coffee table before Elaine.

All other colours leached away, all sounds became distant.

'Oh, no,' Ruth said, staring at the innocent-looking little machine. 'No, please.'

The man in charge said, 'I suggest you wait in another room. You're probably going to find this distressing.'

Someone touched her arm. It was Tom Diaz.

'Ruth?' he said.

He guided her through a door into another part of the house. She went without resistance. Elaine was looking bewildered as she left her; she was clearly wondering what was going to come next.

Diaz closed the door behind Ruth. Now she was alone

in the hallway. But she could still hear their voices from here, so she went on through into the kitchen and closed that door as well.

She sat at the kitchen table, put her head right down, and covered her head with her arms.

But the tape ran in her mind anyway.

42

I feel no pain, she told herself emptily. I feel no fear. Those two thoughts echoed around inside her head, meeting no resistance. I am a shell, she thought. All that once filled me is gone. It was as if pathways had been stopped, the nerves disconnected.

Feeling nothing, she could function.

Aidan was dead. He'd failed to return to their motel room because Peter Michaud followed them there and had been waiting and had taken the chance to abduct him. The killing part had come later. Michaud had waited and then, when Ruth had returned home, he'd called her on the phone and begun to slaughter Aidan like a beast while she listened helplessly.

This was the tape that they were now playing to Elaine.

The recording had been taken from a legal wiretap on Aidan Kincannon's line, set up within hours of Ruth telling her story to the small Maryland community's Chief of Police. First the State Police had become involved, and then the FBI. Of Aidan, there had been no sign. The unregistered farm truck had been found run into a drainage ditch alongside a dirt road about two miles out of town. The bottle of California champagne was in the back, unopened. It had been wiped clean of prints. Ruth had answered questions for what seemed like a day and a half, and then they let her go home. The phone had been ringing when she'd arrived, but she hadn't reached it in time. The caller had hung up before the machine had kicked in. It rang out again ten minutes later, and when she picked it up she first heard the voice of Peter Michaud. He'd reassured her about Aidan and promised her information on where to find him. He'd tried to get Aidan to speak, but Aidan had refused to play along. But he was there in the room for sure because Michaud had then begun, audibly, to torture him, shouting encouragement to Ruth to keep on listening. Which Ruth had somehow managed to do, even though she was in no doubt that Michaud was going to break his promise of information just as he was now breaking his pledge over Aidan's safety.

As he did.

They'd told her afterwards that the call had lasted a little over twelve minutes. Twelve minutes. They'd locked open the line and traced it to an unoccupied office suite where nothing was found other than two phone lines linked together in what they called a cheesebox hookup. It was an arrangement most frequently used by drug dealers to avoid being located. Michaud could have been calling from anywhere. The call coming out was the one that they'd traced; but the source of the incoming line was now impossible to determine.

The kitchen door opened. Ruth raised her head from the table. Elaine was standing there, looking pale and shaky like someone who'd just walked away from a serious road accident and who was only now beginning to realize it. She took a step over to the water cooler and drew herself a cupful which, trembling, she almost spilled as she drank.

'I'm really sorry,' she said. 'I'm really sorry.' Ruth said nothing, and Elaine said, 'Who was he?'

'His name was Aidan,' Ruth said. 'He was also the best thing that could have happened to me, and I never took the chance to let him know it.'

'I don't know what to say.' Elaine was almost in tears. Ruth was calm.

'I wish he was here,' she said.

'I didn't lie to you. I never did see my brother and he never was in touch. I kind of wondered, but . . . anyone can wonder.'

A little of the iron reappeared in Ruth. She almost

resented Elaine's grief. That right was hers, even if she'd made a deliberate choice not to claim it.

She said, 'What exactly made you do that?'

Elaine took in a big sigh and let it out. 'Squatters in the old house,' she said. 'Nobody there, but . . . just signs. I only went out there a couple of times. Me and Lou had this dream about fixing it up and moving in, but the house is too far gone. And people know what happened there. That'll never go away.'

'What did you see?'

'Someone had been sleeping in Pete's old room. There were other rooms in better shape, but that was the one he'd used. And then the one time this year I went out to the cemetery, someone had been tending Momma's grave. I'm the only one of us left. If I didn't do it, who else would?'

She pulled out the other chair, and sat with Ruth at the table.

She said, 'They're telling me all kinds of stuff about him. I don't want to believe any of it. The problem is, I almost can.'

Ruth said nothing, but waited for her to go on.

'He never did think like ordinary people,' Elaine said. 'I think that could be what it was. We had this cat, once. It had kittens. One of them was stillborn but the rest of the litter came out fine. Daddy said we'd have to find them homes, so the three of us made a sign to hang out at the side of the road. We had this argument because Pete wanted to hang out the dead kitten with the sign, like a way to show people the merchandise. He wanted to fix it on there with a staple gun. We voted him down. But he still snuck out there later and hung it up on a stick.'

She looked at Ruth.

'Will you help him, Ruth?' she said, and then she must have seen the disbelief on Ruth's face because she added, 'You must have seen something in him. I mean, to do whatever it was the two of you did at the beginning.'

'You can say that? Even after what you just heard?'

'He's still my brother,' Elaine said, and then she lost

288

it completely and started to cry. Ruth sat and watched her for a while. It wasn't any ladylike sobbing but good old ugly-crying, something much closer to the real, ropes-of-snot bawling of a child. They must have been able to hear her elsewhere in the house, but nobody came in.

Ruth hesitated for a moment longer. Then she slid her chair along and put an arm around Elaine's shoulder.

'We lost everything,' Elaine said when she was able. 'One piece at a time. It got so we couldn't even keep our own name any more.'

'I know,' Ruth said.

'It's God's honest truth, I never even think about those things we did. It's like it all happened to someone else. It used to be like a movie that ran every time I closed my eyes. That's how I came to deal with it.'

I know, Ruth thought. I know.

Ruth said, 'Where's Lou? What does he do?'

'He drives a truck for Kaiser Aluminum.'

'Do you still want to call him?'

'He'll be home tonight. I don't want them bothering him while he's working. We're saving money. We're gonna get married next spring.'

'Does he know about what happened?'

'He knows everything I could ever think of to tell him,' Elaine said, and then she suddenly looked at her watch. 'Are they going to let me go back to work?' she said. 'I don't want to lose this job. I was only supposed to come home on my break to let the puppy out.'

But they didn't seem to be ready to let her go back. Once she'd composed herself, the Agency people came and took her into the sitting-room again. Ruth was left with Tom Diaz, who ushered her out of the kitchen and into the open air.

They walked up the driveway toward the road. Tom Diaz said, 'Come and get in the car, Ruth.'

'I've got a car of my own.'

'Just get in,' Tom Diaz said. 'Please.'

She got into the back of one of the official cars with him. It was a dull-looking day. Ruth still couldn't get to grips with it. A day as overcast as this should not, according to her internal wiring, be so hot and close. She'd look at it from an air-conditioned house or a refrigerated vehicle, and she'd reach for a coat on the way out. Then she'd open a door and it would hit her.

Diaz said, 'I've been assigned the job of keeping you out of the way.' And he said it with some weariness.

'Is that your entire function around here?'

'I got sent down to brief the local FBI on what we know. That's done, so now they take over the train set. Now I'm gathering background stuff on Michaud so I can take it back pre-trial to Pennsylvania. It's federal now, but the state wants a piece of him too.'

'For how long?'

'Another day. Maybe two.'

'I think he's down here.'

'Maybe.'

Ruth glanced toward the house.

'Nobody seems too interested in hearing what I got told.'

'They've got the place bugged, is why. They know it already.'

'What's going to happen to me?'

'Well, now that you're potentially a material witness, I have to warn you not to attempt to leave the United States.'

'Jesus,' Ruth said. 'Don't times change fast.'

Most of the official cars had now been moved away again, spirited back into the surroundings to leave the place apparently unobserved once more. Get rid of this car and her own, and there would be nothing to make anyone suspicious. For herself, Ruth had considered this to be something of a long shot. Yet they were here in force, and they'd wired the place for sound.

'The deportation order's only on hold,' Tom Diaz warned her. 'It could still happen after.'

'Not worth worrying about, Detective,' Ruth said. 'We may never see the day.'

And meanwhile . . .

43

Theresa McCall lay in the darkness, and counted the breaths that she took. Hours had passed. Or it might have been days.

She had no sense of time, down here. The darkness was total and the sludge in which she lay was close to blood heat. She didn't know how long it was since she'd seen daylight. The battery in her key-ring flashlight had died after only a few minutes and then her house keys had dropped into the muck at the bottom of the water, where she was disinclined to search.

It was unlikely ever to work again. There might be a few more seconds' life left in it, no more. And what it would show her, she was disinclined to see.

She'd lost her watch, as well. It had been disappearing into the flesh of her bad arm as it had swelled, and she'd unpicked the band with her teeth. It occurred to her after that maybe she could have broken the crystal and then felt the hands like a blind person. If her fingers were too numb, then with the tip of her tongue. But what would it tell her? She didn't even know if it was daytime or night-time. Or how many hours or days had passed already.

Better to let it go.

Theresa counted.

One arm, she'd decided, wasn't broken after all. She'd already had some limited use of it and, though stiff, it now seemed to be showing a little improvement. The other was busted like a branch, and quite definitely so. She'd been feeling along it, gingerly checking its shape with her good hand, when she'd found a terrifying sawtooth of protruding bone on the inside of her forearm. One of the ends had pushed right out through the skin, and she hadn't even known it. She'd seen enough to know that she was lying in filth. But to think that she was lying in filth with an open wound was almost too much for Theresa to bear. All that she could do was to hold it close to her like a little tyrannosaurus arm, shortened and bent over like the limbs of the long-term comatose, and try to keep it above the water.

Her breathing was steady. She concentrated on keeping it steady. Panic wouldn't improve her situation, and screaming would only make her head ring and her throat hurt even more. She'd tried both, she knew they brought her nothing. What she'd also found was that despair, like any intense emotion, could only be sustained for so long. After a while it would flag like any other passion, its energy spent, and she'd be left with only feverish, machine-gun thoughts that hammered at the subject of her prospects without actually getting her anywhere.

This was not the end. This could not be the end. She had unpaid bills on her hallway table. Stuff in her freezer she'd bought and hadn't used. A new pair of shoes with a broken heel that she was determined she was going to get some satisfaction out of. The list was trivial, but it was endless. She could add something to it with every minute that went by.

Ten breaths to the minute, she reckoned. Twice that when she wasn't so calm, or wasn't trying so hard enough to keep herself under control.

The inescapable conclusion was that if she were to accept that this couldn't be the end, then it would follow that there had to be some way out for her. There hadn't been for those who had gone before, that much was clear. They were still in the tank with her; menacing presences at first, the horror of them dulled by familiarity now. But perhaps they'd given up on themselves too easily. Christopher, or whatever his name might be, entered the lives of his victims through a channel of lowered self-esteem. Like any successful disease, he mimicked the answer to a need and then, once established, he clung on and let nothing else get through.

Theresa had never thought of herself as a strong woman. She didn't think of herself in such terms now.

But she was damned if she was going to just lie down in darkness and die because it suited someone else.

The count reached one hundred.

She'd lost one shoe in the fall. She'd kicked off the other. She'd been using her feet to conduct an inch-by-inch barefoot exploration of her place of entombment. There had to be weaknesses. The air was foul, but it didn't run out. And she'd noticed that the level of water in the place wasn't constant, but seemed to rise and fall to a pattern. It wasn't salt water, so the effect couldn't be tidal. But what was of most interest was the fact that it happened at all.

There was no way of knowing what she might find herself touching next. She didn't worry, because nothing could disgust her now. Disgust had been burned out of her in a day, or a week, or however long it had taken.

The walls were of block. Above her was concrete. The space was roughly that of a small, flooded storeroom. Whatever else might be in here with her, she would soon know.

Probing, she found her marker. Her marker was a jewelled brooch pin that had been worn by one of the women who had gone before. Theresa had jammed it into a crack between the blocks as a way of ensuring that she didn't go over the same stretch twice to no new effect. Touching the pin, it was as if she felt a charge. Something positive. A latent echo of the hopes of the dead.

She would have to prevail.

For all of us, she thought.

And then, buried alive and unaware that she was slowly being eaten by gangrene, Theresa continued to map out the limits of her grave.

44

Tom Diaz was blazing. It wasn't his job to nursemaid Ruth Lasseter, and no-one here had the authority to order him to do it. He wasn't responsible for her. He didn't even want to be here. Where was the point? Where was the glory? The federal boys had taken over, and now everybody else got to hold the coats. If Pete Michaud were to run out onto the Clearview Parkway and impale himself onto the hood ornament of Tom Diaz's car right now, Diaz still wouldn't get to take him home. Diaz wanted to do what he had to do, turn in his car, get on his plane and go back. Additions to the list were less than welcome. He'd extracted a promise from Ruth that she'd behave, and then he'd turned her loose. He'd found out where she was staying, and he would check on her later. What more could he do?

He couldn't decide what to make of the woman. He'd thought her damaged, neurotic perhaps, maybe even one of those born victims who'd failed to get herself sufficiently punished the first time out. Not that he hadn't been attracted to her when he'd met her back at the beginning. There had been a definite trembling of the compass needle, but the attraction hadn't lasted. Not beyond the sight of her in that pimp hotel, sitting on the bed with her empty stare while three of his men aimed guns at her head and a fourth took the revolver from her hand. These were the women that dragged guys down. The sirens. The Snow Queens.

Ask Aidan Kincannon about *that* notion.

The Medical Center was a severely geometrical structure off Clearview, three storeys of pure white with angles and corners as sharp as creases. Across the street stood one of its satellite buildings, the more modest Medical Plaza for which Diaz was heading. This had the look of an old apartment block that had been spruced up and refurbished, its brickwork painted a dusty pink and white shutters fitted to its windows. There was a red vinyl awning above the entranceway and a lot of well-cared-for plants all around it. Diaz went in through tinted glass doors and found himself in a passageway that was like a corridor in a very expensive hotel. Nobody was around. Only the noise made by the elevator as he ascended betrayed the actual age of the building underneath it all.

Diaz took a deep breath, heaved a big sigh. What was the point of anger? It would chew him up and get him nowhere. He was the only one who'd suffer. Which kind of took away the purpose of it.

Nobody around up here, either. He checked the number, found the suite. In the clinic reception area he looked through the glass and said, 'Hi. I'm Tom Diaz, down from Philadelphia for the Michaud family files?'

'Can you just wait one moment, please?' the receptionist asked him, and she hit the screen saver on her Apple Mac and went out of the office on the other side of the window. The quiet whirring of computer fans seemed to be the only sound in the place.

The door through into the main part of the suite opened. A young man in shirtsleeves and a necktie was standing there.

'I'm Jeff Hirsch,' the young man said. 'We talked on the phone. You want to come in?'

Tom Diaz went through. 'I've got some paperwork for you to check over and sign,' he said to Hirsch as the door closed behind them.

'Me too,' Hirsch said. 'We can borrow my boss's office.'

'Don't you get an office of your own?'

'Yeah, but hers is nicer.'

The office into which Tom Diaz was led had a calculated sense of comfort about it. This was the place to which the Michaud children had come, week after week, first for assessment and later for therapy. There was a low divan-style couch and a couple of reproduction antique chairs, a pendulum clock, a doll's house. The lighting was indirect and there was a stuffed knitted duck along with a small pink teddy bear on a side table. A pleasant room. A room where whispered secrets could come out in safety at last. Only the files and the bill spike and the out-tray and the businesslike phone on the desk gave it away.

Tom Diaz looked at the stack of papers. His name was attached to the top of it, scribbled on a page from a notepad headed *Freudian Slips*. 'Is that all for me?' he said.

'I'll find a box for you to put them in before you go,' Hirsch said. 'The originals were kind of messy, but some of the copies are clearer. There's a lot of handwritten stuff in there.'

They went through the formalities and the permissions, and Hirsch gave Diaz a rundown of what he would find in the pile.

Diaz said, 'Did you work with the Michauds?'

'No. I haven't been here that long. But if you want me to, I can fix up for you to talk to one of the doctors who did.'

'I don't need a doctor for this,' Diaz said, looking through the first dozen or so pages on the top of the heap. They consisted mostly of test scores and multiple-choice gradings, nothing that Diaz could follow at all. 'I need an interpreter.'

'There are summaries as well,' Hirsch told him. 'What I *will* say is, try to get an overview. The kids changed their stories more than once.'

'I'm used to that.'

'But not to make themselves look better. They were desperate to get their father off the hook.'

'That's what I'd heard. Do I have the father's records in here as well?'

'We don't have those. You'd have to apply to the State Hospital in Mandeville.'

Jeff Hirsch went away to find him a box. Diaz riffled through the papers, stopping here and there to read a few lines. Face it, he was no trained psychologist. He was a practical man, with a practical man's suspicion of all this stuff. A few pieces were in the handwriting of the children themselves, but apart from the tests the bulk of the text appeared to consist of typed interview transcripts.

He stopped and read a few of the words on one double-spaced page. He didn't know from whom they'd been taken:

We all lined up and got a grip on the coat, and we started to drag. The coat collar began to tear at first, so we had to stop and rearrange everything before we tried again. It was slow progress but we got her across the floor where a doorway led through to the kitchen, and there we had a problem because the three of us all got bunched together and we couldn't squeeze through.

It was clear that the children had been desperate to say anything to keep their daddy out of jail. They'd probably worked on their stories together. But the man was way beyond help at that point, and had been a walking shell for months. He hadn't even been considered fit to stand trial, and so the story had faded from national attention and had never developed into quite the circus that it might have.

Diaz laid the papers down and glanced around the office. At the doll's house, and the child-friendly touches. He imagined them coming in here, one at a time. Three spooky little kids, fresh out of hell and all scared of the future. Elaine had survived it. Her older sister hadn't. And Peter – well, it seemed that Peter had been hit the worst and was still spiralling down in flames. That didn't excuse him, in the eyes of Tom Diaz. It simply made him more dangerous.

Jeff Hirsch came back with an empty box.

Diaz said, 'I want to ask you something. You don't have to answer. Can I do that?'

Hirsch was unruffled. 'Depends on the question,' he said.

298

'Do you think there are monsters?'

'Oh,' Hirsch said. '*That* kind of a question.'

'Do you?'

'No.'

'Even in spite of some of the stuff that you'll get coming through here?'

'Well,' Jeff Hirsch said, 'we don't see it quite so much in the raw like a cop would. By the time they get to us, they tend to have quietened down. They're not monsters, they're deeply screwed-up people. Some of them are total train wrecks. But they're still people.'

Tom Diaz got to his feet, and reached for his cardboard box.

'That's pretty much what I thought you might say,' he said.

45

So this was the area where the Michaud children had spent their early years. These were the roads along which they were driven to school. These were the roadside bars where their father hung out in the evenings, so quiet in the corners that almost no-one ever registered his presence. The Sports Shack, a long, low and windowless cabin with a huge radar-like satellite antenna on its roof and dirt-lot parking to the side. Ronne's Roadhouse, a falling-down shed with a sign over its entranceway reading MUST BE NINETEEN. PICTURE ID REQUIRED.

Ruth was north of Lake Pontchartrain, inland across the water from New Orleans and into the beginnings of rural Louisiana. Mandeville was a few miles along the road from here. In Mandeville was the State Hospital, where Ralph Michaud now had a permanent home. Where he sat so quietly in the corner that almost no-one ever registered his presence.

Ruth had promised Diaz that she'd behave herself and go back to where she was staying.

But she hadn't promised to go back there right away.

Ruth had flirted with the idea of trying to get in to see Michaud, but it seemed unlikely that she'd be allowed. Not without ID and proper authority, which no-one was about to grant her. And what would a visit tell her anyway? The way Elaine had described him, he'd escaped into some inner landscape from which he would never emerge. For her to go and see him would be just a visit to the zoo.

Understanding was required. Ruth felt like somebody standing amid the wreckage of a plane, looking for some evidence of the bomb that had brought it down. A bomb on a plane was a terrible thing. But it was a fact, and as a fact it had to be lived with. But what was unacceptable was the thought that any plane might fall from the sky at any time, and for no reason at all. Like anybody, Ruth needed to sense that there was some underpinning order in life. But for her it was a sense that had been tested to its limits and beyond.

She hadn't cried a single tear for Aidan. Not a one. At least, not since the phone call.

I feel no pain. I feel no fear.

Around here, north of the lake, the country was low and flat and wooded. Deer country. The roads were long and straight, the woodland cleared back from the sides and held there by ditches. Even then the trees, overgrown and dense, leaned in and hung over. The best housing seemed to be the lakefront property. Driving away from the lake she passed a number of modest roadside businesses, more than a few of which seemed simply to have given up trading. In the space of two miles Ruth passed a daycare centre, a Dairy Queen, a ramshackle luncheonette which also sold redwood signs and ceramic animals, Daisy's Pampered Pets, Kirsten's Fried Chicken, an auto sales and service centre, an electrical supply business, Pickett's Seafood with a picture of a crawfish on the side of the building, half a dozen gas stations and the Ozone Motel.

A turn off the main route brought her into different territory. These were the area's real back roads, a loose gridiron pattern of narrow driveways along which building lots had been hacked and cleared. Even smaller roads interconnected these, rough pavement no more than one-and-a-half cars' width that had been potholed and patched and then repatched several times.

It was down one of these, around an unexpected corner, that Ruth found the cemetery.

This was a couple of cleared and less-than-crowded acres, a few trees still standing in among the graves. It had a high wire fence and simple gates that were propped wide open so that one could, if inclined, drive straight through and out the other end. At the centre of the field stood a tin-roofed, open-sided shelter where visitors could rest on wooden benches in the shade. Some county workers were taking a break under this, their pickup truck alongside with its driver's door open and its radio playing. The truck was loaded up with sacks full of cuttings.

Ruth stopped her car outside one of the gates. Could this be the place that Elaine had talked about, where Kathy and her mother were buried? It wouldn't take her long to find out.

The graves were of varying ages. The newest were in the neatest rows, and seemed to Ruth to contain a striking proportion of the young. Others were so old and run-down that it was impossible to tell whom they had ever contained at all. One, at the base of a big tree, had all but broken apart as the tree had grown. Through the crack in the stone thrust a riot of ferns and plants. Down in New Orleans, she'd heard that the water table was so high that all burials had to be in brick or marble mausoleums above ground to avoid contamination. There were a few of that design here, but mostly they were the more conventional hole-in-the-ground kind.

Over on this side of the burial ground, the county workers' radio was almost drowned out by the constant sound of crickets. Moving slowly in the afternoon's heat, Ruth walked the rows and read off the markers. Over one, dense with planted flowers, bobbed a foil balloon that read HAPPY FATHERS' DAY. Some bore flags. More than one carried toy cars and animals under which a dead child slept, immune to the grief of those it had left behind.

Mid-row, she found it. No trouble at all.

The surface was a smooth patch of cement over which mosquitoes hung in constant motion, attracted by the glare. The marker was of black polished marble, and before it stood a funerary vase of flowers that were just beginning to wilt and wither.

Ruth stood at the foot of the grave.

She imagined the Michaud family gathered on this spot. They'd once filled this space around her. This very space.

She could almost see them in the damp heat of a Louisiana summer's day like this one, eyes screwed up against the sun and their clothes probably sticking to them as hers were sticking now, little realizing how much they were actually saying goodbye to. Not just to their mother, but to their future happiness as well. Because everything, *everything* would begin to unravel for them from this point onward.

Her eyes moved down the stone to the second carved name and its seventeen-year span: Kathy, beloved sister, Safe in the Arms of Jesus. The edges of these words were a little sharper, the gold a little shinier. Kathy in the grave with her mother, her daddy rotting in another place with his mind a blank sheet, little Elaine forever looking over her shoulder, and big brother Peter a figure stalking the land as grim as any reaper, his head and his heart full of worms.

All because of love, and the sorrow that came with the loss of love. They must have been happy, she thought. They must have been so happy in their time, to fall apart so badly when it all went wrong.

The county workers had gone, now, and so Ruth went over to sit for a while in the shade in the middle of the field. The wooden deck was tilting, and there were creepers forcing their way up through the cracks in the boards. It didn't feel much cooler under the tin roof than it did out in the sun.

Peter was supposed to be dead as well, of course. Dead no less than twice over, and still running around. She wondered if there was some other body taking up his space in the family tomb, or if the cost of another burial was more than Elaine and her savings from the TG&Y had been able to bear. The real Tim Hagan had been half-cremated in that motel fire already. It had probably made sound economic sense simply to finish the job.

She looked around. Something buzzed her, and she swatted it away. The graveyard fell away toward woodland at its quietest corner. The ground was soft-looking; one or two of the big, heavy crosses appeared to have sunk right in. Soft, damp, ferociously fertile. There was a recent interment close by, fresh earth piled up and still unsettled; the mourners' flowers were decaying already, and even now there were green shoots rising out of the dirt.

Ruth frowned.

Then, picking her way carefully through the lush, coarse grass, she went over for a closer look. There was no stone as yet, but a grey metal marker had been pushed into the soil as temporary identification. It had a plastic window on the front, behind which was a typed card with only the sparest details from the funeral home.

She read the date. Then she looked at the condition of the flowers. Then she read the date again, to be sure.

Ruth went back to her car. She drove away from the cemetery and back onto the main road, where she kept on going until she reached the first likely place for a public phone that she could see.

This was a redbrick shopping plaza containing the Calvary Christian Church, a print shop, a video store, a coffee and pastry shop, and a piano showroom. It was backed by forestation crowding up so close that it resembled a lost temple in the jungle. Water had pooled on its parking lot from the rains that had fallen while most people were sleeping the night before. There were two phones, one with an OUT OF ORDER notice hung on it. Ruth realized that she didn't know who to call, and so she called the city police in New Orleans and explained herself to three different people before giving her number and hanging up. Then she took the OUT OF ORDER notice and hung it on the good phone.

She bought a can of soda from the coffee shop and brought it outside, glugging it down almost in one. She didn't want to be too far from the phone. She didn't know how much time would pass before it rang, and she didn't want to be sitting in the car when it happened. She waited around in the heat outside the piano showroom, studying without seeing the bargain notices in the window. Some teenagers came along in a Volkswagen and tried to use the other phone. Ruth tensed as she waited to see if they'd pick up hers, but they only glanced at the notice and then piled back into their car and left.

Eventually the phone rang, and she picked it up. They'd managed to get her message to Tom Diaz.

'What is it, Ruth?' he said, and he didn't exactly sound enthusiastic.

'I was right,' she said. 'He's around here.'

'Did you see him?'

'I saw flowers on the family plot. They're almost fresh. I checked them against some others. They've got to be less than a week old and Elaine said she only came out here once this year.'

'Oh, come on,' Diaz said.

'Who else is it going to be?'

'Anyone. One of the older sister's boyfriends. Anyone can buy flowers. Is that your entire proof?'

'What's the matter with you?' Ruth demanded.

Diaz conceded. Grudgingly, but he conceded.

'Tell me where to find you,' he said.

46

The ridge road out to the old Michaud house was overgrown and unmaintained, but still passable. Tom Diaz had arrived alone. They'd left Ruth's car behind at the shopping plaza, and Ruth came along as passenger. There was a half-hearted roadblock at the end of the track. It had been made out of a couple of crates and some old boards, and it all but fell apart as Tom Diaz dragged it aside. As a barrier, it barely delayed them at all.

The creek that ran alongside the ridge had become something of a local dumping-ground. Where it was at its widest, a sea of old tyres floated. A hundred yards on, about half a dozen cars and trucks had been run down its banks and torched. One or two were still recognizable. Most looked as if they'd been stripped down to rust by a nuclear wind.

Ruth said, 'What do we do if he's there?'

'He's not going to be there,' Diaz said.

'You don't know that.'

'The local cops have been keeping an eye on the place. If there'd been any coming and going, they'd know.'

'So why are we here?'

'For you.'

He looked at her. She shifted uncomfortably. But he couldn't keep his eyes on her for long, because he had to return his attention to the road.

Here was the house, just ahead.

After all the buildup, it was almost disappointing. Just an ordinary-looking place that was halfway to a ruin. One storey with a second-floor addition, decayed and crumbling. A frame house with grey clapboard walls. The windows were gone, the building reamed-out.

But it did have a certain atmosphere. Ruth could feel it as she was getting out of the car.

'Dig around,' Tom Diaz suggested. 'Whatever helps.'

They explored. Tom Diaz went looking around the back while Ruth stepped in through what had once been a glass patio door. Some of the glass crunched underfoot like new snow. She found herself in a mess of a room, stuff piled high on the floor as if several garbage cans had been upended. One corner of the room was blackened in tongues from floor to ceiling, signs that someone had once lit a campfire there.

A sound came from above her. Pressure, the creak of a board. She waited, and it came again. Whoever was up there, he wasn't trying to hide.

'Detective Diaz?' she called out. 'Tom? Is that you?'

'I'm up here,' came his voice down the stairwell. 'I found a few things.'

How had he got up there? The stairs inside were all destroyed, so she went out through the kitchen and there found an outside stairway that led up to a sun deck. She picked her way up, with care. The handrail was hanging loose, and some of the runners had broken through.

She found Diaz in one of the bedrooms.

Part of the room had been divided off with a makeshift screen of rope and blankets. Behind this lay a mattress and a bedroll; next to these was a tote bag with some jeans and other clothing, and a nunchak.

'Is all that his?' Ruth said.

'I don't know,' Tom Diaz said doubtfully. 'It's been here a while.'

She watched as he dug through the tote bag. He pulled out a paperback book and flicked through its pages. The book had swelled with the dampness. There were bird droppings on the mattress and the bedroll, which suggested that whoever had set up this camp had left it unvisited for days. Weeks, even.

Ruth left him loading everything back into the bag, and went to look at the other rooms. The floor had collapsed in one of them. The boards in another began to sag beneath her tread and it was then that she conceded that there was nothing to learn here, and she'd be safer back on the ground.

She descended from the sun deck, and poked around the back of the house. There was a big shed here, almost a barn, that had been stripped of everything including its door. Open land behind the house ran all the way out to a line of trees and the creek. The grass was waist-deep in places, and there was no wind to stir it.

She could hear a car. Couldn't she hear a car?

Ruth went around to the front of the house, where their own car stood. Another vehicle was coming down the track toward her, taking it carefully over the potholes. It was a police car, dark in colour and with a yellow and white diagonal slash across its door. It pulled in behind their own, and the driver got out.

He was a uniformed officer. His moustache was grey and his hair was almost white and he had a noticeable paunch, but he didn't have the look of someone to be messed with. His shirt was dark blue, with yellow piping and an embroidered badge.

He said, pleasantly enough, 'Good day to you. Can I help in what you're looking for?'

But it was pretty clear that he was asking something else altogether; like, what do you think you're doing?

Ruth said, 'We're looking for someone who used to live here.'

'No-one's lived here in a *very* long time.'

Both of them glanced around as Tom Diaz emerged around a corner of the house with the tote bag in his hand, carrying it out at a distance from his body to ensure that it didn't brush against his clothes.

'Hi there,' he said.

He set the tote bag down on the ground and introduced himself, showing his Philadelphia police ID. Then he introduced Ruth by name, but didn't give any reason for her being here.

'We found this stuff in one of the bedrooms,' he explained. 'Somebody left it and didn't come back.'

The policeman picked up the bag and set it on the hood of his car. He looked through it and found some papers that Diaz seemed to have missed.

'I know this boy,' he said. 'I put him in jail last month for stealing a bicycle. He's got to be an all-time loser because it was a police captain's bike. I'll take his stuff.'

He went around to the back of his car to stow the gear, and Ruth walked around with him.

She said, 'Did you ever know Peter Michaud?'

'I knew the whole family,' the policeman said. His name was on his badge. Officer Hearn. 'I practically grew up with Ralph Michaud. I was the one who had to come out here and bring him in.'

'How did it happen?'

'He wasn't careful. He didn't even try to be careful. It was just blind luck and bad fortune kept him going for as long as he did.'

'Can you show me where he put the bodies?' Ruth blurted out before she realized how it must sound. But then it was too late, it was out. Officer Hearn was looking at her coolly. He looked like a wall of granite. He didn't say anything for a few moments and Ruth started thinking how she'd pushed too far, too fast.

But then he said, 'Are you the woman I heard about?'

She'd no idea what he might have heard. But Ruth said, 'I think I probably am.'

He nodded, and slammed down the trunk lid on his car, and then indicated for her to walk with him. Tom Diaz followed, staying a few yards back. They walked around the house.

'You can imagine how this has turned into something of a spot,' Officer Hearn said to her. 'People used to come and take pictures, steal a piece of the house. Kids still come out here Saturday nights for a dare. I gave up chasing them away.'

'What was the mother like?'

'She was a young woman. Younger than him.' Dense as the grass was behind the house, there was a way across it. Not so much a path, more an overgrown parting.

They went across in single file. Of course, Ruth was thinking. The buried pipe from the house to the tank. The grass doesn't grow quite so well directly over it.

'Here's what you've been looking for,' Officer Hearn said.

'That's it?' Ruth said.

'That's it.'

There was a concrete slab over the opening to the septic tank, covering it completely. It was a heavy-looking piece of masonry and it had been sprayed with graffiti like the side of a subway train, over and over and over again. It was somewhere between three and four feet square, and it gave the tank the look of a permanently capped well. Or the lid of the Ark, holding down forces beneath.

Ruth said, 'What are all those marks along the edge?'

'That's from people trying to lever it up to see what's underneath.'

'What *is* underneath, now?'

'Nothing. It all got filled in.'

The three of them stood there, in silent contemplation. This was where Ralph Michaud had stowed the bodies of his victims. Five, in all. They'd established that he'd brought the women home and killed them in the house before dragging them out here; all, presumably, while his children slept on in their rooms upstairs. At least one, the last one, hadn't been properly dead when she'd gone in.

Officer Hearn said, 'Hallowe'en's the only really bad time now. Nobody means any harm. But no-one considers those poor women.'

There was nothing more to say, nothing new to be learned. The stone was bleak and mundane, as was its setting. Ruth shivered, and the two men looked at her. The air temperature was somewhere around eighty degrees.

But not down there, she was thinking, looking at the slab. Down under there, it's as cold as it gets.

They were walking back when Ruth suddenly said, 'I want to look.'

'There's nothing to see,' Tom Diaz said.

'I still want to look,' she said, and she turned to Officer Hearn. 'Is there any way I can?'

'No, Ruth,' Tom Diaz was insisting. 'Come on.'

They carried on back to the house. There was a slight gradient to the ground, not noticeable before. Years ago, one of Ruth's school friends had lived on a dairy farm. They'd had a new septic tank dug, right in the yard. She'd told everyone how it worked. She'd told everyone how her father had thrown in a maggoty rabbit to get the bacterial action started. They'd gone to the farm in twos and threes and levered up the lid and peeked inside, but no-one had ever actually seen the rabbit.

They got into their cars. Hearn backed his away, so that they could turn around to get out again.

But before Diaz had moved, Ruth was opening her door and stepping out.

'What do you think you're doing?' Diaz said, leaning forward and calling through the open car door.

'I have to,' Ruth said.

'Why?'

'I just do.'

She was walking toward the tank on the far side of the house again, and she could hear that Diaz was following her. That was fine, it didn't matter. Just as long as he didn't try to take her back.

He said, 'You heard what he told you. It's all filled in.'

'I thought we came here for me,' Ruth said. 'Well, this is what I want.'

At that point, Officer Hearn trudged past and overtook them both.

'Come on,' he said. 'It'll be quicker than talking about it.'

He and Diaz took a side each, and together they got ready to lift the slab. Diaz wasn't enthusiastic, but he squared up anyway. The concrete looked as if it was going to be too heavy to be moved at all. The eroded-looking edges were evidence that others had tried, mostly with tyre irons or other, similar tools. But there was kind of an unspoken challenge between the two, neither of them being willing to be the first to give up. It wasn't unlike an arm-wrestling contest between the older and the younger man.

Once they'd found handholds, they strained like a couple of horses. Hearn flushed red and Diaz went purple. The cords in their necks stood out like piano wires. Ralph Michaud could never have managed this on his own. Back then, the tank had probably been covered with a regular iron lid like the one Ruth remembered.

Ruth moved to help, but they'd already got it started. The slab lifted as if hinged.

They stood it on its end and balanced it there.

'Do you feel any better now?' Diaz said as soon as he was able.

The tank had been filled with what looked like builders' rubble, all the way up to within inches of the rim. On top of the rubble lay the blackened but still identifiable remains of a wreath. Some litter had been poked in through gaps around the sides.

Ruth nodded, and they let the concrete fall back into place. The air rushed out from under like a soft explosion. She felt awkward. But she wasn't sorry.

Nobody said anything to her until they were walking around the house to get back to the cars.

That was when Officer Hearn said, 'You wouldn't believe it, but this used to be one of the happiest places I knew. There's no happiness here now. You've seen what you came for and you know it's nothing special. So walk away and leave it and get on with your life. Don't let it suck you in even further than it already has.'

Too late, Ruth thought.

Too late for that.

47

In another hole, in another place, Theresa rested.

She more or less had the measure of her prison now. Inaccessible to her sight, she held it like a model in her mind. She could turn it, inspect it, check it from any angle. It was a deep double-chamber like two squares together, lower at one end than at the other. A below-ground storage tank of some kind, as far as she could tell. It might once have been open to the sky, but it had been roofed-over with concrete blocks like railroad sleepers. There were twenty-five of these, and they fitted together so closely that there was no gap between any of them. Where she reached up and got her fingernails in, she found only dirt. She reckoned that some had been lifted to make a gap and that was how she'd been pitched in here; but which ones, and at which end, she couldn't say.

Most of the mess and the debris was down at the lower end under a couple of feet of water. Round stones and rubble at the bottom of the tank had formed a soakaway, but these had been partly excavated as if by a tunnelling dog. In among the stones, she'd found some kind of a mesh cover. It was eighteen inches across, and circular, and it wasn't attached to anything. This had been no church picnic. Everything was under a deep layer of sludge as well as the water, and in the sludge had been some of the most appalling matter imaginable. She'd found rings and shoes and the clasp of a bag. She'd found a sheet of ribs with a skull still attached. For what seemed like hours, she'd howled and cried.

But then the water level had dropped again, and she'd carried on.

It struck her that perhaps she'd gone mad. She wondered

if she'd know it if she had. Surely no sane person could have kept on going under such circumstances. She didn't know how long it had been since she'd last eaten. And it would have been certain suicide to drink any of the water, but there was some kind of a seepage drip from the roof in one place and she'd managed to catch a few drops of that. She remembered her name, and said it aloud often. Sometimes, the voice didn't sound like her own.

The level was falling. She'd been waiting for it to fall. She'd taught herself patience, but the wait had been hard. The reason for this was that she believed she'd discovered the opening from which the mesh cover had been prised, but then she'd been forced back from it before she'd had a chance to explore.

Theresa slid her way down into the muck. With the accuracy of a blind person in a familiar room, she made her way to the opening.

Memory was so unreliable. She could no longer be sure that she hadn't imagined it.

But it was there.

She knelt at the bottom of the tank, and explored the opening with her good hand. Her other gave her no trouble. She'd pushed it into her blouse, where the double-button held it as if in a sling. At first it had hurt her whenever she'd moved, but now it never hurt at all.

The reason for her wait was that she had to be able to reach right in without putting her face under the surface.

She wouldn't get excited. She wouldn't dare to get excited. The hole was blocked, but only by what felt like a mass of twigs and decaying vegetable matter. Flattening her hand like a blade, she kept on pushing it in. On it went, and on. As if she was forcing it through a mass of fibrous dough.

Then her fingers touched something hard, and she stopped. She felt around it. What she felt was like a handle of some kind. She wrapped her fingers around the handle, but her grip was poor. Theresa found that she could make it rock a little from side to side, but that was all. She'd been holding her breath and she realized now that her face was half-under and she was about to black out.

Something had tangled around her arm like seaweed, and for a moment she was afraid that it wouldn't let her go. But it came out with her, and she fell back exhausted.

She saw lights. But they were just the sparks that popped in her eyes, not real lights at all. It was some time before they subsided, and she was able to consider the implications of her discovery.

There was a way out. The way out might be cleared. And once the way out had been cleared . . .

The water was rising again. Her window of opportunity was a limited one, here. One-handedly she tried to untangle the weed, thinking of how she'd judge it better next time. Her patience might be endless, but her strength certainly wasn't.

And as she was thinking this it started to dawn on her that what she was pulling free wasn't weed, but had metal clasps and buttons. It took her a while to make a certain identification. It was a garter belt.

A garter belt. Theresa sat in the darkness with the garter belt in her hand.

She now knew what the blockage was.

It was one of her predecessors.

The pulp was the sludge of her waterlogged flesh, the handle most probably some part of her pelvic cage. She'd found the hole and she'd opened it up and she'd crawled into it. And there, for whatever reason – exhaustion, lack of oxygen, sheer lack of space to get through – she'd died.

Someone was laughing.

The voice wasn't hers.

48

It was evening, and Ruth was back in her room when the phone rang. She wasn't looking forward to switching on her lights. The room light was a wall-mounted tube that gave the place an even dingier look, like the bottom of the stairway to a really seedy nightclub. Her music-loving neighbour had moved on, but her air-conditioning unit was making almost as much noise. She'd pulled off the bed cover and was lying on the sheets which carried, for no reason that she could imagine, the legend MEDICAL CENTER HOSPITAL OF VERMONT.

She looked at the phone. There was a five-dollar deposit for its use that she hadn't paid, so she wondered who might be calling her and how.

She picked it up, and said a cautious hello.

'It's me, Tom Diaz.'

Ruth swung her legs off the bed and sat upright. 'What is it?' she said.

'I'm right here,' Diaz said. 'I'm on the house phone in the motel office. Are you presentable?'

'I was thinking of raising the energy for a shower.'

'What does that mean?'

'It means I haven't done anything about it yet.'

'Is this a desperate need?'

'Meaning what?'

'I mean, does it have to be now or can it wait until later?'

Ruth had showered once already, when she'd arrived back at the end of the afternoon. But her room had stayed hot and sticky for some time and had taken a while to cool, so she'd been thinking of another. It was something to do. Showers and forty-one channels of TV. The place offered nothing else.

She said, 'It can wait.'

'Get yourself ready, then,' Diaz said. 'I'm coming down.'

'What's the matter?' she said when he arrived. 'Did something happen?'

'Nothing happened,' he said. 'I'm going out to eat, that's all. Do you want to come along? Don't tell me you already ate because I checked your car and the engine's cold.'

'I'm not hungry,' Ruth said.

'Come and watch me, then,' Tom Diaz said. 'Sitting alone in an empty room in a strange city is no-one's idea of a healthy and productive experience.'

'Don't worry about me,' Ruth said. 'I'll be fine.'

Diaz looked around her room, and while he didn't exactly wince, he didn't exactly have to. 'Think about what you're going to do,' he insisted. 'You're going to watch TV or listen to the radio. Do you know what they play on the radio here? Cajun music. Have you ever *heard* Cajun music?'

'Some.'

'I rest my case. Come on. You don't know anybody in town, I don't know anyone in town. If you won't do it for you, do it for me.'

What could she say? She locked up the room and went along with him. It would pass the time even though, like the tramp in the play said, it would have passed anyway. They headed north, up a boulevard that ran along the edge of a city park where police horses were being exercised in the early evening sun. Diaz had changed his clothes, losing his wilting suit jacket in exchange for some canvas trousers and a cotton shirt. He had the car radio on and it was playing, not Cajun music, but golden oldies from one of those stations that were obliged to play 'Unchained Melody' every twenty minutes or so.

From the beginning, Ruth had been convinced that Tom Diaz hadn't liked her. She couldn't have pointed to any detail and explained why, but it was a strong impression she'd had. Nothing in his manner had altered and he wasn't making any attempt to ingratiate himself, but something seemed to have changed. Almost as if she'd switched sides, gone through fire, and was now being accepted.

She said, 'Why'd you pick me up?'

He was checking his rearview mirror as they made a turn to run parallel to the lake shore. They weren't yet in sight of the water, but over walls and buildings could be glimpsed forests of yacht masts and flags. 'I wanted to,' he said without looking at her.

'You don't have to feel guilty,' she said.

'I don't? For what?'

'For not believing me when I told you I'd seen him.'

'I'm a professional disbeliever. If my mother says it's raining, I take a look out of the window.' And then he said, 'And I didn't pick you up. I invited you out. You've lived here long enough, you ought to know there's a difference by now.'

They turned into a dead-ended road, and pulled into a half-empty parking lot that was within a crescent of ramshackle buildings. These were out on decks that had been built on wooden pilings over the water forming a veritable stilt town of seafood restaurants and bars, all of which were reached and connected by a maze of gangplanks and walkways. The lake beyond could be seen through the pilings, choppy and grey and opalescent and barely any deeper in colour than the sky.

'I got a recommendation,' Diaz explained. 'I asked for somewhere the tourists can't find.'

The place was called Bucktown, and the buildings reminded Ruth of the run-down English seaside resorts of her northern childhood. A couple were closed, and one even appeared to have burned down to its decking. The others had been spruced up in Florida pinks and greens but it was all very coastal, pleasantly tacky and with the unbuttoned feel of a place that had been run down just sufficiently to be comfortable.

Ruth got out of the car. The light had faded enough for a couple of the restaurants to have switched on their neon. Two or three skinny-looking cats were roaming the grass verges, and one of them had curled up and was asleep in the middle of the driveway.

Tom Diaz was by the car, hands raised in fists, stretching out all the kinks. Just at the point where it looked as if something was going to burst, he relaxed with a sound of immense satisfaction.

'I always feel the same when I'm on the road,' he said as they walked toward the lights. 'Doesn't matter if it's for one night or a week. I get all excited like I'm twelve years old because it means I'm going to get away from everything and then, when it actually starts to happen, I'm just aching for it to be over so I can go home. You know what my kids do? They make a chart and cross off the days.'

'That's sweet.'

'Yeah,' Diaz said. 'Isn't it.'

'What's wrong with that?'

'There's nothing wrong with it. All I wonder is, if they miss me so much when I'm gone, why aren't they nicer to me when I'm there?'

They were aiming for a building that was a little farther out over the water than some of the others, reached by a covered walkway lit by hanging strings of bulbs. A warm breeze was coming in off the lake through the walkway's open sides. Water lapped underneath them, slow-moving like bright oil.

Diaz said, 'You take any book written for guys to read. The hero always lives on a boat or in a trailer or some crummy rented apartment that you wouldn't call home. He's alone. A good-looking woman walks in and gives him the eye, and he's on her like a dog. It's a fundamental male fantasy to be rootless and have no ties. And yet there's nobody more unhappy than a rootless guy. Jails and flophouses are full of them. From that I get one conclusion.'

'What?' Ruth said.

He opened the door, and stood aside to let her go ahead of him. Which was a courtesy that Ruth had never much appreciated, because it meant always being the first to enter an unfamiliar place. He said, 'The conclusion is that you never know it when you're happy. The best you can hope for is to know when you were. When were *you* happy, Ruth?'

'I don't know,' she said.

'Make an effort. Don't ruin a good theory.'

'Before I met Pete Michaud, I suppose.'

'I don't think so.'

It was as if he'd caught her off-guard. After some of the things she'd been through, the last that she expected was a challenge in the one area where she reckoned she was the world's sole expert.

'Well,' she said, 'there hasn't been much joy since.'

'I saw the life you were leading back then. It was nice, but it was kind of dull. It was like four well-chosen objects in an empty room.'

He was still holding the door for her. Ruth felt the blood drain from her as his words sank in.

She said, 'What did you say?'

'I said,' Diaz explained patiently, 'you had all the basic essentials to hand when you were playing house with Aidan. But you were so obsessed with Michaud, you just couldn't see it.'

Was that it? Was that what he'd really said? Or was he playing some game with her? If he was, he gave no sign of it. Ruth felt a sense of alarm, as if the mask of the world had momentarily slipped. A reminder of how precarious her outer calm actually was.

Feeling a little dazed, she went on in.

Diaz was still talking as he followed her. 'I don't know, Ruth. It was your life, not mine. I'm only telling you how it looked from where I was. Do you miss Aidan?'

'Yes,' she said.

'Did you tell him how you felt, while you still could?'

He was treading on dangerous ground, now. She could only shake her head.

'Point proven?'

'Thanks, Tom,' she said. 'I could have been less miserable in my room for no cover charge.'

'You're still obsessed with Michaud.'

'I'm not.'

'Then why else are you here? It's going to eat your whole life away, Ruth. I once tried to say this to Aidan and now I'm saying it to you. You've turned out to be tougher than I thought you were. But get away from it. Hasn't he taken enough?'

At first it seemed as if they were going to be dining alone. The bar was empty, there was no-one at the gaming machines and no-one watching the TV. But that was simply because everyone had been seated right down at the far end where a room had the best views out over the water, and there was no clear way to this part because the place had been built on and added to in such a haphazard fashion.

A waiter in black pants and a white shirt came to get them. He led them through the empty tables and down a narrow passageway into the dining area. The windows here were grimed and spotted with spray. Out across the lake, Ruth could see the Pontchartrain Causeway down which they'd returned that same afternoon. Seen from here it was like a second horizon. Seventeen miles from shore to shore, and not a yard of it over solid ground.

Ruth gazed at the menu, but couldn't get her head together enough to order. She laid it down and looked around. She knew that whatever she might have, she wouldn't appreciate it. The fate of the restless. Always trying to live in the next moment, and never quite managing it while also failing to live in this one. For most it was a downfall. For Ruth it was a means of survival. Or escape.

'You want anything to drink?' Diaz said.

'Just water,' Ruth said.

This main dining-room had been half-papered with green palm trees on a silvery background. Green neon strips supplemented the concealed lighting, giving the place a submerged feel. Taken together with the general

321

impermanent feel of the place, the impression was of an old ballroom built somewhere down in the Amazon with the tide of civilization having receded, leaving a losing battle to be fought against decay.

Still looking at his menu, Tom Diaz said, 'You thought Aidan was going to be under that slab, didn't you?'

Ruth said nothing, and Tom Diaz laid the menu down.

'It's not as mad as it sounds,' he said. 'The odometer on Frances Everline's car showed a mileage that we've never been able to account for. I'm not saying he brought her down here, it isn't *that* high, but he does seem to take some trouble over his disposals. You want to hear what they've set up at the cemetery?'

Ruth showed some interest.

'They've put a notice on the Michaud family stone,' Tom Diaz explained. 'Something to the effect that the records have been mislaid and if no-one comes forward, the site's going to be reclaimed by the county and resold, and the remains moved to a communal grave. There's a number to call. If mother's boy sees that, it's going to hit him where it hurts.'

'Do you think he'll go for it?'

'I don't know. It's a long shot. But I've known longer that have worked.'

The meal wasn't a disaster, but it was no birthday party either. Ruth picked at her salad and tasted nothing. Every now and again a lake craft would cut by outside, opening up the water like a fast-healing wound. The sky darkened further, tables in other parts of the restaurant started to fill.

Walking out to the car afterwards, Tom Diaz said, 'This didn't work out the way I planned. I had it in mind to try to raise your spirits a little, but I guess I made everything worse.'

'Don't worry about it, Tom,' Ruth said.

'What I'm trying to do,' he admitted at last, 'is persuade you to go home.'

She stood with her hand on the car door, waiting for him to unlock it for her.

'No point, Tom,' Ruth said. 'I don't think I actually have one, any more.'

49

Gus Frick had been the night gateman at the Cameron County Incinerator Company for almost eight years. Prior to that he'd worked for one of the big oil companies and seen the world, returning at the end of two decades with the opinion that the world wasn't everything that some reckoned it to be. He'd been some places and he'd seen some sights, but he'd come to believe that nothing quite compared with finding one patch of ground where one could feel totally at ease.

Well, this was his.

Cutbacks at the plant meant that tonight he was gateman, driver, office assistant and all-purpose drudge as well as duty manager, security chief and catering officer. In short, he was running the place solo. Normally he wouldn't have minded, but in the last couple of weeks the company had taken on a big and not-widely-advertised contract and the burners were running twenty-four hours a day. He had to meet the trucks, log them in and out, supervise their unloading and resecure the perimeter after every delivery. This was apart from running the ovens, loading the ovens, monitoring the ash buildup and disinfecting the yard. Material for destruction was beginning to arrive in a volume greater than the plant could handle. Given the nature of the contract, this was not the most desirable of situations. But complaint, he knew, would get him nowhere with the possible exception of the unemployment line.

He swung back the gates, and the big truck came through. It had a canvas cover and no markings, and it came in slowly with its lights all ablaze. Gus closed up after and then went around to the cab.

'Still got 'em coming?' he said as the driver was climbing down.

'You never saw anything like it,' the driver said. 'They got this big warehouse and they're just bringin' 'em in dead and pilin' 'em up to the roof.'

'In a whorehouse?' Gus said uncertainly.

'A *warehouse*,' the driver repeated. 'I've meant to ask you this before, no offence. Would you happen to be at all deaf?'

'Only in this ear,' Gus said. 'Have they told you what they're dyin' of yet?'

'There's no secret to what they're dyin' of. Bullet in the brain, is what they're dyin' of. But as to what's makin' 'em throw up and foam at the mouth and stagger all over the show, nobody's sayin'.'

'All I want to know is, can people get it?'

'They got doctors there. These doctors say definitely no.'

The two men stared at each other for a moment. Then, as one, both pulled out big handkerchiefs and tied them over the lower halves of their faces before going around to open the back of the truck. Gus had to unpick a little crusty patch out of his, where he'd absentmindedly pulled it out and blown his nose a few hours before.

Together they peeled back the canvas to reveal a solid jam of cattle bodies. They were diseased cattle from two states away, and they'd been coming for weeks. Twos and threes at first. Twenty or thirty here, at least.

The two men pulled the split pins to drop the tailgate prior to tipping.

Slightly muffled by his makeshift face covering, the driver said, 'What they say is, be sure that the brains and the spinal cords burn. Whatever it is that's sending them crazy, it lives in the nerves.'

'How many more loads are they planning to send us?' Gus wanted to know.

'I can only give you my opinion. Which is that there's no sign of an end to it.'

'We're backed-up here already.'

'That ain't my department. Where do you want them?'

Gus indicated vaguely with a sweep of his arm. 'Dump 'em against the wall. I'll remake the heap and then hose it down after.'

The driver exchanged some papers with Gus, and each got the other's signature on forms before the driver climbed back into his cab and backed his truck around until the tail-end of it faced the yard wall with some room to spare. Tip too close, and they'd bounce right over.

Hydraulic rams lifted the back of the truck. Bodies tumbled. Gus saw a calf in there, hardly bigger than a big dog. They came out and hit the ground and piled up like so much sheet rubber.

When the driver had cleaned out the back with the high-pressure hose and resecured his canvas, Gus opened up the gates again and waved him through. Slowing, the driver leaned out of his window and called out, 'What time are you here till?'

'We're on continuous operation now,' Gus said. 'I get off at six, but someone else takes over.'

'Got another run to fit in,' the driver said. 'I may see you later.'

When the back end of the truck had disappeared off into the night, Gus went over to the main building and switched on more yard lights. He wanted to see what he was doing, here. The carcasses were heavy and they were awkward to handle. At first the slaughtermen had been using chainsaws to cut them down into more manageable pieces, but that had been stopped because of the risk of cross-contamination from spraying nerve pulp. For a no-threat disease, it seemed to be causing a lot of anxiety.

Before he left the main building, Gus checked all the gauges. Then, with an iron rod, he lifted the inspection flaps and looked in through the dense glass window into the heart of each furnace. Each blazed almost white, each showed the same animal-shapes lying stacked on their sides like brilliant X-rays. As he watched, one heap shifted and collapsed and flared so brightly that he had to screw up his eyes and let the flap fall again. Then he adjusted his handkerchief and settled his hard hat before he went over and started up the Dumpster.

It would have to be said that the patch of ground he'd once had in mind had more resembled a small farm or a ranch than this. This was like the night shift in Hades after a Rolling Stones concert. But it was gainful employment, and not to be sniffed at. He needed the job. Gus had invested his oil company savings, but it couldn't be said that he'd invested them well.

At least it was comparatively quiet out here, not counting the roar of the plant itself. Nobody had so far been inclined to buy any of the adjoining land and set up next door. The plant was a big, square building clad in lime-green aluminium siding with three big drive-through doors cut into it. The perimeter fence enclosed the yard, which was subdivided into bays by cinderblock walls. Out back was the ash heap. Across the way was the plant's sole neighbour, the still-standing ruin of the Comet Roller Rink. It was grey and blind-windowed and starting to lean, and had a FOR RENT notice out at the front.

The Dumpster revved into life. The plant had two of them, and they were the real workhorses around here. Each had a hydraulic arm at one end and a blade like a snowplough at the other. Usually there was a bucket on the end of the arm, but Gus had unbolted this and replaced it with a three-pronged attachment normally used by farmers for spiking and lifting bales of hay. It wasn't pleasant to use, but once he'd managed to get the hang of ramming it in he'd found that he dropped fewer carcasses and was able to place them more precisely.

He spun the Dumpster around and revved it a little more when it spluttered. Where to start? He tried to put some method into this, but Frank Xilas on the day shift had been going at the heaps haphazardly and in no particular order. Xilas was brother-in-law to one of the co-owners, and no other fact would explain how he came to be holding down a job at all. He had new deliveries dumped on top of old and kept no record, which meant that Gus was depending mainly on a fly count to ensure that nothing hung around for longer than it should. There was a heap of spoiled meat in Bay Three that had long outlasted its welcome, Gus reckoned, and it was due to be bumped to the head of the line before the carcasses got too rotten to hold together.

Two or three rats shot across the yard as the Dumpster came around the corner. Rats were a fact of life around here. They were an amazingly flexible population. There were always exactly as many rats as there was available food. Always. They bred fast, they aged fast. And they'd eat anything, including each other.

Here it was. Bay Three. The carcasses had swelled like balloons, green and black in the Dumpster's headlights. Gus was half-expecting the first to go up with a bang when the points went in, but the flesh had gone hard like a crust. He worked the levers, hoisted it up, drove it around to the next available furnace, and then went back for another.

This was routine. Ram in the spikes, heave them aloft. They felt nothing now. It only had the look of cruelty.

The next one stuck.

The prongs went in all right, but the cow bodies had become entangled and when he tried to lift one, he found that he was lifting them all. The heap rose and shifted, the hydraulics whined in protest, the Dumpster started to rock.

Finesse was required. Gus let the arm drop and saw the rising heap subside, falling into a new configuration like a settling campfire. So now to try again, gently, teasing flesh from rotten flesh.

He started, but without such a good purchase this time. The meat was so far-gone, the points had erupted through the animal's side. This was no good. It was tearing.

Gus reached for the lever to take it back down. But the shock that he received then froze his behind in the saddle and his hand on the control.

He saw a hand.

A human hand.

A hand that burst up through the charnel-heap and, as if grasping the hilt of a sword, caught hold of the end of the spike and held on to it.

50

It held on with one hell of a grip. The spike tore free of the carcass and continued to rise, and the owner of the hand was coming up with it. The determination was almost palpable, like an electricity in the air. There was a sucking sound as the dead meat gave up its prisoner. Head and shoulders first, and then his other arm came free and he was able to make the grip two-handed. It was a man, but he was so daubed with filth that he looked like a totem painted with several thick colours of mud. He was shirtless and in his underwear, the underwear plastered seamlessly to his body. As he pulled his legs free, Gus saw that he was also shoeless.

The man let go of the spike, and slithered down the heap. When his feet hit the ground, he staggered. He managed two steps forward and then he fell to his knees. Gus shut down the controls and then scrambled down from the saddle. The man was braced on his hands, already attempting to rise.

Gus was going to help him, but then the stench hit him like a wall. The handkerchief over his face was no protection. It was as if the heap had belched the man forth in a bubble of deliquescence. Gus was gagging, and the man was rising. Unsteadily, he made it back onto his feet. He swayed, but he didn't fall again. He was like a crude thing of wet clay. All except for his eyes, which were bright and wide open.

Gus said, 'Where in hell did you come from?'

'I want this stuff off me,' the man said, holding out his hands before him and looking at them, and at himself. The dead matter caking him was soot-black and dark red, and streaked with bad-meat green. Pieces of what

330

appeared to be frayed ropes and parcel tape hung from his limbs.

'Are you all right?' Gus babbled. 'I mean . . . oh, hell, follow me. Don't touch anything. How long were you under there?'

'I don't know.'

'Should I call for a doctor?'

Those eyes turned onto him.

'Don't call for anyone,' the figure said.

Gus led the way, and the man followed with lurching steps. Gus had to keep looking back at him, because it was so damned scary to have him plodding along in his wake. In another part of the yard there was a high-pressure shower for emergency use, mainly in the event of corrosive splashes. Gus was leading him toward it. The shower was out in the open, with a metal grid to stand on and a chain to pull. Gus had never actually seen it in use before.

The water came down with such force that it was more like being hit by a fire hose than a shower. It almost dashed the man to the ground again, but he fought it and managed to stand firm. The filth was stripped from him and, as he slowly emerged from his dirt shell under the cascade, he seemed to grow bigger. Gus opened up the safety locker on the wall and brought out a pump-spray like the ones they used to squirt on everyone's wheel trim at the car wash. The spray contained a powerful disinfectant.

The man let go of the chain. The shower stopped all at once. He started to breathe again. Then he shook the water from his hair and held his head in both hands for a while.

'I need something to wear,' he said. 'Can I get that here? I can't pay you anything.'

Talk about hitting the ground running. Gus said, 'I'm going to spray you with this, then you're going to shower again. While you're doing that I'll see what I can dig out. Close your eyes.'

Because the plant was set up to handle just about every kind of waste that there was, they had very strict hygiene

331

procedures in the locker room. Only Frank Xilas failed to stick to them consistently, which was odd in that he'd go home with asbestos dust in his clothes but still believed that one could pick up AIDS from a doorknob. Xilas was about this man's size. So he got to donate one of his clean coveralls.

The man stood out in the middle of the tiles and towelled himself down. Gus couldn't help noticing some of the marks on his body that the clean-down had revealed.

'How'd all that stuff happen?' Gus said.

'I had a few accidents,' the man said, and seemed disinclined to say more. He held out the towel and said, 'Thanks.'

Gus held up his hands, not wanting to touch it. 'Drop it straight in that bag,' he said. He still had the handkerchief tied over his face; only now, a little self-consciously, did he take it off.

He said, 'How did you get to be under that shitheap anyway?'

'I was put there,' the man said, pulling on Xilas' one-piece, 'by a guy who thought I was near enough gone for it not to matter. You were supposed to shovel me in and burn me with the rest of the garbage.'

'Maybe I ought to call the police.'

'I don't need the police. I do need a phone.'

Gus led him out of the locker room and through into the office. It was spare and bare, with a chipped desk and a couple of filing cabinets, but it had a phone. The man moved around the desk. Xilas' clothes were too tight for him. He was still barefoot.

Gus said, 'Call from here. I'll clean it down after. Nothing personal.'

He dialled. Listened for a while.

Then he said, 'Ruth? It's me. Don't be scared. Pick it up.' And listened for a while longer.

Then he hung up.

'She isn't there,' he said.

'I've got to refill the ovens and rake out the ash,' Gus

told him. 'There's nobody with me and I'm all at full stretch.'

'Go right ahead,' the man said, obviously not picking up the note of apology in Gus's voice.

'I can't leave you in here alone,' Gus explained.

Without argument, the man went outside. Gus locked the office and then led him down to the end of the building. There was an outdoor sitting-place here, one that Gus and his co-workers had fixed up and which saw some more regular use in less pressured times than these. Salvaged furniture, threadbare but serviceable, stood out under a lean-to awning. There was a refrigerator and a radio, also rescued and repaired. Light was from a single bulb with a tin shade. Gus switched it on. Midges danced in its beam.

'I'll set everything up and get back to you,' he told the man. 'It'll take me about half an hour. Get rested and breathe some clean air.'

The man dropped wearily onto the couch whose springs had been pushed back in and secured with carpet tape. By the look on his face, it might have been a thousand-dollar mattress.

'Fine,' he said. Eyes closed, he lowered his head back.

Gus hurried to the furnace room and did what he had to do. He felt anxious and uncertain. There might be some kind of liability involved here, he didn't know what. He was going to have to call one of the owners, regardless of the hour. He wondered if he'd done everything right. If the police were going to be involved, it would be better to let the boss make the call.

He reloaded the furnace with new carcasses from the last delivery. They might want to keep the other scene intact for investigation. And damned good luck to them if they did, as long as they didn't expect him to stand too close while they were investigating.

The fact of it was, the shock of the discovery was only just beginning to make itself felt. Practical demands had held it off, but getting back to routine now laid Gus open to it. His concentration was bad. All the evidence of shock

333

was there. He did simple things twice, and then couldn't remember whether he'd done them at all. When he climbed down from the Dumpster, his legs were shaking so much that he almost sat down right there on the ground. It had been quite a thing to witness. Gus was badly spooked.

The only time he could recall feeling anything like this was the time that he'd seen his ghost. And that was a story he'd told nobody. He'd wanted to tell it, nearly had a number of times, but he'd always managed to hold back at the last moment. Gus didn't want to be laughed at, the way they did at people who saw UFOs. He'd believed it when it happened, but the certainty hadn't lasted. He'd been driving home after a night shift and he'd passed someone walking by the road, and in his mirror he'd recognized the figure. It was the Louisiana boy, name of Michaud, who'd worked at the plant for a while. But then when Gus had gone back to see if he'd wanted a ride, there was nobody there. It was as if he'd jumped off the road and hidden himself, which didn't make any sense. He'd later heard that Michaud had died in a motel fire that same night, some five or six hours before Gus was supposed to have seen him.

Weird, or what?

And the weirdness continued. Because when Gus went back to see how the man was doing he found that there was no-one on the old couch, either.

51

Elaine didn't hear the alarm, but she woke when Louis got out of bed. She'd an instinct for his presence, and she always knew it when he moved close to or away from her. It was early, still dark. She listened to him moving around, picking up his clothes so that he could take them and dress in some other part of the house. He was doing it as quietly as he could, but he kept bumping into things. Something dropped, and she heard him whispering to himself in annoyance as he gathered it up again. Then he went.

She gave it a couple of minutes, and then she got up and followed him.

He was in the kitchen with the light on, pulling on his shoes. Lucius was sitting up in his basket. Lucius, Louis. She called them both Lou. Neither of them had thought of it at the time but she was going to have to change the dog's name, before it all got too confusing. Call them Big Lou and Little Lou, maybe. She kept putting it off. But then, Elaine knew that a name was something that one didn't change lightly.

Lou looked up at her. 'You should have stayed in bed,' he said.

'Tell me what you want for breakfast.'

'I don't need any.'

'Anything you want. I'll get it for you.'

'I'll get it on the road. Go back to bed and stop being in the way. I can't think straight this early.'

'When will you be home?'

'I don't know that.' He looked down, to where the puppy was all but falling over his feet. 'You want something to do,' he said, 'see to him. He's working himself around to peeing on my shoes again.'

She let the dog out onto the grass, and went out with him. She sat on the steps and waited as he snuffled around, a small pale shape in the darkness. The first light was beginning to show in the sky. There were no lights in any of the other houses.

A few minutes later, Lou walked out to his truck. It wasn't huge, hardly bigger than a van; Lou delivered parts, and most of them weren't bulky. As he was unlocking the driver's door, she called the puppy back from around its wheels.

'Bye, Lou,' she called in a raised whisper. 'See you later.'

'Don't make so much noise,' he said.

She held the squirming puppy, which licked her at the same time as trying to get away. Lou's truck made a racket as he backed it off the driveway.

As far as a goodbye was concerned, that seemed to be it. Lou wasn't at his best so early in the mornings. That was why he was grumpy, and wasn't always so considerate. Elaine reminded herself of the reasons, but still she felt a little crestfallen as she let the puppy down onto the ground to finish its business and went inside.

Something was waiting for her on the kitchen table that hadn't been there before. There was a present in fancy paper, and there was a card. The present, she found when she took the paper off, was some Eau de Cologne with a French name. The card read *Happy Anniversary, lots of love, Louis.* Elaine sat at the kitchen table and read the verse through twice. She couldn't think what it might be the anniversary of; they hadn't been together for long enough for their lives to have settled into those kinds of conventional patterns. Just about every week was an anniversary of something . . . first meeting, first date, first kiss, first time they did the other thing.

Perhaps it was a year since they'd moved in. She wasn't sure. The house belonged to one of Lou's uncles, who let them have it cheap and expected Louis to fix it up in return. Then it was Elaine's suspicion that they would be pushed out and the house sold or let for rather more.

Whatever the anniversary was, she hadn't realized it was coming up. She'd have to get him something today. She tried to think of something that he might need. Some vitamins that he'd seen advertised in one of his bodybuilding magazines, perhaps? Louis had a bench and some weights in the extra bedroom. He used them all the time and he was as skinny as a pole. He was strong, but he'd never be broad.

She folded the paper. She stood the card where she'd be able to see it and she uncapped the cologne and took a sniff.

Oh, well. The thought counted most.

She went to the doorway, and stepped out again to call the puppy. She couldn't quite decide whether to go back to bed for an hour or to find something useful to do. Lucius was snuffling, and thrusting his face into the earth at the base of one of the trees. Elaine felt a little sad for him, and a little envious as well. He'd grow up and get old and die, and he'd never even know it. Like dogs in really old photographs. They'd been there, they were long gone. And they'd never wondered why.

She called him, twice, in a low but urgent tone. He hung on as long as he dared, started to respond, and then got distracted by something else.

He must have done something by now. She would go out and clear it up when it got a little lighter. Never, Elaine had sworn to herself, would she live in a house with dog's mess out on the grass. Standing in the doorway, seeing the dawn begin to take a hold in the sky, she noticed something that she hadn't seen before. The little flag on the mailbox had been knocked so that it was half up and that was odd, because the mail never got here so early.

Folding her arms across her chest to hold her robe shut, Elaine went down to the mailbox to check it. There was a single white envelope with her name and address on it.

337

The envelope must have been hand-delivered at some time in the night, because it had no stamp.

She opened it as she was walking back into the house, and she started to read it by the light in the kitchen. After the first couple of sentences, she wished she hadn't started. She tried to stop but her eyes went on, sucking it in. Finally she tore it from her gaze and screwed it up.

Hate mail. Someone had sent her hate mail.

It panicked her and she destroyed it, tearing it up and forcing it down the waste. If she kept it, she knew she'd read it all. She wouldn't be able to stop herself. And it was so sick. The sins of the fathers. Whatever Jesus might have died for, it wasn't to provide justification for people like that. It had been, of course, unsigned.

She ran water into the disposal, shredding the paper into a pulp. She put the envelope down after. Then she backed away across the room.

She'd thought it might be from Peter. A secret message from her brother. Now she almost wished that it had been.

Then she wondered if she should have kept it for the police. But then she thought, would the police even be interested? Or would they be in broad agreement with the sender of the note?

She wondered exactly who might have put it there. One of the neighbours, at a guess. Someone who'd seen all the comings and goings and who was aware of all the interest in her. She'd never made public who she was and she'd told her story to nobody other than Lou, but obviously someone knew. And if someone knew, before long everyone would know.

She went to the window and looked out. Surely it had to be someone in one of those houses. The ones that she could see from here and who, in their turn, would have been able to see the arrival of the police and FBI. She'd tried to keep a low profile. But it wasn't exactly witness relocation.

She wondered if the surveillance was still going on. They

hadn't said so in as many words, but she'd the feeling that it was what they'd intended. Which meant that whoever had delivered the note had probably been seen doing it. Photographed, even. Sneaking to the house in darkness, tweaking the mailbox open, slipping it inside.

She could ask the watchers.

But then she realized that she didn't actually want to know.

Elaine sat at the kitchen table, her head in her hands, and it was as if she could see her entire future caving in and falling down the same crack. There was a scratching at the door now, the puppy wanting to come in, but she didn't register it.

She'd shut so much out of her life completely. She hadn't been to visit her father in ages; he was close to catatonic now, had been for years, and he didn't even know her when he saw her. What he'd become was no more than a distressing parody of the daddy she'd had. She bent forward, her shoulders heaving, head to the table, remembering him. She wished he was back; Louis took care of her and swore that he always would, but he was such a boy.

She tried to conjure her daddy in her mind and talk to him, but the shadow couldn't quite make it. It was as if he stood out there in the cold, unable to come forward. There were so many shadows. Kathy, frozen in time at seventeen. Her big sister had always seemed unreachably older to Elaine, and even though Elaine had passed her in years already still she seemed the steadier, wiser one.

Or her mother, forgotten entirely; a stranger in photographs, a name on a stone. Elaine had been so young, and there had been so much to try to forget. Maybe she'd thought that she could pick and choose the memories she'd keep. Well, she'd been wrong.

And Peter.

Peter before her now, hands outspread, leaning over the table. She asked him what he wanted and he said he wanted it all back as it was. Order and meaning again. And he said that he was going to defy God and run through defiling this world that God was so proud of, until he got exactly what he wanted.

All those shadows, that wouldn't come forward.

And Peter, the shadow that wouldn't go away.

52

Although she was a civilian with no actual status in the investigation, Ruth was accepted enough to be allowed a small degree of involvement. It wasn't much. She got to ride the next morning with Tom Diaz, her appointed keeper, as Diaz drove around trying to track down old school friends and acquaintances of the Michauds. Given that Diaz himself was pretty much on the fringe of things, this was clearly a ploy to keep her out of it. She didn't protest. Some tide would carry her where she needed to go, wherever that might be. She and Michaud were fated, she saw that now. She thought about it distantly, as she might of something happening to someone else. Her mistake had been in ever trying to resist the fact at all.

They went out toward Baton Rouge in search of the girl who'd been described by some as Pete Michaud's childhood sweetheart. The search took them to a truck stop town on the highway which seemed to consist almost entirely of gas stations, truckers' motels, and nightclubs with dancing girls. They found the woman running a small roadside business along with her husband on the edge of town. They had hundreds of bicycle frames and a couple of dozen birdhouses lined up on the grass between their house and the traffic. The woman barely remembered Michaud at all, and reacted to the sweetheart notion with disbelief. She'd a vague memory of letting him kiss her once, she said, and that was when they couldn't have been more than six years old.

Diaz checked her off his list.

He made a couple of calls, and then they got back on the road.

As they headed down to pick up a river ferry, Ruth took

a look down his list and said, 'What do you think you're going to get from any of these people?'

'Me?' Diaz said. 'Probably nothing. All I'm here for is to stake out the ground for the prosecution, assuming that we're eventually going to get him back for trial in Pennsylvania. Tell them who's worth calling up and who isn't. I knew an assistant District Attorney subpoena a character witness who'd been in a coma for two years. They had to carry the bed and all the drips and stuff up two flights of stairs to the courtroom, and all he could do was just lie there and drool.'

'Really?' Ruth said. And he glanced at her across the car, and was unable to take advantage of her credulity any further. He shook his head.

'No,' he said.

Ruth laid his notepad down on her knee, and looked out of the window. They were on a wide, dusty, badly kept concrete road, and there was the beacon flame of a refinery dancing atop its chimney on the far horizon.

She said, 'No-one out here can have seen him in years. How much use are they going to be?'

'That depends on what background they can provide. It's all going to come down to one issue. What he did and the fact that he did it, they're not going to be in any doubt.' Tom Diaz shifted in his seat, as if settling down more firmly into his argument. He said, 'What it'll revolve around is, how responsible was he? We're going to be arguing that he made his choices and that what he did gives us a straight picture of what he is. His defence is going to be looking for ways to say that he didn't and you'll have some jury off the street sitting there trying to make sense out of it all. Half an hour ago they were dropping their children off at school, now suddenly they're looking down this long dark pit and the hardest part to take is that there's this face at the bottom looking up, and it's not that much different to their own. People don't expect that. Ordinary people don't ever expect to have to face it.'

'What would you do with him?'

'I don't know.'

He glanced across the car, and saw that she was watching him.

'I really don't,' he said. 'What do you think? Because I'm a cop you think I'd want him run out and strung up?'

'I never said that.'

'I'm not saying I'd cry if he walked in front of a bus. I'd call that God taking care of business. But you tell me something, Ruth. Is Pete Michaud a monster?'

The question took Ruth by surprise, and it was a while before she felt able to give him an answer.

'I don't believe in monsters,' she said.

'Even after what you heard him do to Aidan?'

'That's not fair, Tom.'

Diaz shrugged, as if to suggest that being unfair was simply another way of making a point, and he said, 'So what's a monster anyway? Look what the Greeks did. They put theirs together out of things that were familiar to them. Head of a lion. Tail of a snake. Wings like a bird. A bull's head on a guy's body. Strange on its own doesn't scare us. We get a kick out of strange. But break down someone ordinary and put him back together in some way that shouldn't be . . . that's the kind of monster we turn away from. Like those babies you see in jars. You turn away because if you don't, it just breaks your heart.'

There was a silence.

Then Ruth said, 'Can we talk about something else?'

'Sorry,' Tom Diaz said.

About a mile farther on, they reached the river. The road widened into a red dirt turning area and then dropped down a short hill of white stones to the loading point at the foot of the levee. The ferry was boarding and they didn't have to wait; they were waved ahead by a blonde woman in sunglasses and a dayglo coverall.

The ferry set off about two-thirds empty. It was about seven car-lengths long and had a sheet metal deck. The Mississippi was about three-quarters of a mile across at this point and it was the muddy tan shade of stale, underbrewed coffee. Ruth got out of the car, and went to stand at the rail.

Hands in his pockets, Tom Diaz ambled over to stand beside her. He didn't stand too close, as if wary of invading her privacy and ready to back off if she didn't want company.

He said, 'I'd like to stick around until they catch him, but that isn't what I'm here for. If nothing new comes up, I'm going to be on the evening plane out of here. I'm going to make a suggestion to you. Why don't you turn in the car and come back with me?'

'You know I can't do that,' she said.

'They won't let you *be* there when it happens.'

She left him at the rail, and went back to sit in the car.

He joined her when they were docking on the opposite side.

'Were you crying?' he said.

'No,' Ruth said, and he seemed relieved.

They drove on down country roads and past peach groves and sorghum fields, the sorghum standing at head-height. Occasionally they'd pass someone way out in the middle of nowhere, usually a man on his own walking beside the road in the burning mid-day heat. Once it was a black boy in a loose shirt, no hat, his head almost shaven. Then, later, a beefy white man in a red T-shirt and a tractor cap. Neither looked for a ride. This was a prison area, and nobody stopped for hitch-hikers. After a while they passed a detention centre, a low, neat complex looking like a state-of-the-art chemical plant. It was fenced, and the fence topped with razor wire whose coils resembled the shed skin of some high-tech but barbaric life form.

Diaz checked his watch and said, 'I need the phone again.'

The place that he found was an old service station that Ruth would have mistaken for a derelict building had it not been for the neon window sign that read 'Lite'. Only when she concentrated and looked past this could she see dim shapes moving slightly in the darkness behind it. Diaz was gone for a couple of minutes, and then he returned for her.

'They've got something they want you to listen to,' he said.

She followed him inside. The phone was lying as he'd left it, off the hook. Three or four men were sitting around, but no-one looked up. It was as if they'd died, but still came along here because they couldn't shake old habits.

Tom Diaz had a hurried conversation with whoever was on the other end, and then he handed the phone to Ruth. Not quite knowing what to expect, she took it.

She heard tape rewinding. Then she heard Michaud's voice, filtered by its double-trip through the system but impossible not to recognize.

'*So what* is *this?*' she heard him say in the recording. '*The family paid for perpetual care.*'

And then another voice that she'd never heard before, but which sounded perfectly convincing, replied, '*All I can tell you is, the fees were paid but the taxes weren't.*'

'*What taxes?*'

'*State tax and local tax. The amount still owing is thirty-five dollars and fifteen cents.*'

'How *much? Are you serious?*'

'*I don't make the regulations, sir.*'

Nice touch, Ruth thought.

'*I'll send it,*' Michaud said. '*Just nobody touch them.*'

'*Please get it to this office by close of business today. I can't guarantee processing time if it arrives any later.*'

And then another, different voice came onto the line. This one said, 'Is that him? We think it is.'

'I think so too,' Ruth said.

53

It would, of course, be a trap. In spite of her protests Tom Diaz wouldn't take her there or tell her where to go, but he returned her instead to the motel with a promise that he would get hold of her as soon as there was anything to say. She didn't know how they were going to grab him, or at what point they intended to pick him up. In the office, probably. Deep in some public building, with every exit being watched.

This wasn't how Ruth had seen it. Damn it, she was central to this. She was at the heart of his offences. How could they just shunt her out to the margins? What was the point of any process of justice that left the victims sitting in the dust, ignored and forgotten while everything happened elsewhere?

She tuned the TV to the cable information channel for the sole reason that it gave an accurate reading of the time in one corner of the screen, and she watched the minutes counting down as the last afternoon of Peter Michaud's freedom ticked away.

There was one piece of sense in it, she conceded. If she'd been anywhere around and he'd seen her, the trap would have been blown. But she felt empty. She felt raw.

She felt the need to unload to someone. She sat on the bed and made a half-hearted attempt to summon up the teenager from whom she hadn't heard in so long. But no image came. Nobody spoke to her. Suddenly it felt like a childish game, and a stupid one at that. There was nothing, just a void.

The void that Aidan Kincannon, so perceptively, had once told her that she'd used Michaud to fill.

The phone rang.

She glanced up at the screen. Four-fifty.

So it was over.

She picked up the receiver, and the motel manager said, 'Ms Lasseter? Your friend's arrived. He's on his way down to you.'

'Thanks,' Ruth said.

She replaced the phone. She felt dull. She felt hot. She took the latch off the door ready for the detective's arrival, and then she went into the bathroom to draw herself a glass of water. She'd been ready to deal with anything, or so she'd thought. But how to deal with anticlimax? There seemed to be no equipment for it. She let the water run a while, waiting for it to run cool.

She'd been feeling so little of anything over these past few days; she'd been beginning to think that it had all been burned out of her. But now that it was as good as over she could sense, not quite fear, but something like an apprehension of the return of fear. The future was opening up again, and opening wide. And she had no idea of what her part in it was going to be.

A tap came at the door. 'Wait a moment, Tom,' she called out from the bathroom. 'I'll have to come and take the chain off.'

She took a sip of the water, looking herself in the eye in the bathroom mirror, and then she threw the rest into the basin. For one moment she found herself imagining how she'd feel if she were to open the door and find, not Tom Diaz, but Aidan Kincannon standing there. But she didn't pursue it. She didn't dare.

As she was pulling the cord to switch off the bathroom light there was a bang, along with the splintering sound of screws being yanked out of wood.

And when she quickly stepped through into the bedroom, Peter Michaud was waiting for her.

He'd altered again, but not by quite so much. He'd let his hair grow out a little and he was wearing glasses, the wire-framed kind that had once been old-fashioned

347

but which everybody now wore to look thoughtful. NHS specs, they'd called them back at school in England; the kind the poor children wore because back then, they were free. He still looked good. A little bit too good, in fact, like an actor playing the role of a graduate student. Ruth wondered how she'd ever been taken in by him at all.

She felt herself falter. He'd closed the door behind him, and he was standing patiently.

He smiled a faint smile.

And all that she could say was, 'What are you doing here?'

'I heard you call me, Ruth,' he said.

'What do you mean?'

Michaud put his hand to his heart. 'In here,' he said. 'Don't say you didn't feel it too. Why didn't you tell me? I never would have hurt you if you had.'

'Don't come near me,' Ruth warned.

'I don't blame you for being scared,' he said, ignoring her and advancing around the end of the bed; she had to back away to keep the distance between them. The problem was, he was backing her into a corner. He went on, 'What do I have to say? Your boyfriend was right. You, me . . . we're each what the other needs.'

'And how did you get him to tell you about that?' Ruth demanded. 'Did you torture it out of him?'

'I've given you enough reasons to hate me already. I don't want to give you any more.'

Ruth felt herself bump into the bedside table, and knew that she couldn't retreat any further.

'Stay back,' she said.

He stopped, and held up his hands.

'I'm not going to touch you,' he said. 'I'm going to prove you can trust me. The phone's right behind you. Pick it up if you want to. I won't do anything. I've got no weapons. There's just me.'

Nothing happened for a few moments.

Then Ruth said, 'What if I tell them you're here?'

348

'I'm taking the chance that you won't,' he said.

So they stood there, in stalemate.

They walked out to the motel office together. I won't be scared, she kept telling herself. I won't ever be the way I was before. But she *was* scared, and it was inevitable that she would be. Her heart was hammering and her legs were weak. The difference was that this time, she was choosing to go with him. She believed that. And in a minute or so, she was going to get the chance to test it.

She felt as tight as a wire. The motel manager computed her bill and gave her a credit card slip to sign. He was a middle-aged Asian Indian and he wore a gold chain around his neck, a gold watch on his wrist, and two hefty gold rings on the fingers of his right hand.

Making a real effort to steady her voice, Ruth said to him, 'I'm going to leave my car here. Could you phone the hire company and have them pick it up?'

The manager seemed reluctant to get involved. 'Well,' he began, and he sighed and he looked at the clock on the wall, and then he ran a hand over the unopened mail that was lying on the counter, and generally trod water while he tried to think of a good excuse not to do it.

'I'd drop it off myself, but it's kind of an emergency,' Ruth explained.

'I hope it's not bad news,' he said, more or less giving in. 'Me too.'

The manager stapled the slip to her bill, and Michaud picked up her bag and made ready to go.

His car was an elderly El Camino Super Sport, the front end of a big sedan married to the rear end of a pickup. It stood outside the office and, in comparison to the one that she was leaving, it had the look of a rolling wreck. She wondered what he'd been doing, where he'd been living. Whether he really needed the glasses he was wearing. But she doubted that she'd ever get to know.

'It doesn't look so great,' he said, 'but it's legitimate and paid for. Do you want to have a say in where we go?'

'They're looking for you all over,' Ruth said.

'I know,' he said, almost sorrowfully. 'They'll never get me, though. They tried some stunt down at the graveyard. They've got no shame at all.'

Ruth said, 'Give me the keys.'

He didn't react for a moment. He was looking at her, and his eyes were like pale empty glass into which she might read anything, anything that she cared.

'I can drive us,' he said.

And Ruth said, 'No.'

She held out her hand.

'They're in the car,' Michaud said.

Ruth walked around to the driver's door, and the two of them got in.

'Where do you want us to go?' he said.

'I'm still thinking about that,' Ruth told him.

She got them onto Veterans Boulevard, heading northward out of the city and looking for a place to pick up the Interstate. The Interstate, the Causeway, she'd take whichever came up first. The traffic was heavy with the end-of-the-day rush. She said, 'How did you know where to find me?'

But Michaud said nothing.

Ruth said, 'Did you follow Tom Diaz? Were you watching us in the restaurant?'

'What does it matter?'

'Oh, my God,' Ruth said suddenly. 'You went to see Elizabeth, didn't you?'

He looked out of the window.

'What did you do to her?' Ruth said.

'Nothing,' Michaud said tersely. 'Elizabeth's fine.'

Ruth gripped the wheel harder. She said nothing more about it, but her disbelief must have been perceptible.

'I swear to you, Ruth,' Michaud said, 'whatever I may have done in the past . . . this is going to be different. I'm letting you take charge, aren't I? How much different can it be?'

'You think it's going to be that easy?'

350

'Why not? It happens all the time. They call it being born again. I tried it before but it's never worked out. Something catches up with you. Or something goes wrong, and it all turns to shit because you don't have the right help. But I knew you'd be the one.'

'You killed the ones who weren't,' Ruth said drily.

'Please, Ruth.'

The ramp went under the Interstate, through its shadow and then around to join it. Ruth checked over her shoulder as she cut into a gap in the traffic and said, 'You can't be born again, Peter. That's a myth.'

'So why do they say it?'

'Because it's what people want to hear. Like fat people want to be thin people but they don't want to work on it.'

They progressed through a complex of overpasses and then, almost immediately, the Interstate was out over the Bonnet Carre spillway. For a while it was like being on an emergency slipway thrown over a drowned forest, and then the wetlands opened up around them. Acres of marsh gave way to acres of open water.

Michaud said, 'What am I going to do?'

'Leave it to me,' Ruth said, and she started to put on speed.

After a while, Michaud said, 'Hey, Ruth. It's not a new car. It won't get us anywhere if you shake it apart.'

She had the pedal right down to the floor. The El Camino was responding, but it was taking its time. At around seventy, everything started to vibrate. She got over into the lane with the fastest-moving traffic, and stayed there. Anyone who didn't get out of the way, she gave them the lights.

'Ruth!' Michaud protested, and it started to dawn on him that something here wasn't exactly as he'd planned it.

'Look, Peter,' she said as they passed a temporary sign. 'Construction work ahead. Remember the road works? We had some fun there, didn't we?'

Michaud's face had set. He was watching her, not even looking at the road.

'You're disappointing me, Ruth,' he said.

'I'm sorry,' Ruth said. And then she hit the first barrier.

The barrier made the El Camino weave, but it barely slowed them and it certainly didn't stop them. She'd wondered how solid it was going to be but it was just lightweight reflective paddles standing upright on the hardtop, and they'd scattered with a thunderclap sound as the car exploded through. In her mirror, she could see them showering down onto the road in their wake like so much debris.

Now they were in an isolated lane running parallel to the traffic flow. They had a clear run, nothing ahead of them at all. Unlike the lake causeway, which ran straight on and for ever, this road wound its way through the wetlands. The two directions of traffic were separated by a gap of about sixty yards, with a long drop between. There was nowhere to go but onward.

Ruth kept the pedal down. Something in the El Camino's engine began to whine. On the edge of her vision she could see Michaud's hand braced against the dash. His knuckles really were white. She was ready in case he made a grab for the ignition key or tried to fight her for control, but he wasn't moving. He seemed rooted.

They shot onward past the single line of traffic that was moving at a more-or-less legitimate speed. She didn't even see the highway patrol car in the line, but she heard its siren winding up belatedly when they'd already left it some way behind. No matter. She sensed Michaud turning around in his seat to look back. Her own eyes were fixed on the road before them.

There was a big highway resurfacing vehicle in the lane about a half-mile ahead. From here, it didn't appear to be in motion but it was impossible to be sure. She hoped there was no-one on board. It was a huge yellow Tonka toy of a wagon, one of those used in quarrying or highway construction that dwarfed their drivers and looked as if they'd been built to reshape the landscape of Mars. Whenever they transported them from one site to another, they had a police escort and they stopped all the other cars on the road.

Well, Ruth thought, it would serve to stop this one, all right.

The distance closed.

The highway patrol car had set up pursuit, but the sound of its siren was a faint and forlorn thing and she couldn't even see the car in her mirror at all. In the fraction of a second that it took her to check, the big truck seemed to take a leap forward and to fill their windshield from side to side.

Ruth closed her eyes.

And Michaud grabbed the wheel.

He must have been waiting for his chance. He broke her grip, and she felt the car swing. She opened her eyes and tried to get back control of the wheel, but the huge tyres of the wagon were already sliding by and she felt a second impact as the El Camino burst through the breakaway barrier and re-entered the flow. Cars braked, tyres screamed. It was like being in some weird and wild theme park ride where cut-up footage was being projected onto the windows from all sides at high speed, and no part of it related to any other.

They hit the concrete of the outer barrier, side-on. The bounce made her neck snap and her teeth rattle as if she'd been punched in the back. She could hear, like gunshots falling back behind them, the chain-effect of a multiple shunt that sounded as if it had the makings of a major highway pileup. Michaud had one hand on the top of the wheel, and he was trying to steer them straight; but he was overcorrecting and they were weaving.

Ruth got her hands back onto the wheel and tried to slam the car into the side of the causeway again. They recrossed the shoulder, tyres juddering on the diagonal white studs, but Michaud pulled back and they swerved out before they hit. The barrier looked from here as if it was no more than three feet high. They might not go through, but if she could get the angle right it might be possible to plane up against it and go over. Once in the water, assuming that Michaud survived, there would be no way back for him. The road was on concrete stilts, the stilts were tall and sheer.

She tried again, he pulled back again, and an entire row of the reflective paddles were ploughed into and mown down like soldiers. Then, suddenly, the works were at an end and they were out into two lanes of empty road once more. The El Camino swerved along drunkenly, certain mayhem in its wake.

Somewhere behind them, the patrol car was catching up fast.

Ruth took her foot off the gas pedal and started to brake. The brakes were soft and the car pulled to one side, but at least it responded. She looked in the rearview mirror, but the mirror had been knocked in their struggle. Then the highway patrol car zipped by them like an overtaking fighter plane, and braked so hard that it turned almost fully around and came to rest blocking the two lanes about a hundred yards ahead.

Some of that distance got eaten up as the El Camino finally rolled to a halt and stalled. The lone patrolman was out of his car and running toward them down the middle of the road. He'd taken the safety strap from his holster and he'd pulled out his sidearm. His face was white and sick-looking and when he stopped and levelled the gun at the car, his hands were shaking.

'Both of you, out!' he yelled, even as Ruth was sliding out from behind the wheel. She moved around the door and started toward him, and as she did this he swung the gun about to cover her alone.

'You,' he said. 'Stop right there.'

Ruth stopped in her tracks and said, 'Officer, listen to me. You've got to arrest this man.' She started to indicate Michaud behind her in the car, but then became aware that he'd emerged and was walking toward her with his hands outspread in appeal.

'I beg you, Susan,' he was saying loudly, almost shouting over her. 'Please don't make it worse than it already is.'

She turned back to the patrolman and said, with renewed urgency, 'He's wanted. Check on that, right now.'

Michaud was shaking his head and looking stricken.

'She's under a doctor's care,' he said, almost wailing. 'But she hasn't done anything like this in ages.'

'He's wanted by the FBI!'

The patrolman was backing off before them, unable to decide where the greater threat lay and getting no time to think it through. Michaud was almost in tears, now. Real tears, as well, that he seemed to have summoned up for the occasion. He said to Ruth, 'Oh, God, Susan, *listen* to yourself for a minute! You're not well. Everything's going to be all right but you're going to have to trust this man.'

'I'm not Susan!' she said. 'I'm Ruth! I'm Ruth!' And Michaud looked at the patrolman and made a helpless gesture as if to say, You see what I mean?

'Everybody, here,' the patrolman said. 'Shut up.' He didn't look so old. Mid-twenties, maybe, and looking a little younger for being so shaken. He kept on backing off before them, trying to keep a manageable space around himself and letting nobody get too close. The patrol car behind him had some rear-end damage, as if he'd been clipped getting through. The road was utterly empty now. Clear of traffic ahead, blocked and backed-up some way behind them. Cars and trucks too far back to see the reasons for the holdup were sounding their distant horns.

Michaud was still moving, circling around Ruth as if to get over onto the patrolman's side and into the safety that his presence represented. He was saying, 'Call Dr Prendes at Tulane Medical. Tell him she's hearing voices again. It's been more than a year. That's supposed to be over.'

'I said shut up,' the patrolman said, but his eyes were on Ruth and it was clear that he was being swayed. She had, after all, been the one at the wheel of the car.

'He's Peter Michaud,' Ruth said quickly. 'His daddy killed all those women.'

She was banking on some recognition. The patrolman wasn't quick to take it aboard, but he got it.

Too late.

Michaud had moved in too close. Even as the patrolman was turning to him, he slid out his foot and hooked the man's legs from under him. The patrolman fell back heavily against his own car, his head banging hard on the side. Michaud crouched over him and took the gun from his hand and, right there in front of Ruth, he stood up and shot the young man twice as he lay on the ground.

The young man hunched into a ball. He was squirming, and was still alive. Michaud had the patrolman's weapon in his hand, and he turned and walked toward Ruth.

That's it, she was thinking. It's done. I tried for it and I failed.

She closed her eyes once more, and waited for the terminal light.

The scene was clear in her mind. The road, empty as an airport runway. The two cars, the boy on the ground, the two figures standing. And one big sheet of wide grey water all around them, all the way out to the edges of the world.

The basics of the endgame, in all its bare essentials.

And then something slammed her hard across the head, and that was all that she knew for a while.

54

Ruth's head hurt, the air was so hot that it almost burned her to breathe, and she'd come around with a desperate thirst. She was lying face-down. He'd put her into the open back of the pickup, but she was in darkness. There was canvas stretched tight above her head. Her face was full of the smell of machinery. Every time the wheels hit a rut, she was jarred and her headache got worse. She tried to move, but he'd bound her.

She closed her eyes and beat her forehead gently against the floor. It didn't help.

She'd had her chance, and she'd failed. It hadn't been a failure of nerve, because when the moment had come she'd been ready. But she'd fumbled the catch. Dropped the ball. Such chances were rarely offered at all, and almost never twice. Ruth had managed to decline one and to mess up a second.

She doubted that she'd ever get another.

The car was in a bad way. Even worse than her, by the sound of its engine and the way that something broken seemed to grind against itself whenever they hit a bump. Wriggling like a caterpillar, she managed to get over onto her back. The pounding in her ears subsided a little.

She wondered how long she had left. Part of her almost hoped that it wouldn't be long. She didn't want to die, never had. But she'd been left with so little to hang on to. She'd stripped it all down to one final sense of purpose.

And it hadn't worked out.

'I'm sorry,' she whispered in the confined space of the empty load compartment. But to whom, she wasn't sure.

With a sudden, thrashing sound, something sheared.

She couldn't tell from here whether it was in the engine

or the transmission, but it sounded loud and final. It was like somebody had dumped a sack of nails into the works. The El Camino came to an abrupt halt, and Ruth slid and fetched up against the bulkhead behind the driver's cab. She stuck there at an awkward angle, unable to move, and through her entire body she could feel the straining of the ignition as Michaud tried to get the engine going again.

She felt the car bounce, the door slam. And outside, she heard him starting to curse.

That slight hesitation in his speech had returned, she noticed, and she was intrigued; it had never occurred to her such a thing might still happen when no-one was supposed to be listening. There was a bang and the car rocked, and she guessed that he'd kicked the side.

There was a long silence for a while, and she began to wonder if he'd simply abandoned her. But then, without any warning at all, the snap-cover overhead was suddenly torn aside.

The light hit her, and it hurt. She screwed up her eyes, and turned her face away.

She sensed him leaning over, looming above her.

'Are you awake?' he said.

'Yes,' Ruth said, still not yet able to open her eyes.

'That was cruel, Ruth,' Michaud said.

Which, coming from him, was kind of rich. All that Ruth could say was, 'Oh.' She was so dry and raw that even that much barely came out.

'I believed you. And now that's it, is it? I get one look at the gates and then I'm turned away. I'd rather things had stayed the way they were.'

She was able to look up at him now. Behind him was the sky, filtered through the foliage of an overhanging branch. His hair was messed up as if he'd been running his hand through it, over and over. He still had the glasses on. He did need them, she realized. He needed them to drive. It was probably the reason why he'd made her take the wheel on that first long journey, way back when all of this had begun.

She said, 'What now?'

'I'm going to untie you so you can walk. You've already shown me you're not scared of dying. So I'll just remind you, that isn't all I could do. I could also hurt you a lot.'

'Would you do that?'

'Don't try me.'

He rolled her over and she guessed that he was cutting through the cord with which he'd bound her, although she'd lost so much sensation in her limbs that it was difficult to be sure. When he sat her upright she realized that her hands were still tethered, but at least not as tightly as before.

He got her out and onto her feet. Her legs immediately gave way, but he caught her. She steadied herself by leaning against the side of the car, and she waited a few moments for feeling to return.

It was hardly a wonder that the track had felt and sounded so rough. Seen from outside the car, it was almost nonexistent. They were on what passed for high ground deep in swamp country, a few feet above the duckweed and no more. Along a piny ridge hardly more than a dozen feet wide, two vague lines marked out the passage of the occasional truck or four-wheel-drive. Along the ridge, shading it, grew oaks and magnolia trees. Their branches were hung with Spanish moss, pale and silver like maidenhair seen by moonlight.

It was like being on the banks of a secret river. Except that the river surrounded them, and the bank was a sinuous maze that ran through its heart, and the swamp country went on with more of the same for miles all around it. Cypress and Tupelo, Black Gum and Maple; big trees with soft bark rising straight out of the water, permanently sodden and stained permanently dark. Ruth had no idea of where they were, or how far into this near-wilderness they'd travelled. Wherever she looked, it was the same. And it went on and on.

'Come on,' he said, and started to walk her.

Ruth did her best, but within half a dozen strides her

legs folded under her. She sat, heavily, and she stayed on the ground and couldn't get up.

She said, 'I need water.'

'Not now,' Michaud said, pulling at her arm.

'I'm going to faint if I don't.'

'You can't drink the water here,' he said. 'It'll make you ill.'

Ruth started to giggle, and then she tried to shut up when she could see how much it was annoying him. He walked back the short distance to the car and returned with something: a soda can, which sprayed when he popped the ringpull.

'Here,' he said. 'I know it's warm, I'm sorry. It was in the car since yesterday.'

He had to hold it up for Ruth while she drank. His free hand was behind her shoulders, steadying her. Despite the presumed brutality of his intentions, it felt like a moment of inescapable tenderness.

'Thank you,' Ruth said, and then failed to suppress a belch. The stuff was too warm and gassy for her to do otherwise.

'More?' Michaud said, and she shook her head and tried to straighten her legs out from underneath her. It wasn't easy without the use of her hands and she almost toppled sideways, but Michaud brought her back.

He said, 'Why did you try that stunt with the car?'

She closed her eyes as sensation flooded through her cramped lower body like a wild flow of undirected current. It was pain and bliss, all mingled.

She said, 'I thought it would be the kindest thing for us both.'

'Is that all you can see for us?' he demanded almost plaintively; and Ruth was tempted to counter in kind, and ask exactly what kind of future he saw for them now. He hadn't brought her here to look at the wildlife, of that she was sure.

She couldn't help recalling what Tom Diaz had said to her. About how Michaud always seemed, in a disturbing piece of understatement, to take some trouble over his disposals.

Ruth said, 'We've got no future, Peter, together or alone. You killed me already. I'm just lingering on. And you say you want to stop what you do, but you're never going to. What you are now is what you'll always be. If I thought I could change you, I would. I'd spend the time. But you've gone too far and now I can see that it's never going to happen.'

He took her arm, and started to help her to rise. Her legs felt weak, but at least they were back under her control again.

He said, 'It would be a big load off my shoulders if they caught me. You wouldn't believe how many times I've been close to it. I've had them stop the car and look it over and still they let me go. I've even had the police help me out. It's true. The car broke down and they helped me get it started and they never even looked in the back. I played it straight. I treated it like a test. Do you believe there's a God, Ruth?'

She looked at him, and saw that the question was an earnest one. But she didn't know how to answer it.

'You clearly don't,' she said.

'I do,' he insisted. 'But I seem to be invisible to him. Nothing I do ever gets a response. What does that make me?'

'I don't know,' Ruth said. Because how could she tell him what she really thought, that only one term existed to describe a soul that raged against heaven and still went unnoticed?

She'd said it once already, to Elizabeth Vermot.

He was lost.

Michaud said, 'Can you try to walk, now?' and Ruth believed that she could.

There was a whistling sound all through the swamp. Birdsong, she supposed. The ridge descended to a sandy bar, almost level with the water but firm enough to walk on. The water wasn't clear, but looked like soup. The swollen bases of the trees all around them were evidence of a higher level of flooding. Cypress knees were exposed a few yards out from the banking like sharpened stakes in the water.

Michaud said, 'I've seen people die in two different ways. If there's more than two ways, I don't know what the other one is. With some it's like you snap your fingers and they're gone, and you can't quite believe it. It's like something small and stupid happened that no-one ever intended, and the life just left them and you can't bring it back. Other times it takes for ever, and they just won't go. And the worse *they* get, the worse *it* gets. Because you see what it's doing to them and you wish you hadn't started, but already you've gone too far to turn back. You could stop it. But the way you'd leave them, that isn't mercy.'

'How was it with your mother?' Ruth said, not even thinking, and only realizing how the question must sound to him when she heard the long, long silence that followed.

He said, 'She died looking the way she did in her wedding pictures. I saw her just ten minutes before. That's what I'll always remember.'

'I've got to stop for a minute,' Ruth said.

He found a fallen log and lowered her down to sit on it. The end of the log was soft and decaying and had been eaten out by termites, but the middle part of it was solid enough. Ruth sat with her head down between her knees, feeling sick. Having her hands behind her back made it even more awkward.

When finally she was able to raise her head, he was waiting for her and watching. She looked him in the eye.

She said, 'What are you going to do with me?'

'I'd prefer not to tell you,' he said.

And he said it kindly, as if not wanting to cause her unnecessary distress.

55

Four kids in a stolen car had run into the side of a bus no more than half a mile from the hospital, and the emergency room was noisier than a cattle auction. People were walking around and holding their necks and their backs and groaning, claiming whiplash injuries and looking for a lawyer to handle their demand for compensation. It didn't matter that more than half of those present hadn't been on board the bus and a few of them hadn't even seen it happen. Loud bangs and lawyers on contingency fees could always guarantee a steady supply of victims.

Tom Diaz checked all the cubicles and talked to some of the doctors, and after being told to get out of the way for the third time he found the nurse in charge. He showed her the name on his paper and was redirected upstairs.

The smell hit him as he came out of the elevators and headed down the corridor toward the Intensive Care unit. Hospitals always had that weird scent like new plastic, that reminded him of childhood visits to relatives that he'd barely known and hadn't wanted to see. He came from a large family, and at one time it had seemed as if there had been an entire ailing generation whose clocks had all been running out together. Little Tom got dragged along to see them all and say goodbye, and had nightmares about oxygen masks for years after.

He looked into one of the side-rooms. An elderly woman lay on the bed, hooked up by various tubes to a forest of drips that hung overhead. She was on her side, and her face was turned away. Her body bucked, gently, to a steady rhythm, as if under the regular application of mild electric shocks.

Up here it was supposed to be one nurse to every patient,

plus the attending medical team. He ought to be able to find someone who could give him an answer.

But then he found the whiteboard, and spotted her name immediately. It gave her time of admission and the number of her bed. Diaz went around into the curtained-off bay that had been indicated, and found only a piece of empty floor.

So then he went to the nurses' station.

'What happened to Theresa McCall?' he said.

'You just missed her,' the supervisor in charge told him. 'She went into surgery about twenty minutes ago.'

'Did anybody talk to her first?'

'Are you kidding? They were all over her. They didn't even shut up when the anaesthetist put her under. Who are you?'

Diaz showed his ID. 'Detective Diaz, Philadelphia police,' he said.

'Diaz,' the nurse mused. 'Good Pennsylvania name.'

'Don't start me off on that. Did you catch anything of what was said?'

'No, but they all got excited and ran out. They left one man to sit with her for when she comes around.'

'Is he in the OR with her?'

'I think he went to get some coffee.'

Diaz went looking. If they were operating on Theresa McCall now, then it would be hours before they could hope to get any more sense out of her. Diaz could only hope that they'd got what they needed before she went under. Without seeing her, it was hard for him to imagine the state that she must be in.

Two oil company employees had found her. The oil companies, Texaco in particular, had unmanned oil and gas terminals throughout the swamps and they had to be checked out every day to ensure that they were pumping. Theresa McCall had been found clinging on to one of the wooden platforms by a two-man team making their rounds of the wellheads. She'd been exhausted, befouled, and seriously dehydrated. One arm had been pumped up like a balloon and the other had looked as if someone had been trying to burn it off.

She was blinded. She'd been in total darkness for days. She was in a bad way, but she knew her own name. She'd been reported missing by her maid. She'd been on a list of possible victims compiled by the FBI team who were working on the case of Peter Michaud, and as the helicopter was bringing her down across the lake alarm bells were already beginning to ring.

Michaud had never shown up, and the trap hadn't been sprung. But word came in that a patrolman had been shot following a multiple accident out on the spillway road and his weapon stolen. The patrolman had survived the shooting and had been able to repeat the names of his assailant and the woman in his company. Meanwhile, across town, Theresa McCall had been flown in looking barely alive and talking deliriously about sharing a pit with the dead.

There was a day room for waiting relatives at the end of the corridor, and that was where Diaz found the officer who'd been left to await the return of Theresa McCall. He was a uniformed policeman, pale and red-haired, and he looked about fifteen years old. Tom Diaz opened the door and caught him with cake crumbs on his face.

'Where did they all go?' he said.

'I don't know,' the young man admitted.

So then Diaz turned and headed back by the nurses' station.

'Is she going to be all right?' he asked the supervisor. There would be nothing to stick around for here, the parade had all moved on. Gamely, he would do his best to catch up. He felt responsible. He didn't know why, but he did. Ruth Lasseter was back in the hands of her captor, and for him it was like witnessing the crashing-down of a dam because of a tiny leak that he'd once failed to stop.

The supervisor leaned out to speak, because Tom Diaz

was already backing off and halfway along the corridor to the elevators.

'You're the first one of them to ask that,' she said. 'As it happens, she's going to lose the arm.'

56

Michaud knew the area pretty well, that much was obvious. Now and again he'd stop Ruth and hold her by the shoulders while he searched out some landmark or some memory, but otherwise he seemed to know where he was going. Ruth stumbled a little, but her head was clear. She felt sharp now, and she felt bright. Unnaturally bright, as if she was burning up all her reserves like in the last incandescent flaring of a chemical fire.

Michaud wasn't so well-balanced. More than once he wished aloud for a boat, but the closest to it that they saw was a boat graveyard in a backwater where vessels too old to run or be repaired had been scraped of their identification and sunk. They'd passed it in silence, almost in respect. Prows and cabins stuck up above the waterline at unnatural angles. They'd been junked, that was all, and no dead men lay below. But it was impossible to see those drowned hulks, rotted to the bones and awash with floating vegetation, without thinking of the slow decay of some lost civilization deep in the jungle.

But they were, in truth, just so much backwater debris. The fact of it was that the swamp, though seemingly vast, was no wilderness at all. It was a working area and a playground, and a well-used one at that. It was simply the nature of the place that it took no permanent mark. Out across the water, Ruth saw the occasional houseboat or transitory structure that had been pitched out in the middle of nowhere for weekenders' use. All looked derelict, none actually was. They floated on oil drums, leaned into the water, had sagging decks with car seats or threadbare old lounge furniture set out for relaxation. None was without its outdoor barbecue. All had docking space, one or two even appeared to have electricity.

None was presently occupied.

Ruth said, 'I went to your old house.'

'Everybody goes to the old house,' Michaud told her. 'People are sick that way.'

'I heard you tried to live there, once.'

'I tried.'

Suddenly, he dropped to the ground and dragged her with him. Ruth panicked as she went, afraid that she was going to fall on her face without being able to put out her hands and stop herself. But his hand clamped over her mouth and he guided her down, dropping her into the undergrowth and falling beside her just as the high whine of a boat's engine came fully into earshot. He held her there, one hand still over her mouth and the other pressing her body tight against his own. Through a veil of grass, she saw a boat go by. In it were three huntsmen in green flotation vests over army surplus camouflage; their image flickered through the stems and then was gone, the pirogue's engine note fading after.

In the stillness that followed, there was a whistling sound so close that it was almost deafening. Its source seemed to be only inches away, but there was nothing in sight. But then she saw it, black and grey, clinging to the underside of a broad, long blade of green.

She'd taken the sound for birdsong, but it wasn't. And its source was nothing that had ever taken flight.

It was a frog. A tiny frog. A frog with the voice of a bird.

Dazed with wonder, Ruth allowed herself to be helped back onto her feet.

Without either of them mentioning the boat that had passed, they walked on.

'Tell me something,' Ruth said suddenly.

'What?'

'It doesn't matter what. It can be anything. But it's got to be something you never told anyone else.'

'I spent years talking,' Michaud said darkly. 'They filled up books with the stuff. There isn't anything left.'

The ground was soft and spongy for a way. It seemed that they'd again picked up a part of the route that was just about navigable for a vehicle. Ruth saw tyre tracks that had filled up with water like long, narrow troughs. They walked between them.

After a while Michaud said, 'How does this work? Then do you have to tell me something back?'

'If that's how you want it.'

He thought for a while. Then he said, 'What if I never told anyone because it's something I don't like to remember?'

'Tell it anyway,' Ruth said. 'You'll feel better.'

She stumbled slightly, her foot sinking into the turf. He was still holding her arm, and she didn't fall.

'I don't think I like the idea,' he said, but Ruth half-shrugged and said nothing.

They walked on for a while.

And then suddenly Michaud said, 'I caught a fish in a jar one Sunday afternoon. My sisters had gone to Bible class, which was something I used to do anything to get out of. I wasn't very big. I don't know if Kathy was at school yet, but Elaine could just about walk. This fish was nothing to look at, but I was proud of it. I carried the jar all the way home and took it upstairs to show it to someone. What did I know? Kids don't think. I heard them in the bedroom and I pushed open the door. She was sitting on top of him and moving around, but I had no idea what they were doing. They both shouted at me to go away. I went out into the yard and I sat down on the ground. I emptied the jar out and the little fish just lay there on the dirt. I watched it while it flipped around for a while and then it lay there gasping and then it died. Nobody ever said anything about any of it. Your turn.'

Ruth looked up. It had to be well into the evening by now. The sky was turning a deep, creamy peach colour as the sun went down behind dense cloud.

She said, 'I nearly had a baby once, but I lost it. But

then I was never quite able to feel like it was dead. It was more like he was growing up in some other place and I might turn a corner one day and there he'd be. I'd talk to him. Not like when you pray, more like when you really talk to someone.'

'That doesn't count,' Michaud said.

Ruth was not pleased. She looked at him, hard.

'Why not?' she said.

'It's supposed to be something you never told anyone else. You already said all this to Aidan.'

Ruth actually chilled at the mention of his name. 'How would you know that?' she demanded.

'We discussed a lot of things,' Michaud said.

'When?'

But Michaud didn't say.

Ruth said, with a growing anger that she'd been determined that she wouldn't show, 'You mean, the night you killed him. What was he like, Peter? Was he quick? Or was he one of those who hangs on and hangs on and just won't go?'

She wasn't sure whether his silence indicated that he was being sullen, or whether it hinted that there was some reservoir of well-hidden shame that might even now be tapped. Decency, even. The dimmest spark would be better than nothing. Better than a darkness that truly didn't end. Ruth felt the stirrings of a faint hope. For him, if not for herself.

But then he said, 'It doesn't matter, anyway. I made mine up.'

And then he added, 'Nothing's going to make any difference now.'

Aidan Kincannon was less than five miles away.

He moved stiffly, and not without pain. It hurt him to sit in one position in the car for too long, and on the puddle-jumper flight coming down he'd alarmed the cabin staff with the cold sweat and grey pallor that had overtaken him at the prospect of being strapped into his seat. Even the captain had emerged from the flight deck and taken a look, from a distance, before one of them had come down and asked if everything had been all right. Aidan had invented some reason for his apparent distress, he'd already forgotten what. Then he'd gritted his teeth and gone through it.

Anything could be endured. Anything.

Most of the time it was simply a matter of determining whether the damage was worth the goal.

He'd been home. But only to get clothes and money. He'd grabbed what he needed from the house and gone on. He didn't know whose car he'd taken to get him there. He'd left it by the terminal and mailed the keys to the airport police before boarding.

While the authorities moved in on Pete Michaud by carefully piecing together elements of Theresa McCall's garbled story and matching them to the ever-changing landscape in which she'd been discovered, Aidan was on the fast track. Aidan knew things about Michaud that Michaud would never have told the living. But Aidan, by Michaud's reckoning, had been as good as dead by then. Physical extinction was a mere formality, the delay of which would ultimately alter nothing. Hearts had opened.

By choice or under duress, they had opened.

Down a dead-end road, Aidan drove.

And though his eyes were wide open and his mind was awake, he dreamed of being buried. Of being inert and unable to move, with the rank meat piled high and pressing down in a suffocating darkness. Ton upon ton of it, claustrophobic as a filled-in mine. Where he lay at the bottom, unknown, unnoticed, and miles from the daylight.

The flight attendant had suggested that he might try to sleep. But then he'd looked up into her eyes, and she had backed away.

Dead-ended or not, the road was a well-surfaced and maintained stretch of blacktop that ran in by the side of the river whose overflow backed up and fed the swamplands. Every now and again he'd pass a mailbox on a post, and behind each mailbox there would be some land with a house on it. Some of these were neat, some were shabby; some lots were fenced and some were not. The unfenced properties had stuff spread out all across them, almost as if there had been a flood and all the junk in the world had been dragged out here to dry. Boat trailers with the grass growing through them, canoe sheds and stacks of logs, oil drums and lobster nets. Across the road from each place was a section of river frontage of equal width. This would be marked out with stakes and poles and sometimes string, and would have some kind of a mooring or a ramshackle jetty.

What had sounded like a distant speedboat turned out to be a man mowing his lawn. Aidan stopped the car and backed up fifty yards or so to be level with him. He got out, and the man leaned on his mower and watched him with its engine idling.

'Excuse me,' Aidan said.

And the man said, 'Help you?'

His was a big modern house on an acre of land, with two garages and two cars and a pickup standing in the driveway. The entire family of four was out in the garden hoeing weeds. The children were thin and tough as whips, tanned brown by the sun; their father in his knee-length shorts was not so trim, nor so tan.

Aidan said, 'I'm looking for a place I heard about. You can drive to it if you know the way, but almost nobody ever goes there. It's close to an island where there was an old church that burned out.'

'What was the church called?'

'That, I don't know. But it was raised up enough to have a little graveyard to the side. This person I know used to play there when he was a boy.'

'We haven't lived here that long,' the man said. 'I'm sorry.'

Aidan looked around. The evening was drawing on, and the light was starting to fade. He was aware that the rest of the family had stopped working and were watching him.

He said, 'Do you know if any of your neighbours might be able to say?'

'I'd try the boat tour people right down at the end of the road,' the man suggested. 'You go three, four miles on and take a left where there's a sign, then you cross a bridge and keep on driving till the road runs out. You see a big dock with an awning and some animals in wire cages, that's them. They know this entire area better than anyone. It's their business.'

'Thanks,' Aidan said. 'Sorry if I've bothered you.'

'You haven't bothered me,' the man said.

Michaud said, 'I read about Italian perspective in one of those art magazines of yours. You know what it is?'

'Kind of,' Ruth said. What the hell would she know about Italian perspective? She'd sold ad space. She was plodding along, concentrating on putting one foot in front of the other. It didn't sound like much, but every time that she did it the achievement felt slightly greater. She still felt bright and hard-edged. But she'd begun to wonder whether feeling it and being it were always the same thing.

Michaud, showing no awareness of her state, said, 'It's a convention, that's all it is. You pick a point on the horizon. The vanishing point. And all your straight lines head toward it, and that makes your picture look real. Then you rub out all the guidelines and the vanishing point, because it was never actually there in the first place. It doesn't exist. Except it must do, because it's implied in everything else. Nothing in the picture could happen without it, but you still couldn't go there.'

'I'm going to fall down,' Ruth said, and then proceeded to begin a demonstration.

He caught her and supported her. He said, 'Am I making any sense to you?'

'I don't know. What are we talking about?'

'I'm telling you about God. Haven't you been listening?'

Ruth couldn't quite focus. 'What about him?'

'For fuck's *sake*, Ruth!' Michaud exploded, and he

hustled her onward with diminished patience. Prisoner and escort, walking in the twilight. Walking the last mile, to who-could-say-where.

'I can hear a car,' Ruth said, and Michaud didn't respond.

'Two cars,' Ruth said a moment later.

'No-one ever comes down here,' Michaud said. 'You must have heard a boat.'

'Stay in the middle of the track, then,' Ruth suggested. 'We'll soon find out who's right.'

They walked on down the middle of the track, and then Michaud suddenly hauled her across and almost threw her into the swamp. The two of them skidded and slid down the light clay banking and into the shallows at the bottom of the low ridge. The swamp wasn't deep. At no part was it deep, except in those main channels where it had been dredged and this was some way away from those.

The first car came into view, bouncing and labouring its way down the track. It was a big white sedan, completely out of its element, and it was followed by a second. There were at least five people in each. All men, as far as Ruth could see from here, all in suits. She recognized the style of them, even if they passed too quickly for her to be able to pick out any individuals that she might be able to identify. Confirmation came with the next vehicle in line. A police car. They crashed onward into the swamp, unnaturally smooth with their unnatural shine, creatures of the open road being forced into primitive byways.

'Shit,' Michaud said. 'I think this means they found my secret place.'

They crouched down for a while longer, but no other vehicles came by. Boat engines could be heard approaching from somewhere, but they weren't in any waterway that had direct line of sight from here. Their sound came through the trees, beating like a distant chant.

Ruth said, 'What do we do now?'

'I've got to think,' Michaud said.

He gripped her by the arm again. Whether he was

helping her or forcing her up the bank was a matter for interpretation. He was squeezing her arm hard enough to hurt it, that much she knew. He looked both ways, and then started to push her along in the wake of the cars. He was keeping a watch all around them, now. They'd have seen the El Camino. They would know that he and Ruth were probably somewhere close.

Ruth said, 'Well?'

'We have to get onto the water,' Michaud said. 'Out here like this, it's the only chance we're going to have. They'll be watching the road and we can't walk out.'

'Who could have told them where to find us?' Ruth said.

'I don't know. Nobody could.'

'Maybe someone worked it out.'

'That's not possible.'

They walked on. The landspit on which they were walking divided in a big Y. The tracks went one way, the grass already springing up where the undersides of the vehicles had crushed it flat. They went the other. This was no more than a finger of land, yards wide in places and arched-over with exposed roots.

Ruth said, 'Then somebody survived. They got away and told someone. Could that have happened?'

'No,' Michaud said. Too quickly. It was obvious that the same possibility had entered his own mind, and his denial was abrupt and contained a hint of panic.

Ruth was filled with a fierce certainty. It flooded into her, mapping out the shape of the matter that she occupied. Big wheels turned. Forces moved. And sometimes, some hint of the machinery's purpose could be glimpsed like the movements of a great war in the skies overhead.

'Seems like the dead won't lie down, doesn't it?' Ruth said. 'They're coming up out of the ground for you now.'

Michaud was about to speak.

But then his face set, and he hustled her on.

57

'They found a hideout,' the man on the roadblock had told Tom Diaz as he'd handed back his ID and waved to his companions to move back the barrier and let him through, 'but they didn't find him. Put your car over there and leave the keys inside. You can get out on the boat next time around.'

'Can't I just drive out there?' he'd said.

'Not if you don't know the area. There isn't even a track for most of the way.'

So Diaz parked his car in the shade of a big overhanging tree, and was left to kill time around what passed for a base camp until the return of one or another of the local craft that had been pressed into service. They'd set up a communications point here, on the front porch of a house that was little more than a single-storey plywood cabin with its back end out over the swamp on cinderblock stilts. The owner had planted flowers and shrubs in pots and hanging baskets all around it, making a sudden fistful of colour in among the drab browns and greens. Diaz contemplated a yellow and white butterfly that was almost the span of his hand, moving from flower to flower.

Messages came in over the radio, terse and garbled, but nothing much seemed to be happening this far out. Diaz stuck his hands in his pockets, and looked at the swamp. He'd never even *seen* a swamp until this week. Somehow he'd thought of it as being something like quicksand. This was more like a dead backwater, green and still and shaded. They had alligators in there, didn't they? Which meant that Theresa McCall had been doubly lucky. First in getting out of her underground prison, and then in avoiding being sought out and eaten.

Well, she'd been due for some luck.

If you could lose an arm and still call it that.

A big power boat came in, slowing and bobbing and creating turbulence as it swung around in the basin under the house. Its propeller raced as it briefly left the water, betraying the shallowness of the boat's draught. Diaz followed a path of broken shells down to a wooden jetty, and there he helped to load a number of equipment cases before getting his ride out. The boat's pilot was a local man, thin and deeply tanned in a blue shirt, faded and pressed blue jeans and a pair of new-looking white Nikes. He might have been fifty or seventy, it was impossible to say. He had a pencil-thin moustache and gold chain around his neck, and his eyes were shaded under his cap. He swung the boat around in a tight circle, and Diaz grabbed hold of the rail.

It was a ten-minute ride out to the investigation site, the first and fastest part of it being straight down a wide river with the power boat's nose rising high into the air and its back end skipping along the water as if only on kissing-contact with the surface. Diaz had been half-expecting something along the lines of a theme park jungle cruise, but that was rudely knocked out of him in a matter of moments. He hung on, and realized with a rising sense of dismay that he'd spent his entire life up until this moment without ever discovering what a lousy sailor he'd make. Relief came when they swung into a side-channel and slowed, entering the maze of backwaters that was the swampland proper. Diaz tried to keep his bearings, but in minutes he was lost.

He could hear them, though. A shout, a crash of timber, something revving. As they came out and around in a wide stretch of gum bayou, Diaz was confronted with the sight of the promontory that had been Peter Michaud's hideaway since he'd last dropped out of sight.

Slowly, the boat chugged down its length.

Hours ago, this would have been one of the most deserted-looking places on planet Earth. Now it was swarming like a pirate dock. Two or three vehicles had made it through and they looked incongruous and alien amid the tall, dark trees and the lush hanging growth. Diaz stood up in the boat to get a better view, his queasiness forgotten. There, through the changing perspective of the trees, stood a burned-out church. He strained to see, but already it was gone. Before him instead was a much closer scene, a dozen or more men and women around and inside an uncovered pit that was near to the water's edge. They'd only partly uncovered it, and they'd dropped a ladder into the water so that one man in waders could get down to a discharge opening that was all but submerged. Up on the land, they were carefully lifting something out on a plastic sheet. Whatever it was, it didn't look heavy; but five of them were doing the lifting, and doing it with exaggerated care.

Diaz looked at the opening again, only the upper part of its rim visible above the water.

That must be where she got out, he thought as the boat chugged around to the other side of the promontory and the pilot hauled it into reverse to swing it in. Theresa McCall. They were dismantling what was to have been her tomb.

Two of the FBI's people jumped down into the boat and started to unload the equipment cases and Diaz, neither acknowledged nor required, got himself onto land and left them to it. He sidestepped someone who was coming through with an armload of poles and canvas screening, barely giving them a glance. He was drawn onward. Onward, to where the church in the swamp now stood in ruins.

It had probably never been much to look at. It might have been a white shed or a barn, but for the crude bell tower at its end. Diaz walked toward it through the trees, feeling a faint awe that he couldn't explain.

It was no more than a shell. The roof had gone, and the building couldn't have seen any practical use in decades. Where the window openings had been, black tongues of soot showed where flames had once raged upward. Most of one end wall had been destroyed. As Diaz got closer and circled around, he could see inside.

There was plenty going on; measuring, photographing, and at least three people making notes with video cameras. The scene resembled that of a suddenly discovered archaeological site, where frantic efforts were being made to unpick the secrets of a lost city in the shadow of some impending disaster. Diaz stepped over the splintered remains of the end wall. The deck that had once been the church's floor had mostly burned or fallen through. A young magnolia tree was growing straight up through the middle of it.

Nothing at all was left of the roof but across from Diaz, in the far corner, a makeshift lean-to had been put together out of timber and blue plastic sheet and a salvaged door. A different kind of sheet plastic had been laid out on the ground before this, and a man and a woman in pristine white coveralls and latex surgical gloves were carrying out items from the lean-to and laying them down. For a moment, Diaz was reminded of a garage sale. Every item was being inspected, described onto tape, numbered and then tagged, like a lot. Investigators were like buyers-to-be browsing, pointing, considering significance; occasionally one of them would lean forward for a closer look, inspecting without touching.

Tom Diaz moved around behind them. A couple of people glanced his way, but no-one challenged him. When he was in line with the doorway he craned to look inside, not wanting to risk getting any closer.

'I thought you'd gone home,' someone said from just behind him.

He turned. It was Hanratty, one of the people from the Elaine Michaud surveillance team. He didn't know her first name.

Diaz said, 'You make life too interesting for me. Is this where he used as a base?'

'Something like that.'

It didn't look much. Just a mean, dark little cell, its

secrets being exploded and put onto display; like an autopsy by proxy, in the absence of the deceased.

'Mr Blandings builds his dream house,' Tom Diaz said.

And Hanratty half-smiled, barely polite, and moved down to the other end of the rolled-out sheet where a marked-up gas station roadmap was causing some interest.

While they clustered, Diaz looked over the rest of the stuff. Packets of dried food, of the kind sold to campers and climbers. Faded T-shirts, and a solitary sweater. A pair of black baseball shoes, well-worn and split. A kerosene lamp. A cardboard box, lid off and with about half a dozen photographs laid out alongside it. Diaz crouched before these, to take a closer look.

Somewhere behind him, he heard a young man's voice muttering curses. He glanced back briefly. One of the agency's people was picking his way across the floor, his good shoes ruined and his pants legs stained with the mud into which he'd obviously stumbled. Diaz returned his attention to the pictures.

One of them was a photograph of the entire Michaud family together, the first that he'd seen. Michaud's mother was seated in the middle of the group, probably because she'd been too weak to stand. Tom Diaz had heard her described as a good-looking woman. This must have been taken only weeks or days before she'd died. She looked shocking. Literally, it was a shock to see her there. She was down to sixty or seventy pounds, no flesh on her bones at all, a caricature of a person among the living. Her eyes were haunted, and they stared directly into the camera. Her hair had been styled and carefully set. But looking at her ruined face, Diaz couldn't help feeling that it was as if Death had anticipated his guest and had taken up his residence early.

'Excuse us,' a voice said. And then: 'Detective Diaz? We need to get in there.'

Belatedly, Tom Diaz became aware of the people

behind him and moved aside. Beyond the blind windows, generators started up and new light flooded in. Diaz felt disconnected, disoriented. He made his way out of the church, and looked back down the promontory.

There had been a graveyard behind the church. Some of the stones were visible, most were overgrown. The point of a stone was to be a monument. The point of having a monument was to be remembered. But if even the stones meant nothing in the end, then what mark did a life leave at all?

He suddenly wanted to be home. Not here. Not anywhere that wasn't home.

He went back down to the dock. The boat that had brought him had gone, but another was moored there. He climbed into it and sat down.

No-one was around.

But he waited.

58

They'd been walking for half an hour or less. Ruth could hear things happening in the distance some way back, but the sounds grew more remote as the natural tranquillity of the swampland re-established itself around them.

When it looked as if they were about to run out of solid ground to walk on, they came to one of the abandoned-looking cabins.

This had clearly been their destination, as it stood on the end of their spit of land with only open water beyond. It had been built out of old wood that had turned silver, and it had a net-enclosed porch and a floating dock with steps and a walkway lashed to poles that had been sunk deep into the swampbed. None of the lines was straight, and it all had a leaning-dangerously look. There were old armchairs set out on the planking, and a light on a pole over the water.

It was clearly meant to be approached by boat, and never by land. There was almost no way through. Ruth had to be helped again.

She said, 'Tell me something, Peter. I'm really curious. I know it's easy not to care about strangers. But how can you do something like this to someone you know?'

'I don't know you,' Michaud replied. 'I thought I did, but I don't. It's always the same. You're talking like this, but what's happening in your mind? It's whirring away, I can hear the fucking clockwork. You're looking for a way to dump me or drop me in it or somehow turn me in. So don't talk about us knowing each other. Nobody knows anyone. Nobody cares, except for themselves.'

'You know this for a fact.'

'I've collected the evidence.'

'So why don't you do it to me now? I'm tired, and everything hurts. You could do it and leave me right here. Sit me in one of those chairs. What difference will it make if you hide me? They'll find me anyway.'

He pushed aside a branch, which cracked and split and came away in his hand. It had been almost completely hollowed-out by decay. He let it fall to one side.

'Shut up,' he said.

'*Can't* you do it?'

'I'm not going to tell you twice.'

'Does this mean there's some hope for you?' she said. 'I don't believe it.'

'If you've got to talk, make it about something else.'

Now there was a fallen cypress that she couldn't negotiate without the use of her hands. She sat on the trunk and swung her legs over, and Michaud had to steady her so that she didn't fall backwards. Once she'd swung around, it was hard to get going again. She sat there without trying to rise, putting off the moment for as long as she could.

She said, 'My daddy used to tell me a story about a pathway through the woods. Do you want to hear it?'

Michaud said nothing, so Ruth went on, 'It wasn't just one story. It was different stories, but they always started the same. He'd say, what if a pathway didn't lead you to the same place that it always leads you? What if there was one day in every year when a path could take a day off and go to somewhere else? And then the story would be about a little girl, who was always like me, and how she went down this familiar path but it took her to somewhere strange that she'd never been. She'd have some strange adventures and then always at the end, she found her way home. She always had to find her way home. There was one story where she didn't, and I had nightmares for a week until he told it to me again.'

And then suddenly she leaned forward, and threw up all of the warm soda that she'd drunk earlier. It splashed on the leaves and some of it came back onto her. There was a drop still on her lips, and she couldn't use her hand to wipe it off. But then it didn't matter, because she threw up again.

She had to force herself to look up at him. She was miserable and embarrassed and she knew that she must look a sight. There could be few things worse, she was thinking, than having someone watch you puke.

'Do *something* with me, Peter,' she said. 'Or let me do something with you. This can't go on.'

But it seemed that, for a while at least, it could.

He let her sit in one of the armchairs while he went into the cabin, which wasn't locked. Ruth could see that there was a gas grill that the owners had stowed away from general sight and thrown a cover over, but otherwise there was nothing here worth stealing. She heard the bang of another door over on the far side of the cabin, and a couple of minutes later Michaud came around from the back dragging a blue fibreglass hull. It was a one-piece moulded boat that looked as if it had been rescued after too many years of service on a lake in some park. He set it onto the water and tied it off while he went back to get the oars. Ruth watched it from her place on the dock as it drifted out the length of its rope and then fell still. The hull had a split that had been patched with silver tape.

She wondered if it was safe. But then, thinking of how she'd tried to drive them both into the back of a truck not so long ago, it seemed like an absurd concern. So instead, she wondered what it might be like to sink into the blood-heat embrace of the swamp.

Death by drowning. She'd heard that it was a blissful way to go. But she couldn't imagine it, somehow.

It was getting late.

When they were out on the water, Ruth lay back as best she could and looked up at the emerging stars. She'd feared that the motion of the boat might make her feel worse, but instead it seemed to soothe her. Rather than rowing, Michaud was using one of the oars like a paddle. The onset of night didn't seem to faze him at all.

Ruth said, 'This is home ground for you, isn't it?'

He was a dark shape against darkness.

He said, 'We used to rent that place. We spent the weekends there. It was ours.'

'Did you go exploring with your sisters?'

'I came out here alone.'

Ruth said, 'Don't you ever wish you could go back? Turn back the clock, and do everything different?'

'No,' he said, as if she was suggesting something so impractical that it wasn't even worth his consideration. 'How's that ever going to happen?'

'I didn't say it was going to happen. But it's not wrong to wish. That's what people do.'

'I don't.'

'Don't lie to me.'

There was silence for a while, punctuated only by the even lap of the paddle as he swung it first on one side and then across for a while to the other.

He said, 'Wishing's like praying. Praying never got me anything. I'm sorry if you got hurt. I try to be kind.'

'You don't seem to try very hard.'

'Which proves you don't know.'

'You don't have to do what you do,' Ruth said. 'You could always walk away.'

'I've tried to do that, as well,' Michaud said.

Ruth said, 'Think about this, Peter. You can't hurt me more than you already have. Which means that you can't hurt me at all. There's nothing you can do to me now that I can't forgive.'

'I don't care about that.'

'I think you do,' Ruth persisted. 'I think it's the one thing you've been looking for.'

Forgiveness.

She left it there, like bait.

For now, the bait remained untaken.

59

Aidan could see the lightbars on the police car before he reached the bridge. They were pulsing in the darkness, sending weird-coloured shadows out through the ironwork. The patrol car's doors were open, its headlights on, its engine running. The bridge was narrow, and there was no room to pass. Its ironwork was rusty, its wooden trestles worn. The car sat there, purring, daring all comers.

Aidan slowed.

He'd been following his directions. He'd made the turn, he'd found the bridge. Along the way he'd passed dense woodland with occasional cleared areas that had been churned up by logging vehicles that had left a few oil drums and other rubbish behind. He'd passed a school bus that had been turned into somebody's home. He'd passed houses that looked as if they'd been nailed together by weekend carpenters with only the haziest idea of what they wanted to finish up with, some with basketball practice nets and one with an immense satellite dish that could probably have pulled in signals from alien civilizations.

But it seemed that he was unlikely to get any further.

He brought his own car to a stop about thirty yards from the bridge. He could see no-one. He wasn't sure of what to do.

The patrol car spoke.

'Step out of your vehicle, please, and place your hands on the roof.'

The voice came from the built-in PA system, a megaphone sound that carried clearly in the night air. Moving slowly and making no fuss, Aidan complied. The car roof felt warm under his hands.

The patrolman moved forward now, from behind his

vehicle and into the silhouetting halo of his own headlights.
Aidan could see that his handgun had been drawn and was
being held down by the man's side. He'd heard the news
on the radio about the highway officer who'd had one bullet
taken out of his arm and four ribs broken by the one that
had been stopped by his armoured vest. They were clearly
taking no chances.

The patrolman said, 'Is this your car, sir?'

'It's a rental,' Aidan said. 'I've got ID in the back pocket
of my pants if you want to see it.'

'Take it out slowly and place it on the hood of the vehicle,
please.'

Again, Aidan did as he'd been asked. This was nothing
personal. He could remember times when he'd been on the
other side in very similar situations, and he could recall the
varying ways in which people had reacted. Guilty with no
reason, scared sometimes, angry often. He'd never been
on the receiving end before. It felt strange.

'Return your hands to the roof of the vehicle, please.'

Aidan stared patiently at the roof of his car, and waited
as the patrolman scooped in his wallet and stepped back,
flipping it open one-handed.

'Would you like to tell me your full name and your home
address, please,' he said in the same neutral, formal tone.

Aidan recited his details as the patrolman checked, before
closing the wallet and laying it back on the hood.

'Thank you,' he said. 'Retrieve your ID now.'

Everything loosened slightly as Aidan completed the
procedure. The patrolman said, 'This is a dead-end road.
Can you tell me where you were heading?'

'I've been told there's a place down here runs swamp
tours,' Aidan said.

'I'm sorry, but there won't be any tour boats out
tonight. You're going to have to turn around and go
back.'

'Can I ask why?'

'Police operation,' the officer said. 'It's for your own
safety.'

They're in there, Aidan thought. In there, and running loose. Within limits.

He said, 'Covering what kind of area?'

'There are plenty of other boat companies,' the patrolman said, sidestepping the question as if it hadn't been asked. 'Try one of those.'

'I will,' said Aidan, and he got back into his car.

About a mile and a half away from Aidan, Ruth Lasseter and Peter Michaud were on foot once again. The boat had begun to leak, but it had got them out of the swamp and across the river to dry land. Michaud had let the river carry it away and they'd continued upslope, climbing the riverbank into open fields.

'This is ridiculous,' Ruth said. 'Are we going to walk all night? Or are we going to keep on walking for ever?'

'I've got a place in mind,' Michaud said. 'Nobody lives there and no-one's going to find us. It isn't far from here.'

Ruth stumbled on. The field had been tilled and they were making their way through some young crop that was pale and which reflected the moonlight like a beach of white sand.

Ahead of them, on the horizon, burned another light. It was yellow and feeble, and it caused Michaud to stop in his tracks and stare.

'There's someone in the house,' he said.

But Ruth kept on going. The way that she was feeling, she reckoned that if she were to stop then she probably wouldn't be able to start again. Michaud caught up with her and said, 'Someone must have been fixing it up. I hadn't planned for this.'

'I don't care,' Ruth said.

'There's nothing else for miles.'

'I still don't care.'

'I'm going to untie you,' he said. 'We'll see if we can do this without anyone being hurt. Don't spoil it, now.'

Ruth swayed as he worked on the cords, unpicking the

knots in the dark. They probably looked like a couple of scarecrows, she was thinking, out here in the middle of the moonlit field like this. When her arms came free, she couldn't believe it for a moment. She flexed her fingers. Her shoulders wouldn't move. But then, as if stirring into life, her arms came forward and she felt her body creaking back into a more natural posture.

'Thank you,' she said, feeling pain and relief in equally huge doses.

They walked on up toward the house. It had the look of a small mansion or plantation house, and it stood alone on the rise apart from a couple of outbuildings and a single big tree. They were approaching it from the back. The light was from an unshaded outdoor bulb.

There was a Hibachi grill on the grass lawn, a faint smoke rising from it. One man sat in a cane chair. He wore work pants and a checkered shirt. Michaud hailed him from a distance, and Ruth saw him stand and peer uncertainly into the darkness.

They reached the house. Three kittens were playing on the wooden deck close to where the man's chair stood.

Michaud said, 'Hi there.'

'Hello,' the man said. Ruth could see that he was unshaven.

Michaud said, 'We're sorry to be walking in on you so late. I remembered there was a place somewhere around here but I wasn't sure if it was abandoned or not.'

'It's never been abandoned,' the man said. 'It stood empty for a long time, though.'

Michaud stepped up onto the deck and pulled Ruth along with him, drawing her into the light. He said, 'We ran our car off the road. This lady got hurt and we're looking for help. Are you the owner?'

'I'm the caretaker,' the man said, staring at Ruth. Even though he was the one who'd been surprised, he had a shy and nervous smile. Ruth knew that she probably looked the part of an accident victim and she looked away, self-conscious. He added, 'Mr Walker's the owner.'

'He's the one I need to speak to,' Michaud said. 'Is he home?'

'No, there's just me working on the place and we didn't get the phone line in yet.'

'Where did he go? I mean, will he be back tonight?'

'He's out of town.'

'That's what I wanted to know,' Michaud said, and he reached around behind him and drew the highway patrol officer's pistol out of his waistband and clubbed the man down with it. He went onto one knee. He looked tough but it was work-toughness, not aggression toughness. He grabbed at Michaud's arm and Michaud slammed a knee into his side. Ruth was yelling 'No!' as the man went down, but Michaud continued to rain blows onto him as he went into a foetal crunch, arms over his head, until Ruth was able to catch Michaud's hand and stop him.

Michaud wrenched his hand free, but he didn't continue. Instead he leaned down close to the man and bellowed in his ear, 'Can you still put a lock on the attic? Can you?'

'Yes,' the man said.

Michaud held the gun out before the man's face, where he could see it.

He shouted, 'You see this? Look at it.'

'I can see it.'

'Am I serious?'

'You're serious.'

'Come on, then.' Michaud looked back over his shoulder at Ruth, as he prodded and pushed the handyman to get back onto his feet. 'Stay with us, Ruth,' he said. 'You do anything, he suffers.'

'Don't hurt him any more,' Ruth said and Michaud, with a good handful of the handyman's shirt collar, pulled his face close and shouted, 'Am I hurting you? I'm not hurting you, am I?'

The handyman shook his head vigorously, and Michaud said, 'See?'

They went into the house, Michaud switching on the lights. A hallway with a staircase ran all the way through;

various rooms could be seen off to either side. The place had been stripped mostly to the bare wood, everywhere. Some walls had been stripped even further, to the timber framework. And yet it was furnished, after a fashion, and quite clearly being lived in. There were paintings hung on the boards, books piled against the walls.

Driving the handyman ahead of him, Michaud clattered onward up the uncarpeted stairs. Ruth followed. The man was scared, and Ruth was scared for him. Two flights up, right at the top of the building, Michaud shoved the man through a door on which there was a hasp with a big padlock. He slammed the door shut and locked the man in. There was a light switch on the outside, but Michaud didn't turn it on.

As Michaud and Ruth were descending the stairs, they could hear the handyman bumping around above. But Michaud shouted once, and he went quiet.

They went from the hallway into one of the rooms. It was a sitting-room, and at one end connecting doors had been folded back to open it up into the adjacent dining area. The sitting-room had chairs and a dresser, some well-worn rugs, and an empty gilt frame above the fireplace. In the corner stood a glass cabinet filled with stuffed birds that had been posed on a branch. There was a stuffed puffin on top of a stack of books and, for variety, a porcelain ram with gilded horns on the mantel. In the dining-room there stood a long oval table on a bare board floor.

'Sit down,' he said, and she lowered herself onto a gilt-backed chair. Footsteps ringing hollowly, he walked off into the house.

She was alone. She supposed that she could make a break for it.

He returned with some water in a bowl and a cloth, and an economy-sized bottle of antiseptic.

'You probably think I'm completely heartless,' he said, crouching before her and uncapping the bottle.

'Everyone thinks you're heartless,' Ruth said. 'I'm the only one who may not.'

'I shouted at him so I wouldn't have to do worse. You have to control a situation. That's all it is.'

She sat, passively, as with the cloth and the water he started to clean up her face. It hurt when he touched her cheekbone, which felt swollen. It was the place where he'd caught her when he'd first knocked her down. There was blood on the cloth when he rinsed it and refolded it. Just a trace.

He said, 'I'm sorry, Ruth.'

'For what?'

'For everything. I can't undo it, though. I'm too far in. I can only go on.'

'Until somebody stops you.'

He almost smiled, but it didn't quite happen. 'You once had the chance,' he said.

Touching her chin, he turned her face to check his work.

Ruth said, 'Do you think we'll get away from here?'

'Don't you?'

Ruth looked him in the eyes, and she slowly shook her head. This made him uncomfortable, and he looked away and got to his feet. Leaving her with the cloth to use as a compress against the side of her face, he picked up the bowl and went back toward the kitchen.

'The food outside will have burned by now,' he said. 'I'll see what else there is.'

'I don't want to eat,' Ruth called after him.

'You ought to try.'

She eased herself up onto her feet, and followed him. The kitchen had the look of a new addition, with a doorway cut through from the dining-room. Kitchen work in the early years of the house would probably have been carried out by slaves in one of the outbuildings, and the food brought across. This room was only half-fitted, with walls of new ply.

He glanced up warily as she entered. Ruth went to the basin and ran some water, rinsing and re-wetting the cloth. She placed it again to the side of her face.

'Is that better?' he said.

'Just a little.'

There were no drapes, no shutters. In the glass of the window she could see herself and the room behind her reflected and also, in a second image, that part of the outside where the light from the windows fell. Part of the building's exterior was covered with a painter's scaffold. Did something move out there? She couldn't be sure. She strained to see into the darkness beyond the house, but nothing solid took form.

Michaud said, 'How about this?'

He was holding up a can of something. It looked like clam chowder. Ruth shrugged, and he took it for acceptance. He turned away, and worked at the ringpull on top of the can.

With his back to her, he said quietly, 'I seem to have painted myself into a corner here, don't I?'

'I suppose you have.'

'I'll get out of it. I always do.'

There was something in his manner. Something too jaunty. Too much like whistling in the dark.

Ruth said, 'It's got to end sometime.'

'But not tonight,' he said, and then he exploded. 'Fuck it,' he said, 'I can't do this.'

Ruth moved in beside him, and took the can from his hand. He'd been trying to twist the lid off with force, and the ring had jammed. She straightened it out gently and peeled it back, using less force but pulling steadily.

'Tell me something about her,' she said, handing it back opened.

'I've done with that game.'

'It's not a game. I just want to know something about her.'

'Who?'

'You know who I'm talking about. This mother you're supposed to miss so much. She must have been something.'

He was looking down at the can, holding it, not seeing it. 'Don't talk about her,' he said.

'I'm not. I want *you* to.'

'Why?'

'Enough people have suffered because of her. I nearly died for her once, and God knows what's ahead of me now. So give me something that makes sense of it. One thing. One detail. Just one thing you remember that was her and no-one else.'

'Shut up,' he said, with a growing air of desperation.

'Can you? Can you, Peter? You were very young.'

'I said shut up.'

'Don't be ashamed if you can't. Things slip away over time. You try to keep them alive in your mind, but they just slip away all the same. Why did you think I was the one? Was I supposed to be something like her?'

'Ruth,' he said tersely, 'I'm only going to say this once. Stop working on me.'

Ruth backed off.

'You know I can't remember,' he said, and he shoved the can across the worktop and stalked out of the kitchen.

She caught up with him standing in the hallway, as if there was no one place that he wanted to be. She took his arm and sat him on the stairs and said, 'It's all right.'

She sat beside him.

He said, 'Nobody could take her place. I never wanted that. I don't know what Daddy thought he wanted when he brought those awful women home.'

'Maybe he was just looking for someone to be close to for a while.'

Michaud looked at her then.

'He had us,' he said miserably. 'What was so wrong with having us?'

She put her hand to his head. Hesitantly, stroking his brow.

For a moment he let her, leaning into it like a dog to his master's touch.

But then he abruptly pulled away, and got to his feet.

60

Aidan could see that there was somebody below him at the boat dock, working. Whoever it was, they had lights to see by and a radio to listen to. He called out, but no-one responded. So then he went down.

He'd no idea where he was. He'd backtracked, he'd followed the river, he'd looked for somewhere else to cross it and then he'd backtracked again. He'd seen a hand-painted sign and he'd followed where it pointed, down a track alongside which stood an abandoned Mardi Gras float from God only knew how many years before. By his headlights he saw that it was painted blue with fish and mermaids all around it, and it listed hard to one side as if its legs had been kicked out from under.

A narrow and uneven walkway led out along the edge of a shallow bay and then finally over the water to the roofed floating deck. The boat within it was flat-bottomed like a landing craft and had a vinyl bench down its centre for tourists to sit facing outward. Its engine cover was raised. The boat showed up a dull green under the lights, but its handrails were worn down to the bare metal.

Aidan called out again.

The woman who came out from under the cover couldn't have been more than twenty-three or four. She was wearing a burgundy-coloured T-shirt and shorts and she'd an adjustable wrench in one hand. Her mid-length brown hair had once been dyed blond, and now it had almost all grown out. Below the line, it was the colour of old brass.

She said, 'Who're you?'

'I called out from back there,' Aidan said, 'but I don't think you could hear me. Is your boat for hire?'

'Not tonight,' she said, watching him warily. 'Try me in the morning.'

'Well, maybe there's some other way I can go. I've been trying to get to a place and I've had no luck at all.'

'Getting to it?'

'Finding it. I don't even know what it's called.'

He gave her the same description that he'd given earlier to the man cutting his lawn, and she said, 'I know where you mean. That's Tidewater Point. They had the Jesuit graveyard there?'

'I wouldn't know about that,' Aidan said, but inside him something soared. He was close. He was almost there.

She said, 'Nobody goes to it now.'

'Can it be reached, though?'

But a shout distracted the young woman before she could answer. It came from the darkness beyond the boat, from somewhere out across the water. 'Hey!' a man's voice was calling. 'You over there!'

For Aidan, this was not a welcome interruption. The young woman switched on a spotlight beside the pilot's saddle and swung its beam around in the direction of the noise. It raked across black water and then up onto the bank on the far side of the channel. There it nailed a figure, standing.

It was a man in work clothes, unshaven, dazed-looking. He appeared to have taken a recent beating and, bad as he looked, he'd probably look worse in the morning. He seemed unsteady on his feet.

The boat pilot called out, 'Henry Clay?'

'Get the police for me,' the man called over. 'I just got attacked and locked up. I had to poke up some of the shingles off the roof to get out. They're still in the plantation house and the guy's got a gun.'

'What are you talking about, Henry?'

'You deaf or something, Louise?'

'My name ain't Louise.'

'There's people in the house!' the man insisted. 'Get the police!'

The young woman was shaking her head and turning away. She switched off the light, sending Henry Clay back into the darkness.

Aidan said, 'What place is he talking about?'

'That's Henry Clay,' the young woman whose name wasn't Louise said, as if the man being Henry Clay explained just about everything. 'He's handyman for Mr Walker.'

It was clear that she wasn't going to take him seriously. The man was shouting some more, now a lone and lost-sounding voice in the darkness. Now that he couldn't be seen, he seemed to be calling from much farther away.

Turning her back and without listening to what he was saying, she called out, 'Go home and sleep it off, Henry.'

'He's called somethin',' Henry Clay shouted almost pleadingly, 'and she's called Ruth!'

Aidan said to the woman, 'Where's he from?'

'You see the big gates on the road you came down? That's Covington. Gates are bigger'n the house behind 'em.'

'Call the police like he says,' Aidan told her. Henry Clay was still yelling his case to an audience of clouds and stars as Aidan sprinted back up the gangway toward his car.

61

Ruth was sitting across from Peter Michaud at the table in the big, unfinished dining-room. They were dining on canned soup by candlelight, but Ruth hadn't touched hers. The candlelight was no romantic impulse. The power had failed when the fuses had blown, the uncompleted wiring overloaded by the electric ring in the kitchen. It must have happened before, because the candles were ready to hand.

The patrolman's gun lay on the table before Michaud. He wasn't eating, either.

Ruth said, 'If you're just going to stare at that, put it somewhere else.'

Michaud sat back, but he didn't take his eyes off the gun. The candles flickered, all at the same time as if at some imperceptible gust. This was like supper in the haunted house. Ruth had glanced at the hung portraits on the walls around them, wondering who the subjects might have been. All were men. Every single one of them looked like Edgar Allan Poe.

Michaud said, 'I was thinking. Daddy took me hunting once. I was really into it and I ran to the first thing he shot but then I cried because it wasn't dead. He said I was too soft and he wouldn't take me again. What do you think he'd say now?'

'I don't know,' Ruth said.

He glanced up from the weapon to her. 'Did you know he's still alive?'

'Yes,' she said.

'He pees himself and a nurse has to clean him up. He doesn't know where he is or what day it is. He's been like that for years.'

'I know.'

'You can go, Ruth.'

She didn't hear. Or rather, she heard, but his tone hadn't varied and it took her a moment to catch up with his meaning. She still didn't understand it.

She said, 'What?'

'I'm telling you to go. Get up and walk out. I'm not going to stop you.'

'Then what?'

'Then nothing. Just go.'

Ruth didn't move. She said, 'So then how do we end it?'

'You've stopped me,' Michaud said with a kind of bitter irony, as if it wasn't only clear that she hadn't stopped him at all but also that she'd failed him in some more important way. 'You've saved me,' he said. 'Job's over. Now go.'

And still Ruth didn't move. So then he reached over and picked up the gun, and she felt herself tense. But there was no way she could have prepared herself for what he did then. Because he raised his other hand, jammed the muzzle of the sidearm into his open palm, and fired.

Shreds. Rain.

A sheet of flame roared straight out through the back of his hand, and blood sprayed onto them both.

'What do I have to do?' he roared at her. 'Go!'

Part-deafened by the blast, she tottered to her feet. She heard the chair fall backwards onto the boards behind her. His hand was still raised, a perfect red hole blown through its centre. Ruth felt that she was going to puke again, and for all-new reasons.

Suddenly he lurched up and, swinging his undamaged gun hand in a ferocious arc, he swept everything within reach across the table and onto the floor. Then he started around the table toward her.

'Turn around,' he said, 'walk out, end of story. Do this for me, Ruth. If you ever felt anything for me at all. Leave now.'

Stiff, scared, and dazed, Ruth turned and ran.

She hit one of the walls in the hallway, and bounced off it. She didn't even feel it happen. Her legs carried her to the main door, big and ornate with a glass fanlight above, and she flung it open and dived out through it.

She was on the porch. In the style of so many of the old plantation houses, this one had a set of columns and steps to create the effect of a Greek temple frontage. She stumbled and almost fell as she ran down to the driveway.

Darkness enfolded her. The darkness of deep country. The stars above were cold points more intense than any that she'd ever seen before. She began to slow, the wave of her energy abating. Ruth wondered, sluggishly, if Michaud would run also as soon as he knew that she was out of the way. But to that, she already knew the answer. There could be no real doubt as to what his intentions now were. Such a shocking act of self-mutilation could hardly be a prelude to anything else.

Two of the stars fell, and began to sweep toward her. They resolved themselves into a car's headlights on the driveway, and with them came the approaching sound of an engine being driven hard. The driveway might have been half a mile long or even more; it was impossible for Ruth to say with any certainty.

They were coming for him.

She knew that she couldn't leave him to face them alone. Not now.

And so, steadying herself, she turned around and went back inside the house.

The dining-room was empty. The debris was all on the floor exactly as they'd left it, but Michaud and the gun were both missing. Ruth went from room to downstairs room, calling his name.

There was no reply.

From the kitchen, she could see the approaching car through the window. Then it left her line of sight as it went around toward the front of the house. She'd no idea who might be in it. Probably no-one that she'd met. Some trained squad, family men with their own lives and no interest in Michaud except as a logistical problem. They'd take him in one piece if they could. But it wouldn't worry them overmuch if they couldn't.

A board creaked above her, clearly heard through the unlined ceiling. She ran for the stairs.

Ruth heard the shot as she was ascending. In spite of itself, her heart dropped.

She was too late.

Ruth had a brief impression of makeshift bedrooms off to either side as she headed toward the one from which the sound had come. She was following the light from a candle that he must have carried up with him. The door at the end of the landing was half-open, and it flew all the way back and slammed into the wall as she skidded through.

Michaud was sitting beneath the window with his back against the wall. The candle had been set down on the floor beside him. There was a powerful smell of cordite in the air. He looked up at her.

This was an almost-empty room, the work of restoration not yet begun; there was cracked plaster scattered all over the floor and a haze of dust still filtering down from the shot that Michaud had fired into the ceiling only moments before.

From somewhere outside the house, Ruth heard the slam of a car door.

'I can't do it,' Michaud said miserably.

His damaged hand lay useless and leaking in his lap. The gun in the other was pointing down at the boards.

'Oh, Peter,' she said. 'Is that really what you want?'

He was shaking his head. 'I'm not that brave.'

'Come here.'

She knelt before him, and took the gun from his hand. He offered her no resistance. Somebody downstairs began trying to kick their way in.

'Can you do it for me?' he said.

She took hold of his sleeve, and pulled him away from the wall. He didn't understand what she was doing, but he went along with whatever she might want.

'You're not alone,' she said. 'Neither of us ever has to be alone again. Do you understand me?'

She took his wire glasses off him. Then she pulled him up so that his forehead touched her own. They were eye to eye. She brought her hand up behind him and placed the muzzle of the gun against the back of his head. She tried to imagine a line all the way through so that the one shot would take them both. There probably wouldn't be time for a second.

She said, 'Are you ready?'

He closed his eyes.

Something crashed in, and she heard running footsteps in the house down below.

'Don't be afraid,' she said, and without opening his eyes he gave the barest nod.

There was nothing left for either of them here. If there was going to be anything beyond the next moment, then everything they had ever valued would be waiting for them in that.

Whoever was approaching, he was now coming up the stairs.

Ruth squeezed on the trigger.

Aidan came through the front door and into the hallway. He'd had to kick out the lock to get in. The lock had held, but the framework hadn't. He'd seen Ruth turn, and go back inside. He couldn't imagine why. There had been nobody with her.

The place looked like a gutted whale. Dark, and full of secrets. He went through a doorway toward what little light there was, and found himself in a room with a long oval table. One of the chairs was lying on its back on the floor and there was mess everywhere. Through the next door, he found a kitchen. He thought he saw something moving at him, but it was only his own reflection in the window-glass looking out onto the night. There was a light switch on the wall and he knocked it up and down a couple of times, but nothing happened.

Back in the dining-room, he grabbed up one of the candlesticks from the table. As he raised it, the shadow of the table dipped away and the light fell across the wall. The big stain that glistened wetly on the boards was unmistakable, even by candlelight.

'Shit,' he said stonily, and he almost tripped himself as he turned and rushed from the room.

He had to shelter the flame with his hand as he went from one room to another, to keep it from being blown out as he moved. Nothing. Nobody. He heard a creak and he forgot and turned quickly, and suddenly he was in darkness.

But there was a glow. A glow filtering down from somewhere upstairs. He let the candle fall and ran for the stairway.

Aidan hit the stairs and started to ascend. Time was stretching. He could sense it beginning to happen, and there was nothing he could do about it. He tried to call out, but the call bubbled up slowly and seemed to take for ever in coming.

The landing. They were in the room at the end of the landing. Pushing as if against resistance, he fell through the air toward it.

The door burst inward. The light beyond it cowered.

There was the scene. The two of them before the window, heads pressed together for what Aidan instantly realized was to be a once-through double-suicide shot. He was thinking Thank God, believing that he'd made it just in time; but then, with great dismay, it registered with him that the hand holding the gun was not Michaud's, but Ruth's own. Michaud's one good hand was in a trusting grip on Ruth's shoulder.

No matter. He was here. He could stop this.

Aidan had no more than ten feet to cover.

He'd barely started it when there was a single shot, muffled by bone and further silenced by brains as the erupting spray hit the wall behind the two of them.

PART FOUR

Ghosts

62

Ruth was deaf. She was blind. She knew that it had happened, and this was the void. She was going to have to open her eyes if she wanted to see what was going to come next.

She opened her eyes.

She saw Michaud falling away from her, the messy exit wound from the spun bullet still spraying out of the side of his head – what remained of it. His face was a blank as he dropped. It showed nothing but emptiness, a place from which the tenant had been yanked.

As he fell sideways from her view, she saw herself. It was her own thinned-out reflection in the window, and she wasn't alone. Someone stood behind her, above her, leaning down over her as if to take hold of her, and her recognition of him was instantaneous. She knew then that she'd crossed over. She'd crossed over, and Aidan had been waiting.

But then the hand that reached over her shoulder and quickly folded around her own, pulling the gun out of her fingers, was solid. And the pain as her own finger twisted in the trigger guard was sharp and real.

Michaud hit the floor. Slackly, belatedly, down in a heap. He shuddered a couple of times. It resembled life, but it couldn't be; half of his head was completely gone. This was no more than the signature that life tried to scrawl in its last moments on the way out.

There was blood everywhere. It was all over her. But she looked up at Aidan as he turned her, and there was no blood in him at all. He looked as pale as any ghost.

'Ruth!' he was shouting. 'Can you hear me?'

His voice was barely making it through. She realized then

that her deafness had been caused by the closeness of the blast. She never got to hear the clatter that the gun must have made as Aidan slung it across the boards to rest, way out of reach against the far wall. Now he was holding her by the shoulders, and squeezing her too hard.

It was too much to take in. But Ruth took it in all the same. It was like the last note of a raging symphony where everything crashed together and fitted and left the listener breathless.

'I'm still here,' she said, disbelievingly.

And if the crushing force with which he held her left any doubt over the fact that she was alive, the sudden hunger with which she hugged him back was no less an affirmation.

63

It was getting light, now, but it was still very early. Aidan was beginning to lose sight of how long he'd been here. It might have been an hour, it might have been for ever. In reality it was somewhere less than the latter. Six or seven hours, perhaps, he thought as he stretched while descending to the gravel drive. The stretching felt wonderful. From the mid-evening to the dawn, seven hours would probably be about right.

The young woman with the swamp tour boat had called in the police as he'd asked, and they'd all arrived at the plantation house in numbers at some indeterminate period later. Aidan had been told that it had been about twenty minutes after the shooting, although he couldn't have argued it either way. Michaud's body was still lying up there. They'd been working on the room solidly for all this time, and only now was the mortuary car being made ready to take him away.

Ruth had been too much in shock to be questioned at first, but she'd refused to leave the scene without Aidan. Aidan had been interrogated, relentlessly, for more than three hours. His head was ringing from it. And he'd probably have to go through it all over again, and a lot more often than once.

The police doctor had checked on Ruth and given her some first aid for her injuries, but then when he'd cleaned most of the bits of Michaud off her she was given the all-clear. Aidan got antibiotic shots and the promise of a hospital check as soon as they made him available. Aidan didn't see why they couldn't let him go right now. Michaud's activities were at an end, and the rest of it would take an age to unravel.

He couldn't see Ruth, either.

He started to panic for a moment, but then he realized that she was sitting in his car. He could see her there, with her head down as she studied something in her hand. She was looking at it with intense interest. Aidan couldn't make out what it was.

He went over to the car, opened the driver's door, and got in beside her. One of the young officers in charge of controlling the area watched them incuriously, but Aidan didn't make any move to start up the engine. He'd only come to sit, not to drive. It would be a while yet before they'd be allowed to leave.

He knew that she was aware of him. Although she didn't look up.

He said, 'What have you got there?'

She opened her hand and turned it slightly, so that he could see.

It was a cartridge case from the handgun. Almost certainly the one from the final discharge. The soft dawn light gleamed on the yellow brass.

Aidan said, 'Guys are on their hands and knees up there, looking all over the room for that. They're just about to start ripping up the floorboards.'

'I know,' Ruth said and she turned it, this way and that. The metal shone warmly.

And still looking at it, she said, 'Isn't it the most beautiful thing you ever saw?'

Aidan lifted his hand, as if to touch the back of his fingers to her cheek. But he didn't, quite. And he resisted the urge to knock away a tiny fleck of bone that was still clinging to her hair.

He leaned back against the door, where he could continue to watch her.

'No,' he said. 'No. It doesn't even come close.'

THE END

ACKNOWLEDGEMENTS

I'll try to keep this simple. Everything has to begin somewhere, and the roots of *Red, Red Robin* lie in a story called 'Homebodies' that was written for a collection called *Dark at Heart*, edited by Karen and Joe Lansdale. To them, and to Keith and Kasey Lansdale whose instant friendship with my own daughter on that summer's visit was the *real* start of it all, many thanks.

In Philadelphia, the linchpin and all-round heroine of my research programme was Sharon Pinkenson of the Greater Philadelphia Film Office. Help and guidance was given to me despite difficult circumstances by Corporal Joseph McQue of the Philadelphia Police's Department of Public Affairs. Thanks are also due to Detective Lieutenant Mike Hasson, Sergeant Terry Young, Firearms Officer Caruthers, and Peggy Trush of Personnel. J. Scott Blackman, District Director of the US Department of Justice Immigration and Naturalization Service, gave generously of his time, as did Lucy Jablon in helping me to find a suitable apartment for Ruth. My visits to the city were made all the more memorable by the hospitality of Sandy Jablon of Bump In The Night Books along with Samantha, Philip and Spencer, and the Elfreth's Alley welcoming committee of Frank X. Smith, Larry McHugh, Maria Di Rienzo, Bill Sheehan, Roman Ranieri, Gary Potter and Darrell Schweitzer. Thanks also to Patti Klein of the Barclay Hotel on Rittenhouse Square.

Sometimes the work on one project can pave the way for another, as was the case here after time spent looking at plantation houses under the guidance of Phil Seifert of the Louisiana Film Commission back in June 1992. In New Orleans, further thanks to long-time friend and ever-patient source Dr Michael Chafetz, to Marjorie Esman, Attorney at Law, and to Hannah Chafetz from her 'temporary occupant'.

In New York, I'm indebted to the Ballantine team of Linda Grey, Joe Blades and Bruce Little and to my US agent Ellen Levine. A similar debt is owed to Mark Barty-King, Broo Doherty and Bill Scott-Kerr at Bantam Press in London, and to my wife Marilyn. To Imogen Parker, champion, guide and navigator from *Valley of Lights* to *Nightmare, with Angel*, and who now has boats of her own to sail, and to Caradoc King, my agent in London:

'*I no doubt deserved my enemies, but I don't believe I deserved my friends.*'

– Walt Whitman

A SIMPLE PLAN
by Scott Smith

'That rare and satisfying combination: a compulsive thriller which also happens to be a beautifully-written and original work of art'
Robert Harris, author of *Fatherland*

Every New Year's Eve, Hank Mitchell and his older brother Jacob make a pilgrimage to their parents' grave. This year Jacob's friend Lou comes with them.

As they drive through thick snow towards the cemetery, a fox runs across the road, and they skid on the ice and crash. Jacob's dog chases the fox, followed by the three men. Beating their way through the drifts, they come upon a small plane, belly down in the snow. In the pilot's seat is a dead man, his eyes pecked out by crows. In the back they discover a duffel bag. *In the bag is over four million dollars in cash . . .*

A seemingly foolproof plan to keep the money, without fear of discovery or anyone being hurt, begins Hank's nightmare. From this moment on, his hitherto ordinary and ordered life unfolds into an inevitable and doomed spiral of events, through murder, betrayal and mass killing.

From its deceptively simple beginning, to its horrific and surprising conclusion, *A Simple Plan* will have you on the edge of your seat.

'Astonishing . . . A harrowing exploration of the banality of evil'
Vanity Fair

'Chilling . . . The inexorable progression from greed to betrayal, from betrayal to violence, is handled with icy skill'
Jack Curtis, author of *Conjure Me*

'Makes an enormous impact . . . A classic story of crime and punishment '
Mail on Sunday

0 552 14143 7

A SICKNESS OF THE SOUL
by Simon Maginn

'It was a bigger story than I'd imagined, and at the centre of it was Teacher. I was determined now, more than ever, to get the story, the whole story. I would do whatever was necessary.'

When Robert, an investigative journalist, tunes into a phone-in programme while driving through the Midlands, he immediately realizes he is on to something. He goes undercover to infiltrate a bizarre bikers' cult, the Sons of the New Bethlehem, led by the charismatic Teacher. It is Teacher whom Robert has heard on the radio, giving advice to distraught callers and praying for their salvation. Teacher's ministry is a fully-fledged crusade, in leather. Astride their Harleys and Hondas, the gang – Spider, Loverman, Stroker, Biceps and the rest – gather in shopping centres and car parks with the aim of winning converts for Christ.

Robert's cover, however, is not as good as he'd thought, and he finds himself prisoner of the Sons, cooped up in an eerie hotel. Trying to penetrate the enigmatic facade of Teacher, and to discover what, *exactly*, is the man's method of healing his followers, he becomes involved in a series of deaths before he can escape. And when he's back in London with his partner, Fiona, he can't settle into his former life. The memories of Teacher's weird regime haunt him, and before long he's on the road to the Midlands once more . . .

'A name to watch'
Ramsey Campbell

0 552 14250 6

JIGSAW
by Campbell Armstrong

The spirit of *Jig* lives on . . .

On a bitter winter evening a bomb explodes in a crowded London underground train. People are senselessly slaughtered. Who planted the murderous device? And why?

A few hours later in a Mayfair flat a young prostitute is brutally killed and an enigmatic message written in blood is left in her room. It is addressed to Frank Pagan, counter-terrorist specialist, and it draws him into the most terrifying case of his career.

Pagan finds himself pitted against two extraordinary adversaries: the lethal Carlotta, a woman whose appetite for blood is matched only by Pagan's hunger for justice – and the ghost of Jig, his most famous antagonist, whose death has given birth to new demons . . .

From London to New York, Berlin to Venice, *Jigsaw* weaves a breathtaking story of conspiracy and power, passion and betrayal – a magnificent follow-up to Campbell Armstrong's worldwide betseller *Jig*.

'Armstrong creates electric tension'
Daily Telegraph

'Campbell Armstrong has outdone both Frederick Forsyth and Ken Follett with *Jigsaw*. *Jigsaw* features a villain to die for, plus the most unusual and haunting romance I've encountered in a thriller'
James Patterson, author of *Along Came a Spider*

'Armstrong has created a thriller where the sex is sexy, the horror horrific, and the plot is, as it should be, the skeleton for a well fleshed-out piece of storytelling'
The Times

0 552 14168 2

A SELECTED LIST OF FINE WRITING
AVAILABLE FROM CORGI BOOKS

14054	6	THE DOLL'S HOUSE	Evelyn Anthony	£4.99
13817	7	EXPOSURE	Evelyn Anthony	£4.99
14241	7	BLOODSTONES	Evelyn Anthony	£4.99
14168	2	JIGSAW	Campbell Armstrong	£4.99
13947	5	SUNDAY MORNING	Ray Connolly	£4.99
14227	1	SHADOWS ON A WALL	Ray Connolly	£5.99
13827	4	SPOILS OF WAR	Peter Driscoll	£4.99
12550	4	LIE DOWN WITH LIONS	Ken Follett	£4.99
12610	1	ON WINGS OF EAGLES	Ken Follett	£5.99
11810	9	THE KEY TO REBECCA	Ken Follett	£4.99
13275	9	THE NEGOTIATOR	Frederick Forsyth	£5.99
13823	1	THE DECEIVER	Frederick Forsyth	£5.99
13990	4	THE FIST OF GOD	Frederick Forsyth	£5.99
14043	0	SHADOW PLAY	Frances Fyfield	£4.99
14174	7	PERFECTLY PURE AND GOOD	Frances Fyfield	£4.99
14295	6	A CLEAR CONSCIENCE	Frances Fyfield	£4.99
13598	4	MAESTRO	John Gardner	£5.99
14223	9	BORROWED TIME	Robert Goddard	£4.99
13840	1	CLOSED CIRCLE	Robert Goddard	£4.99
13839	8	HAND IN GLOVE	Robert Goddard	£4.99
13869	X	MATILDA'S GAME	Denis Kilcommons	£3.99
12433	8	A COLD MIND	David Lindsey	£4.99
13215	2	SPIRAL	David Lindsey	£4.99
13489	9	HOOLET	John McNeil	£4.99
14122	4	SHEEP	Simon Maginn	£4.99
14249	2	VIRGINS AND MARTYRS	Simon Maginn	£4.99
14250	6	A SICKNESS OF THE SOUL	Simon Maginn	£4.99
13918	1	THE LUCY GHOSTS	Eddy Shah	£4.99
14145	3	MANCHESTER BLUE	Eddy Shah	£4.99
14290	5	FALLEN ANGELS	Eddy Shah	£5.99
14143	7	A SIMPLE PLAN	Scott Smith	£4.99